**Pokémon ADVENTURES
BLACK AND WHITE**
Volume 4
Perfect Square Edition

Story by **HIDENORI KUSAKA**
Art by **SATOSHI YAMAMOTO**

© 2014 Pokémon.
© 1995–2014 Nintendo/Creatures Inc./GAME FREAK inc.
TM, ®, and character names are trademarks of Nintendo.
POCKET MONSTERS SPECIAL Vol. 46
by Hidenori KUSAKA, Satoshi YAMAMOTO
© 1997 Hidenori KUSAKA, Satoshi YAMAMOTO
All rights reserved.
Original Japanese edition published by SHOGAKUKAN.
English translation rights in the United States of America, Canada,
United Kingdom, Ireland, Australia and New Zealand
arranged with SHOGAKUKAN.

Translation/Tetsuichiro Miyaki
English Adaptation/Annette Roman
Touch-up & Lettering/Susan Daigle-Leach
Design/Shawn Carrico
Editor/Annette Roman

The stories, characters and incidents mentioned
in this publication are entirely fictional.

Printed in the U.S.A.

Published by VIZ Media, LLC
P.O. Box 77010
San Francisco, CA 94107

10 9 8 7 6 5 4 3 2 1
First printing, July 2014

PARENTAL ADVISORY
POKÉMON ADVENTURES
is rated A and is suitable
for readers of all ages.

POKÉMON™
ADVENTURES
BLACK & WHITE

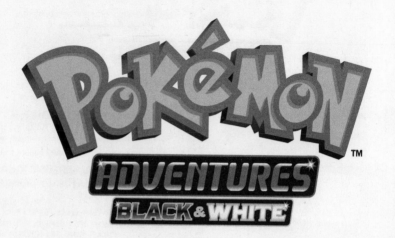

Pokémon ADVENTURES
BLACK & WHITE

4
VOLUME FOUR

Story by
Hidenori Kusaka

Art by
Satoshi Yamamoto

& WHITE

A STORY ABOUT YOUNG PEOPLE ENTRUSTED WITH POKÉDEXES BY THE WORLD'S LEADING POKÉMON RESEARCHERS. TOGETHER WITH THEIR POKÉMON, THEY TRAVEL, BATTLE, AND EVOLVE!

SOME PLACE IN SOME TIME... A YOUNG TRAINER NAMED BLACK, WHO DREAMS OF WINNING THE POKÉMON LEAGUE, RECEIVES A POKÉDEX FROM PROFESSOR JUNIPER AND SETS OFF ON HIS TRAINING JOURNEY TO COLLECT THE EIGHT GYM BADGES HE NEEDS TO ENTER NEXT YEAR'S POKÉMON LEAGUE.
ON THE WAY, BLACK MEETS WHITE, THE OWNER OF A POKÉMON TALENT AGENCY, AND ENDS UP WORKING FOR HER. BLACK EARNS HIS SECOND BADGE, AND THEN, DURING THE BATTLE FOR HIS THIRD BADGE, BLACK'S TEPIG EVOLVES INTO A PIGNITE! BLACK WINS THAT BADGE AS WELL AND HIS JOURNEY WITH WHITE CONTINUES... BUT UNBEKNOWNST TO OUR HEROES, TEAM PLASMA IS SCHEMING TO GET AHOLD OF THE LEGENDARY POKÉMON ZEKROM AND THE DARK STONE. WHAT FOR...? AND HOW WILL OUR TWO HEROES GET DRAWN INTO THEIR DASTARDLY PLOT...?!

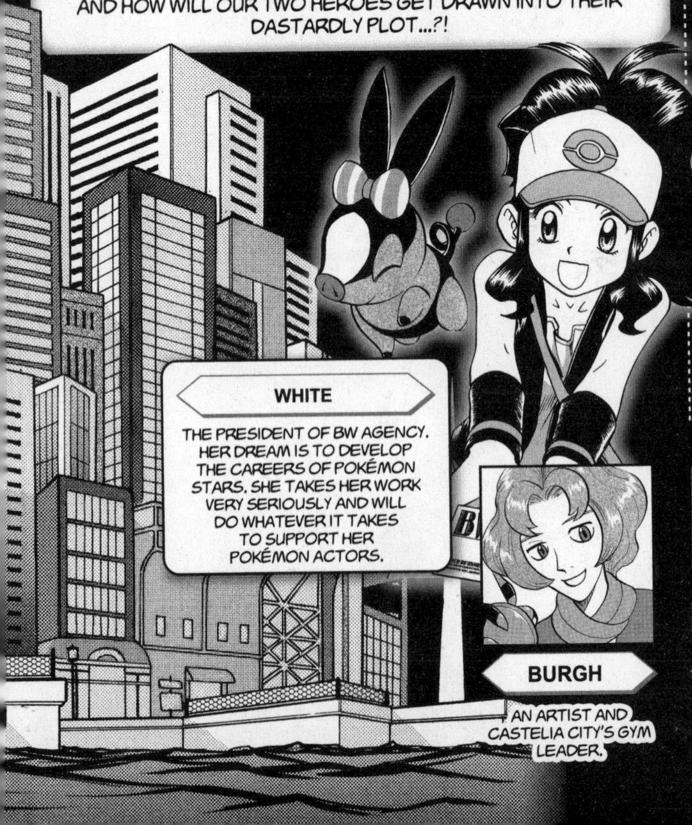

WHITE

THE PRESIDENT OF BW AGENCY. HER DREAM IS TO DEVELOP THE CAREERS OF POKÉMON STARS. SHE TAKES HER WORK VERY SERIOUSLY AND WILL DO WHATEVER IT TAKES TO SUPPORT HER POKÉMON ACTORS.

BURGH

AN ARTIST AND CASTELIA CITY'S GYM LEADER.

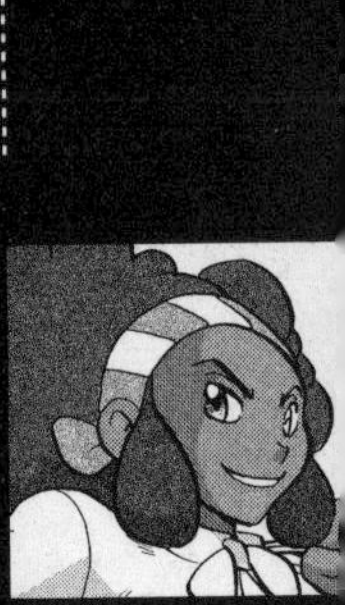

LENORA

THE NACRENE CITY GYM LEADER AND NACRENE MUSEUM DIRECTOR.

POKÉMON ADVENTURES
The Tenth Chapter 10 BLACK

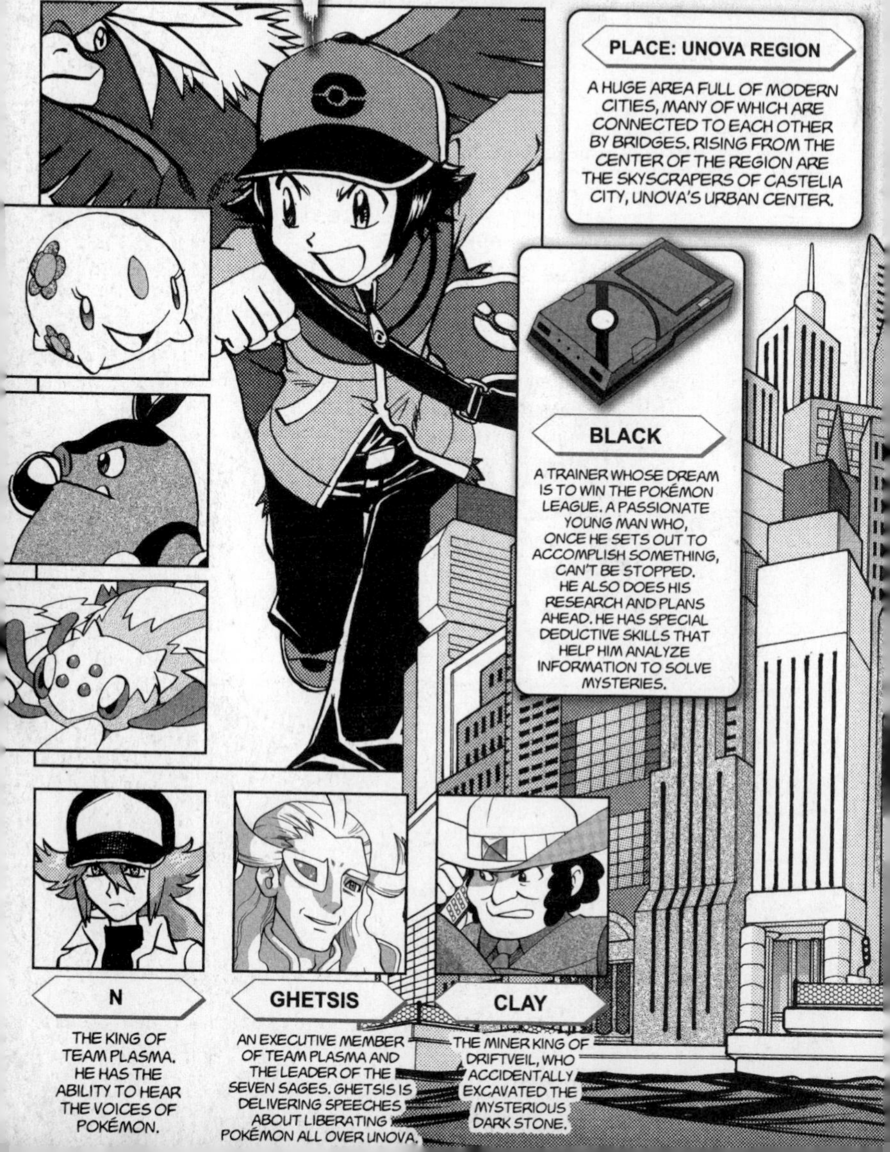
PLACE: UNOVA REGION
A HUGE AREA FULL OF MODERN CITIES, MANY OF WHICH ARE CONNECTED TO EACH OTHER BY BRIDGES. RISING FROM THE CENTER OF THE REGION ARE THE SKYSCRAPERS OF CASTELIA CITY, UNOVA'S URBAN CENTER.
BLACK
A TRAINER WHOSE DREAM IS TO WIN THE POKÉMON LEAGUE. A PASSIONATE YOUNG MAN WHO, ONCE HE SETS OUT TO ACCOMPLISH SOMETHING, CAN'T BE STOPPED. HE ALSO DOES HIS RESEARCH AND PLANS AHEAD. HE HAS SPECIAL DEDUCTIVE SKILLS THAT HELP HIM ANALYZE INFORMATION TO SOLVE MYSTERIES.
CLAY
THE MINER KING OF DRIFTVEIL, WHO ACCIDENTALLY EXCAVATED THE MYSTERIOUS DARK STONE.
GHETSIS
AN EXECUTIVE MEMBER OF TEAM PLASMA AND THE LEADER OF THE SEVEN SAGES. GHETSIS IS DELIVERING SPEECHES ABOUT LIBERATING POKÉMON ALL OVER UNOVA.
N
THE KING OF TEAM PLASMA. HE HAS THE ABILITY TO HEAR THE VOICES OF POKÉMON.

CONTENTS

ADVENTURE 20
At Liberty on Liberty Garden......................7

ADVENTURE 21
Sandstorm......................34

ADVENTURE 22
To Make a Musical......................56

ADVENTURE 23
Special Delivery......................78

ADVENTURE 24
Battle on a Roller Coaster......................96

ADVENTURE 25
Gigi's Choice......................122

ADVENTURE 26
Unraveling Mysteries......................146

ADVENTURE 27
A New Perspective......................168

ADVENTURE 28
Growing Pains......................190

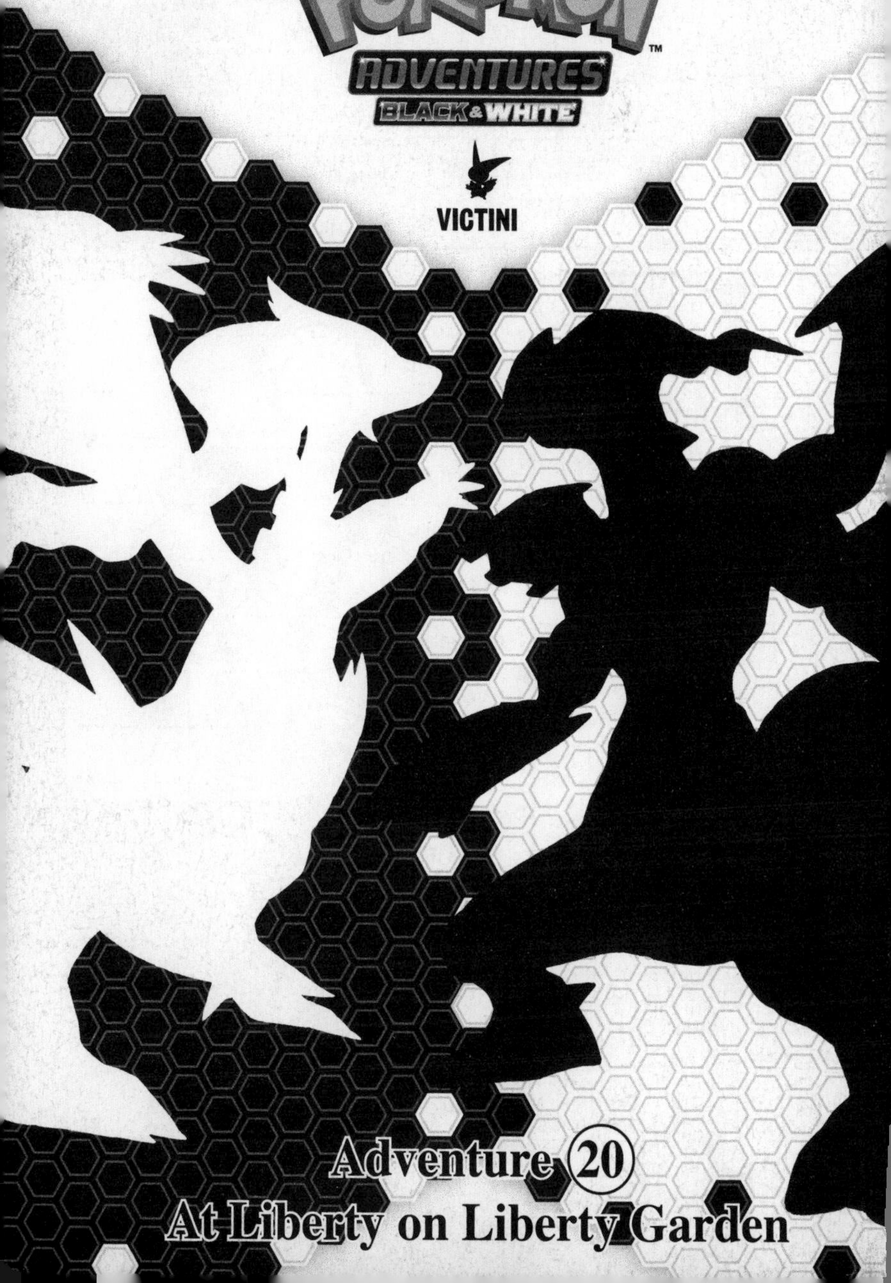
Pokémon Adventures Black & White
VICTINI

Adventure 20
At Liberty on Liberty Garden

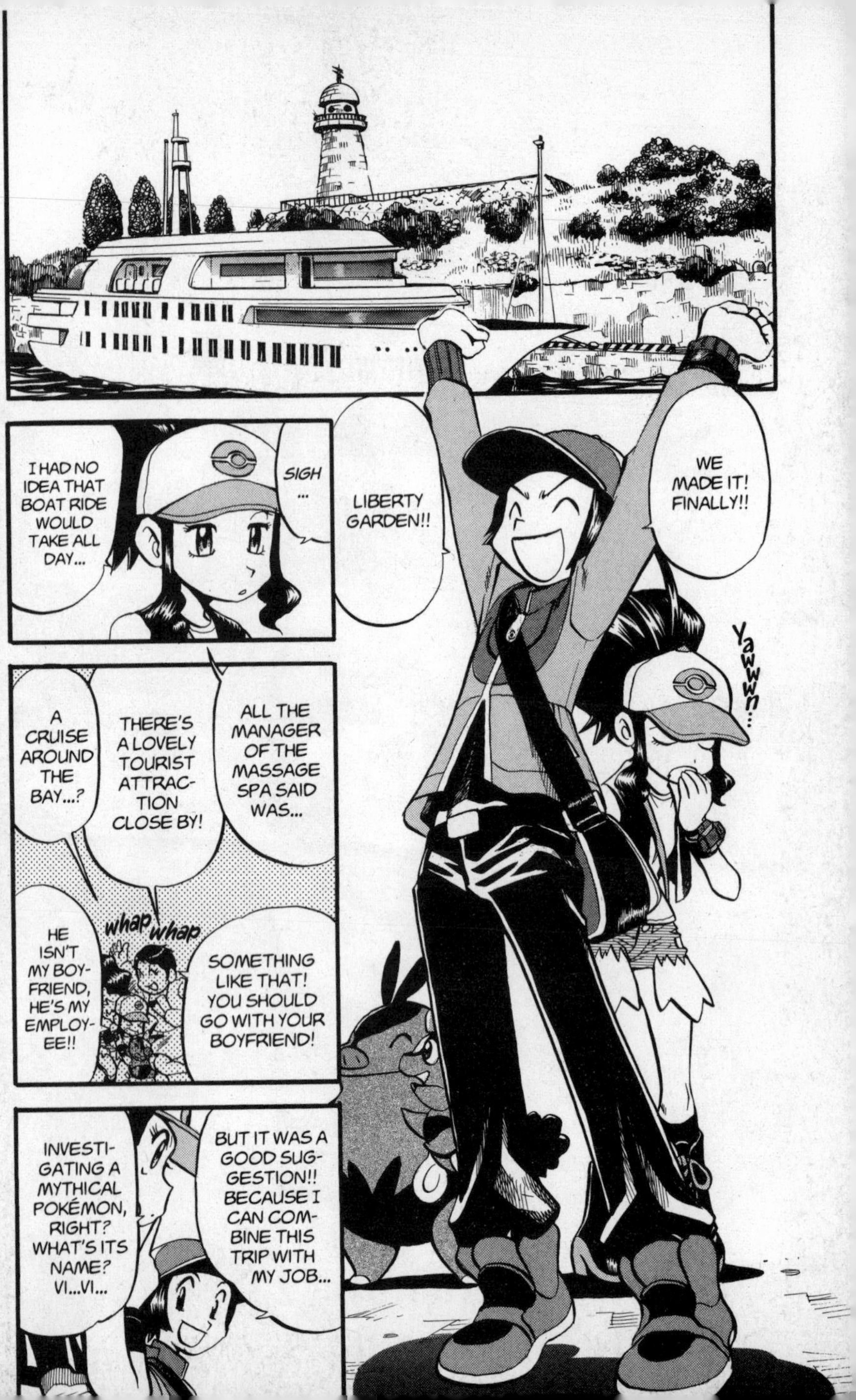
WE MADE IT! FINALLY!!
LIBERTY GARDEN!!
Yawwwn...
SIGH ...
I HAD NO IDEA THAT BOAT RIDE WOULD TAKE ALL DAY...
ALL THE MANAGER OF THE MASSAGE SPA SAID WAS...
THERE'S A LOVELY TOURIST ATTRACTION CLOSE BY!
A CRUISE AROUND THE BAY...?
SOMETHING LIKE THAT! YOU SHOULD GO WITH YOUR BOYFRIEND!
whap whap
HE ISN'T MY BOYFRIEND, HE'S MY EMPLOYEE!!
BUT IT WAS A GOOD SUGGESTION!! BECAUSE I CAN COMBINE THIS TRIP WITH MY JOB...
INVESTIGATING A MYTHICAL POKÉMON, RIGHT? WHAT'S ITS NAME? VI...VI...

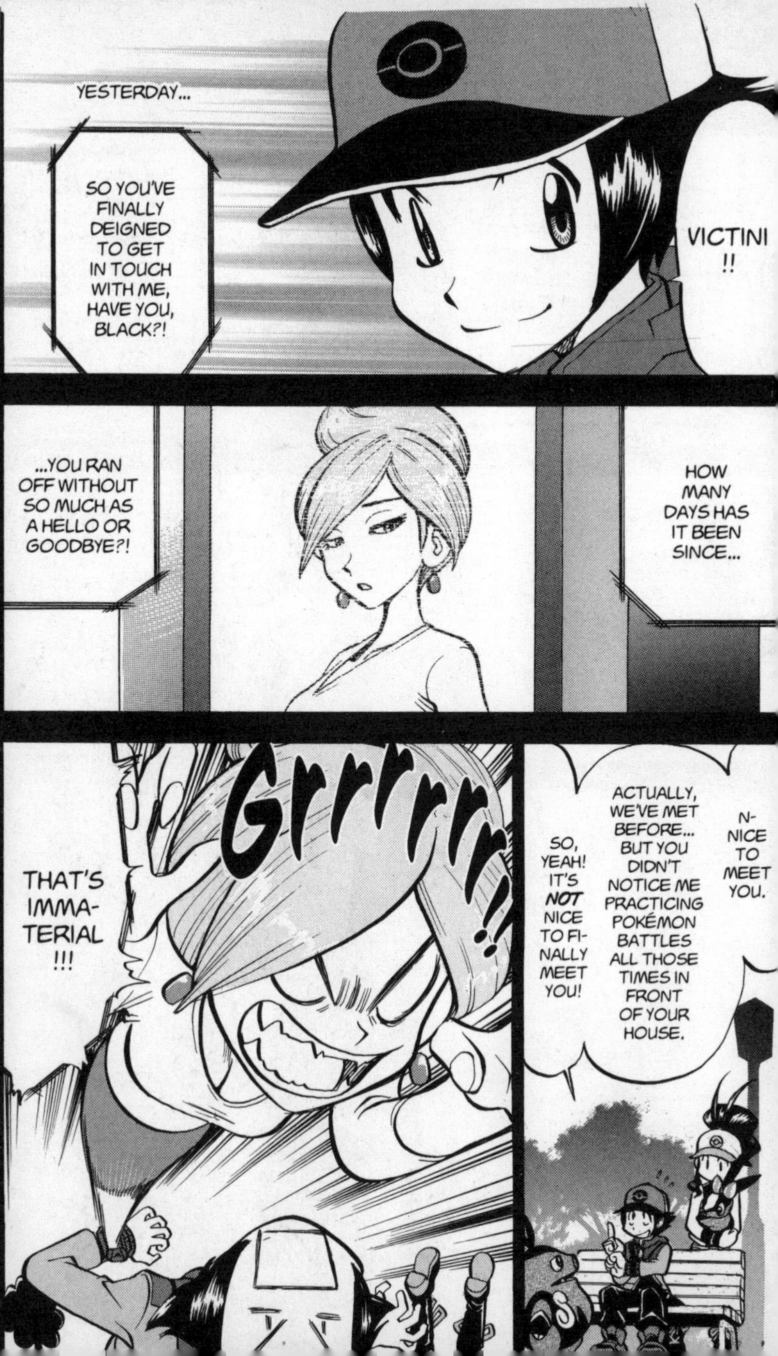
YESTERDAY...
VICTINI!!
SO YOU'VE FINALLY DEIGNED TO GET IN TOUCH WITH ME, HAVE YOU, BLACK?!
HOW MANY DAYS HAS IT BEEN SINCE...
...YOU RAN OFF WITHOUT SO MUCH AS A HELLO OR GOODBYE?!
N-NICE TO MEET YOU.
ACTUALLY, WE'VE MET BEFORE... BUT YOU DIDN'T NOTICE ME PRACTICING POKÉMON BATTLES ALL THOSE TIMES IN FRONT OF YOUR HOUSE.
SO, YEAH! IT'S *NOT* NICE TO FINALLY MEET YOU!
Grrrrr!!
THAT'S IMMATERIAL!!!

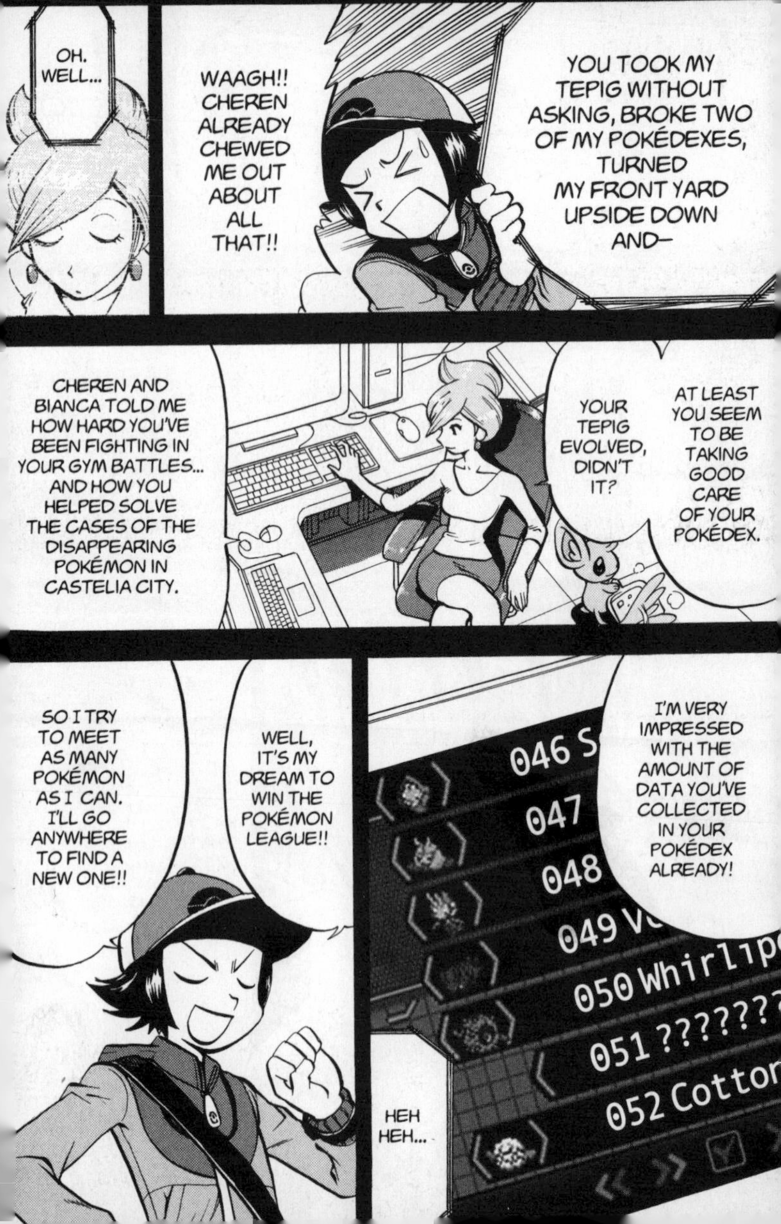
YOU TOOK MY TEPIG WITHOUT ASKING, BROKE TWO OF MY POKÉDEXES, TURNED MY FRONT YARD UPSIDE DOWN AND—
WAAGH!! CHEREN ALREADY CHEWED ME OUT ABOUT ALL THAT!!
OH. WELL...
AT LEAST YOU SEEM TO BE TAKING GOOD CARE OF YOUR POKÉDEX.
YOUR TEPIG EVOLVED, DIDN'T IT?
CHEREN AND BIANCA TOLD ME HOW HARD YOU'VE BEEN FIGHTING IN YOUR GYM BATTLES... AND HOW YOU HELPED SOLVE THE CASES OF THE DISAPPEARING POKÉMON IN CASTELIA CITY.
I'M VERY IMPRESSED WITH THE AMOUNT OF DATA YOU'VE COLLECTED IN YOUR POKÉDEX ALREADY!
046 S
047
048
049 Ve
050 Whirlip
051 ???????
052 Cotto
HEH HEH...
WELL, IT'S MY DREAM TO WIN THE POKÉMON LEAGUE!!
SO I TRY TO MEET AS MANY POKÉMON AS I CAN. I'LL GO ANYWHERE TO FIND A NEW ONE!!

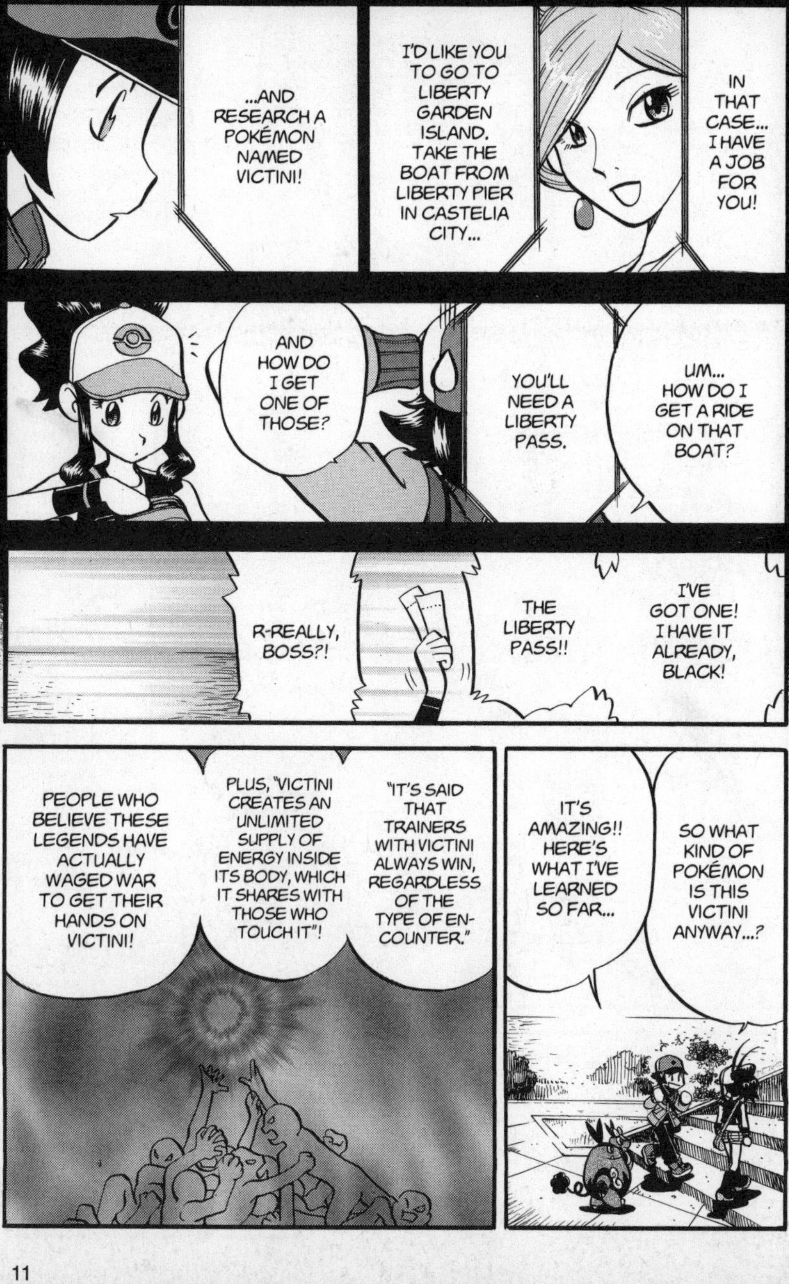
IN THAT CASE... I HAVE A JOB FOR YOU!
I'D LIKE YOU TO GO TO LIBERTY GARDEN ISLAND. TAKE THE BOAT FROM LIBERTY PIER IN CASTELIA CITY...
...AND RESEARCH A POKÉMON NAMED VICTINI!
UM... HOW DO I GET A RIDE ON THAT BOAT?
YOU'LL NEED A LIBERTY PASS.
AND HOW DO I GET ONE OF THOSE?
I'VE GOT ONE! I HAVE IT ALREADY, BLACK!
THE LIBERTY PASS!!
R-REALLY, BOSS?!
SO WHAT KIND OF POKÉMON IS THIS VICTINI ANYWAY...?
IT'S AMAZING!! HERE'S WHAT I'VE LEARNED SO FAR...
"IT'S SAID THAT TRAINERS WITH VICTINI ALWAYS WIN, REGARDLESS OF THE TYPE OF EN-COUNTER."
PLUS, "VICTINI CREATES AN UNLIMITED SUPPLY OF ENERGY INSIDE ITS BODY, WHICH IT SHARES WITH THOSE WHO TOUCH IT"!
PEOPLE WHO BELIEVE THESE LEGENDS HAVE ACTUALLY WAGED WAR TO GET THEIR HANDS ON VICTINI!

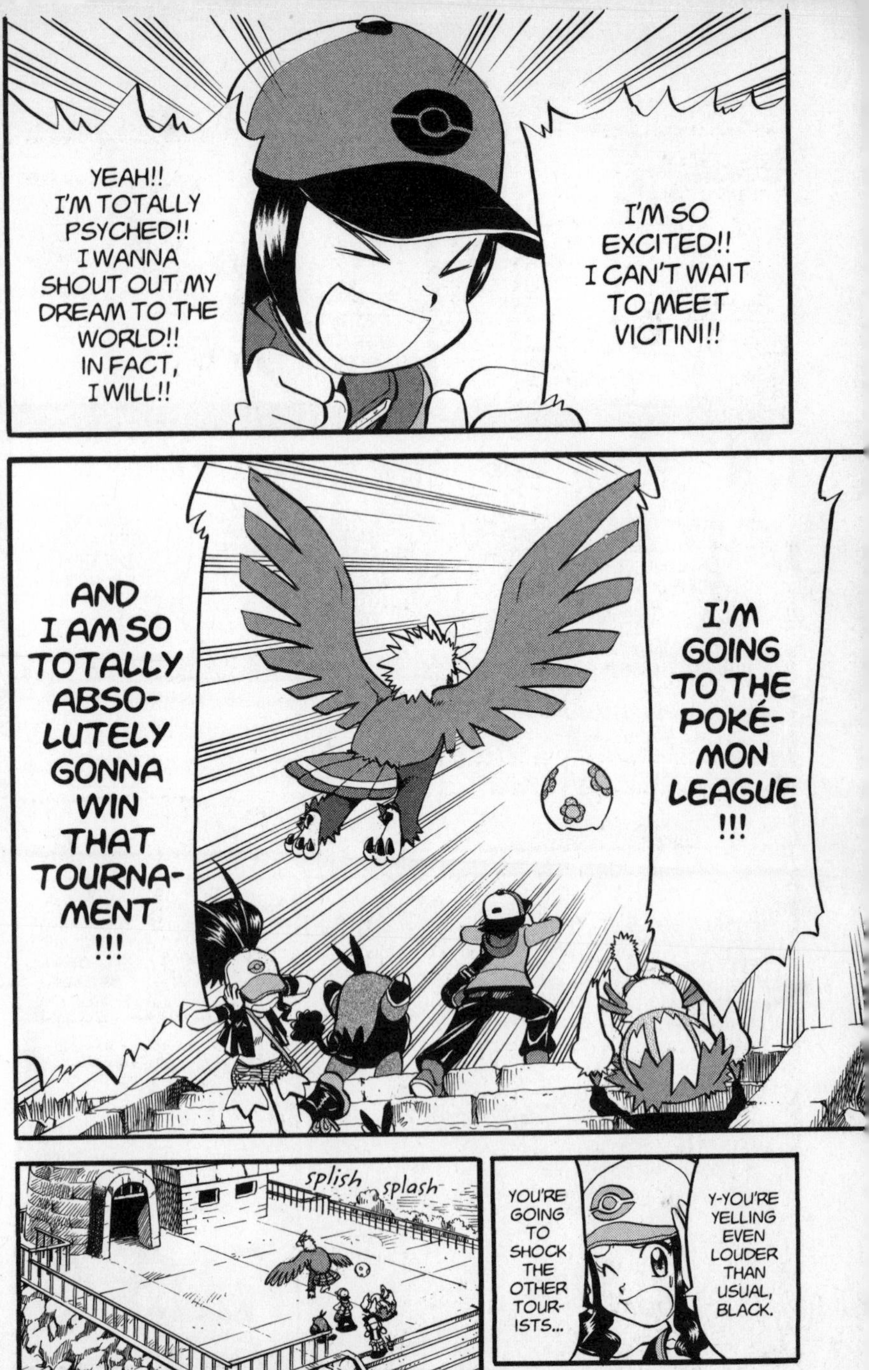
I'M SO EXCITED!! I CAN'T WAIT TO MEET VICTINI!!
YEAH!! I'M TOTALLY PSYCHED!! I WANNA SHOUT OUT MY DREAM TO THE WORLD!! IN FACT, I WILL!!
I'M GOING TO THE POKÉ-MON LEAGUE!!!
AND I AM SO TOTALLY ABSO-LUTELY GONNA WIN THAT TOURNA-MENT!!!
Y-YOU'RE YELLING EVEN LOUDER THAN USUAL, BLACK.
YOU'RE GOING TO SHOCK THE OTHER TOUR-ISTS...
splish splash

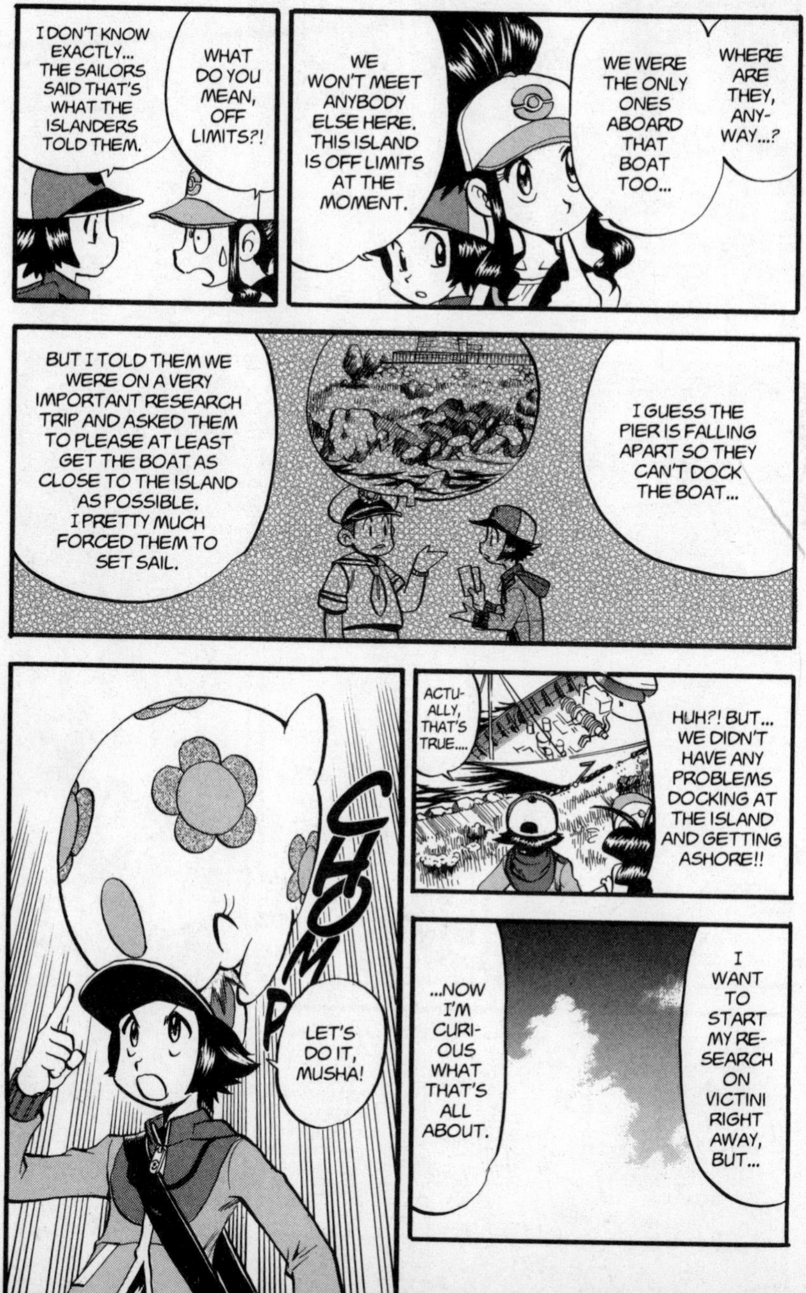
WHERE ARE THEY, ANYWAY...?
WE WERE THE ONLY ONES ABOARD THAT BOAT TOO...
WE WON'T MEET ANYBODY ELSE HERE. THIS ISLAND IS OFF LIMITS AT THE MOMENT.
WHAT DO YOU MEAN, OFF LIMITS?!
I DON'T KNOW EXACTLY... THE SAILORS SAID THAT'S WHAT THE ISLANDERS TOLD THEM.
I GUESS THE PIER IS FALLING APART SO THEY CAN'T DOCK THE BOAT...
BUT I TOLD THEM WE WERE ON A VERY IMPORTANT RESEARCH TRIP AND ASKED THEM TO PLEASE AT LEAST GET THE BOAT AS CLOSE TO THE ISLAND AS POSSIBLE. I PRETTY MUCH FORCED THEM TO SET SAIL.
HUH?! BUT... WE DIDN'T HAVE ANY PROBLEMS DOCKING AT THE ISLAND AND GETTING ASHORE!!
ACTUALLY, THAT'S TRUE....
I WANT TO START MY RESEARCH ON VICTINI RIGHT AWAY, BUT...
...NOW I'M CURIOUS WHAT THAT'S ALL ABOUT.
CHOMP
LET'S DO IT, MUSHA!

BL-ANK...
AND...
...WHITE NOISE COALESCES INTO...
...BLACK!
?!
WELL? FIGURE ANY-THING OUT?!
...
CHECK THIS OUT, BOSS!
A GUIDE TO LIBERTY GARDEN?
I ALWAYS DO MY HOMEWORK BEFORE I MAKE A MOVE!
AND I DID MY RE-SEARCH ON THIS ISLAND.
THE ONLY TOURIST ATTRACTION HERE IS LIBERTY GARDEN AND THE LIGHTHOUSE.
Liberty Garden
Light-house
Liberty Garden
EVERY SINGLE SIGHTSEEING BROCHURE AND GUIDEBOOK HAS PHOTOS OF THE LIGHTHOUSE. I'VE SEEN IT OVER AND OVER AGAIN!

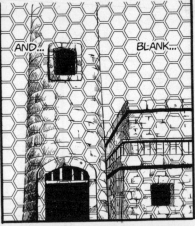

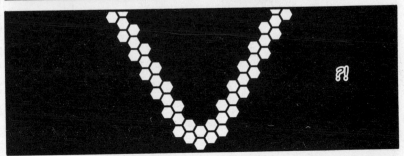

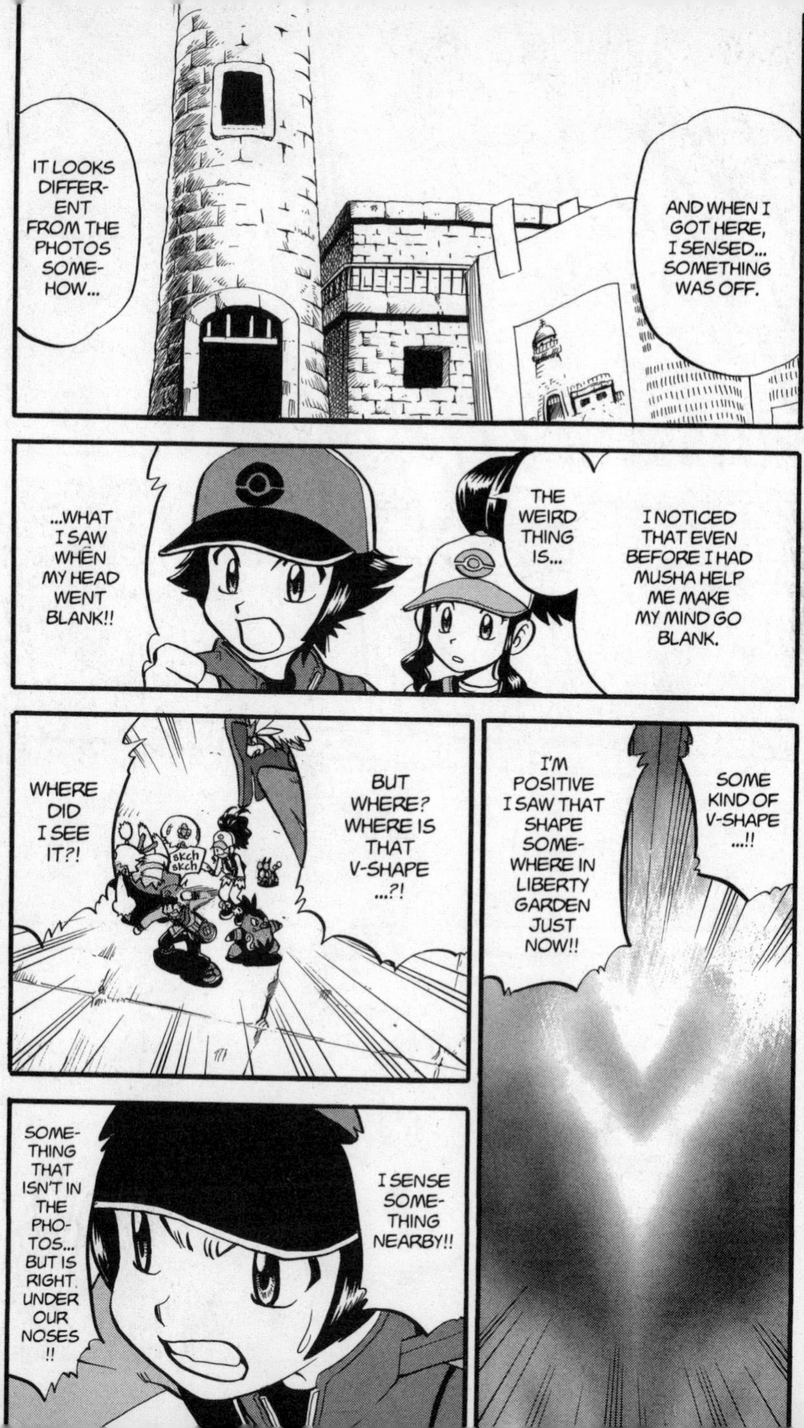
AND WHEN I GOT HERE, I SENSED... SOMETHING WAS OFF.
IT LOOKS DIFFERENT FROM THE PHOTOS SOMEHOW...
I NOTICED THAT EVEN BEFORE I HAD MUSHA HELP ME MAKE MY MIND GO BLANK.
THE WEIRD THING IS...
...WHAT I SAW WHEN MY HEAD WENT BLANK!!
SOME KIND OF V-SHAPE ...!!
I'M POSITIVE I SAW THAT SHAPE SOMEWHERE IN LIBERTY GARDEN JUST NOW!!
BUT WHERE? WHERE IS THAT V-SHAPE ...?!
skch skch
WHERE DID I SEE IT?!
I SENSE SOMETHING NEARBY!!
SOMETHING THAT ISN'T IN THE PHOTOS... BUT IS RIGHT UNDER OUR NOSES!!

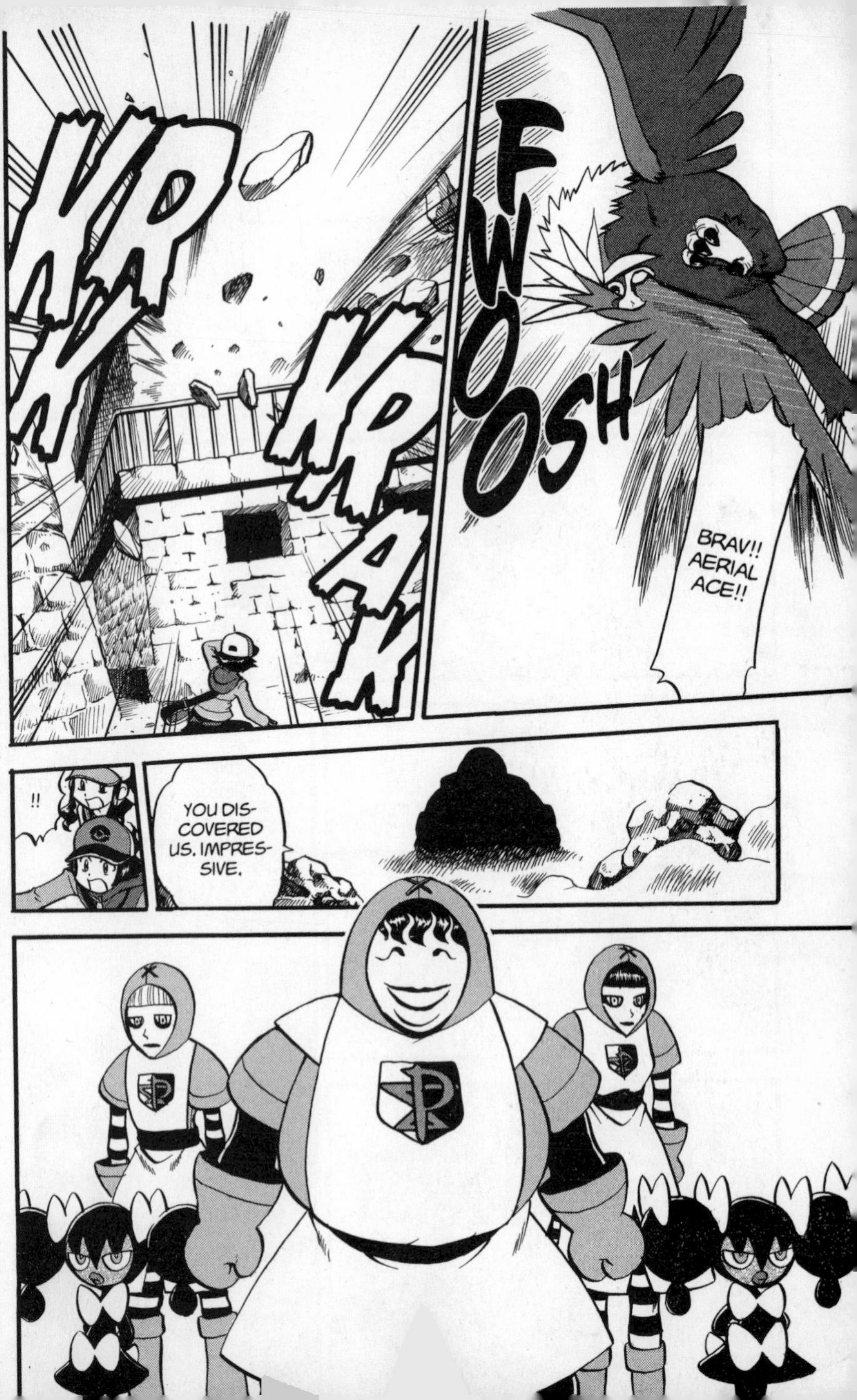
FWOOSH
BRAV!! AERIAL ACE!!
KRAK
KRAK
YOU DIS-COVERED US. IMPRES-SIVE.
!!

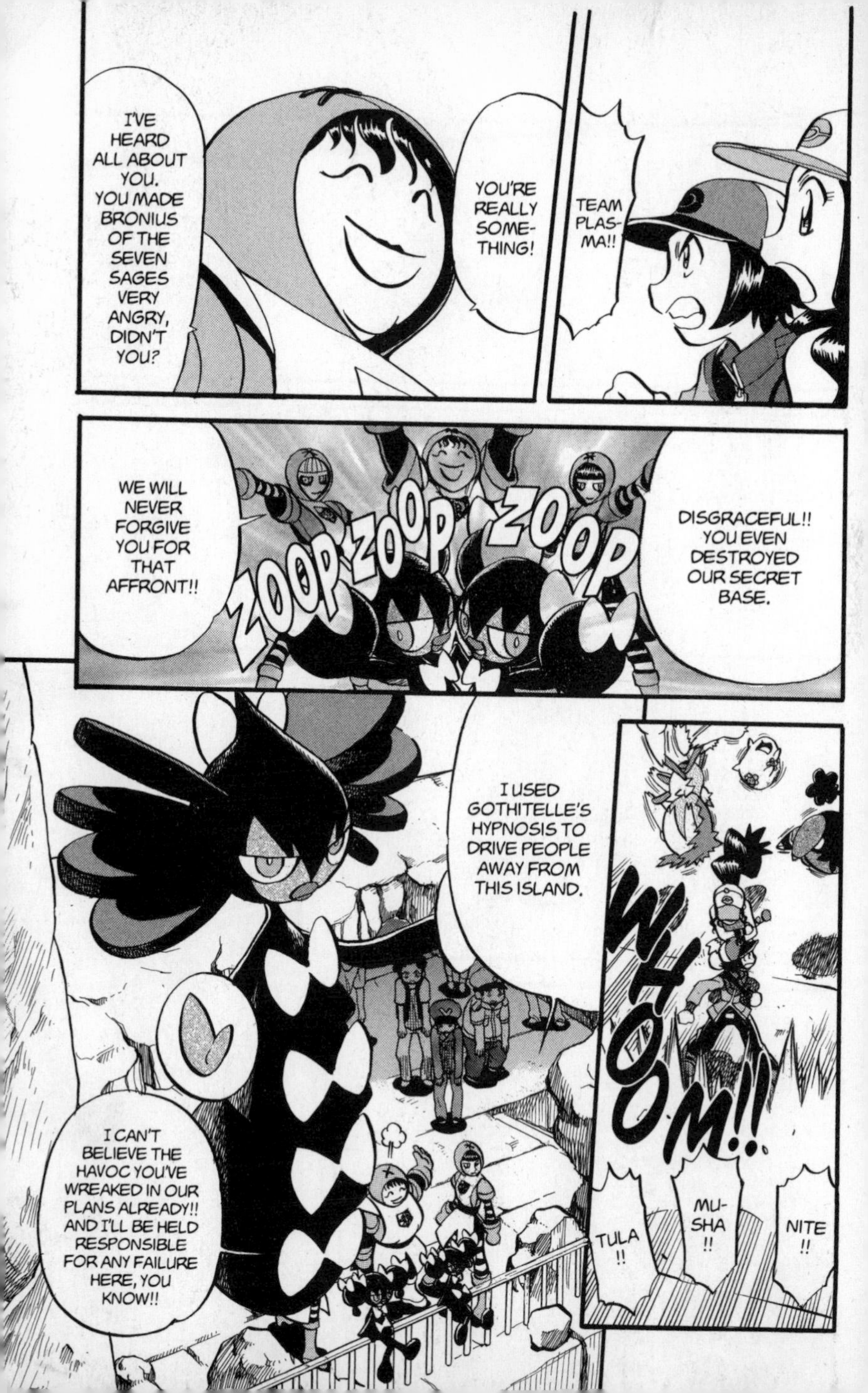
TEAM PLASMA!!
YOU'RE REALLY SOMETHING!
I'VE HEARD ALL ABOUT YOU. YOU MADE BRONIUS OF THE SEVEN SAGES VERY ANGRY, DIDN'T YOU?
DISGRACEFUL!! YOU EVEN DESTROYED OUR SECRET BASE.
ZOOP ZOOP ZOOP
WE WILL NEVER FORGIVE YOU FOR THAT AFFRONT!!
WHOOM!!
NITE!!
MUSHA!!
TULA!!
I USED GOTHITELLE'S HYPNOSIS TO DRIVE PEOPLE AWAY FROM THIS ISLAND.
I CAN'T BELIEVE THE HAVOC YOU'VE WREAKED IN OUR PLANS ALREADY!! AND I'LL BE HELD RESPONSIBLE FOR ANY FAILURE HERE, YOU KNOW!!

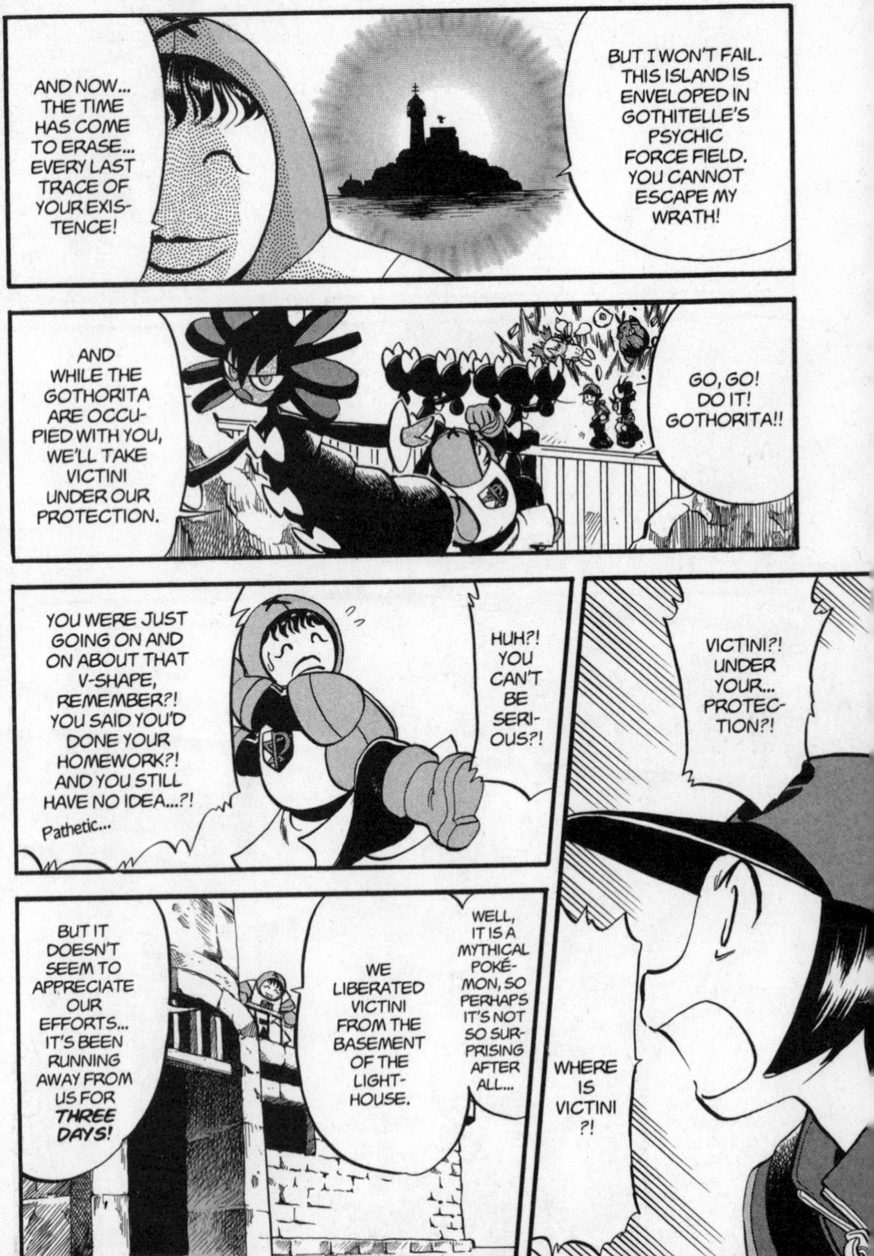
BUT I WON'T FAIL. THIS ISLAND IS ENVELOPED IN GOTHITELLE'S PSYCHIC FORCE FIELD. YOU CANNOT ESCAPE MY WRATH!
AND NOW... THE TIME HAS COME TO ERASE... EVERY LAST TRACE OF YOUR EXIS-TENCE!
GO, GO! DO IT! GOTHORITA!!
AND WHILE THE GOTHORITA ARE OCCU-PIED WITH YOU, WE'LL TAKE VICTINI UNDER OUR PROTECTION.
VICTINI?! UNDER YOUR... PROTEC-TION?!
WHERE IS VICTINI ?!
HUH?! YOU CAN'T BE SERI-OUS?!
YOU WERE JUST GOING ON AND ON ABOUT THAT V-SHAPE, REMEMBER?! YOU SAID YOU'D DONE YOUR HOMEWORK?! AND YOU STILL HAVE NO IDEA...?!
Pathetic...
WELL, IT IS A MYTHICAL POKÉ-MON, SO PERHAPS IT'S NOT SO SUR-PRISING AFTER ALL...
WE LIBERATED VICTINI FROM THE BASEMENT OF THE LIGHT-HOUSE.
BUT IT DOESN'T SEEM TO APPRECIATE OUR EFFORTS... IT'S BEEN RUNNING AWAY FROM US FOR ***THREE DAYS!***

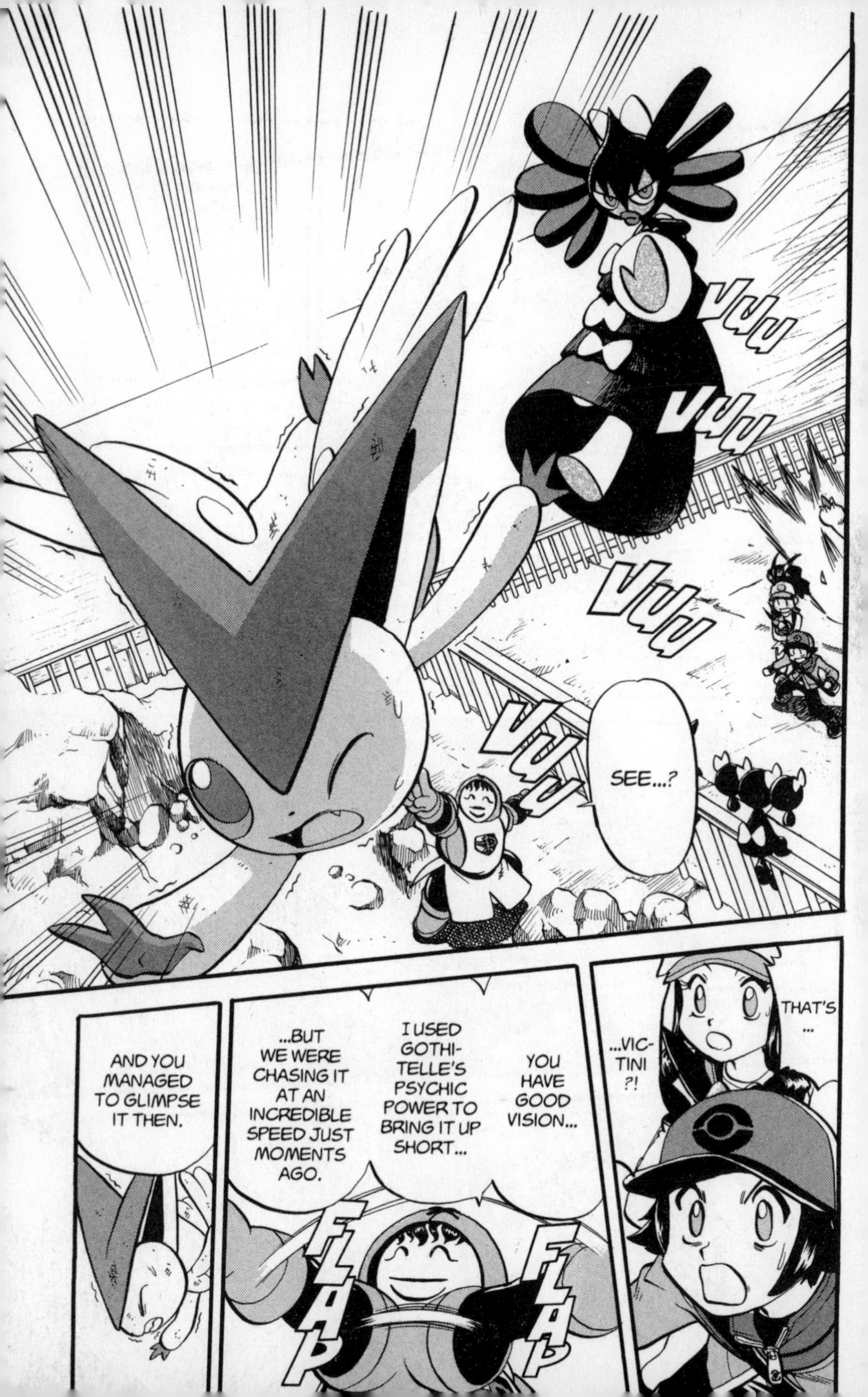
VUU
VUU
VUU
VUU
SEE...?
THAT'S...
...VICTINI?!
YOU HAVE GOOD VISION...
I USED GOTHITELLE'S PSYCHIC POWER TO BRING IT UP SHORT...
...BUT WE WERE CHASING IT AT AN INCREDIBLE SPEED JUST MOMENTS AGO.
FLAP
FLAP
AND YOU MANAGED TO GLIMPSE IT THEN.

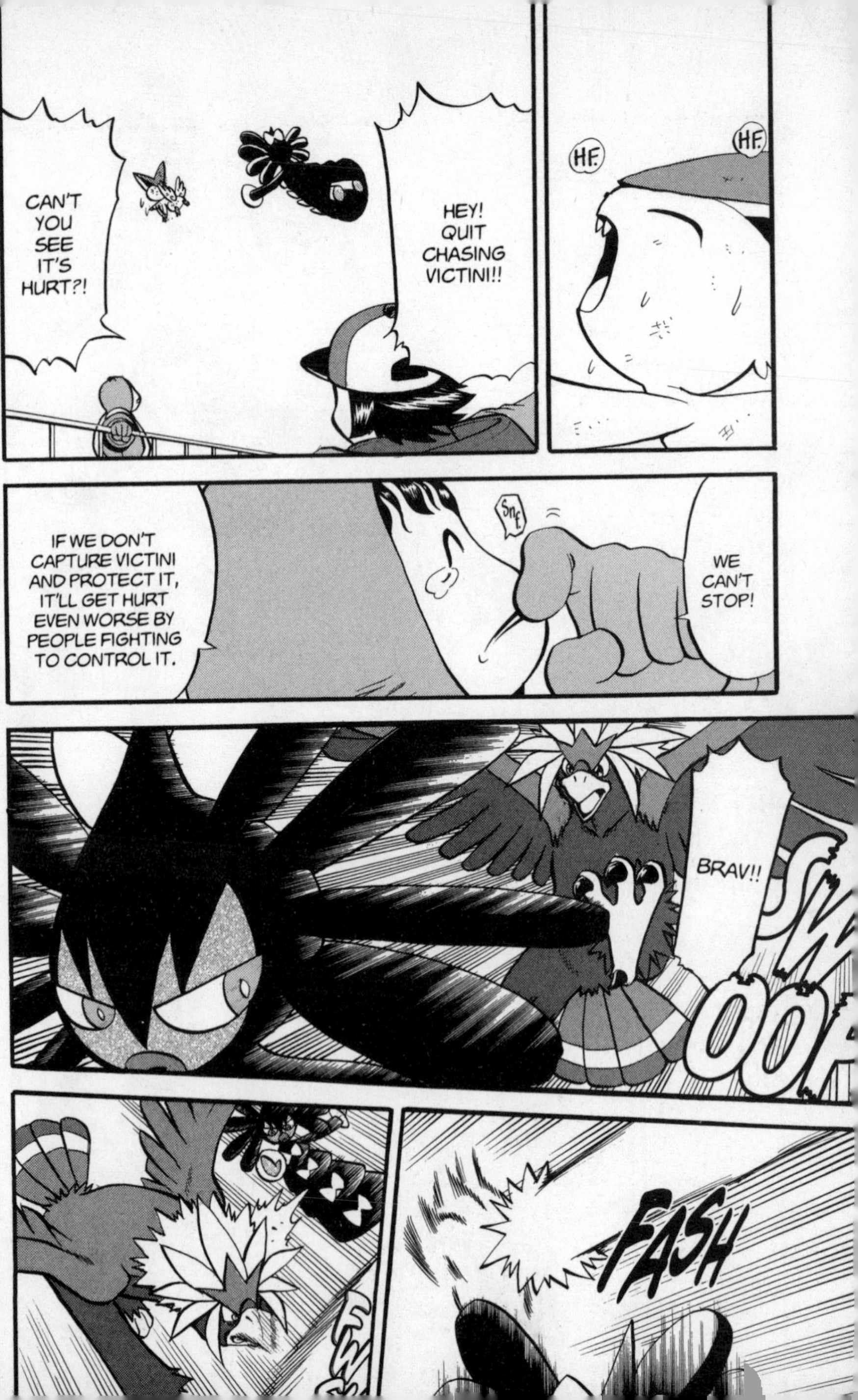
HF.
HF.
HEY! QUIT CHASING VICTINI!!
CAN'T YOU SEE IT'S HURT?!
WE CAN'T STOP!
Snf
IF WE DON'T CAPTURE VICTINI AND PROTECT IT, IT'LL GET HURT EVEN WORSE BY PEOPLE FIGHTING TO CONTROL IT.
BRAV!!
SWOOP
FASH

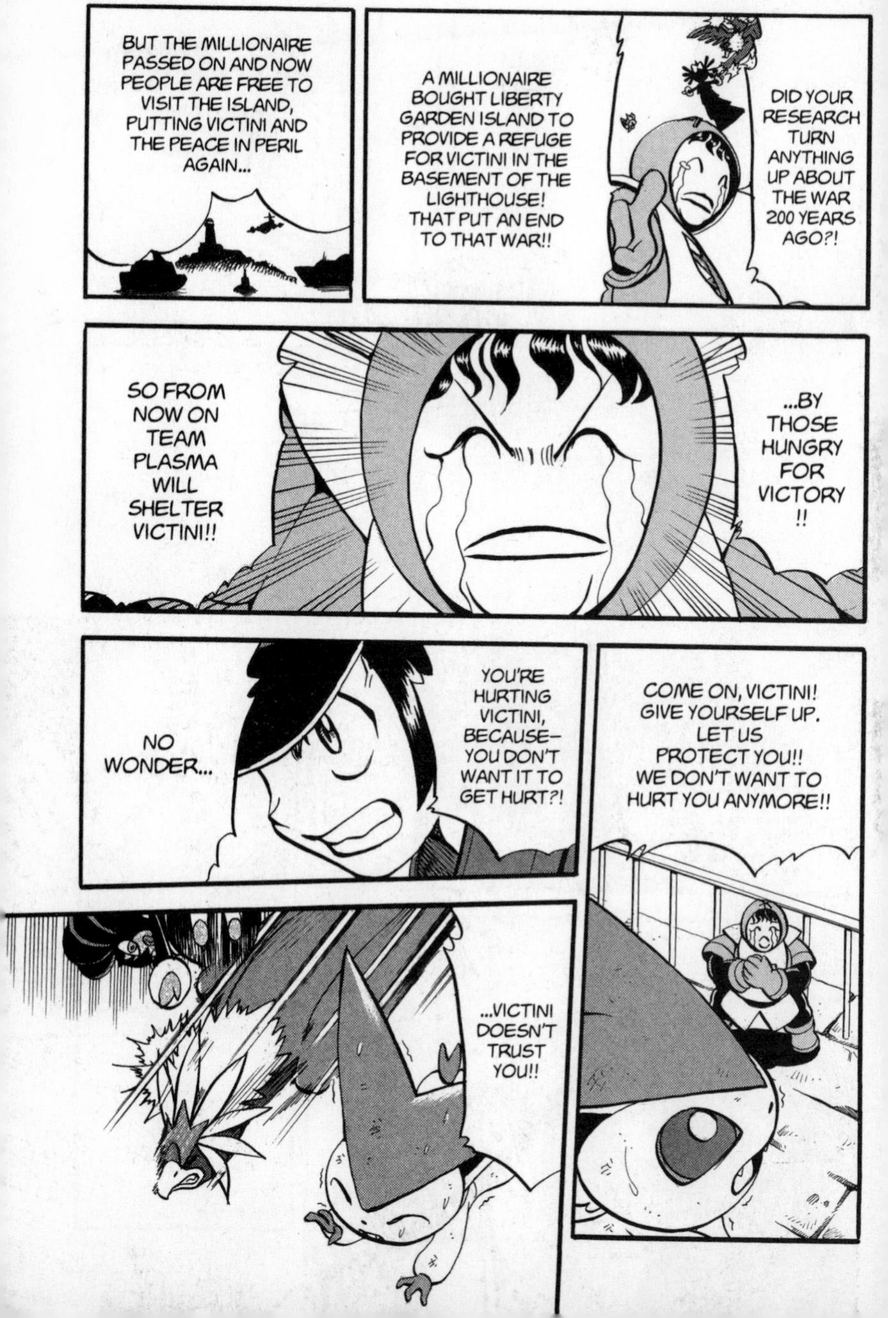
DID YOUR RESEARCH TURN ANYTHING UP ABOUT THE WAR 200 YEARS AGO?!
A MILLIONAIRE BOUGHT LIBERTY GARDEN ISLAND TO PROVIDE A REFUGE FOR VICTINI IN THE BASEMENT OF THE LIGHTHOUSE! THAT PUT AN END TO THAT WAR!!
BUT THE MILLIONAIRE PASSED ON AND NOW PEOPLE ARE FREE TO VISIT THE ISLAND, PUTTING VICTINI AND THE PEACE IN PERIL AGAIN...
...BY THOSE HUNGRY FOR VICTORY!!
SO FROM NOW ON TEAM PLASMA WILL SHELTER VICTINI!!
COME ON, VICTINI! GIVE YOURSELF UP. LET US PROTECT YOU!! WE DON'T WANT TO HURT YOU ANYMORE!!
YOU'RE HURTING VICTINI, BECAUSE— YOU DON'T WANT IT TO GET HURT?!
NO WONDER...
...VICTINI DOESN'T TRUST YOU!!

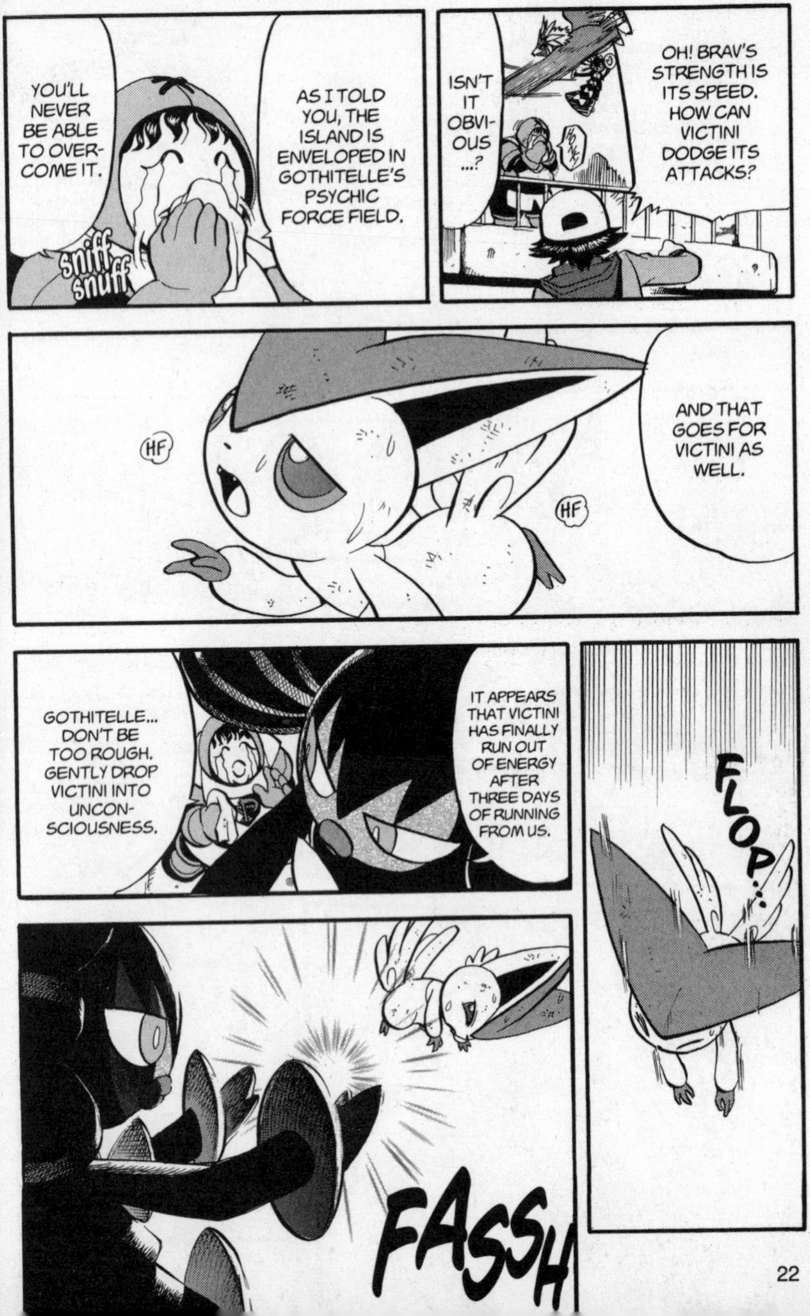
OH! BRAV'S STRENGTH IS ITS SPEED. HOW CAN VICTINI DODGE ITS ATTACKS?
ISN'T IT OBVI-OUS ...?
AS I TOLD YOU, THE ISLAND IS ENVELOPED IN GOTHITELLE'S PSYCHIC FORCE FIELD.
YOU'LL NEVER BE ABLE TO OVER-COME IT.
sniff snuff
AND THAT GOES FOR VICTINI AS WELL.
HF
HF
FLOP...
IT APPEARS THAT VICTINI HAS FINALLY RUN OUT OF ENERGY AFTER THREE DAYS OF RUNNING FROM US.
GOTHITELLE... DON'T BE TOO ROUGH. GENTLY DROP VICTINI INTO UNCON-SCIOUSNESS.
FASSH

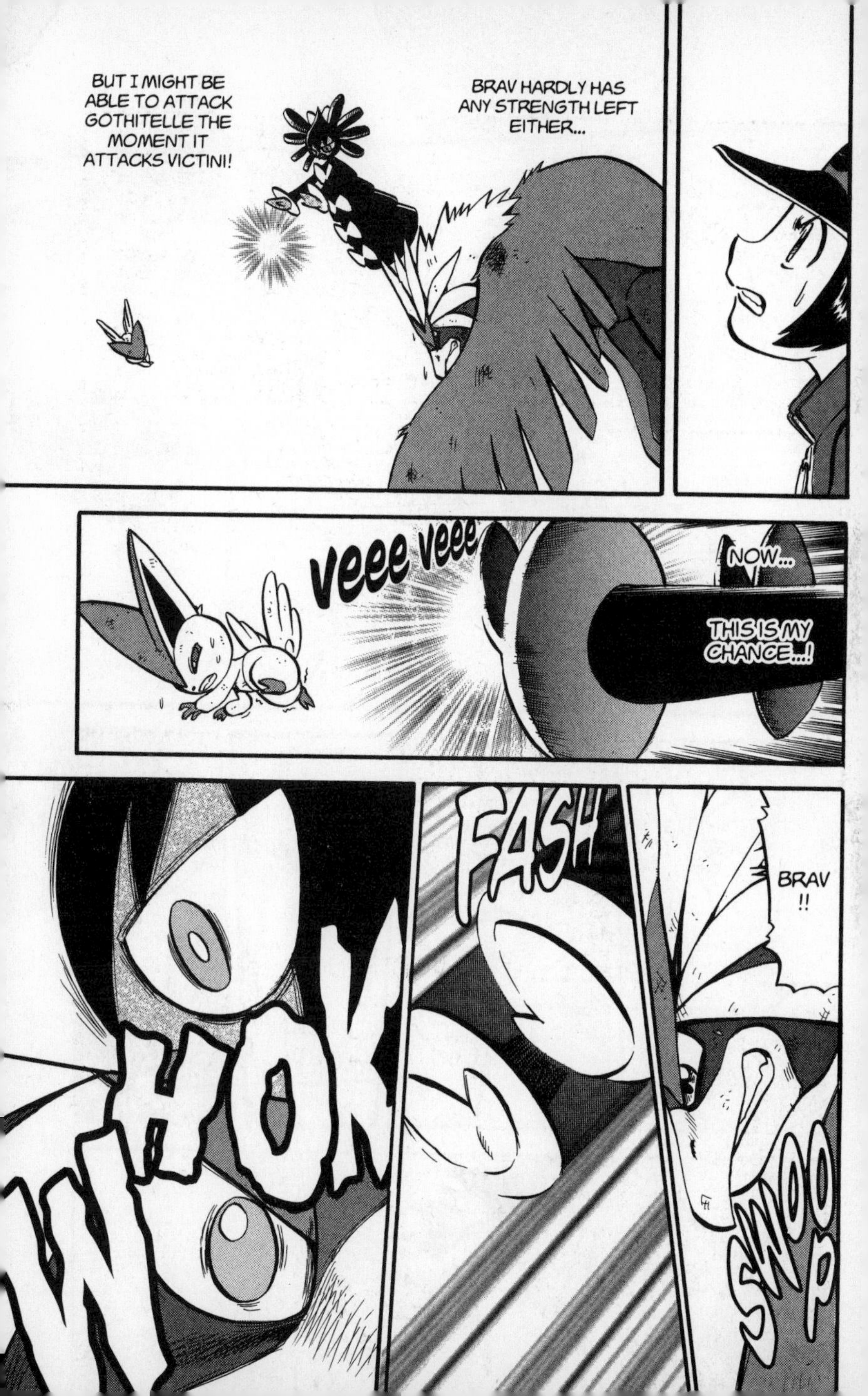
BRAV HARDLY HAS ANY STRENGTH LEFT EITHER...
BUT I MIGHT BE ABLE TO ATTACK GOTHITELLE THE MOMENT IT ATTACKS VICTINI!
NOW...
THIS IS MY CHANCE...!
veee veee
BRAV !!
SWOOP
FASH
WHOK

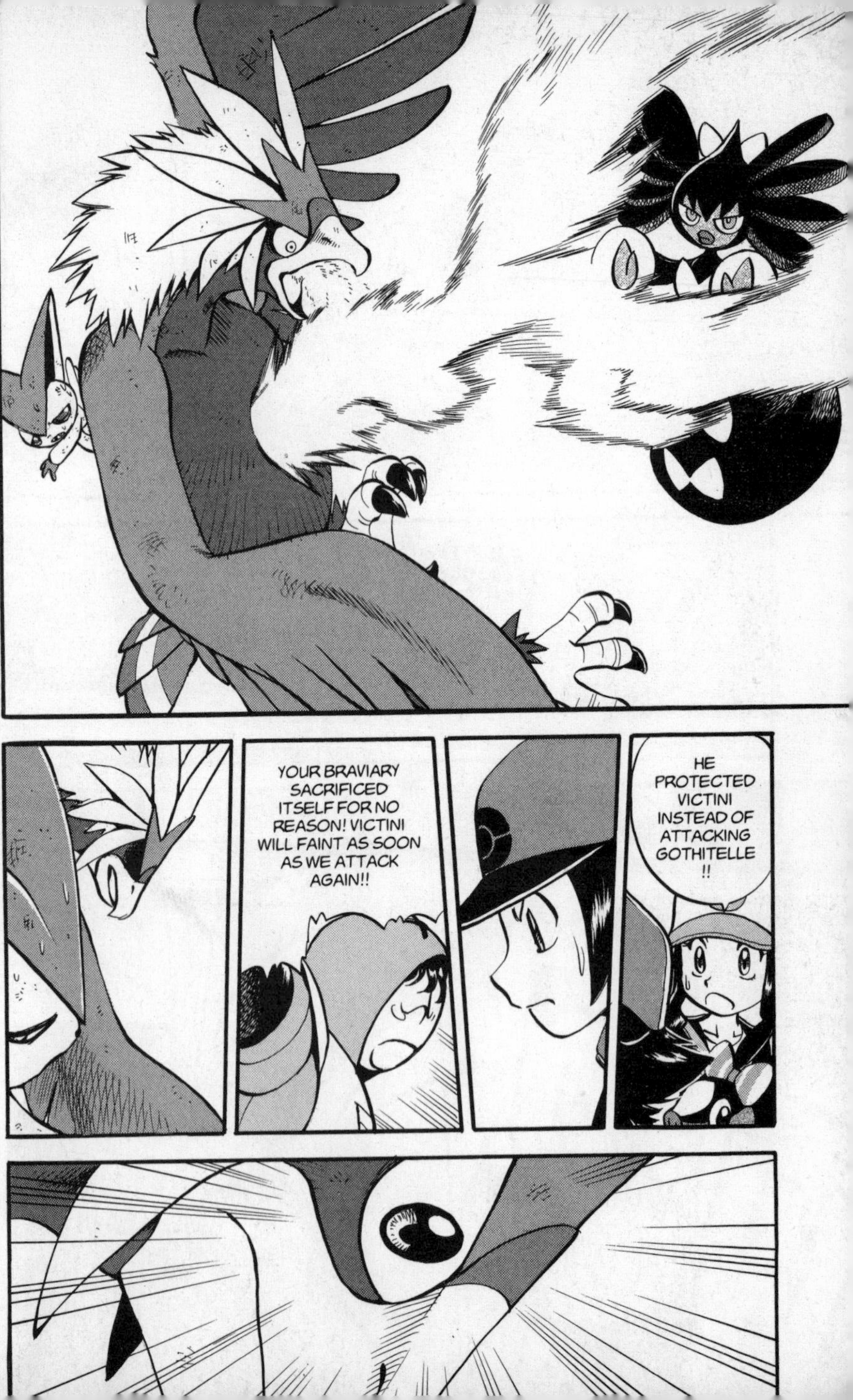
HE PROTECTED VICTINI INSTEAD OF ATTACKING GOTHITELLE!!
YOUR BRAVIARY SACRIFICED ITSELF FOR NO REASON! VICTINI WILL FAINT AS SOON AS WE ATTACK AGAIN!!

FAAAP

...WORKED!!

THE AT-TACK...

HUH?!

H...

CHAK!

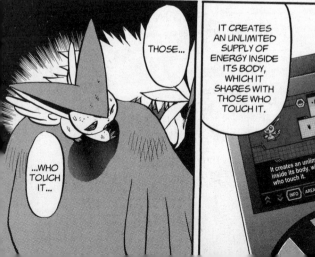

THOSE...

...WHO TOUCH IT...

IT CREATES AN UNLIMITED SUPPLY OF ENERGY INSIDE ITS BODY, WHICH IT SHARES WITH THOSE WHO TOUCH IT.

THIS POKÉMON BRINGS VICTORY.

•000 Victini
Victory Pokémon

PSYCHIC FIRE

HT   1'04"
WT   8.8 lbs.

It creates an unlimited supply of energy
inside its body, which it shares with those
who touch it.

INFO AREA CRY FORMS

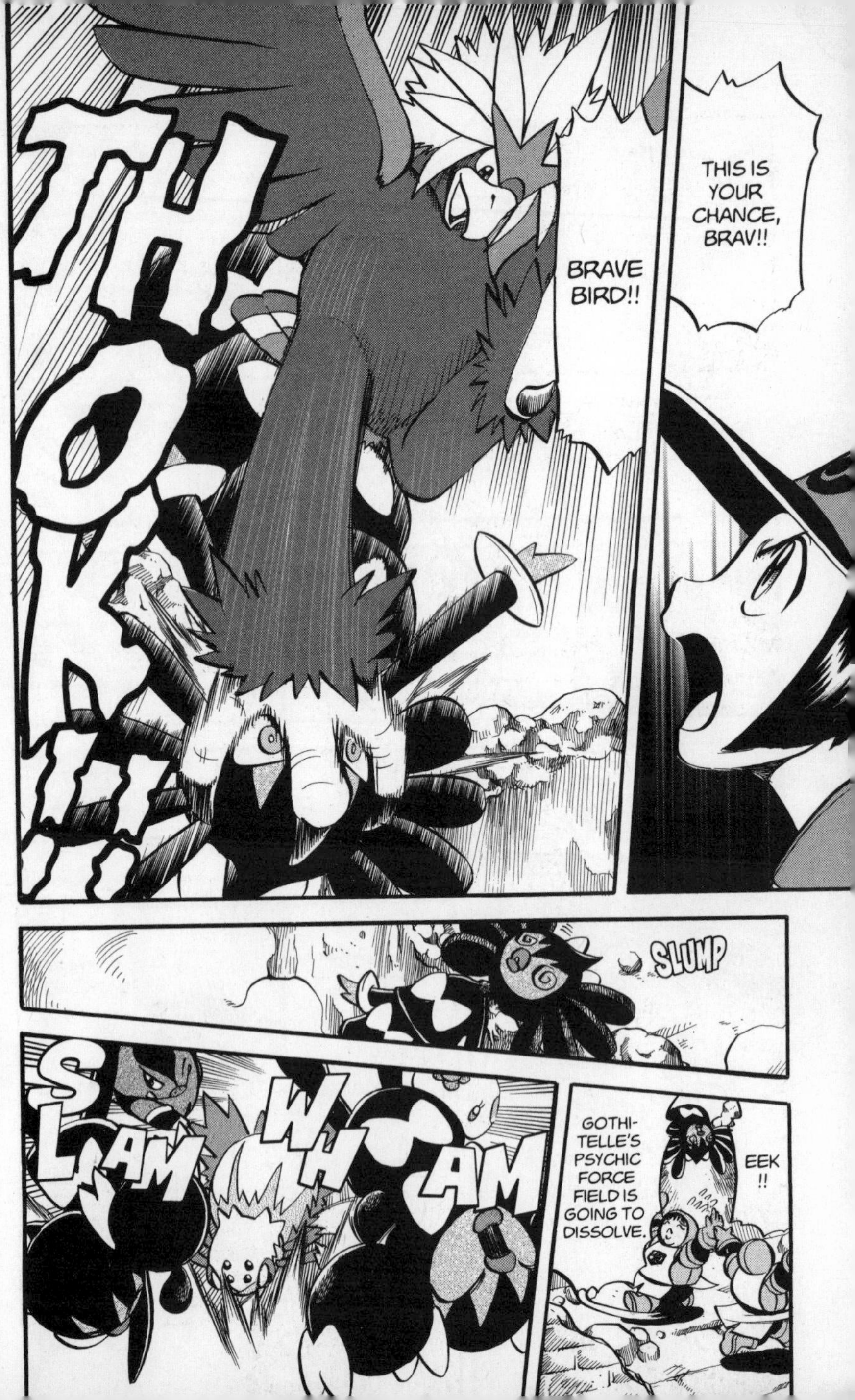
THIS IS YOUR CHANCE, BRAV!!
BRAVE BIRD!!
SLUMP
GOTHI-TELLE'S PSYCHIC FORCE FIELD IS GOING TO DISSOLVE.
EEK!!
SLAM
WHAM

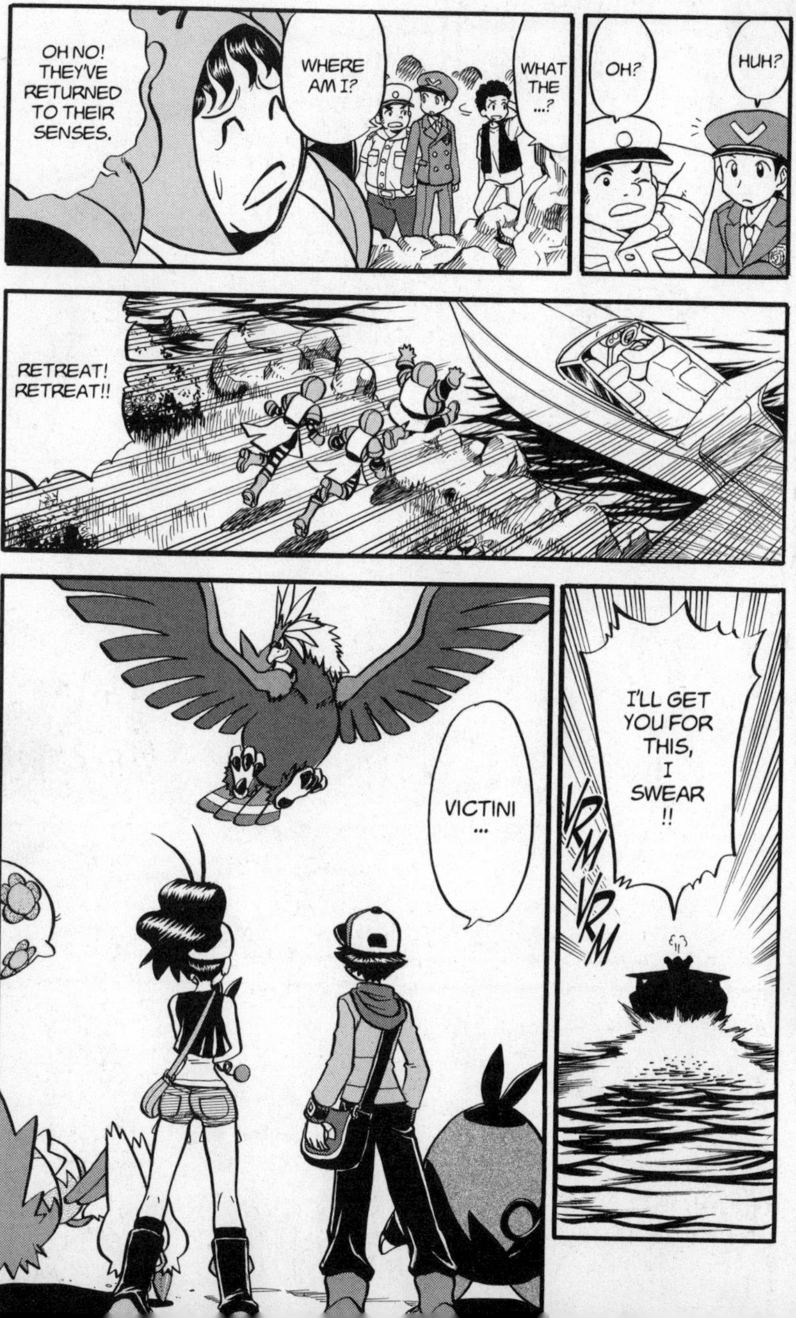
HUH?
OH?
WHAT THE ...?
WHERE AM I?
OH NO! THEY'VE RETURNED TO THEIR SENSES.
RETREAT! RETREAT!!
I'LL GET YOU FOR THIS, I SWEAR !!
VRM VRM VRM
VICTINI ...

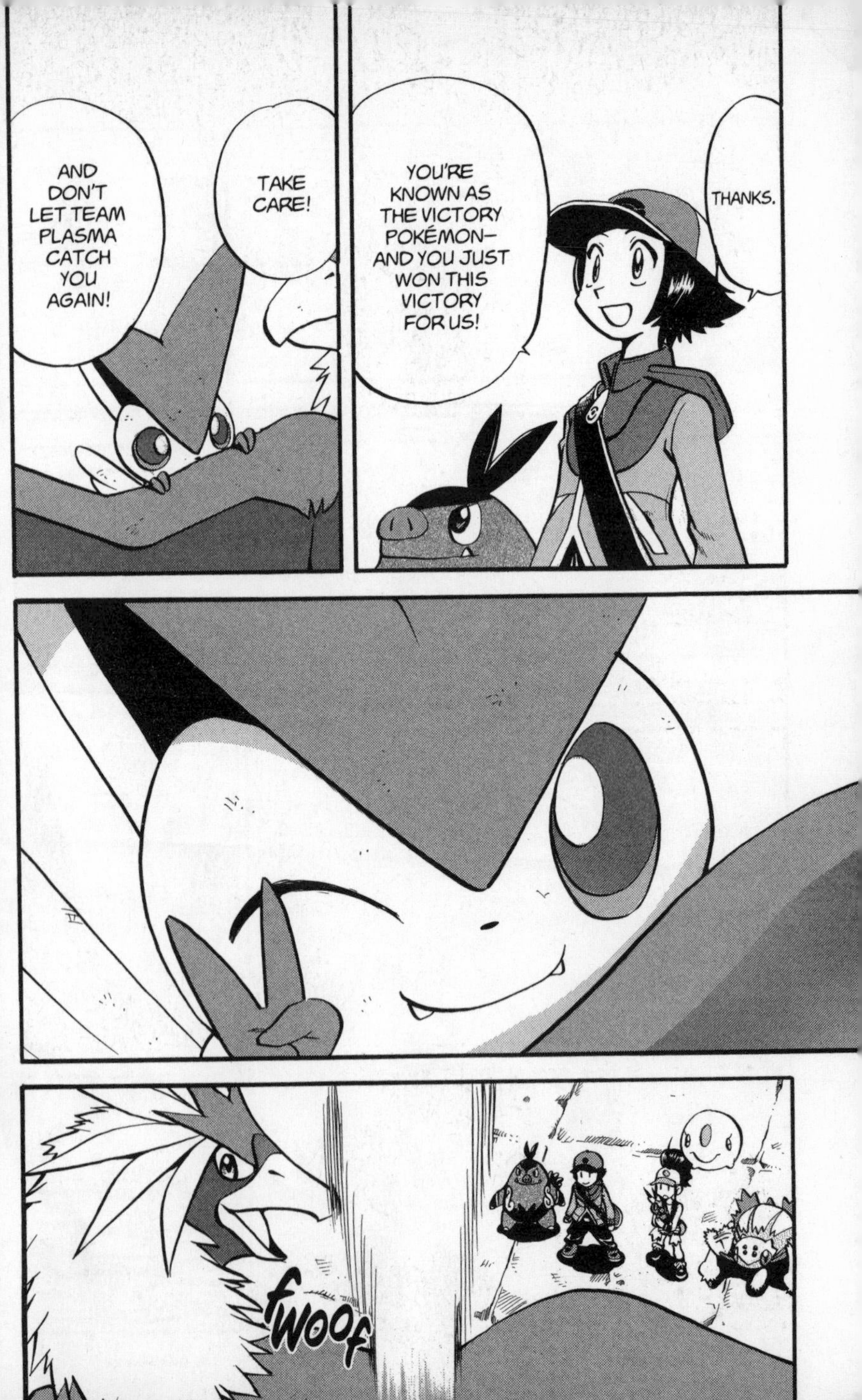
THANKS.
YOU'RE KNOWN AS THE VICTORY POKÉMON—AND YOU JUST WON THIS VICTORY FOR US!
TAKE CARE!
AND DON'T LET TEAM PLASMA CATCH YOU AGAIN!
fwoof

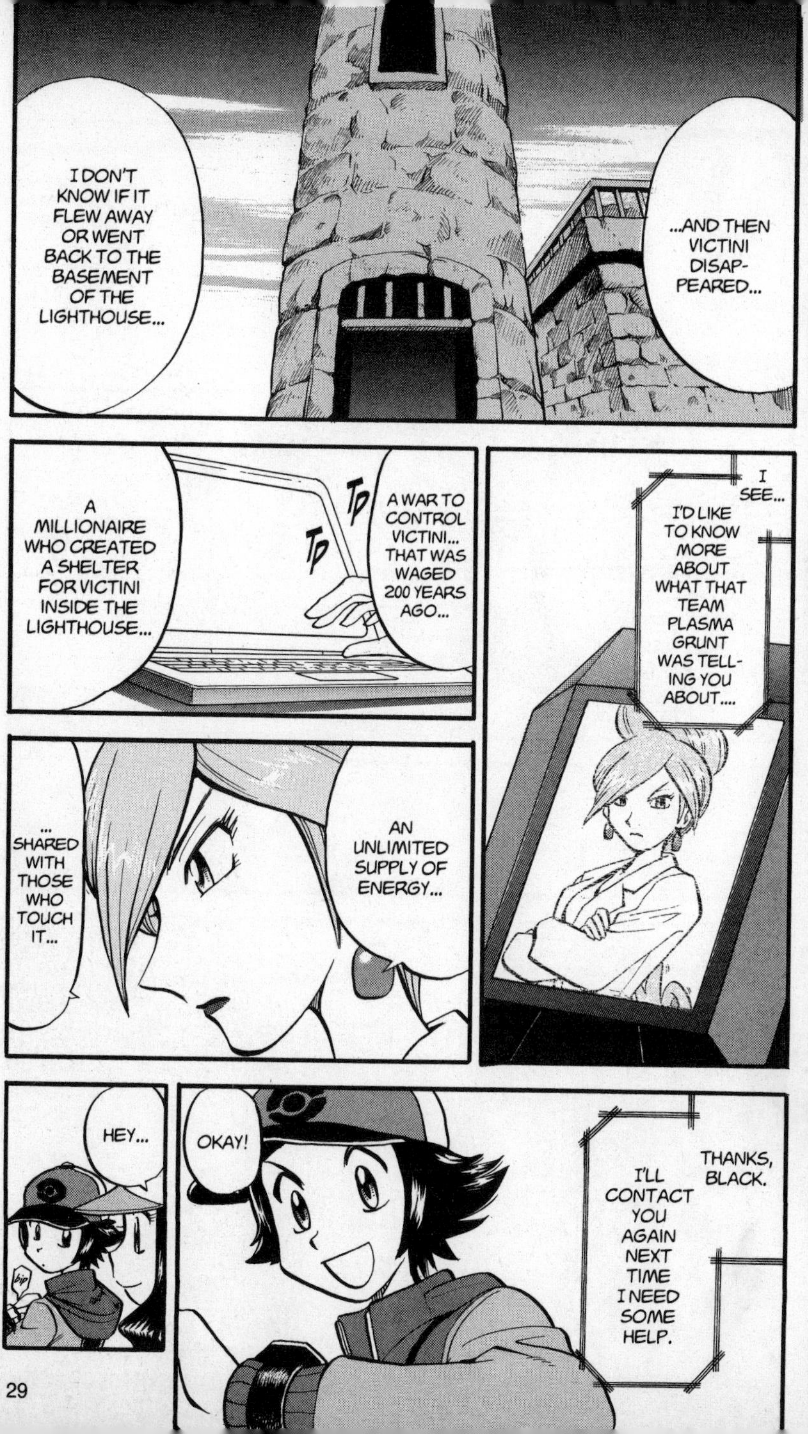
...AND THEN VICTINI DISAPPEARED...
I DON'T KNOW IF IT FLEW AWAY OR WENT BACK TO THE BASEMENT OF THE LIGHTHOUSE...
I SEE...
I'D LIKE TO KNOW MORE ABOUT WHAT THAT TEAM PLASMA GRUNT WAS TELLING YOU ABOUT....
A WAR TO CONTROL VICTINI... THAT WAS WAGED 200 YEARS AGO...
TP
TP
A MILLIONAIRE WHO CREATED A SHELTER FOR VICTINI INSIDE THE LIGHTHOUSE...
AN UNLIMITED SUPPLY OF ENERGY...
... SHARED WITH THOSE WHO TOUCH IT...
THANKS, BLACK.
I'LL CONTACT YOU AGAIN NEXT TIME I NEED SOME HELP.
OKAY!
HEY...
bip

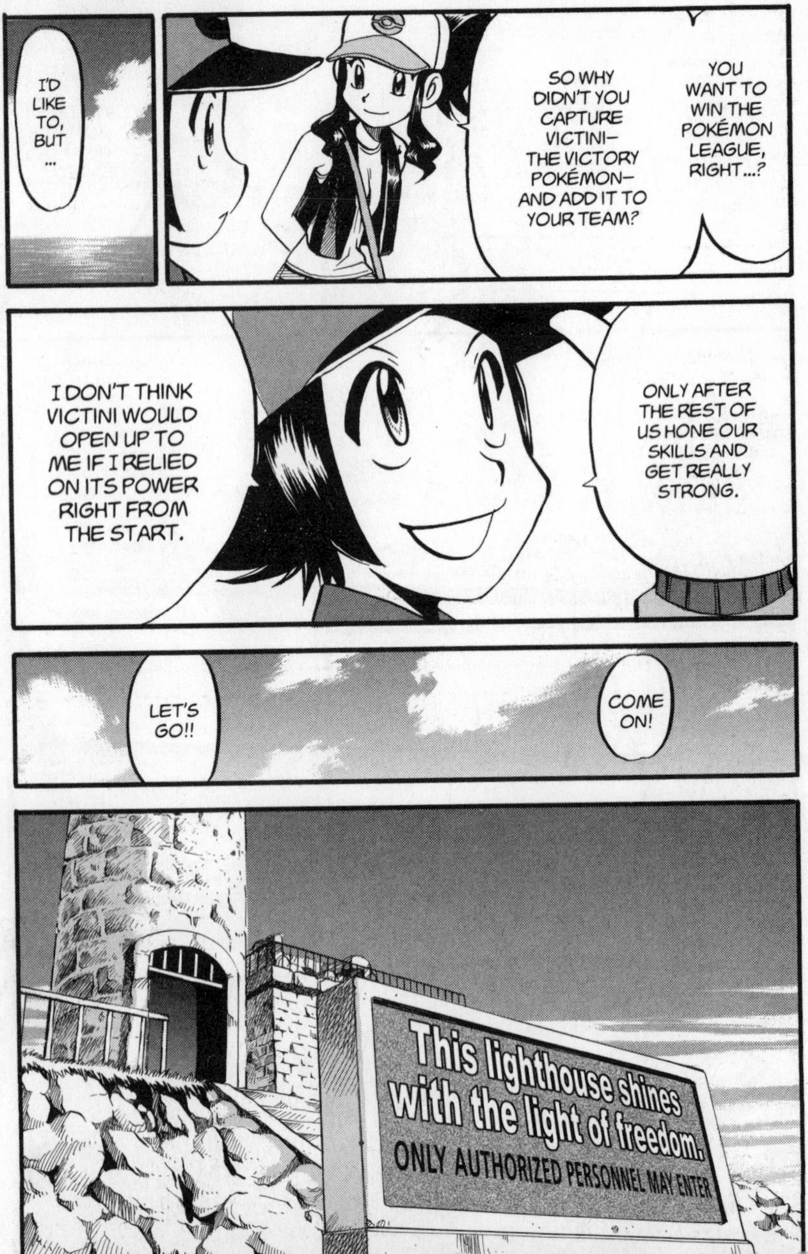
YOU WANT TO WIN THE POKÉMON LEAGUE, RIGHT...?
SO WHY DIDN'T YOU CAPTURE VICTINI—THE VICTORY POKÉMON—AND ADD IT TO YOUR TEAM?
I'D LIKE TO, BUT ...
ONLY AFTER THE REST OF US HONE OUR SKILLS AND GET REALLY STRONG.
I DON'T THINK VICTINI WOULD OPEN UP TO ME IF I RELIED ON ITS POWER RIGHT FROM THE START.
COME ON!
LET'S GO!!
This lighthouse shines with the light of freedom.
ONLY AUTHORIZED PERSONNEL MAY ENTER

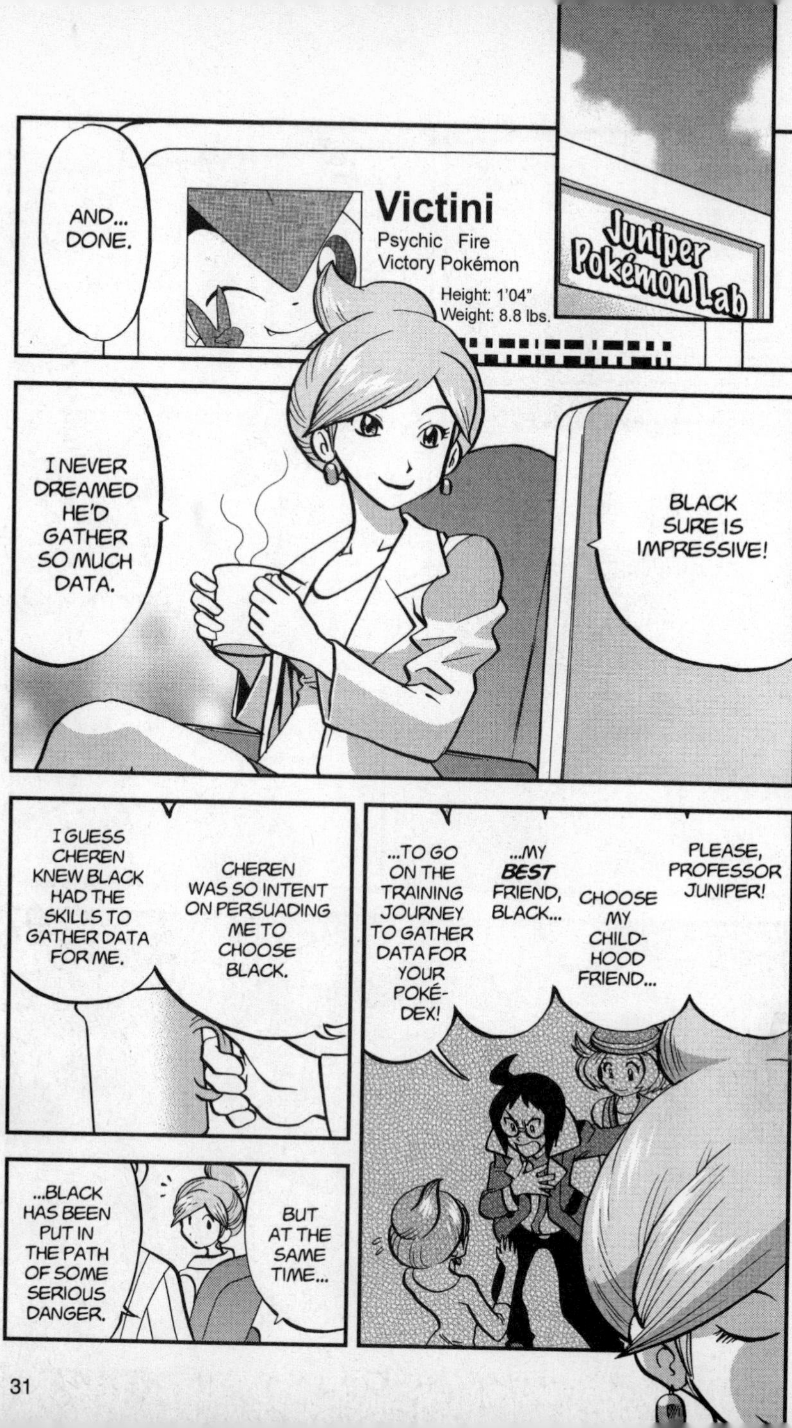
Juniper Pokémon Lab
Victini
Psychic Fire
Victory Pokémon
Height: 1'04"
Weight: 8.8 lbs.
AND... DONE.
BLACK SURE IS IMPRESSIVE!
I NEVER DREAMED HE'D GATHER SO MUCH DATA.
PLEASE, PROFESSOR JUNIPER!
CHOOSE MY CHILDHOOD FRIEND...
...MY *BEST* FRIEND, BLACK...
...TO GO ON THE TRAINING JOURNEY TO GATHER DATA FOR YOUR POKÉDEX!
CHEREN WAS SO INTENT ON PERSUADING ME TO CHOOSE BLACK.
I GUESS CHEREN KNEW BLACK HAD THE SKILLS TO GATHER DATA FOR ME.
BUT AT THE SAME TIME...
...BLACK HAS BEEN PUT IN THE PATH OF SOME SERIOUS DANGER.

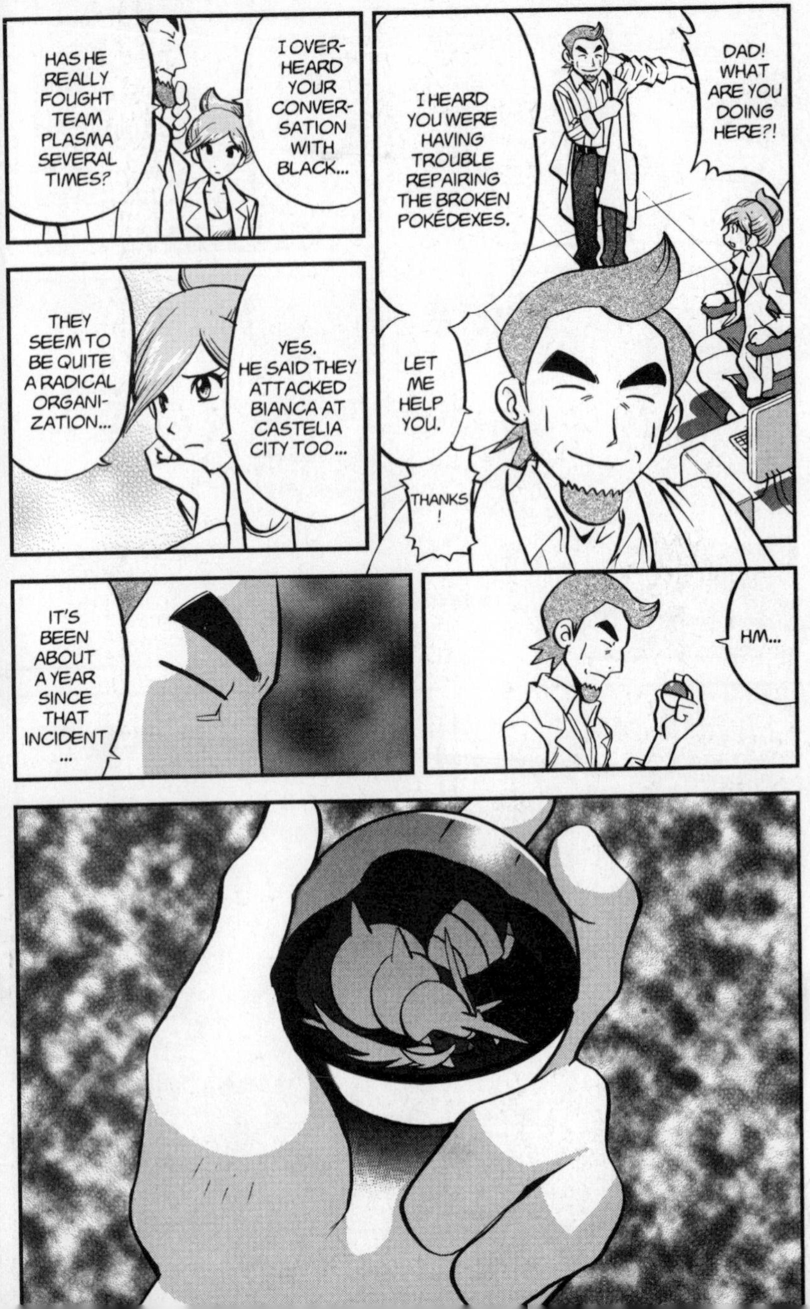
DAD! WHAT ARE YOU DOING HERE?!
I HEARD YOU WERE HAVING TROUBLE REPAIRING THE BROKEN POKÉDEXES.
LET ME HELP YOU.
THANKS!
I OVER-HEARD YOUR CONVER-SATION WITH BLACK...
HAS HE REALLY FOUGHT TEAM PLASMA SEVERAL TIMES?
YES. HE SAID THEY ATTACKED BIANCA AT CASTELIA CITY TOO...
THEY SEEM TO BE QUITE A RADICAL ORGANI-ZATION...
HM...
IT'S BEEN ABOUT A YEAR SINCE THAT INCIDENT...

ADVENTURE MAP

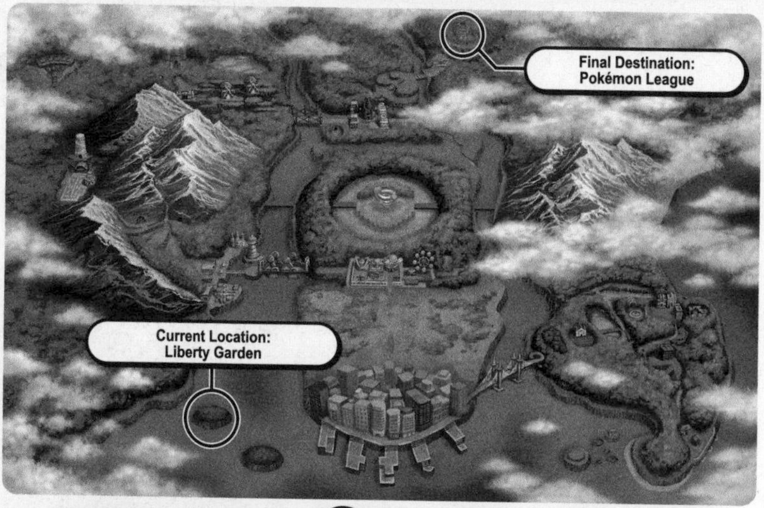
Final Destination:
Pokémon League
Current Location:
Liberty Garden

Fire Pig Pokémon **Nite**
Pignite ♂ Fire Fighting
Lv.19 Ability: Blaze

Dream Eater Pokémon **Musha**
Munna ♂ Psychic
Lv.41 Ability: Forewarn

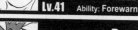

Valiant Pokémon **Brav**
Braviary ♂ Normal Flying
Lv.54 Ability: Sheer Force

EleSpider Pokémon **Tula**
Galvantula ♂ Bug Electric
Lv.43 Ability: Unnerve

BLACK

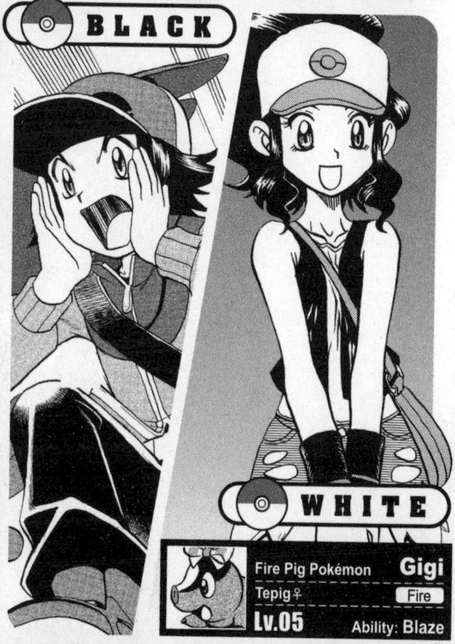

WHITE

Fire Pig Pokémon **Gigi**
Tepig ♀ Fire
Lv.05 Ability: Blaze

TRIO BADGE | BASIC BADGE | INSECT BADGE | ? | ? | ? | ? | ?

Pokémon™ Adventures Black & White

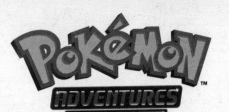

BISHARP

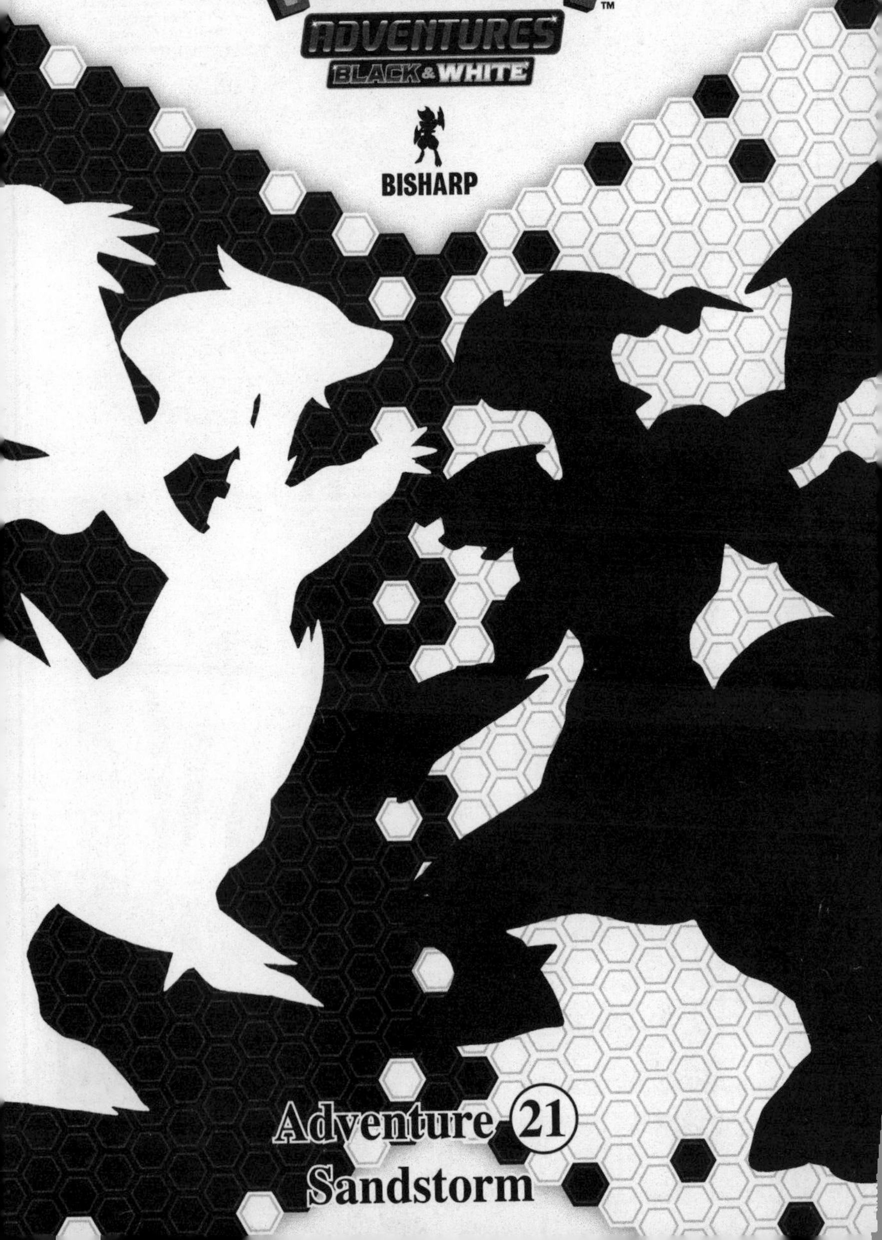

Adventure 21
Sandstorm

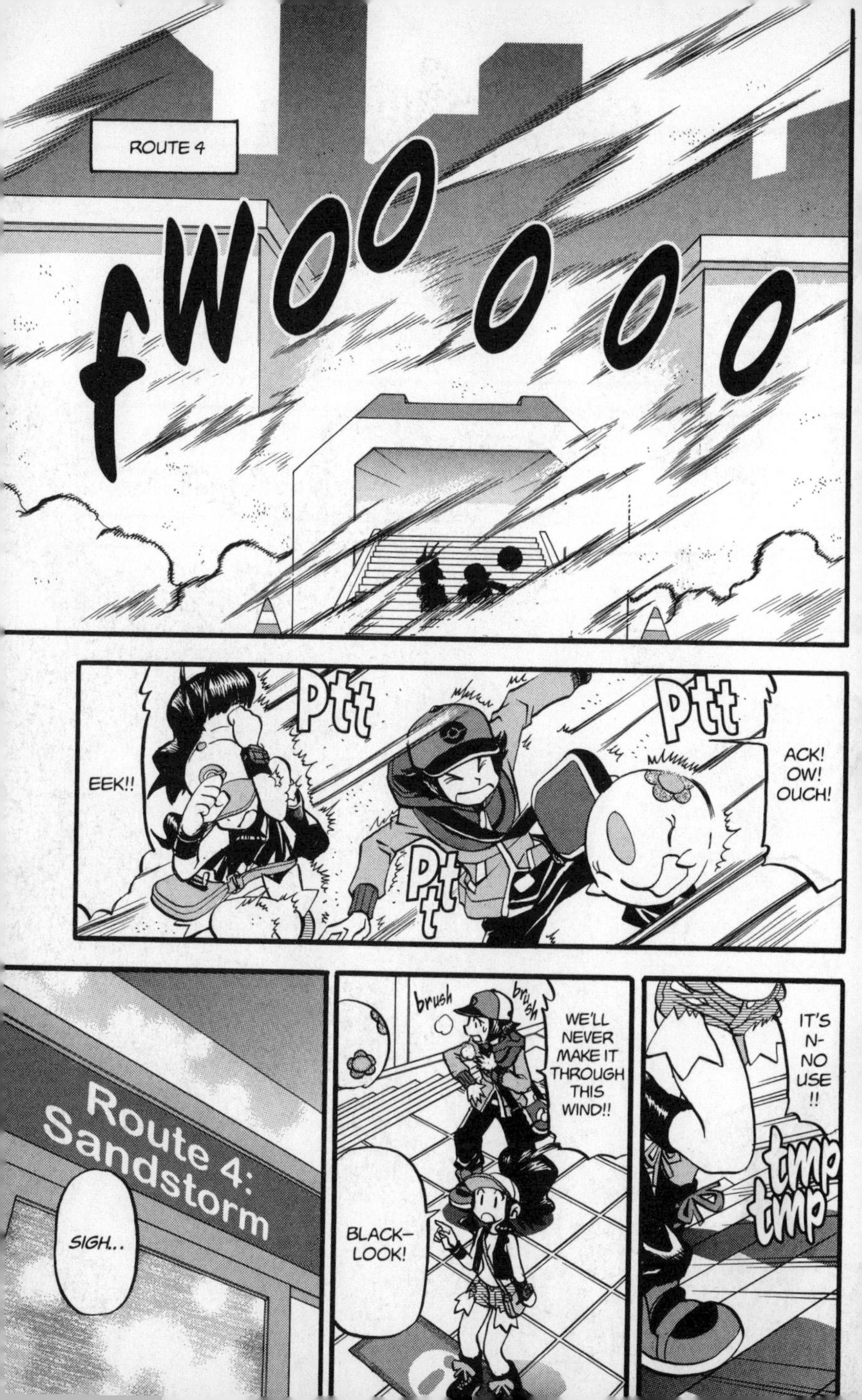
ROUTE 4
FWOOOOOO
ACK! OW! OUCH!
Ptt
Ptt
Ptt
EEK!!
IT'S N-NO USE!!
tmp tmp
brush
brush
WE'LL NEVER MAKE IT THROUGH THIS WIND!!
BLACK-LOOK!
Route 4: Sandstorm
SIGH...

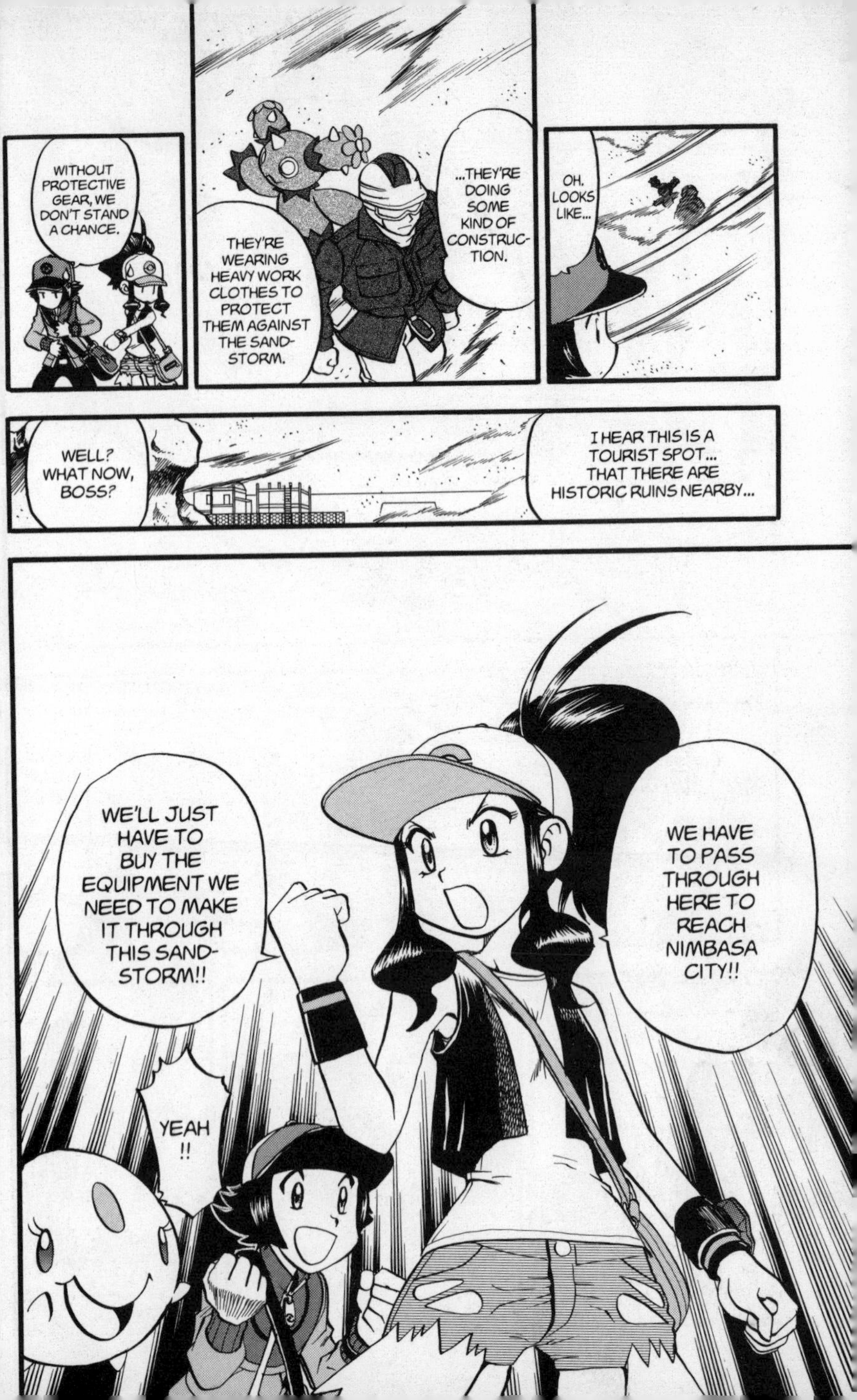
OH. LOOKS LIKE...
...THEY'RE DOING SOME KIND OF CONSTRUCTION.
THEY'RE WEARING HEAVY WORK CLOTHES TO PROTECT THEM AGAINST THE SAND-STORM.
WITHOUT PROTECTIVE GEAR, WE DON'T STAND A CHANCE.
I HEAR THIS IS A TOURIST SPOT... THAT THERE ARE HISTORIC RUINS NEARBY...
WELL? WHAT NOW, BOSS?
WE HAVE TO PASS THROUGH HERE TO REACH NIMBASA CITY!!
WE'LL JUST HAVE TO BUY THE EQUIPMENT WE NEED TO MAKE IT THROUGH THIS SAND-STORM!!
YEAH!!

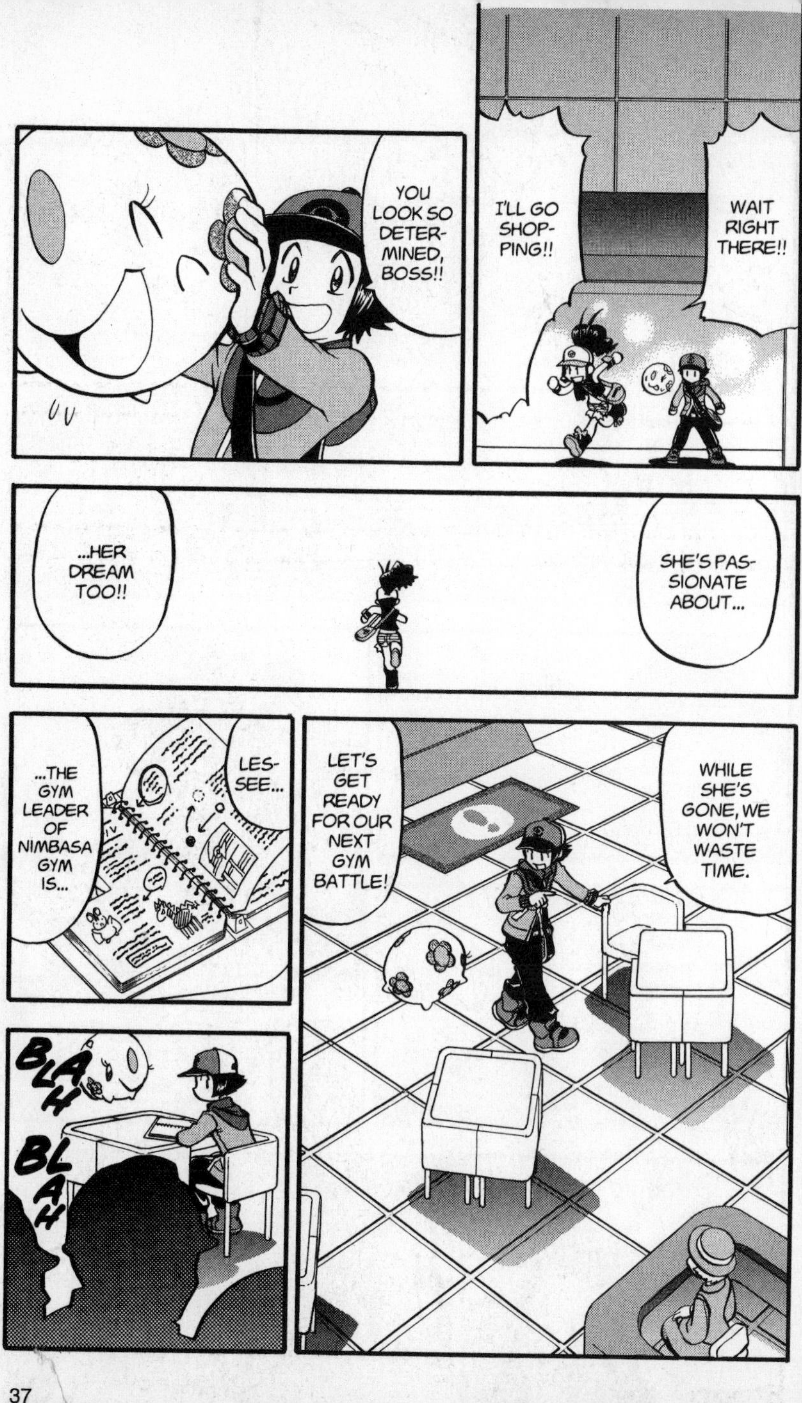
WAIT RIGHT THERE!!
I'LL GO SHOP-PING!!
YOU LOOK SO DETER-MINED, BOSS!!
SHE'S PAS-SIONATE ABOUT...
...HER DREAM TOO!!
WHILE SHE'S GONE, WE WON'T WASTE TIME.
LET'S GET READY FOR OUR NEXT GYM BATTLE!
LES-SEE...
...THE GYM LEADER OF NIMBASA GYM IS...
BLAH
BLAH

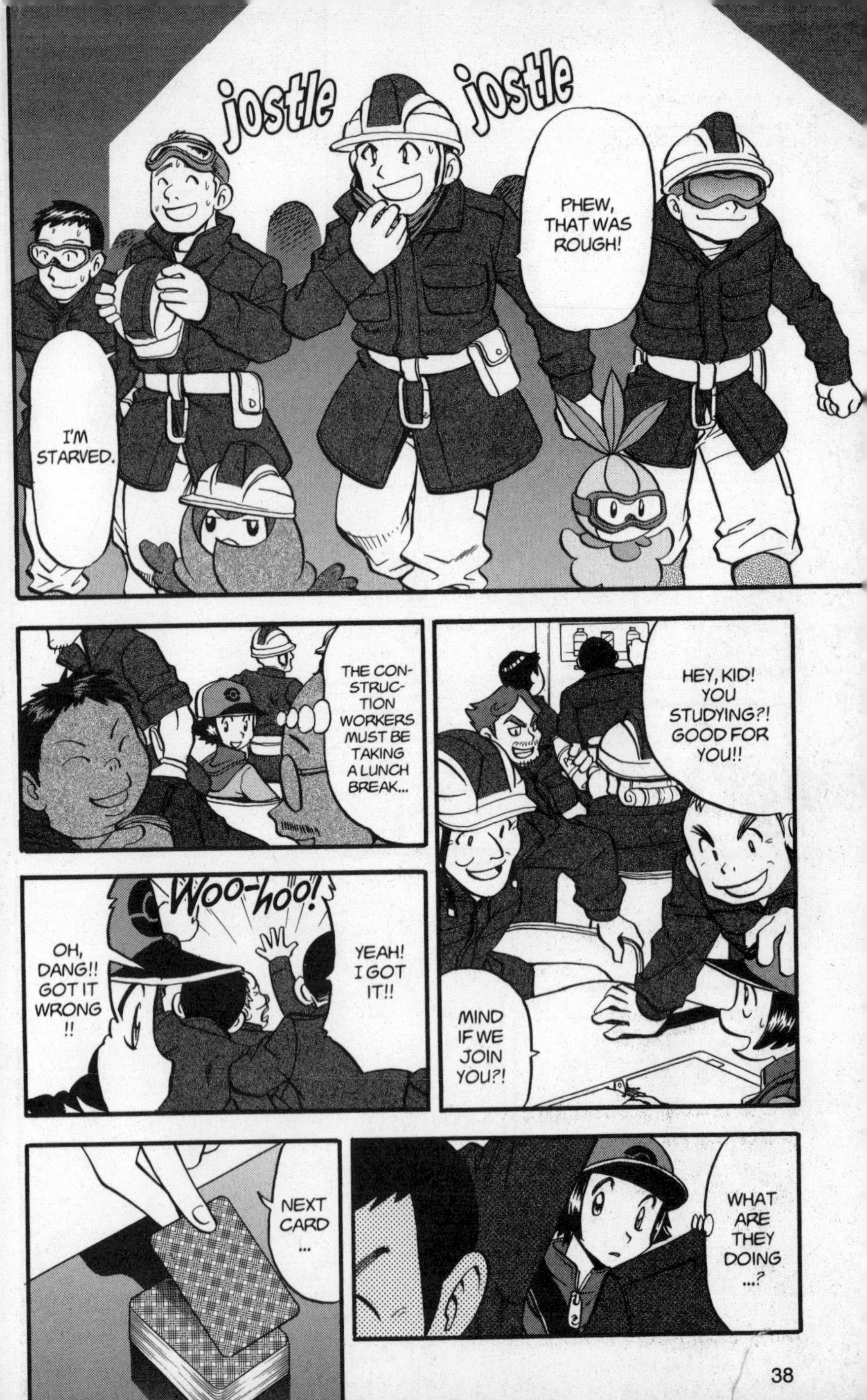
jostle
jostle
PHEW, THAT WAS ROUGH!
I'M STARVED.
HEY, KID! YOU STUDYING?! GOOD FOR YOU!!
MIND IF WE JOIN YOU?!
THE CON-STRUC-TION WORKERS MUST BE TAKING A LUNCH BREAK...
Woo-hoo!
YEAH! I GOT IT!!
OH, DANG!! GOT IT WRONG!!
WHAT ARE THEY DOING ...?
NEXT CARD ...

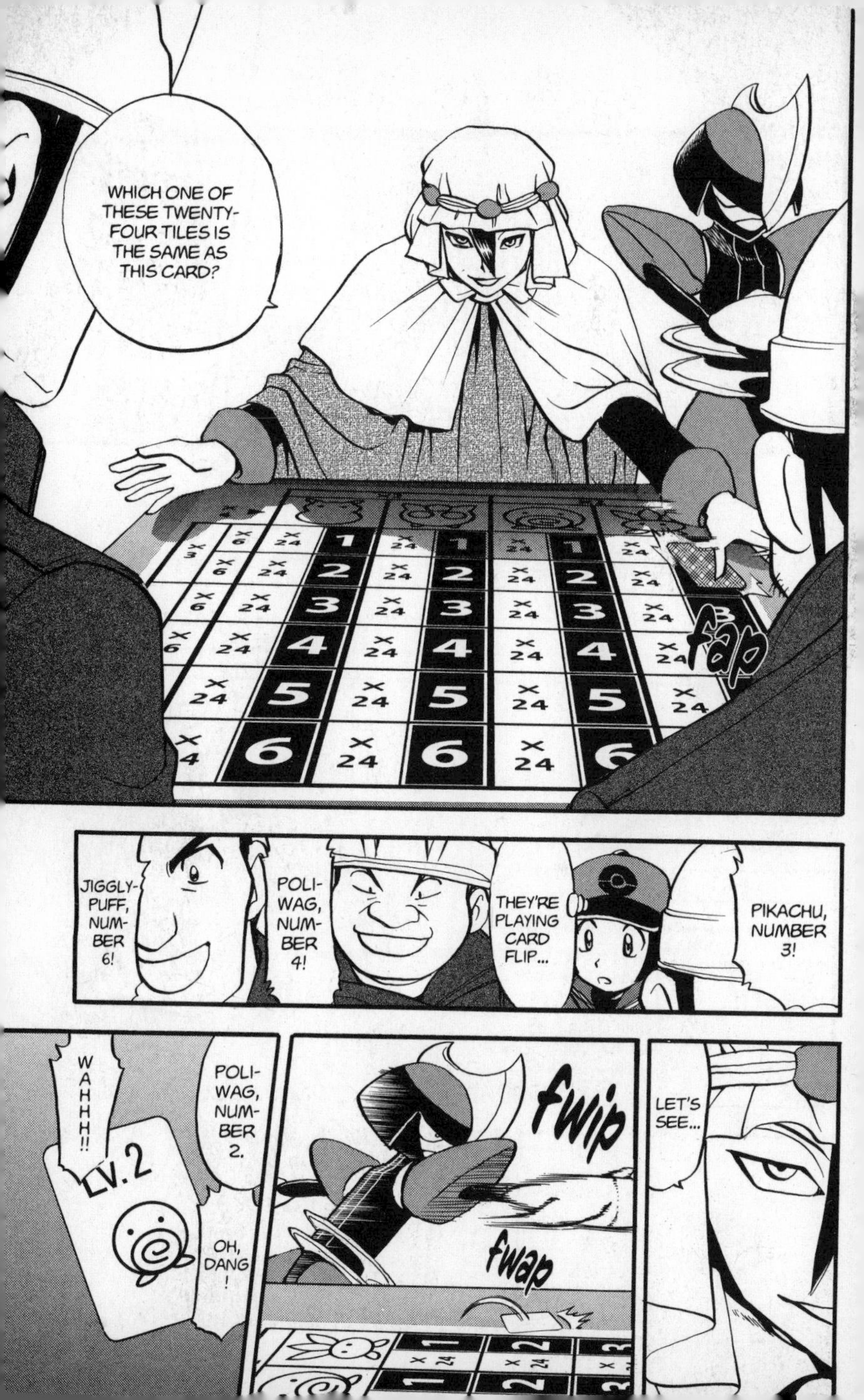
WHICH ONE OF THESE TWENTY-FOUR TILES IS THE SAME AS THIS CARD?
fap
PIKACHU, NUMBER 3!
THEY'RE PLAYING CARD FLIP...
POLI-WAG, NUMBER 4!
JIGGLY-PUFF, NUMBER 6!
LET'S SEE...
fwip
fwap
POLI-WAG, NUMBER 2.
WAHHH!!
LV. 2
OH, DANG!

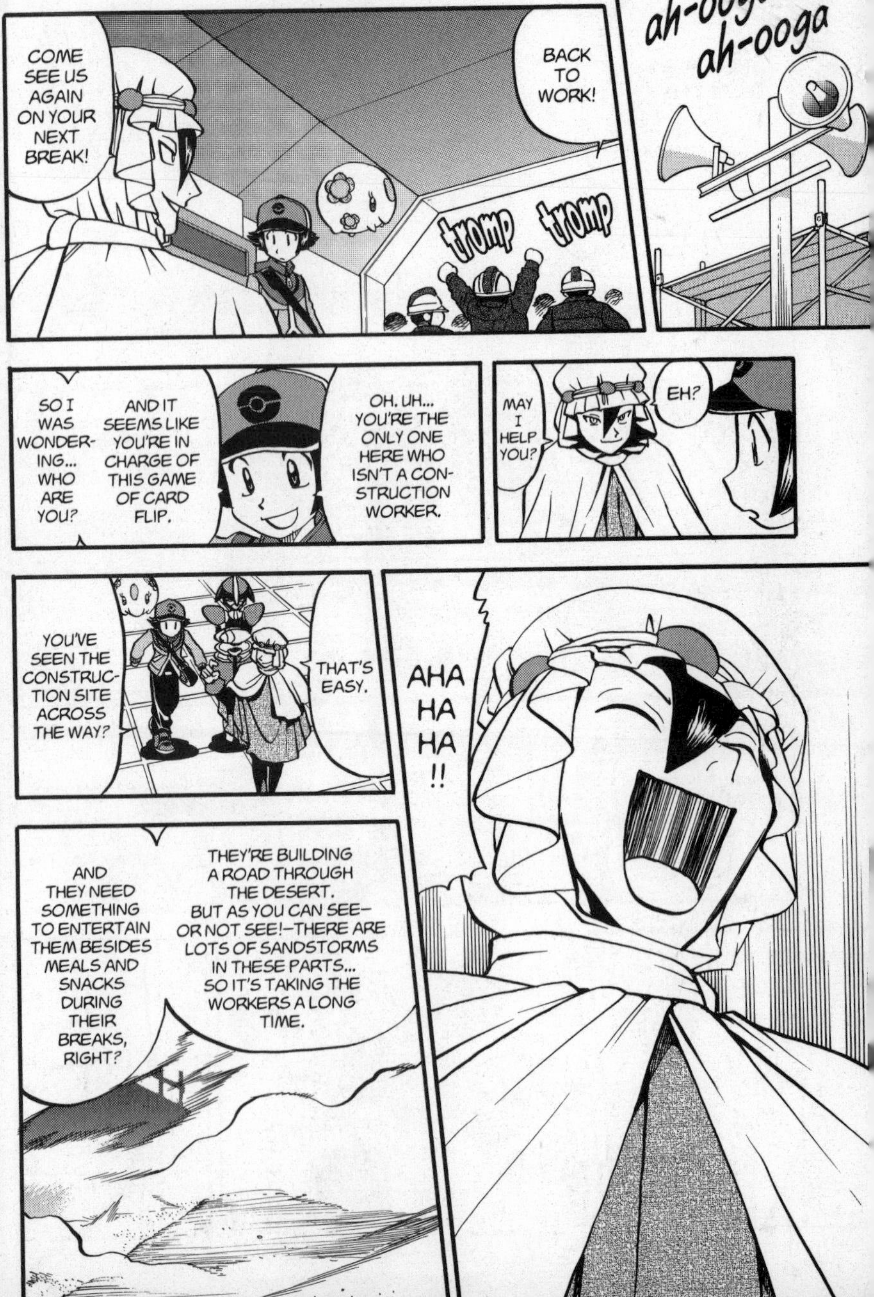
ah-ooga
ah-ooga
BACK TO WORK!
tromp tromp
COME SEE US AGAIN ON YOUR NEXT BREAK!
EH?
MAY I HELP YOU?
OH. UH... YOU'RE THE ONLY ONE HERE WHO ISN'T A CONSTRUCTION WORKER.
AND IT SEEMS LIKE YOU'RE IN CHARGE OF THIS GAME OF CARD FLIP.
SO I WAS WONDERING... WHO ARE YOU?
AHA HA HA !!
THAT'S EASY.
YOU'VE SEEN THE CONSTRUCTION SITE ACROSS THE WAY?
THEY'RE BUILDING A ROAD THROUGH THE DESERT. BUT AS YOU CAN SEE—OR NOT SEE!—THERE ARE LOTS OF SANDSTORMS IN THESE PARTS... SO IT'S TAKING THE WORKERS A LONG TIME.
AND THEY NEED SOMETHING TO ENTERTAIN THEM BESIDES MEALS AND SNACKS DURING THEIR BREAKS, RIGHT?

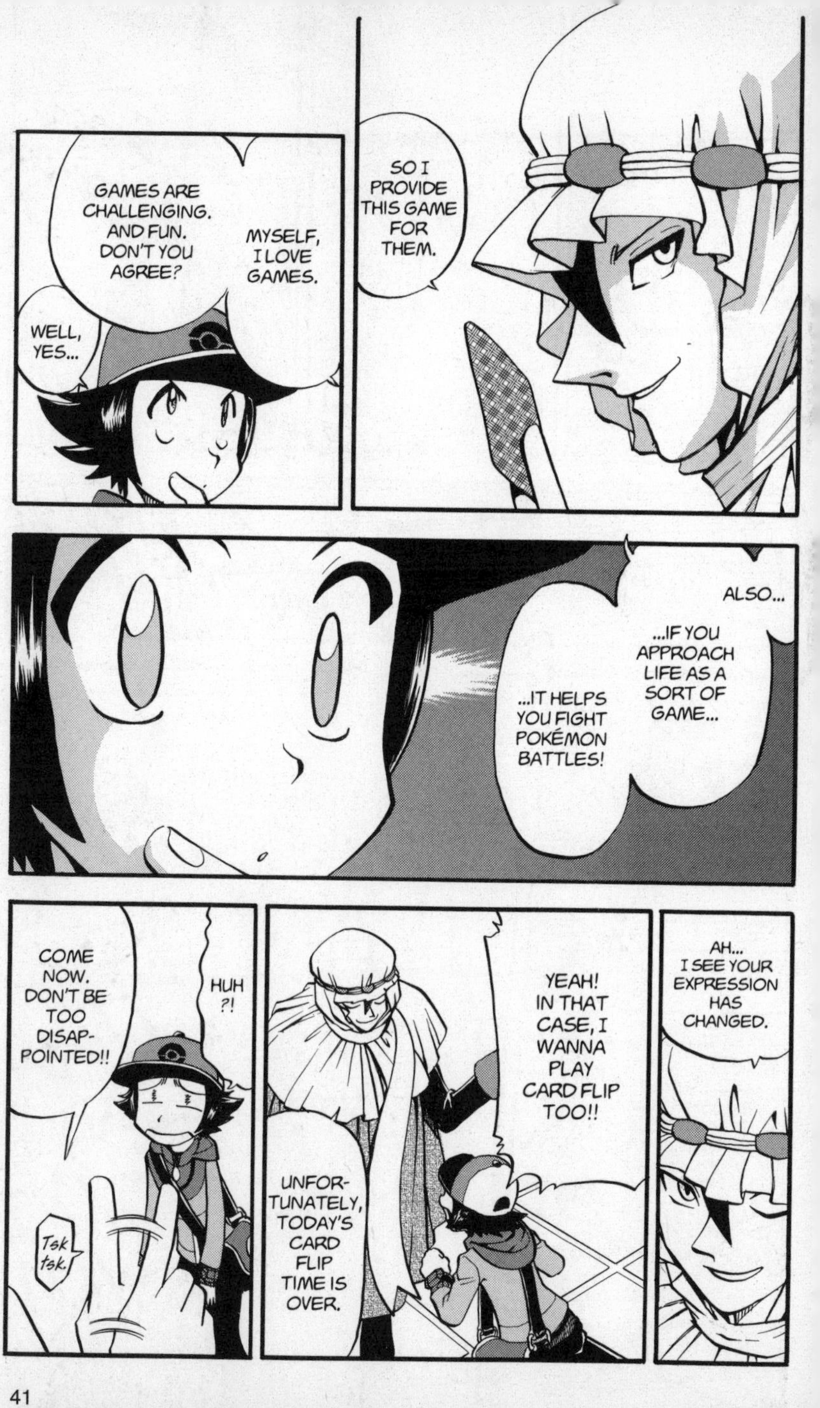
SO I PROVIDE THIS GAME FOR THEM.
MYSELF, I LOVE GAMES.
GAMES ARE CHALLENGING. AND FUN. DON'T YOU AGREE?
WELL, YES...
ALSO...
...IF YOU APPROACH LIFE AS A SORT OF GAME...
...IT HELPS YOU FIGHT POKÉMON BATTLES!
AH... I SEE YOUR EXPRESSION HAS CHANGED.
YEAH! IN THAT CASE, I WANNA PLAY CARD FLIP TOO!!
UNFORTUNATELY, TODAY'S CARD FLIP TIME IS OVER.
HUH ?!
COME NOW. DON'T BE TOO DISAPPOINTED!!
Tsk tsk.

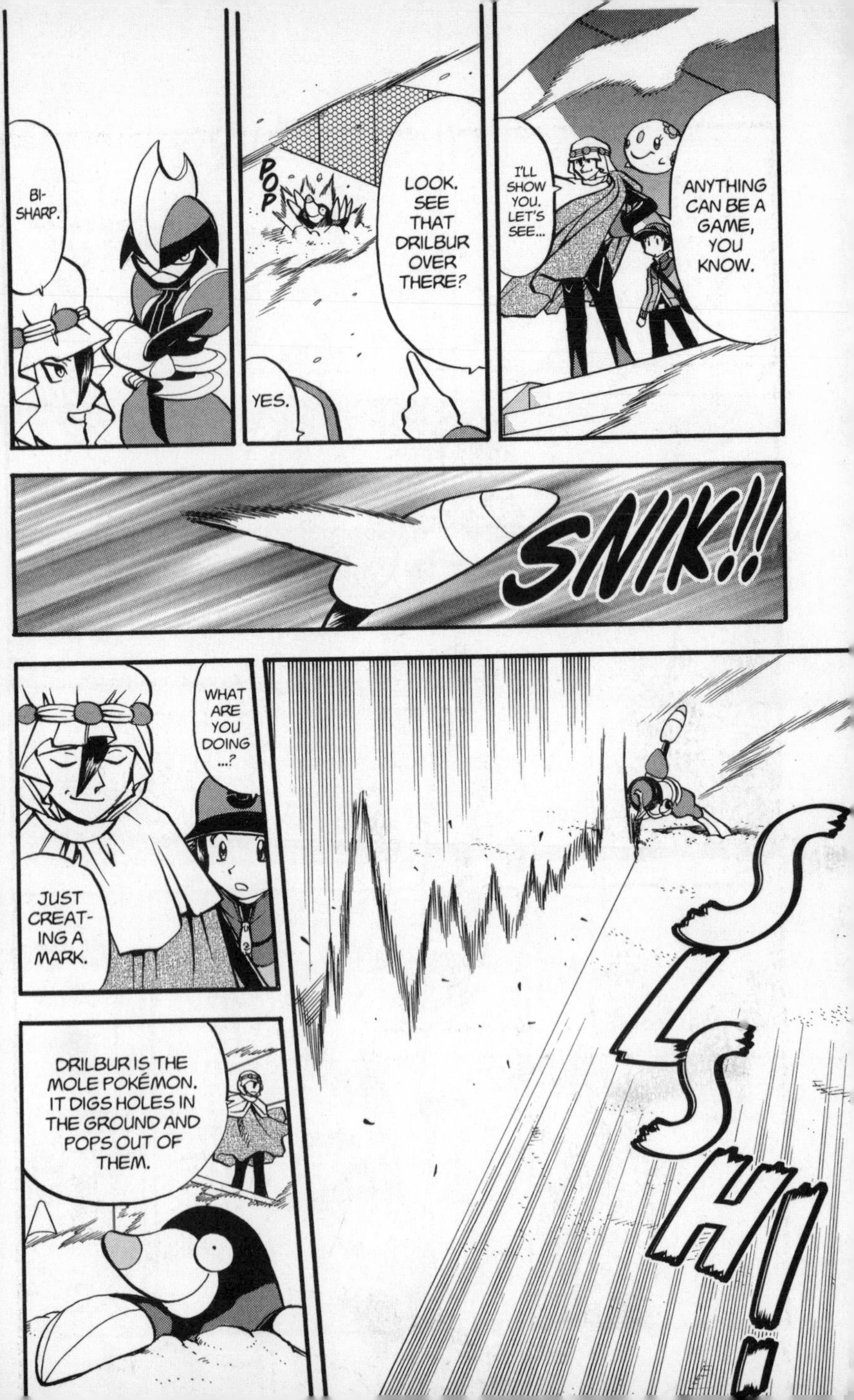
ANYTHING CAN BE A GAME, YOU KNOW.
I'LL SHOW YOU. LET'S SEE...
LOOK. SEE THAT DRILBUR OVER THERE?
POP
YES.
BI-SHARP.
SNIK!!
SLSH!!
WHAT ARE YOU DOING...?
JUST CREATING A MARK.
DRILBUR IS THE MOLE POKÉMON. IT DIGS HOLES IN THE GROUND AND POPS OUT OF THEM.

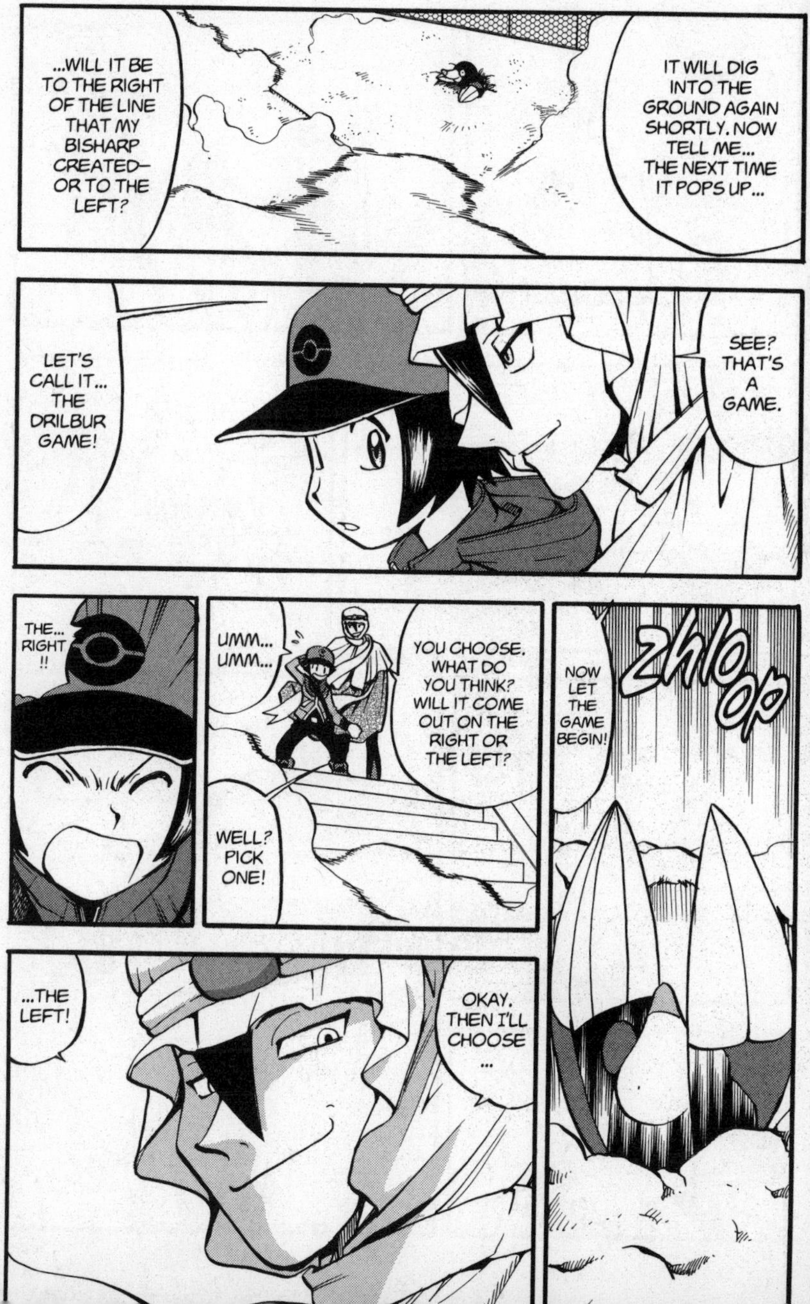
IT WILL DIG INTO THE GROUND AGAIN SHORTLY. NOW TELL ME... THE NEXT TIME IT POPS UP...
...WILL IT BE TO THE RIGHT OF THE LINE THAT MY BISHARP CREATED—OR TO THE LEFT?
SEE? THAT'S A GAME.
LET'S CALL IT... THE DRILBUR GAME!
ZHLOOP
NOW LET THE GAME BEGIN!
YOU CHOOSE. WHAT DO YOU THINK? WILL IT COME OUT ON THE RIGHT OR THE LEFT?
UMM... UMM...
WELL? PICK ONE!
THE... RIGHT!!
OKAY. THEN I'LL CHOOSE...
...THE LEFT!

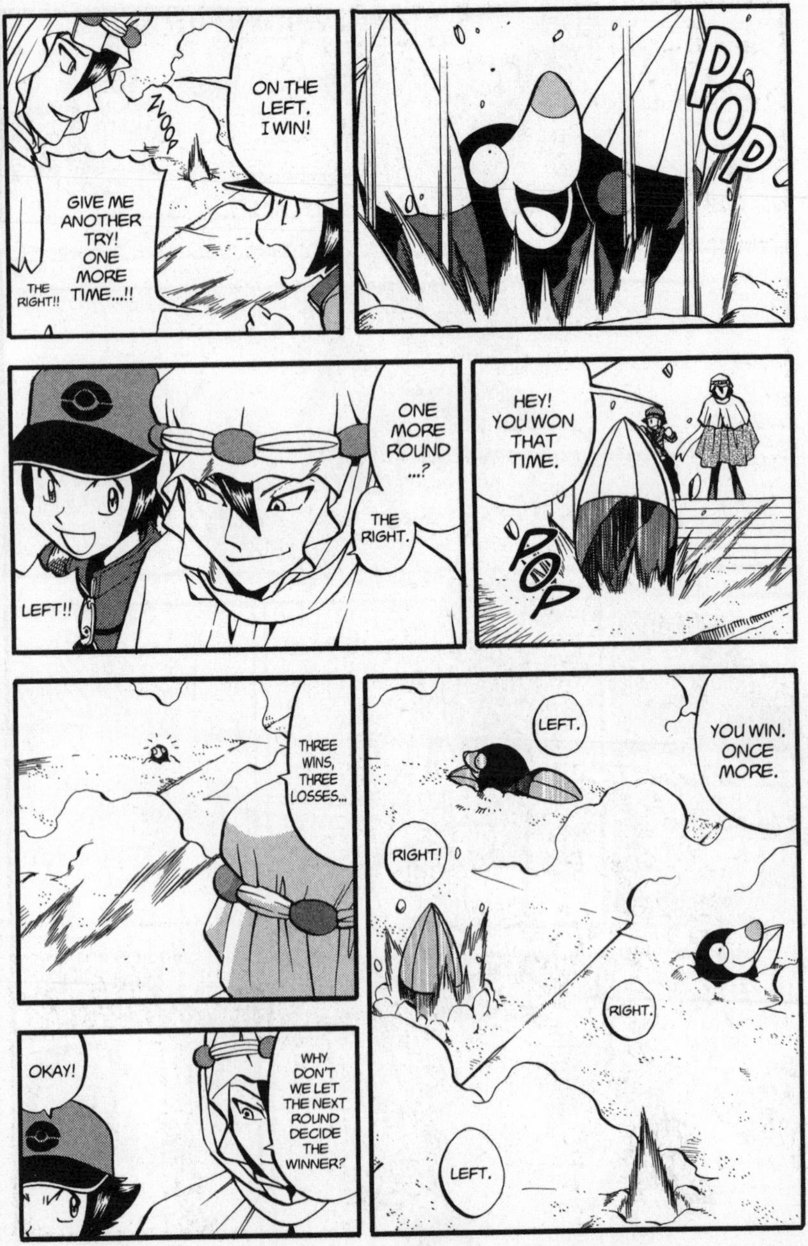
POP
ON THE LEFT. I WIN!
ZVOOP
GIVE ME ANOTHER TRY! ONE MORE TIME...!!
THE RIGHT!!
HEY! YOU WON THAT TIME.
POP
ONE MORE ROUND ...?
THE RIGHT.
LEFT!!
YOU WIN. ONCE MORE.
LEFT.
RIGHT!
RIGHT.
LEFT.
THREE WINS, THREE LOSSES...
WHY DON'T WE LET THE NEXT ROUND DECIDE THE WINNER?
OKAY!

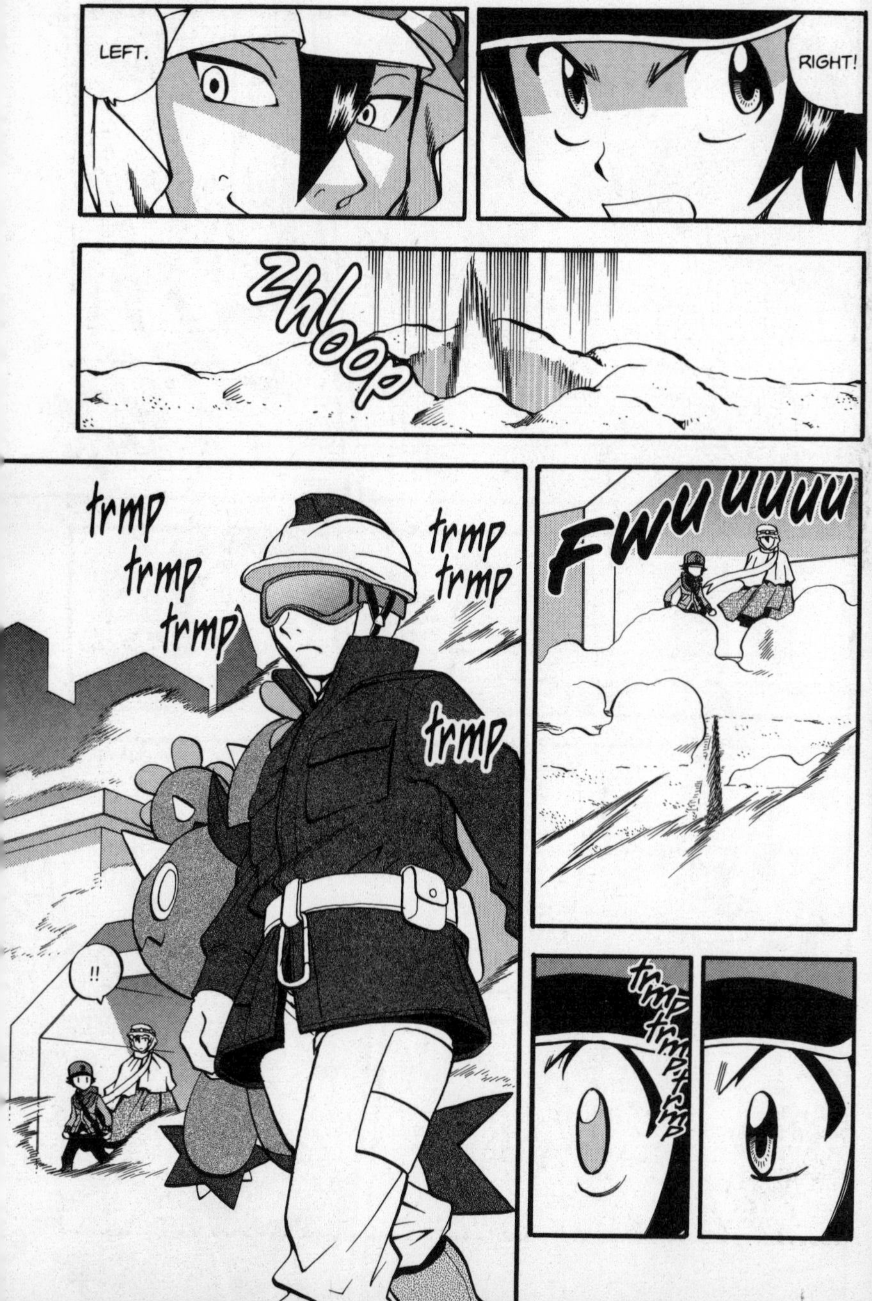

RIGHT!
LEFT.
zhloop
Fwuuuuu
trmp trmp trmp
trmp trmp
trmp trmp trmp
trmp
!!

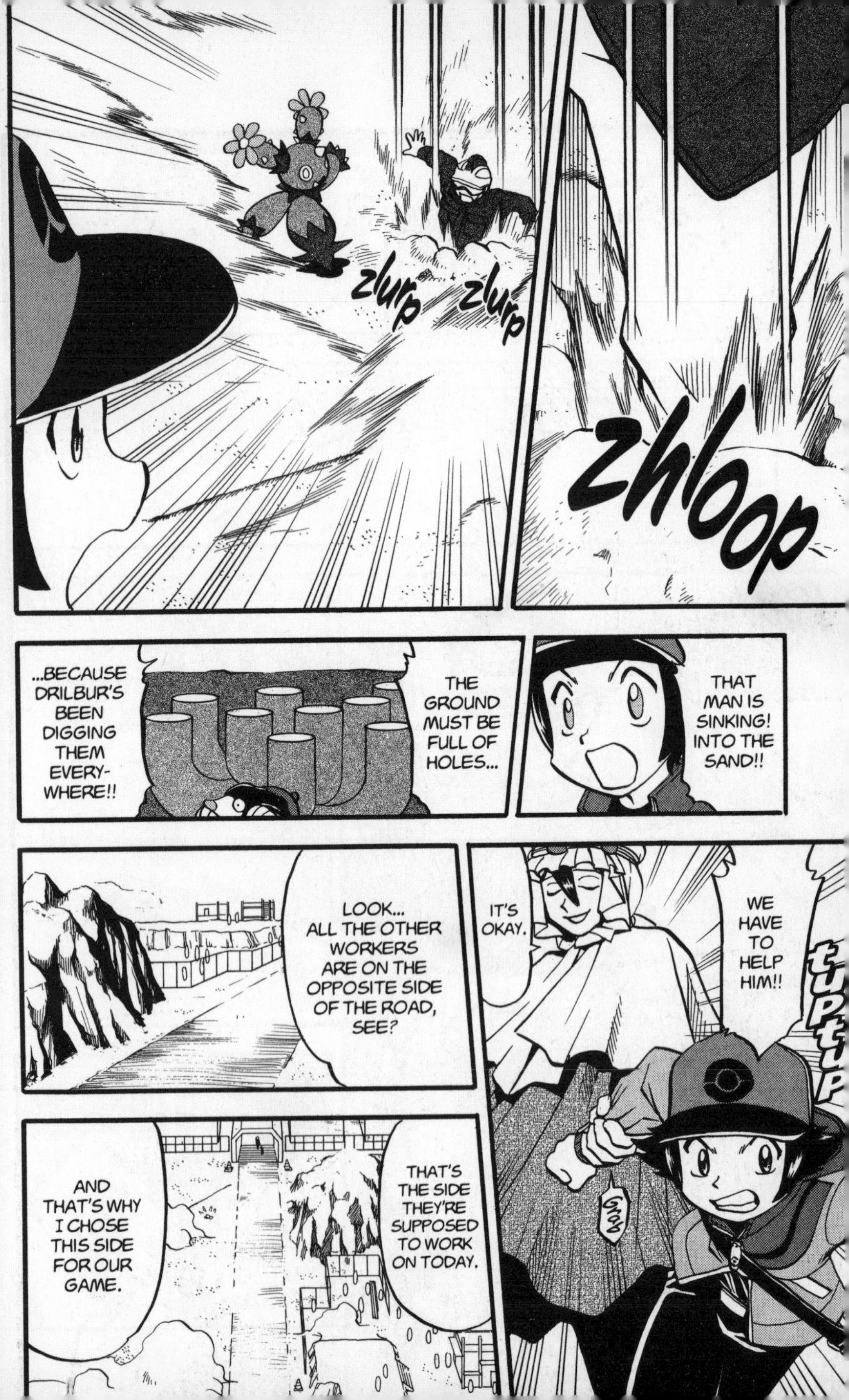
zhloop
zlurp
zlurp
THAT MAN IS SINKING! INTO THE SAND!!
THE GROUND MUST BE FULL OF HOLES...
...BECAUSE DRILBUR'S BEEN DIGGING THEM EVERY-WHERE!!
WE HAVE TO HELP HIM!!
tup tup
IT'S OKAY.
Grab
LOOK... ALL THE OTHER WORKERS ARE ON THE OPPOSITE SIDE OF THE ROAD, SEE?
THAT'S THE SIDE THEY'RE SUPPOSED TO WORK ON TODAY.
AND THAT'S WHY I CHOSE THIS SIDE FOR OUR GAME.

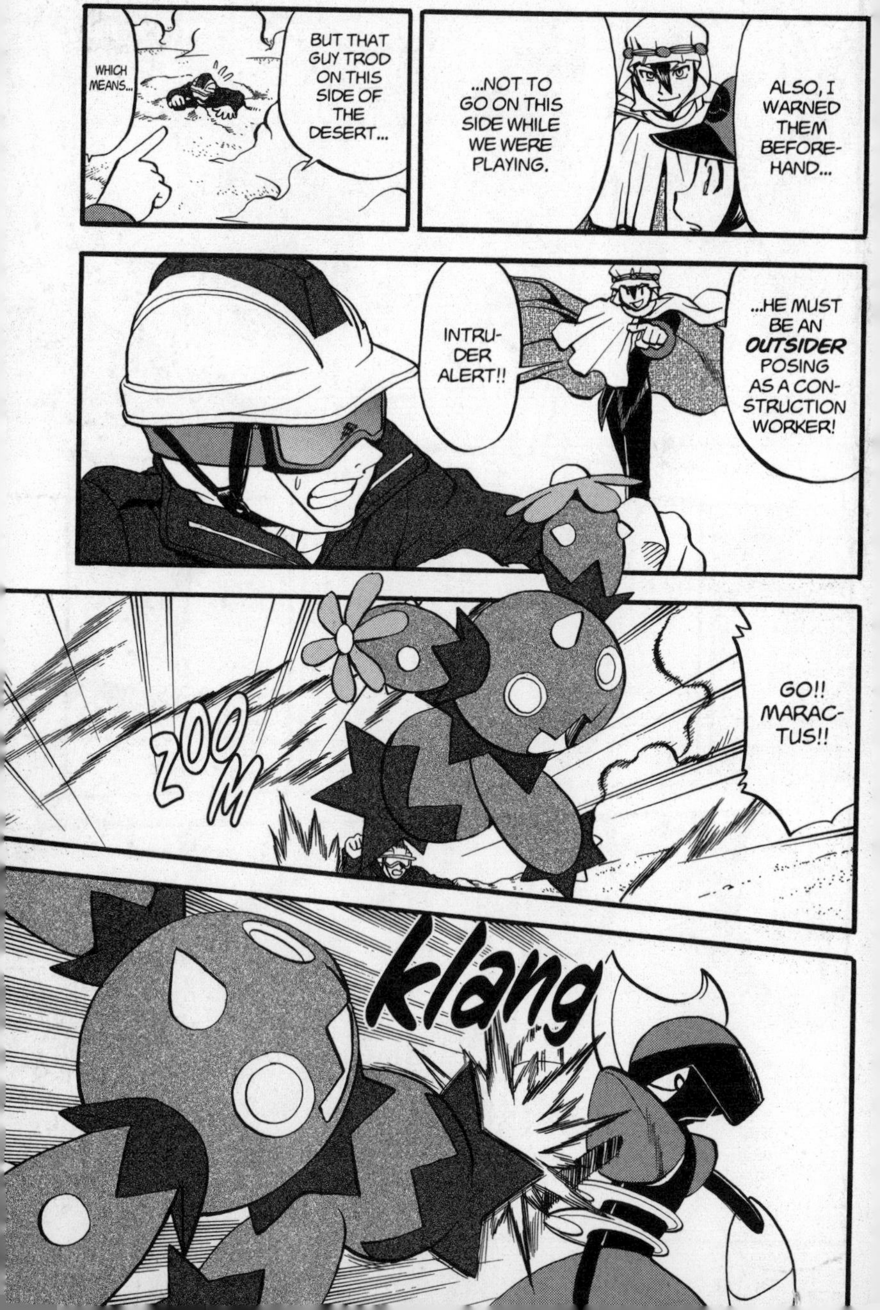
ALSO, I WARNED THEM BEFORE-HAND...
...NOT TO GO ON THIS SIDE WHILE WE WERE PLAYING.
BUT THAT GUY TROD ON THIS SIDE OF THE DESERT...
WHICH MEANS...
...HE MUST BE AN **OUTSIDER** POSING AS A CON-STRUCTION WORKER!
INTRU-DER ALERT!!
GO!! MARAC-TUS!!
ZOOM
klang

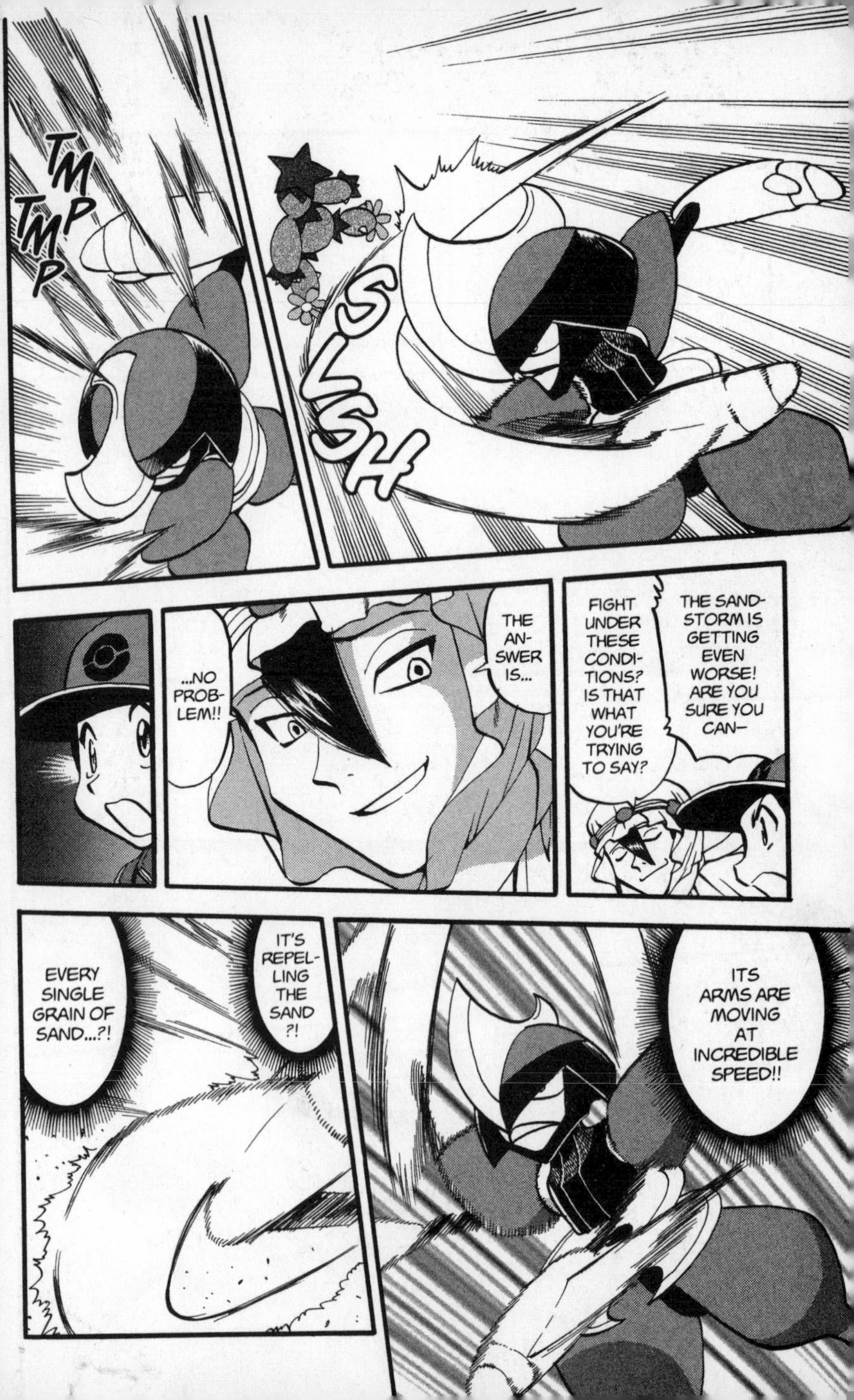
SLSH
TMP TMP
THE SANDSTORM IS GETTING EVEN WORSE! ARE YOU SURE YOU CAN—
FIGHT UNDER THESE CONDITIONS? IS THAT WHAT YOU'RE TRYING TO SAY?
THE ANSWER IS...
...NO PROBLEM!!
ITS ARMS ARE MOVING AT INCREDIBLE SPEED!!
IT'S REPELLING THE SAND?!
EVERY SINGLE GRAIN OF SAND...?!

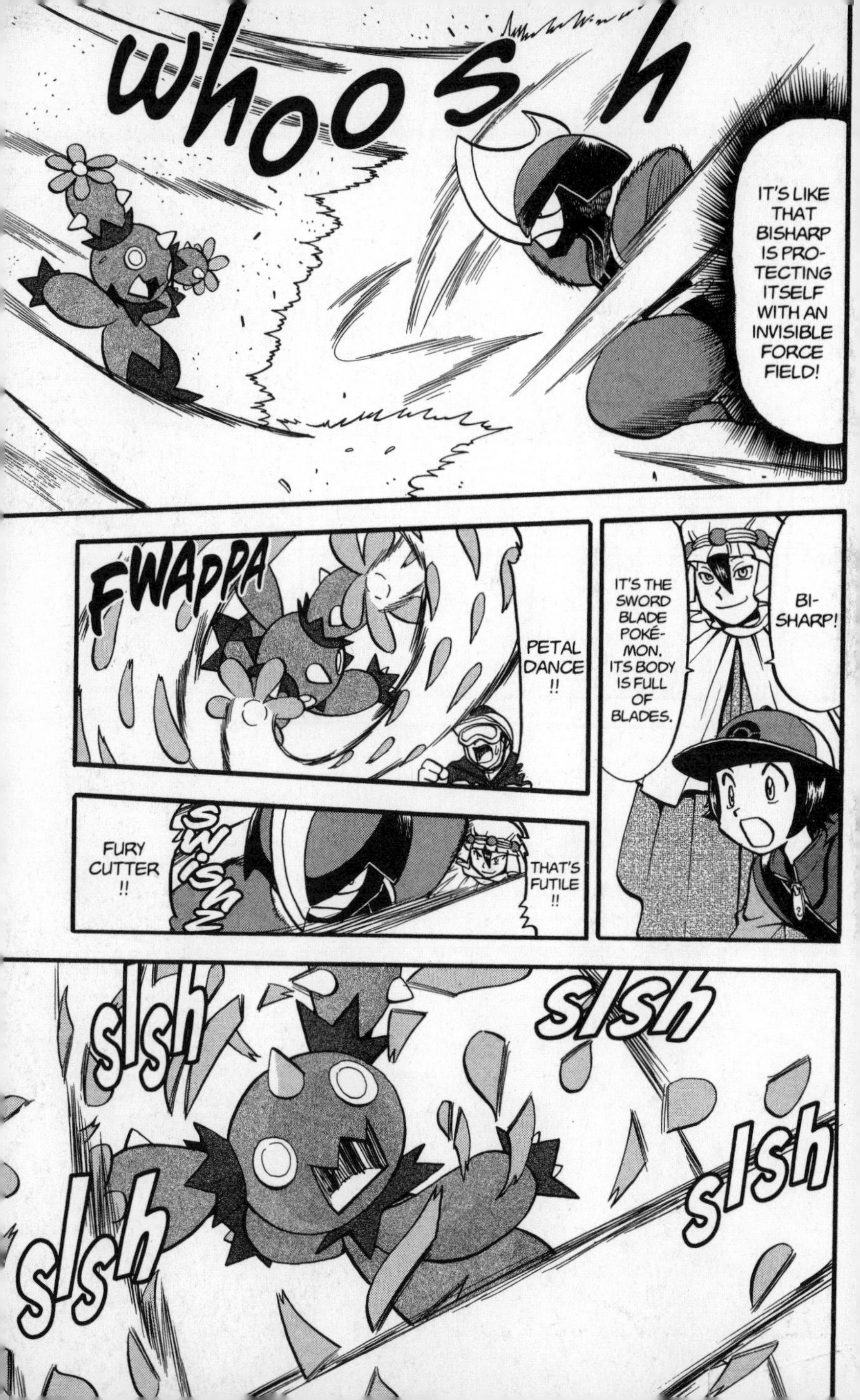
WHOOSH
IT'S LIKE THAT BISHARP IS PRO-TECTING ITSELF WITH AN INVISIBLE FORCE FIELD!
BI-SHARP!
IT'S THE SWORD BLADE POKÉ-MON. ITS BODY IS FULL OF BLADES.
FWAPPA
PETAL DANCE!!
THAT'S FUTILE!!
SWISH
FURY CUTTER!!
SLSH
SLSH
SLSH
SLSH

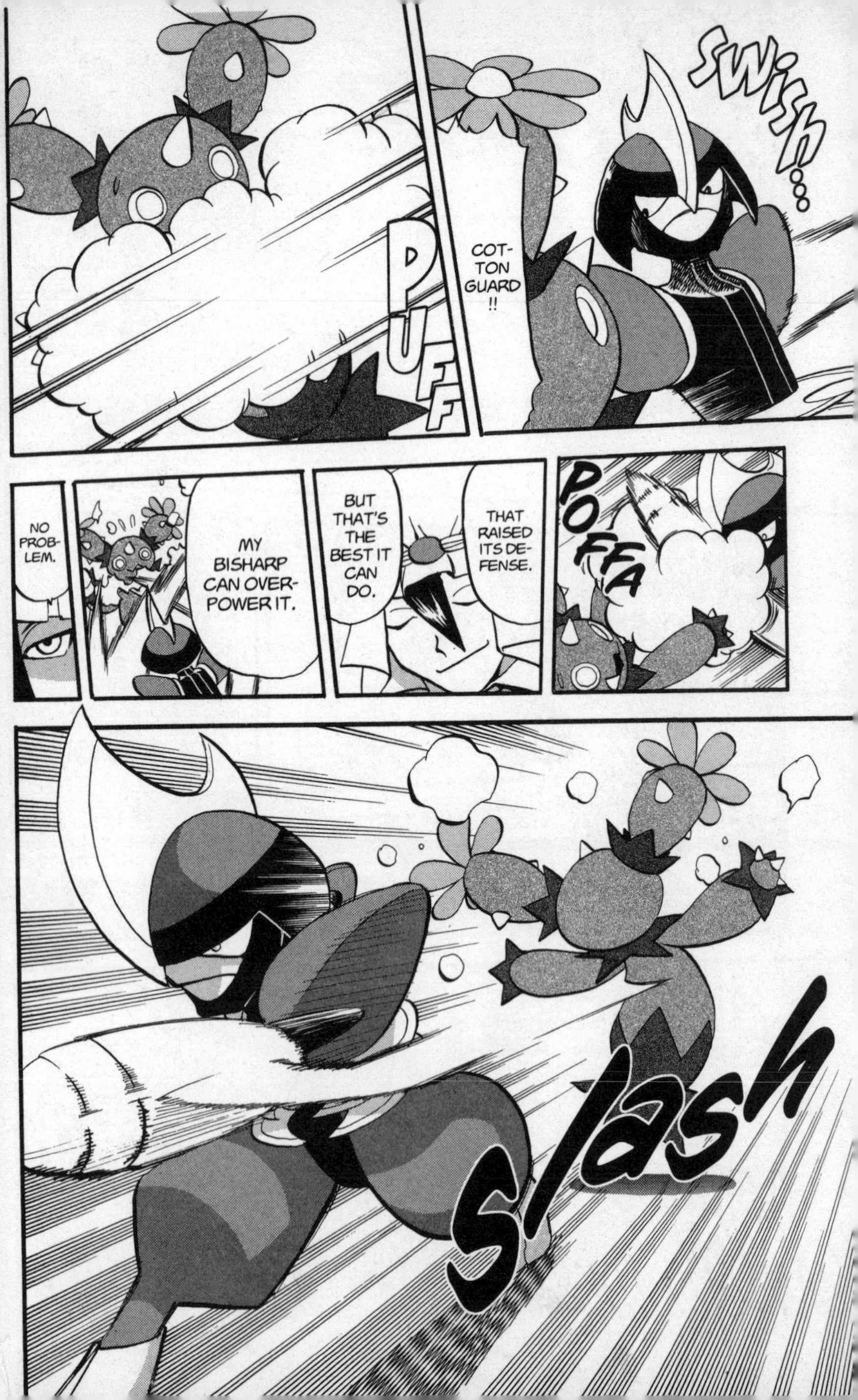
SWISH...
COTTON GUARD !!
PUFF
POFFA
THAT RAISED ITS DEFENSE.
BUT THAT'S THE BEST IT CAN DO.
MY BISHARP CAN OVERPOWER IT.
NO PROBLEM.
SLASH

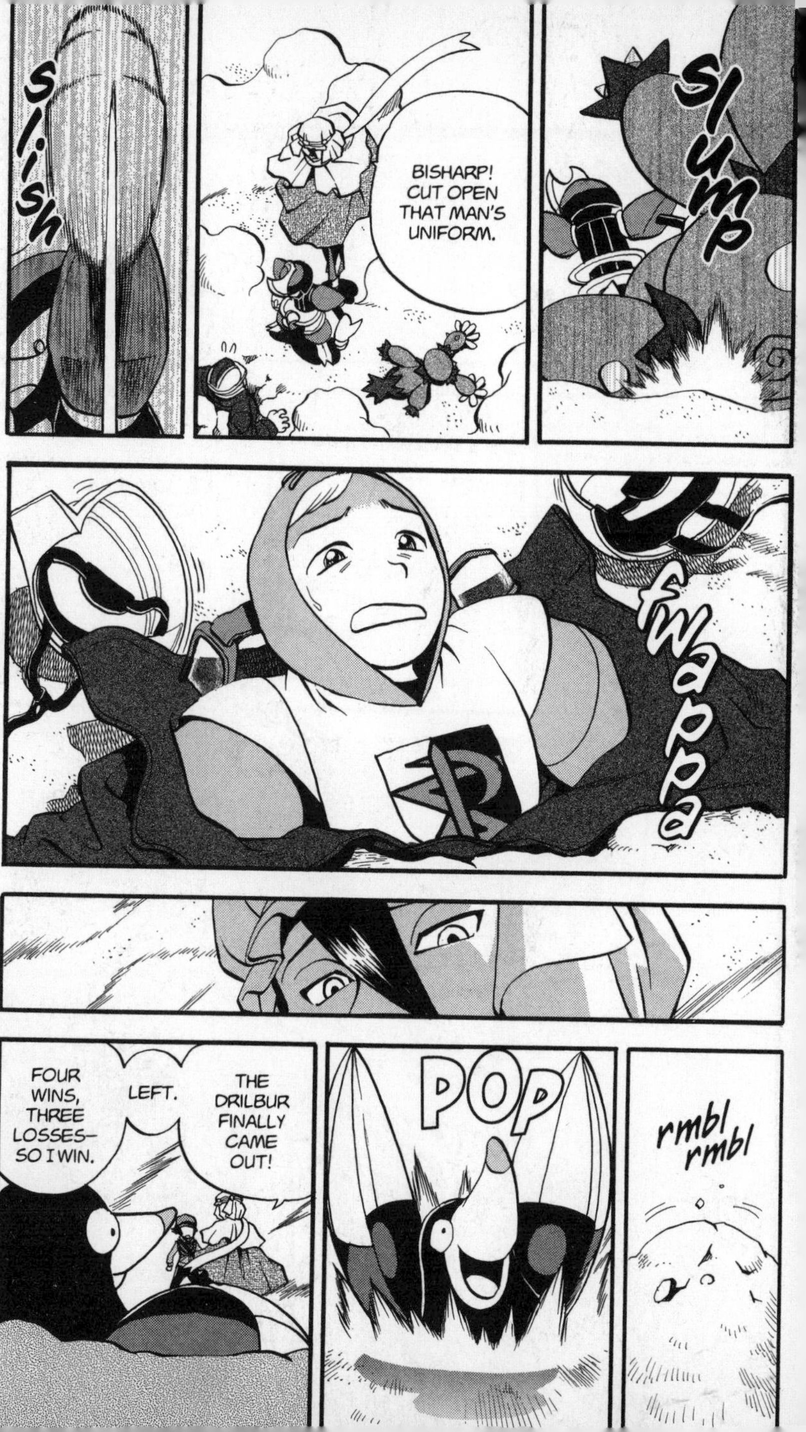
slump
BISHARP! CUT OPEN THAT MAN'S UNIFORM.
slish
fwappa
rmbl rmbl
POP
THE DRILBUR FINALLY CAME OUT!
LEFT.
FOUR WINS, THREE LOSSES— SO I WIN.

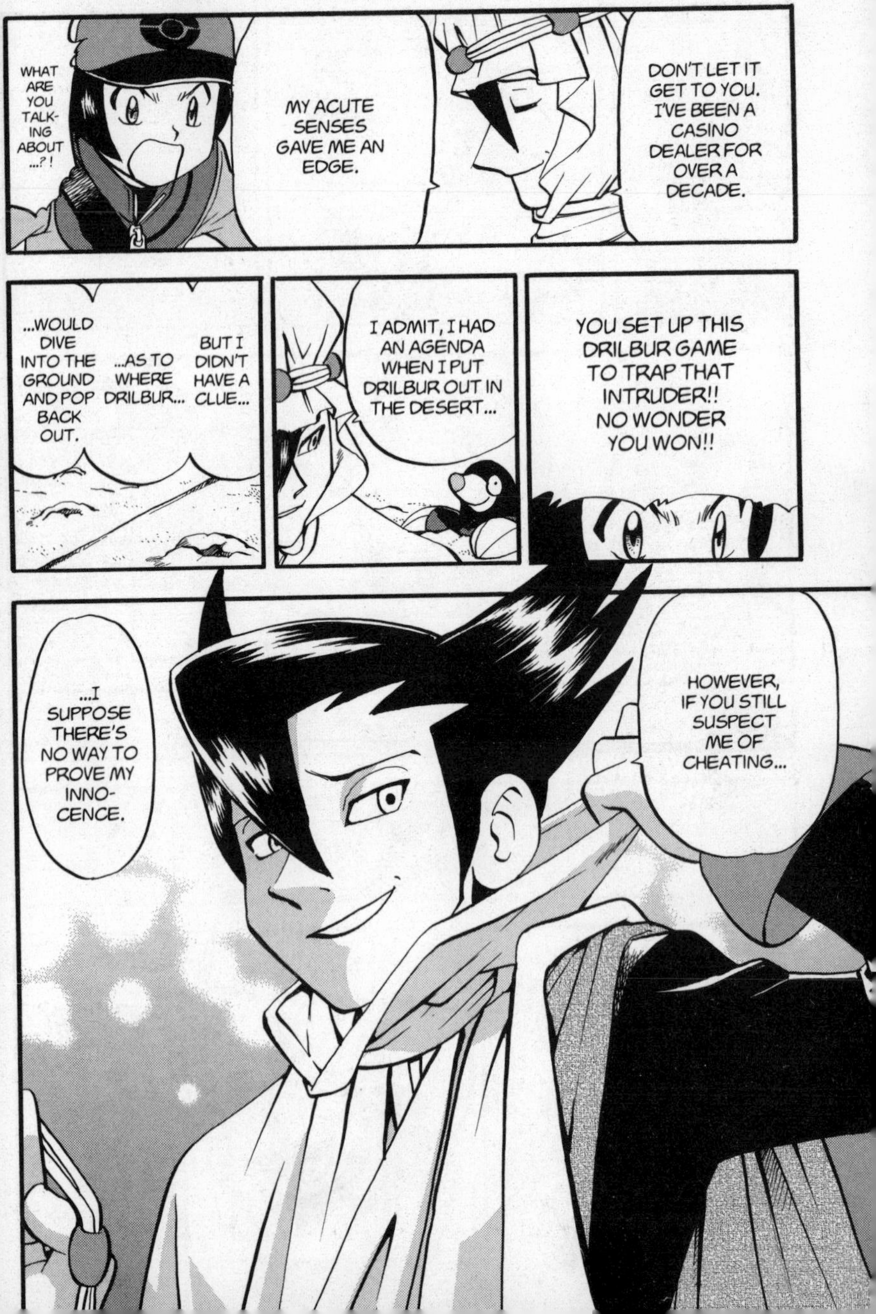
DON'T LET IT GET TO YOU. I'VE BEEN A CASINO DEALER FOR OVER A DECADE.
MY ACUTE SENSES GAVE ME AN EDGE.
WHAT ARE YOU TALKING ABOUT...?!
YOU SET UP THIS DRILBUR GAME TO TRAP THAT INTRUDER!! NO WONDER YOU WON!!
I ADMIT, I HAD AN AGENDA WHEN I PUT DRILBUR OUT IN THE DESERT...
BUT I DIDN'T HAVE A CLUE...
...AS TO WHERE DRILBUR...
...WOULD DIVE INTO THE GROUND AND POP BACK OUT.
HOWEVER, IF YOU STILL SUSPECT ME OF CHEATING...
...I SUPPOSE THERE'S NO WAY TO PROVE MY INNOCENCE.

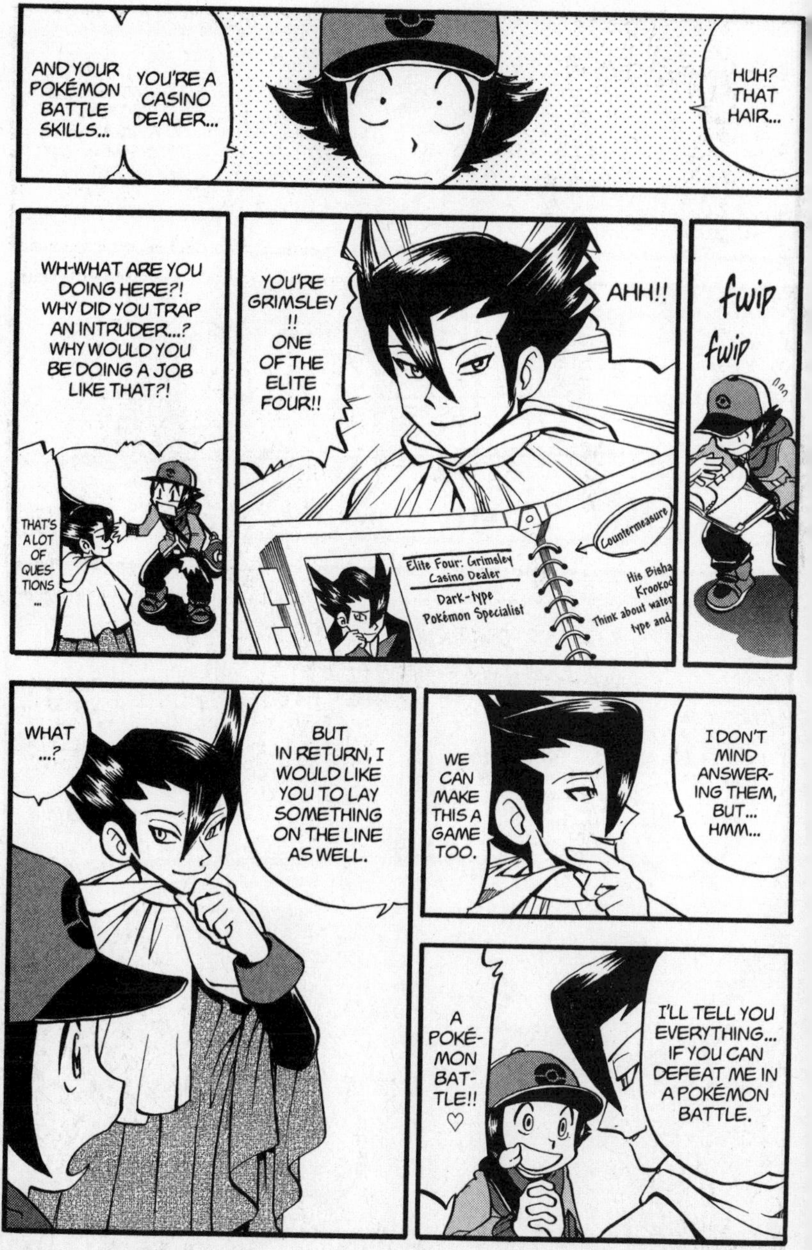
HUH? THAT HAIR...
YOU'RE A CASINO DEALER...
AND YOUR POKÉMON BATTLE SKILLS...
fwip
fwip
AHH!!
YOU'RE GRIMSLEY!! ONE OF THE ELITE FOUR!!
Countermeasure
Elite Four: Grimsley Casino Dealer
Dark-type Pokémon Specialist
His Bisha Krookod Think about water type and
WH-WHAT ARE YOU DOING HERE?! WHY DID YOU TRAP AN INTRUDER...? WHY WOULD YOU BE DOING A JOB LIKE THAT?!
THAT'S A LOT OF QUES-TIONS...
I DON'T MIND ANSWER-ING THEM, BUT... HMM...
WE CAN MAKE THIS A GAME TOO.
BUT IN RETURN, I WOULD LIKE YOU TO LAY SOMETHING ON THE LINE AS WELL.
WHAT ...?
I'LL TELL YOU EVERYTHING... IF YOU CAN DEFEAT ME IN A POKÉMON BATTLE.
A POKÉ-MON BAT-TLE!! ♡

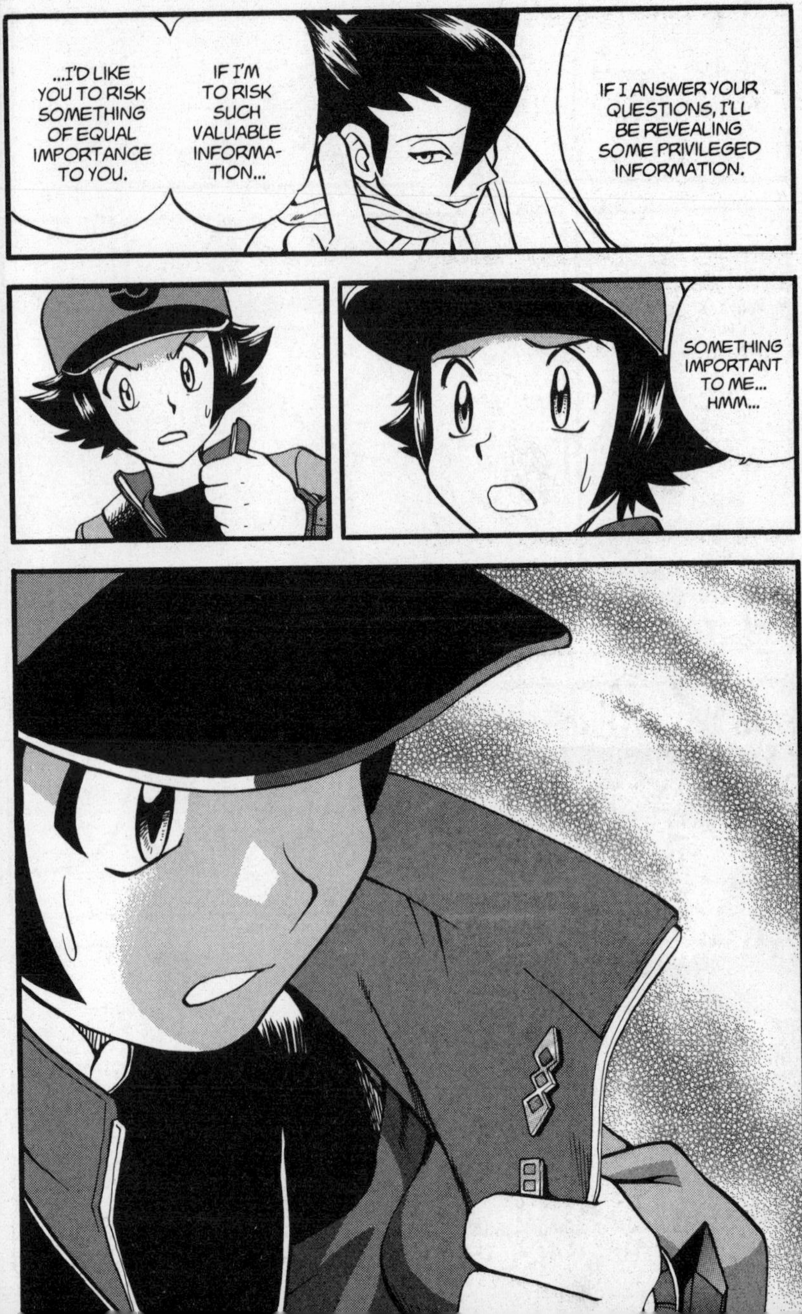
IF I ANSWER YOUR QUESTIONS, I'LL BE REVEALING SOME PRIVILEGED INFORMATION.
IF I'M TO RISK SUCH VALUABLE INFORMATION...
...I'D LIKE YOU TO RISK SOMETHING OF EQUAL IMPORTANCE TO YOU.
SOMETHING IMPORTANT TO ME... HMM...

ADVENTURE MAP

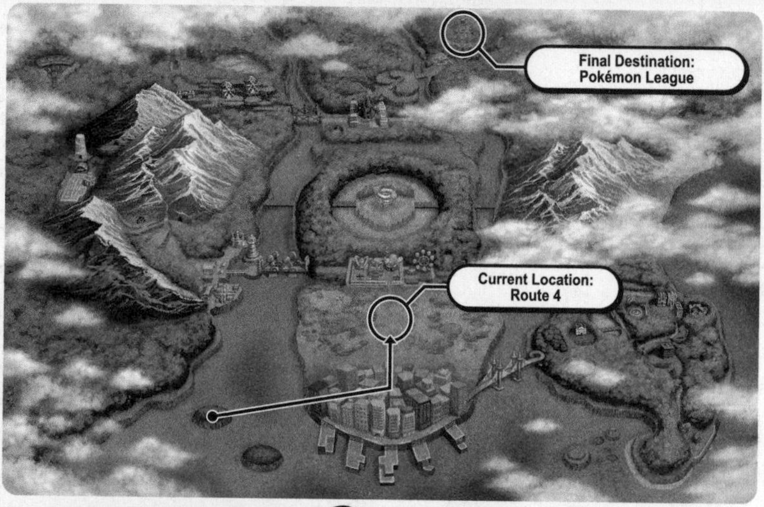

Final Destination: Pokémon League
Current Location: Route 4

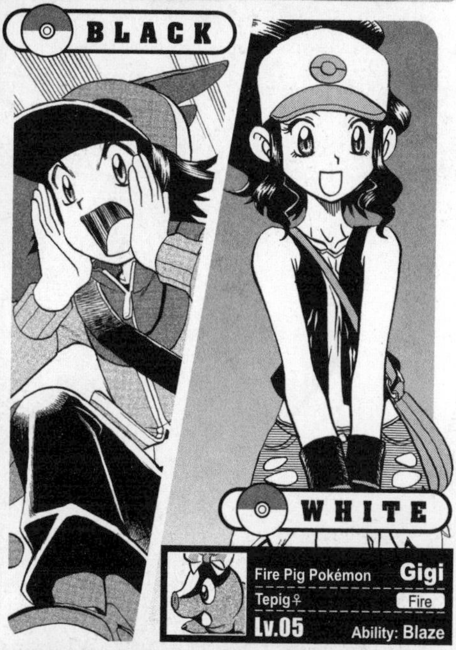

BLACK
WHITE

BLACK

Fire Pig Pokémon **Nite**
Pignite ♂ Fire Fighting
Lv.20 Ability: Blaze

Dream Eater Pokémon **Musha**
Munna ♂ Psychic
Lv.43 Ability: Forewarn

Valiant Pokémon **Brav**
Braviary ♂ Normal Flying
Lv.54 Ability: Sheer Force

EleSpider Pokémon **Tula**
Galvantula ♂ Bug Electric
Lv.45 Ability: Unnerve

WHITE

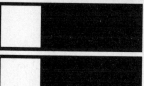

Fire Pig Pokémon **Gigi**
Tepig ♀ Fire
Lv.05 Ability: Blaze

TRIO BADGE | BASIC BADGE | INSECT BADGE | ? | ? | ? | ? | ?

Pokémon Adventures Black & White

MARACTUS

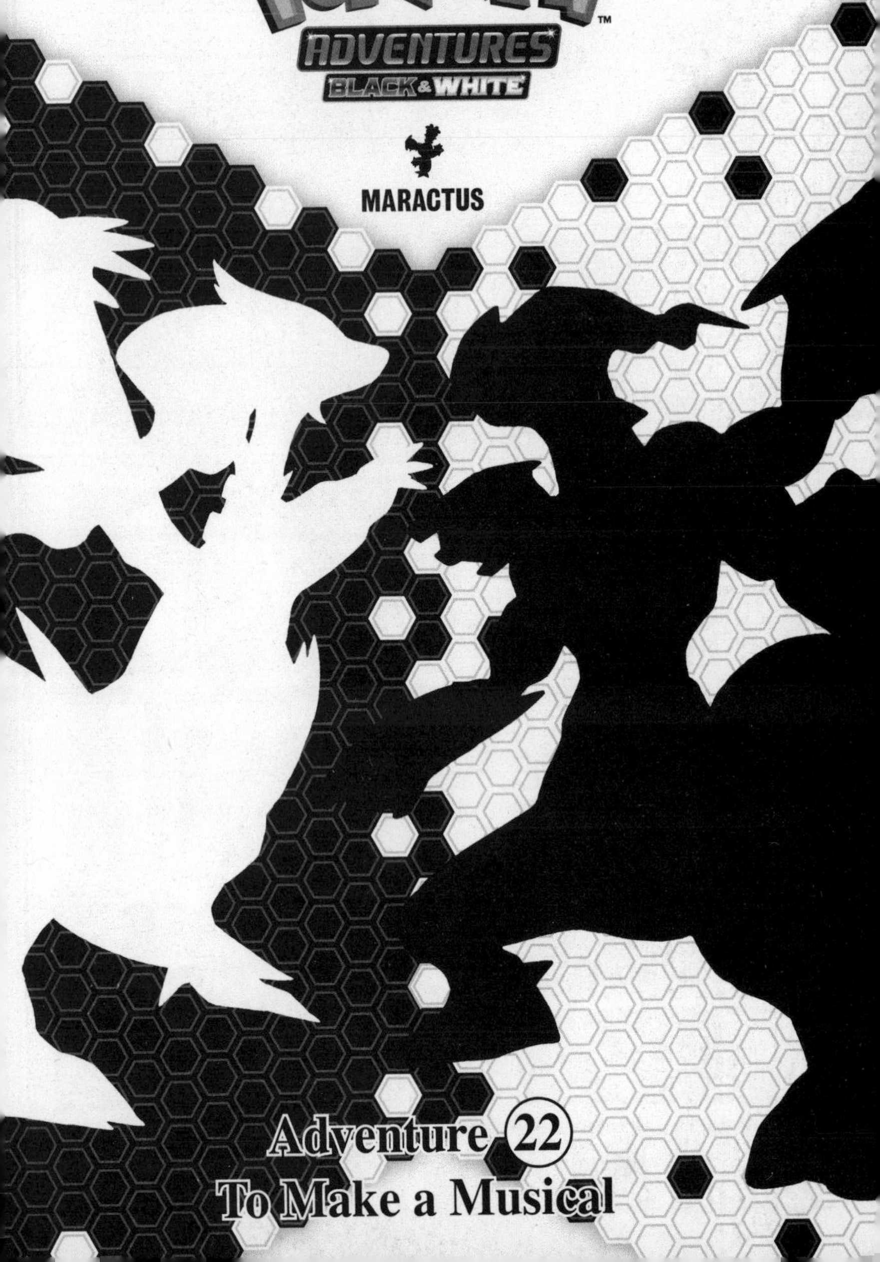

Adventure 22
To Make a Musical

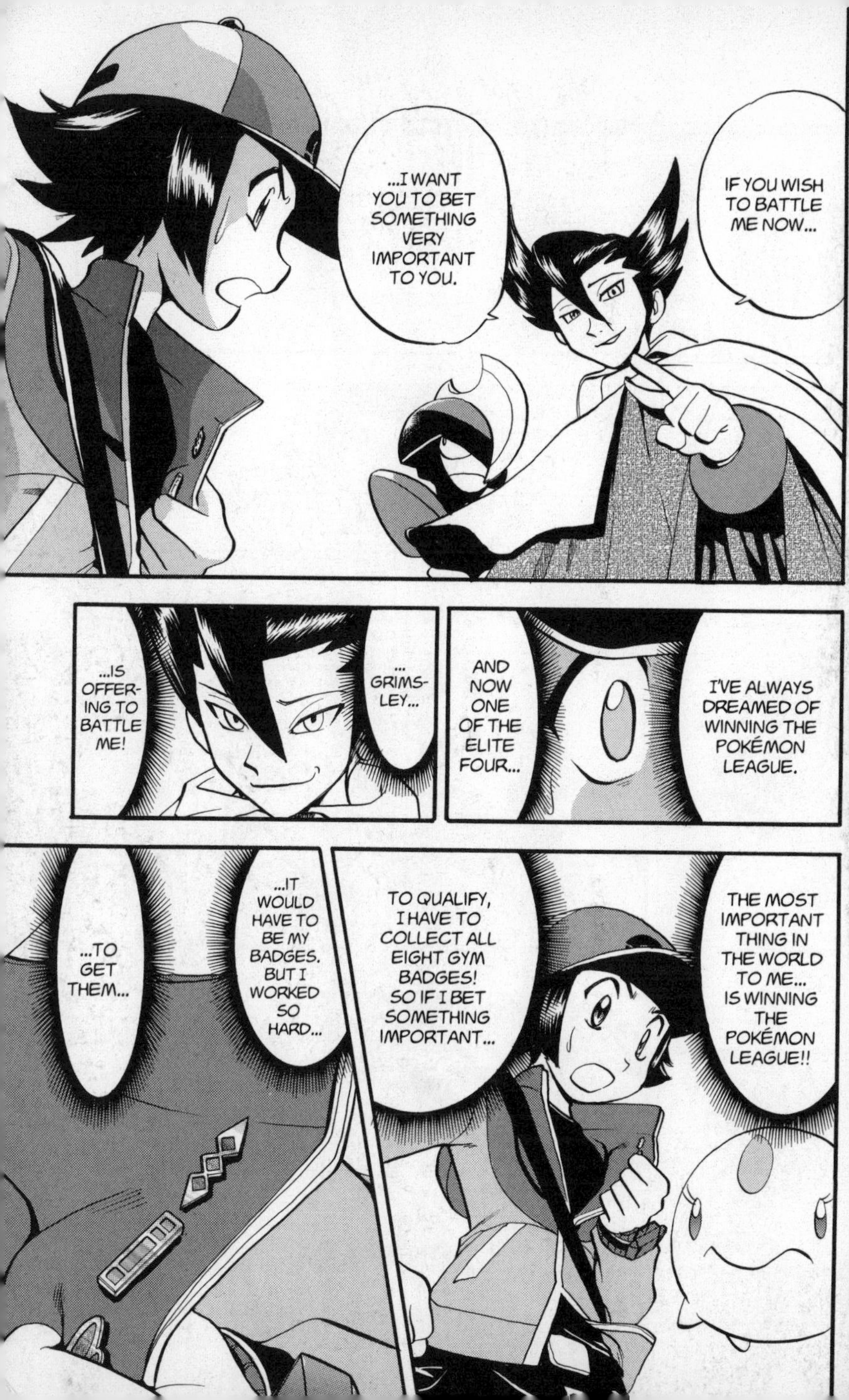
IF YOU WISH TO BATTLE ME NOW...
...I WANT YOU TO BET SOMETHING VERY IMPORTANT TO YOU.
I'VE ALWAYS DREAMED OF WINNING THE POKÉMON LEAGUE.
AND NOW ONE OF THE ELITE FOUR...
...GRIMSLEY...
...IS OFFERING TO BATTLE ME!
THE MOST IMPORTANT THING IN THE WORLD TO ME... IS WINNING THE POKÉMON LEAGUE!!
TO QUALIFY, I HAVE TO COLLECT ALL EIGHT GYM BADGES! SO IF I BET SOMETHING IMPORTANT...
...IT WOULD HAVE TO BE MY BADGES. BUT I WORKED SO HARD...
...TO GET THEM...

...I'D LOSE MY CHANCE OF ENTERING THE POKÉMON LEAGUE!!

AND THEN...

...IF I LOST, I'D HAVE TO GIVE THEM UP...

BETTING THEM WOULD MEAN...

WHAT TO DO?! WHAT TO DO?!

Huf.

Huf.

WHAT SHOULD I DO ...?!

BOOM!

URGH!

to ... a battle but to put my badges on the line won't be my bad... able ...lose but if I lo... my badges I won't ...but I ... ...ut I ...ed to ... badges ... the

H-HEY...

fwump

ARGH!

EH? ARE YOU ALL RIGHT, YOUNG MAN?

Huf.

Huf.

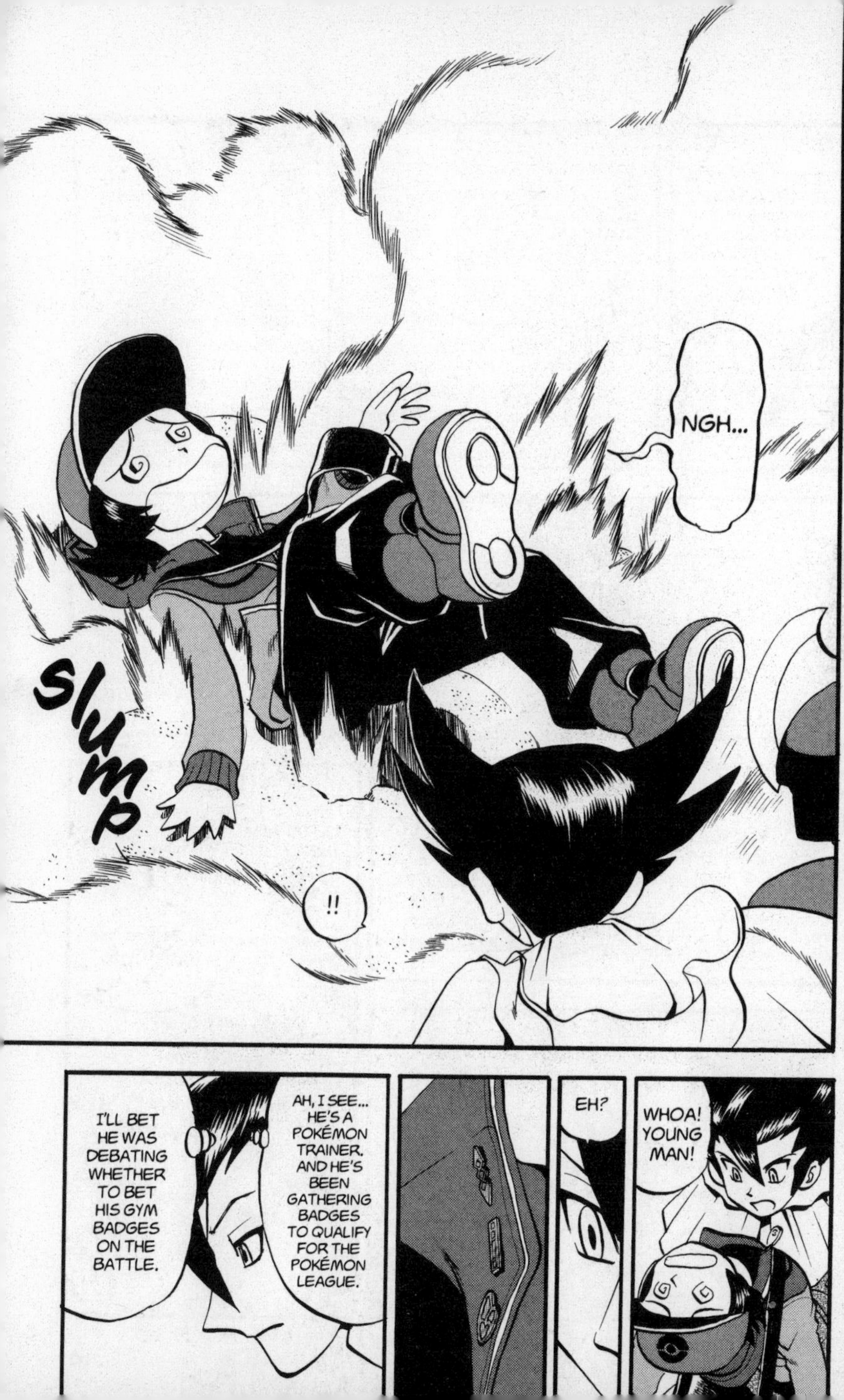
NGH...
slump
!!
WHOA! YOUNG MAN!
EH?
AH, I SEE... HE'S A POKÉMON TRAINER. AND HE'S BEEN GATHERING BADGES TO QUALIFY FOR THE POKÉMON LEAGUE.
I'LL BET HE WAS DEBATING WHETHER TO BET HIS GYM BADGES ON THE BATTLE.

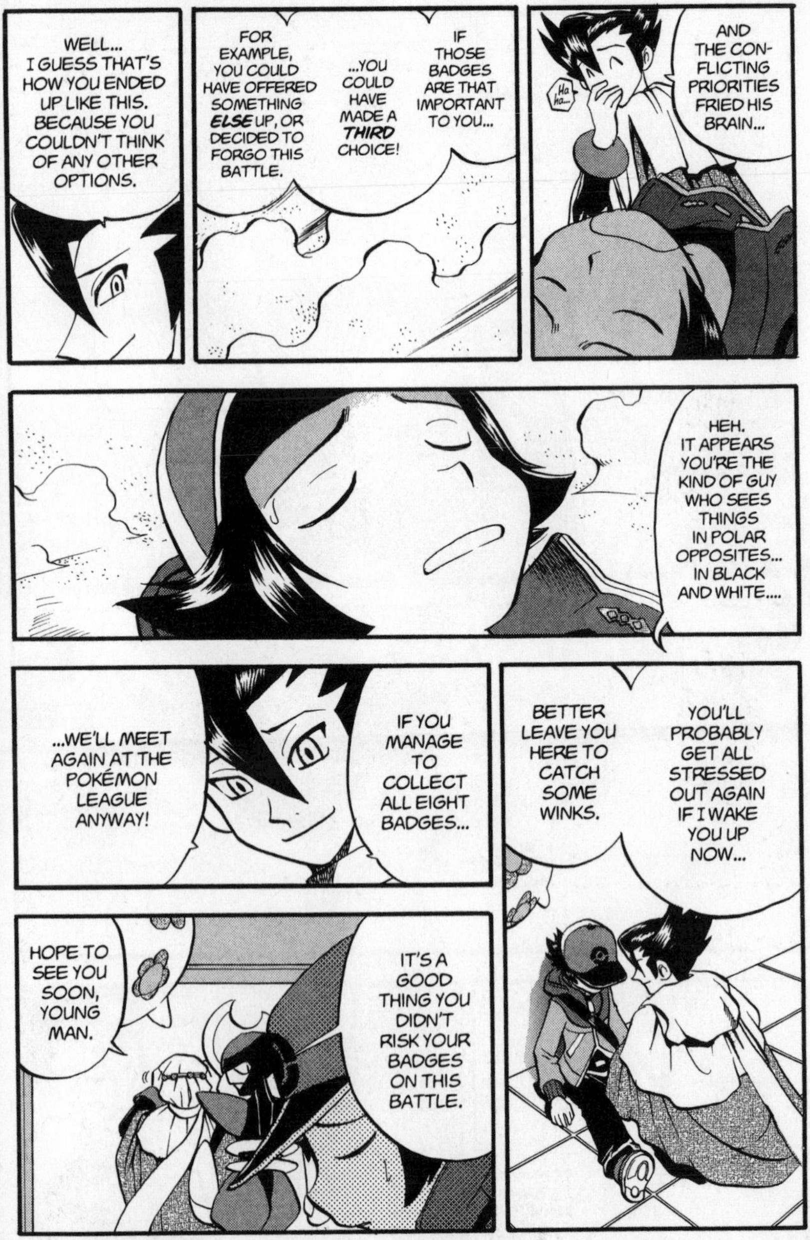
Ha ha...
AND THE CON-FLICTING PRIORITIES FRIED HIS BRAIN...
IF THOSE BADGES ARE THAT IMPORTANT TO YOU...
...YOU COULD HAVE MADE A THIRD CHOICE!
FOR EXAMPLE, YOU COULD HAVE OFFERED SOMETHING ELSE UP, OR DECIDED TO FORGO THIS BATTLE.
WELL... I GUESS THAT'S HOW YOU ENDED UP LIKE THIS. BECAUSE YOU COULDN'T THINK OF ANY OTHER OPTIONS.
HEH. IT APPEARS YOU'RE THE KIND OF GUY WHO SEES THINGS IN POLAR OPPOSITES... IN BLACK AND WHITE....
YOU'LL PROBABLY GET ALL STRESSED OUT AGAIN IF I WAKE YOU UP NOW...
BETTER LEAVE YOU HERE TO CATCH SOME WINKS.
IF YOU MANAGE TO COLLECT ALL EIGHT BADGES...
...WE'LL MEET AGAIN AT THE POKÉMON LEAGUE ANYWAY!
IT'S A GOOD THING YOU DIDN'T RISK YOUR BADGES ON THIS BATTLE.
HOPE TO SEE YOU SOON, YOUNG MAN.

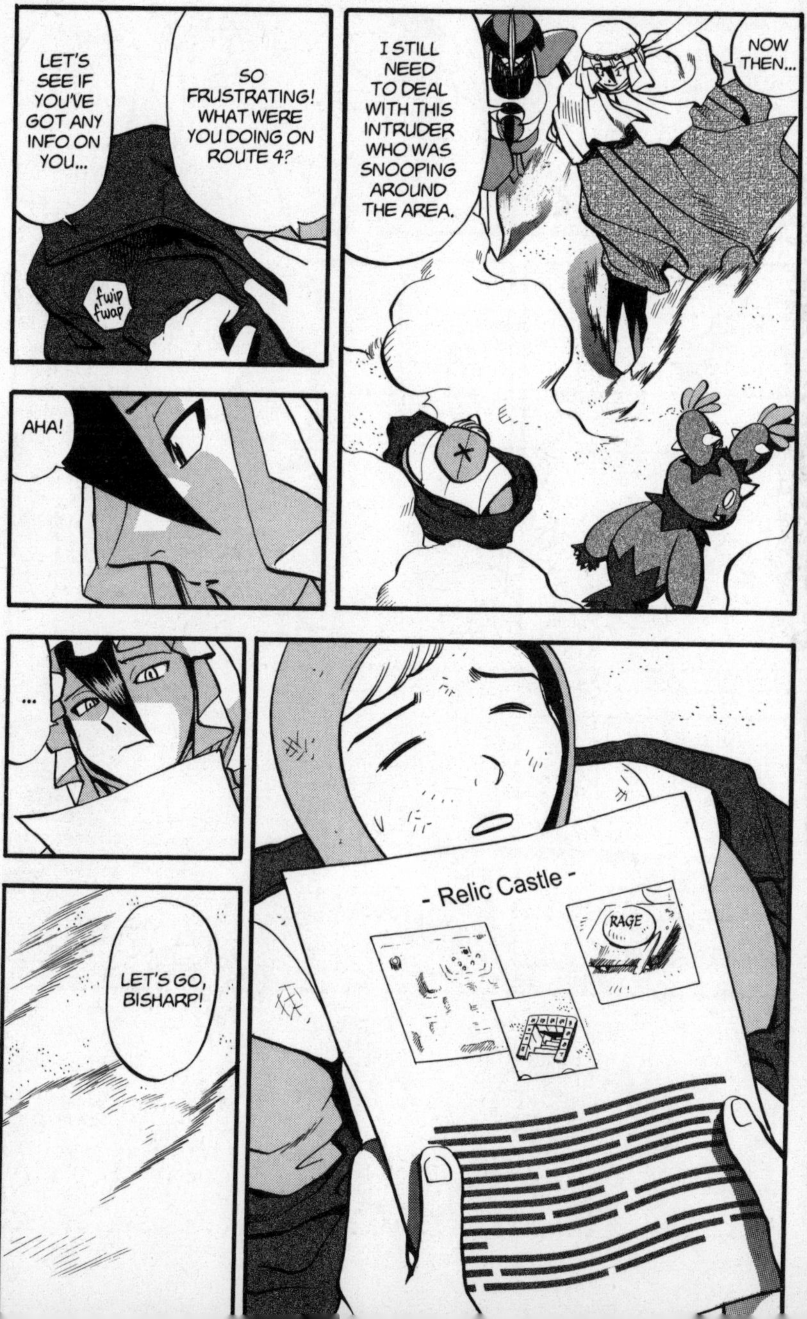
NOW THEN...
I STILL NEED TO DEAL WITH THIS INTRUDER WHO WAS SNOOPING AROUND THE AREA.
SO FRUSTRATING! WHAT WERE YOU DOING ON ROUTE 4?
LET'S SEE IF YOU'VE GOT ANY INFO ON YOU...
fwip fwap
AHA!
- Relic Castle -
RAGE
...
LET'S GO, BISHARP!

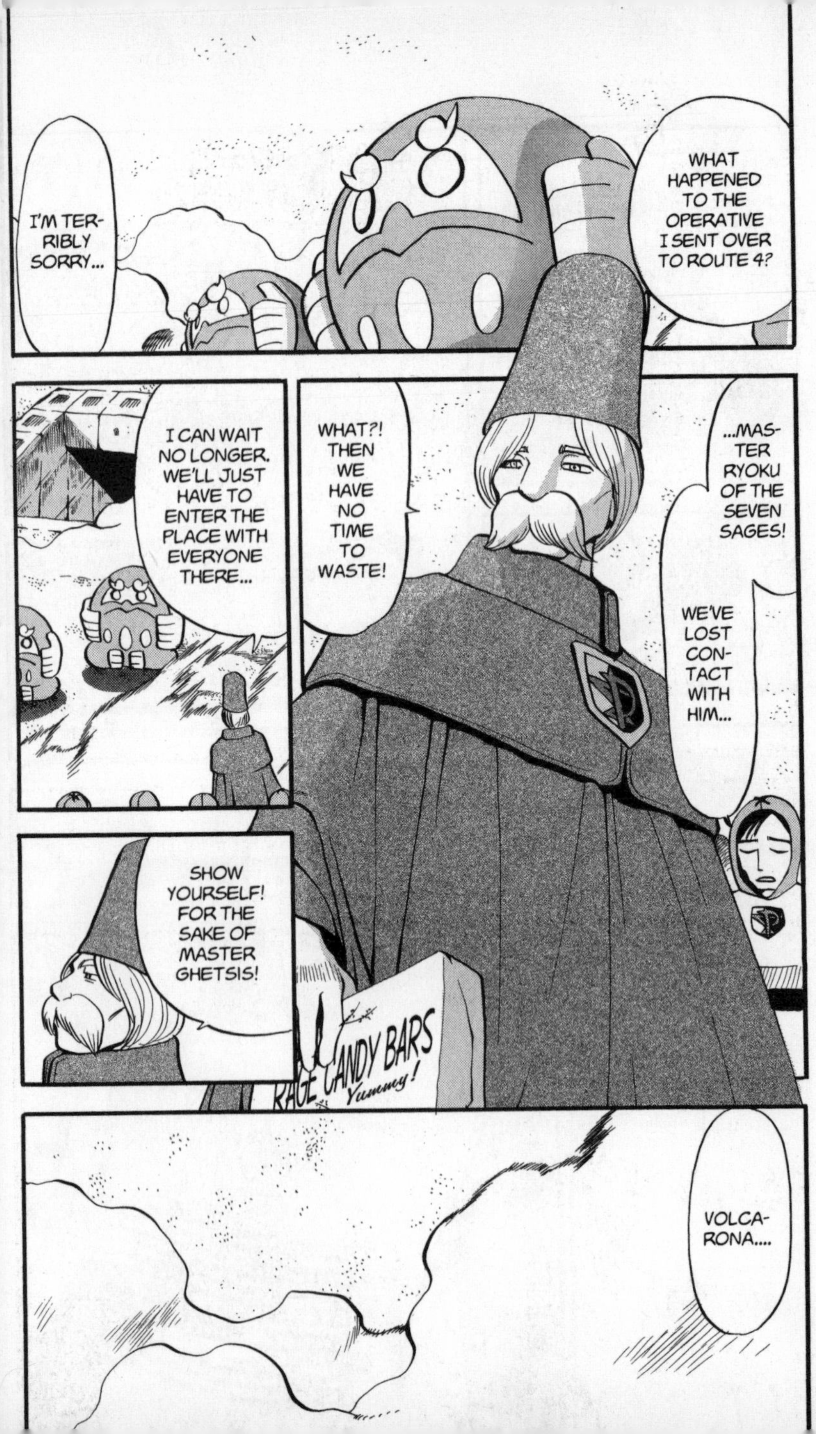
WHAT HAPPENED TO THE OPERATIVE I SENT OVER TO ROUTE 4?
I'M TERRIBLY SORRY...
...MASTER RYOKU OF THE SEVEN SAGES!
WE'VE LOST CONTACT WITH HIM...
WHAT?! THEN WE HAVE NO TIME TO WASTE!
RAGE CANDY BARS Yummy!
I CAN WAIT NO LONGER. WE'LL JUST HAVE TO ENTER THE PLACE WITH EVERYONE THERE...
SHOW YOURSELF! FOR THE SAKE OF MASTER GHETSIS!
VOLCARONA....

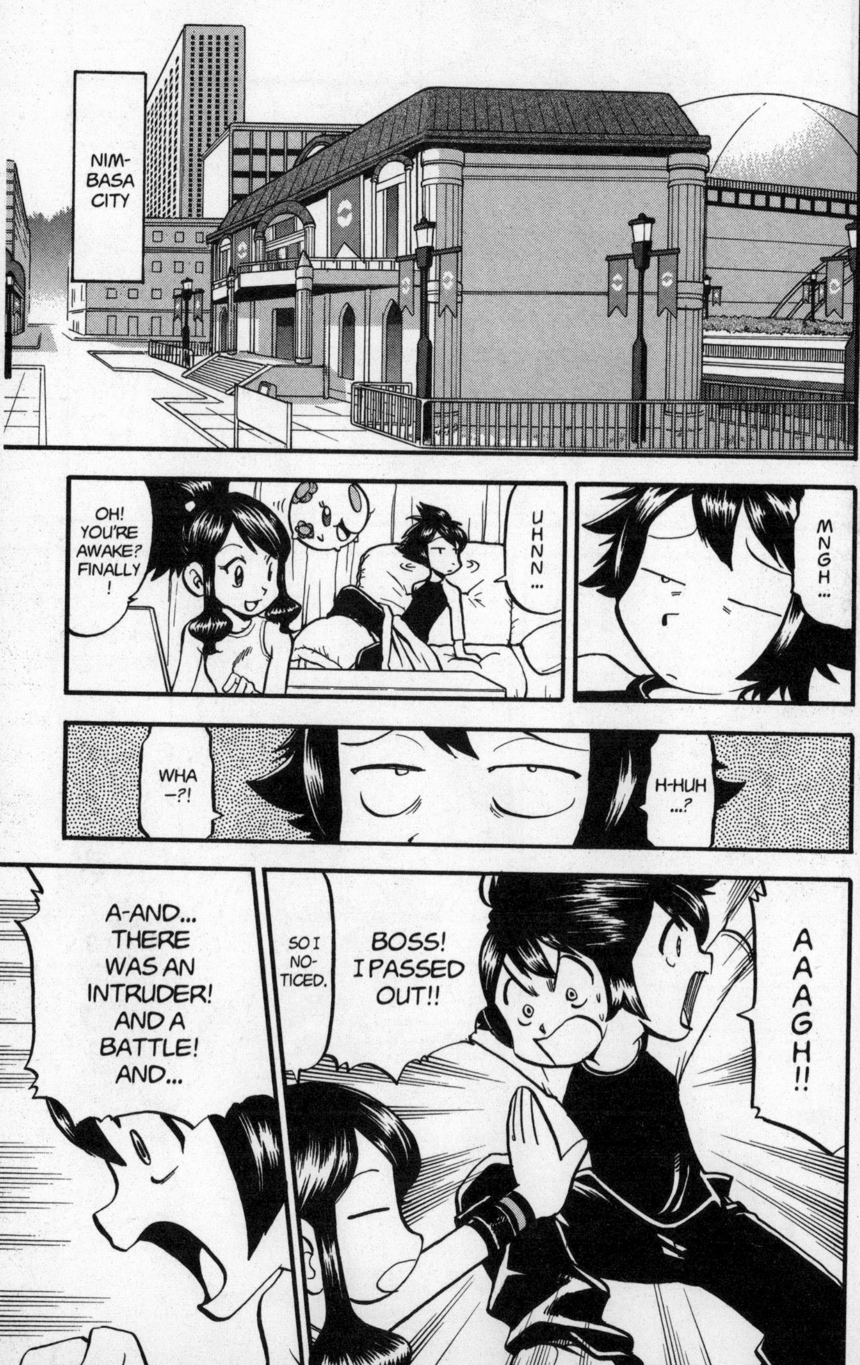
NIMBASA CITY
MNGH...
UHNN...
OH! YOU'RE AWAKE? FINALLY!
H-HUH...?
WHA-?!
AAAAGH!!
BOSS! I PASSED OUT!!
SO I NOTICED.
A-AND... THERE WAS AN INTRUDER! AND A BATTLE! AND...

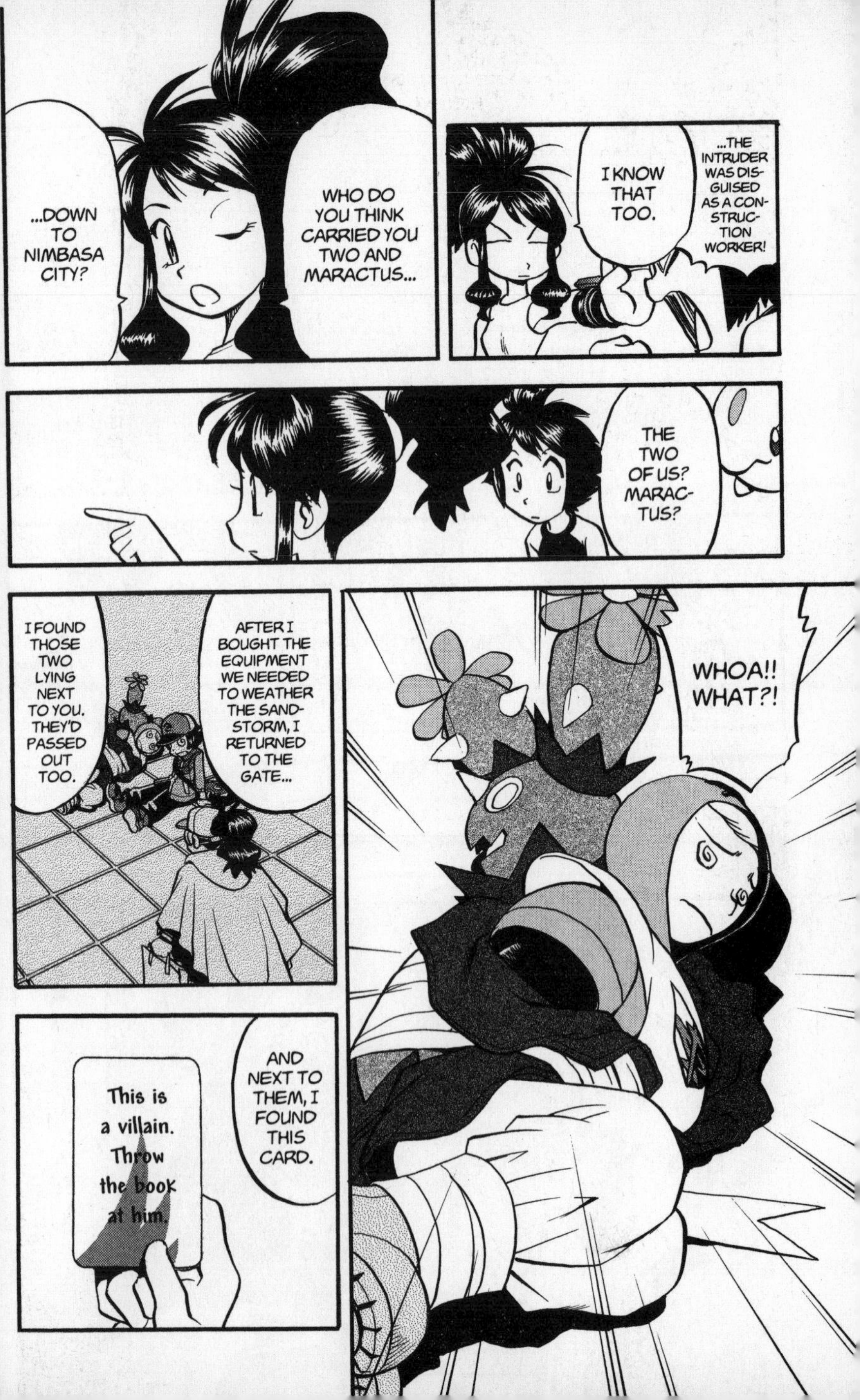
...THE INTRUDER WAS DISGUISED AS A CONSTRUCTION WORKER!
I KNOW THAT TOO.
WHO DO YOU THINK CARRIED YOU TWO AND MARACTUS...
...DOWN TO NIMBASA CITY?
THE TWO OF US? MARACTUS?
WHOA!! WHAT?!
AFTER I BOUGHT THE EQUIPMENT WE NEEDED TO WEATHER THE SANDSTORM, I RETURNED TO THE GATE...
I FOUND THOSE TWO LYING NEXT TO YOU. THEY'D PASSED OUT TOO.
AND NEXT TO THEM, I FOUND THIS CARD.
This is a villain. Throw the book at him.

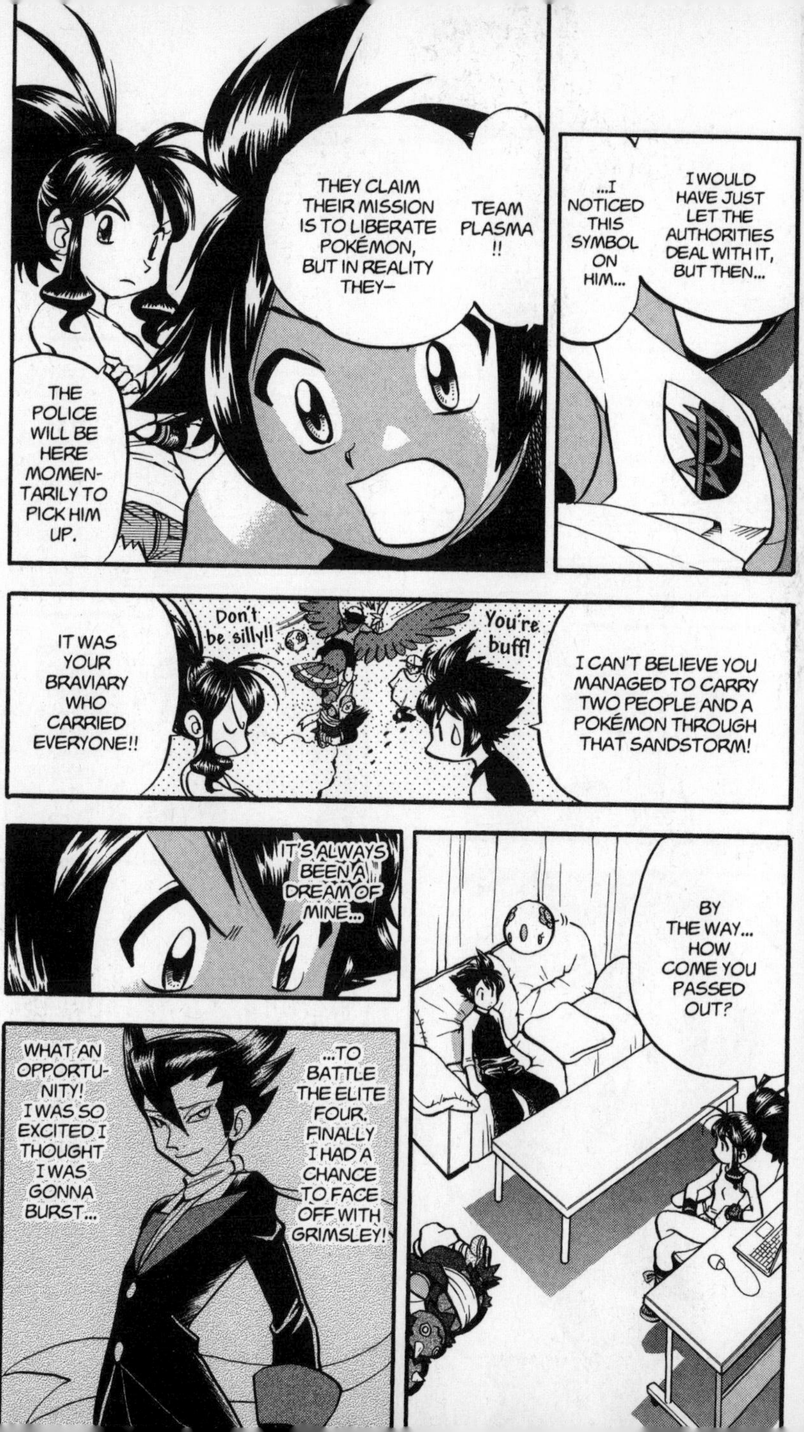
I WOULD HAVE JUST LET THE AUTHORITIES DEAL WITH IT, BUT THEN...
...I NOTICED THIS SYMBOL ON HIM...
TEAM PLASMA !!
THEY CLAIM THEIR MISSION IS TO LIBERATE POKÉMON, BUT IN REALITY THEY—
THE POLICE WILL BE HERE MOMENTARILY TO PICK HIM UP.
I CAN'T BELIEVE YOU MANAGED TO CARRY TWO PEOPLE AND A POKÉMON THROUGH THAT SANDSTORM!
You're buff!
Don't be silly!!
IT WAS YOUR BRAVIARY WHO CARRIED EVERYONE!!
BY THE WAY... HOW COME YOU PASSED OUT?
IT'S ALWAYS BEEN A DREAM OF MINE...
...TO BATTLE THE ELITE FOUR. FINALLY I HAD A CHANCE TO FACE OFF WITH GRIMSLEY!
WHAT AN OPPORTUNITY! I WAS SO EXCITED I THOUGHT I WAS GONNA BURST...

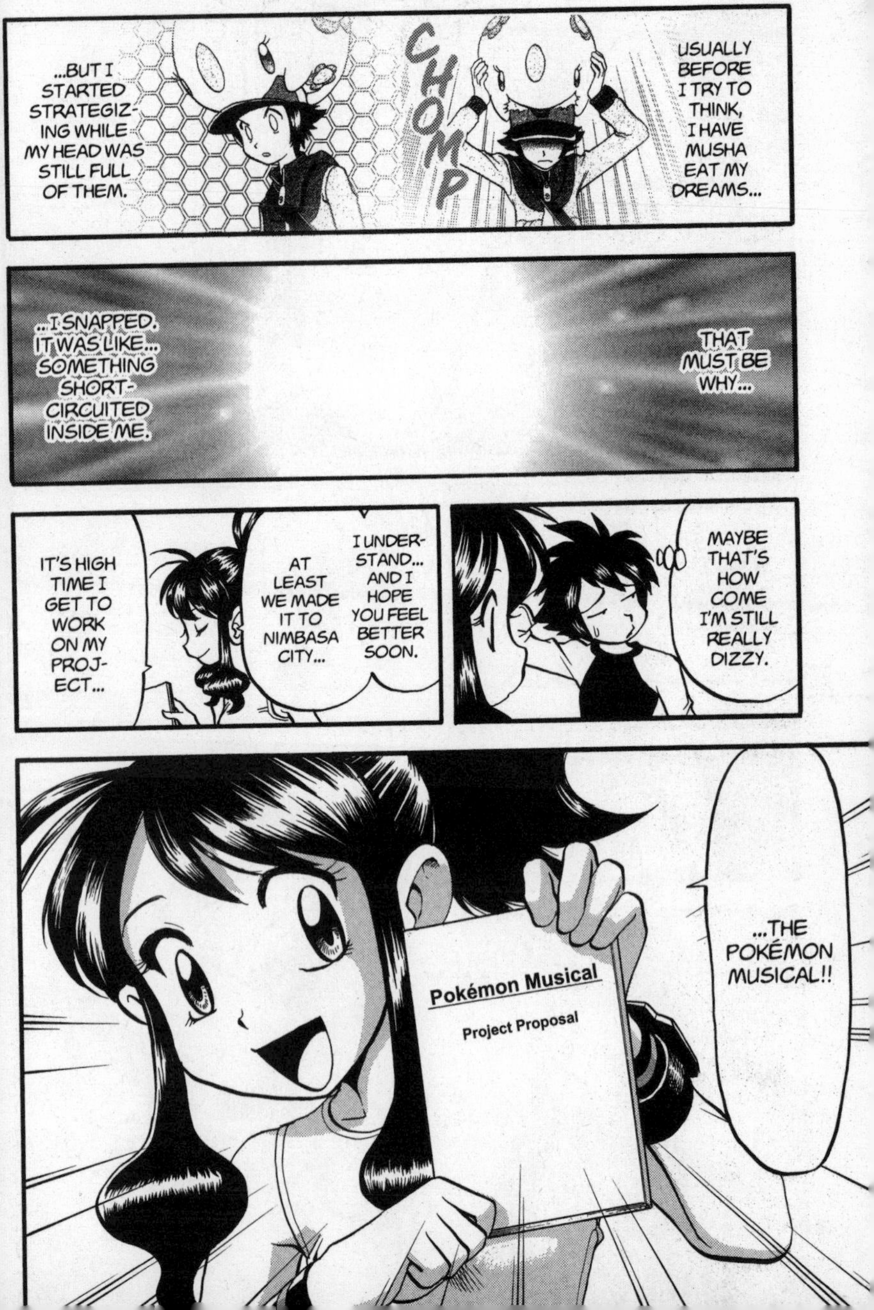
USUALLY BEFORE I TRY TO THINK, I HAVE MUSHA EAT MY DREAMS...
CHOMP
...BUT I STARTED STRATEGIZING WHILE MY HEAD WAS STILL FULL OF THEM.
THAT MUST BE WHY...
...I SNAPPED. IT WAS LIKE... SOMETHING SHORT-CIRCUITED INSIDE ME.
MAYBE THAT'S HOW COME I'M STILL REALLY DIZZY.
I UNDERSTAND... AND I HOPE YOU FEEL BETTER SOON.
AT LEAST WE MADE IT TO NIMBASA CITY...
IT'S HIGH TIME I GET TO WORK ON MY PROJECT...
...THE POKÉMON MUSICAL!!
Pokémon Musical
Project Proposal

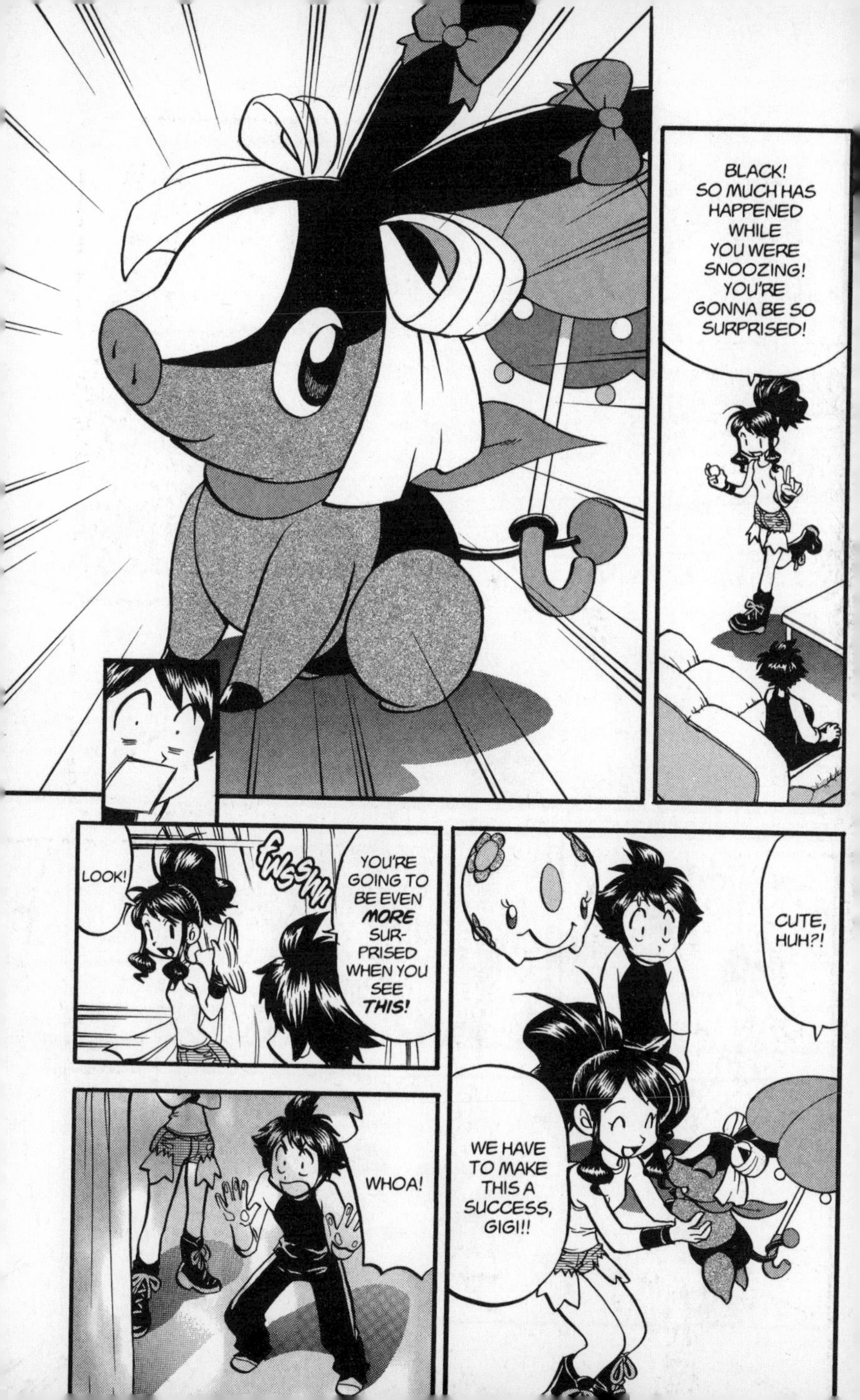
BLACK! SO MUCH HAS HAPPENED WHILE YOU WERE SNOOZING! YOU'RE GONNA BE SO SURPRISED!
CUTE, HUH?!
WE HAVE TO MAKE THIS A SUCCESS, GIGI!!
YOU'RE GOING TO BE EVEN MORE SURPRISED WHEN YOU SEE THIS!
FWSSHH
LOOK!
WHOA!

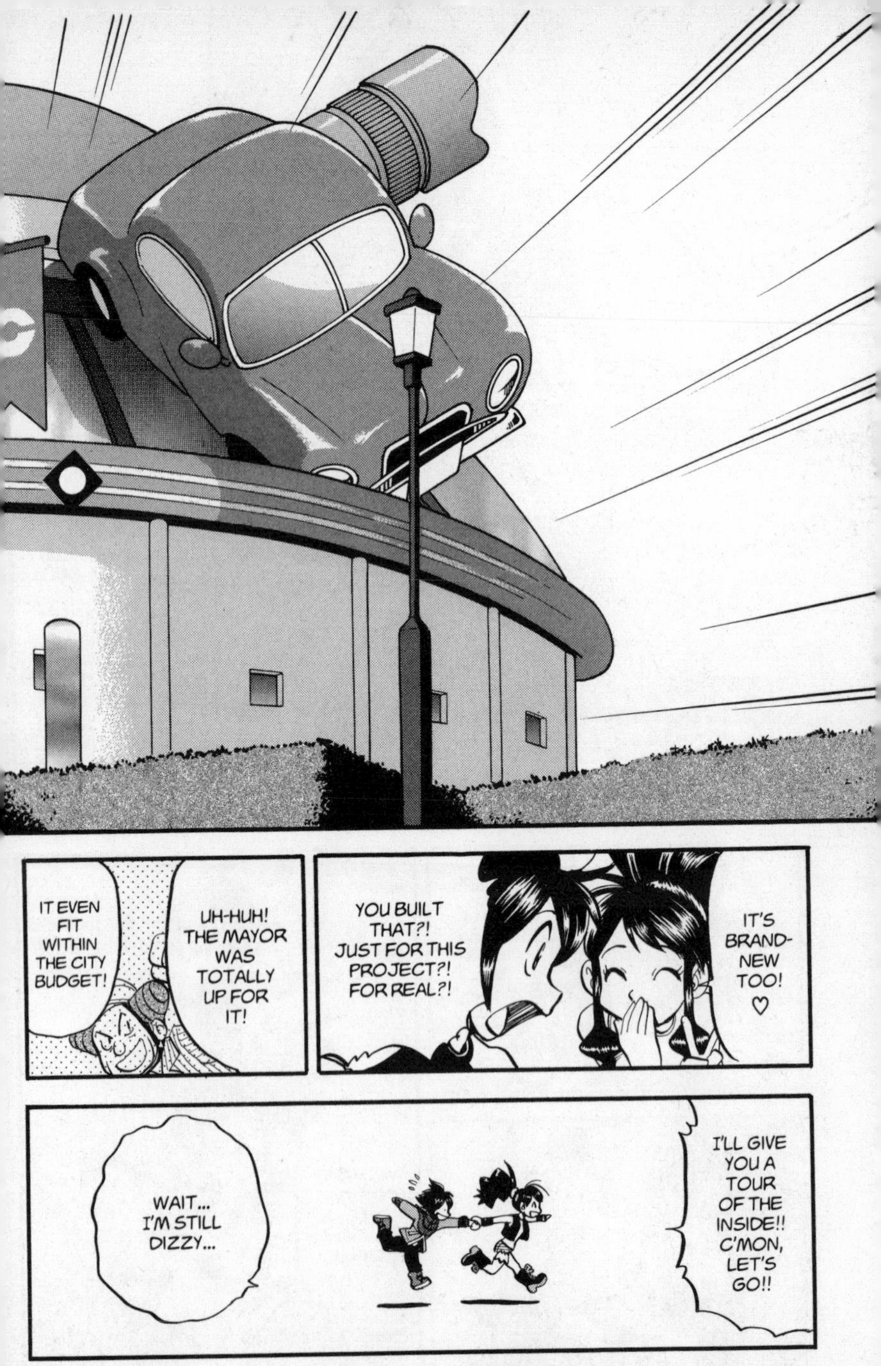
IT'S BRAND-NEW TOO! ♡
YOU BUILT THAT?! JUST FOR THIS PROJECT?! FOR REAL?!
UH-HUH! THE MAYOR WAS TOTALLY UP FOR IT!
IT EVEN FIT WITHIN THE CITY BUDGET!
I'LL GIVE YOU A TOUR OF THE INSIDE!! C'MON, LET'S GO!!
WAIT... I'M STILL DIZZY...

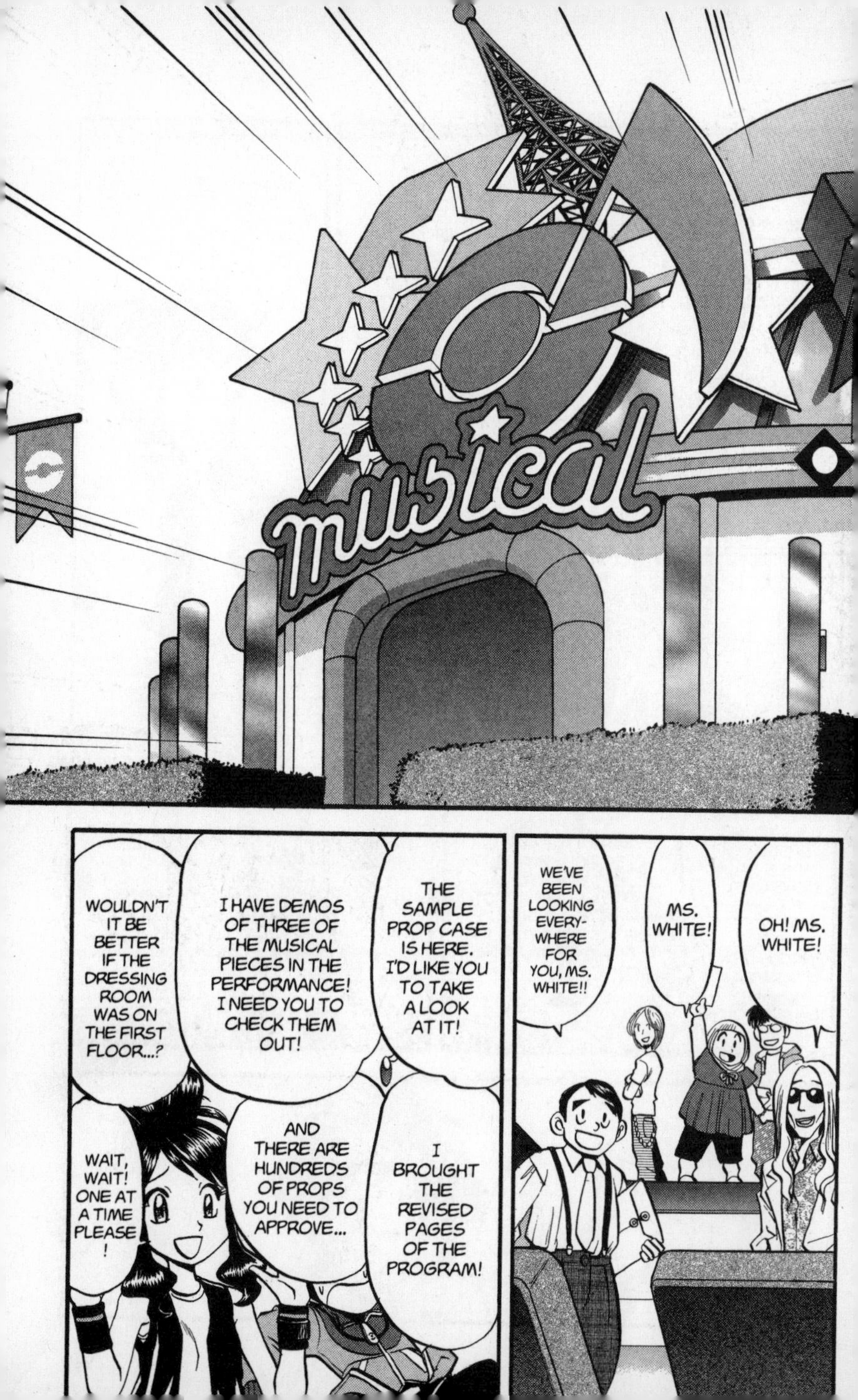
OH! MS. WHITE!
MS. WHITE!
WE'VE BEEN LOOKING EVERY-WHERE FOR YOU, MS. WHITE!!
THE SAMPLE PROP CASE IS HERE. I'D LIKE YOU TO TAKE A LOOK AT IT!
I HAVE DEMOS OF THREE OF THE MUSICAL PIECES IN THE PERFORMANCE! I NEED YOU TO CHECK THEM OUT!
WOULDN'T IT BE BETTER IF THE DRESSING ROOM WAS ON THE FIRST FLOOR...?
I BROUGHT THE REVISED PAGES OF THE PROGRAM!
AND THERE ARE HUNDREDS OF PROPS YOU NEED TO APPROVE...
WAIT, WAIT! ONE AT A TIME PLEASE!

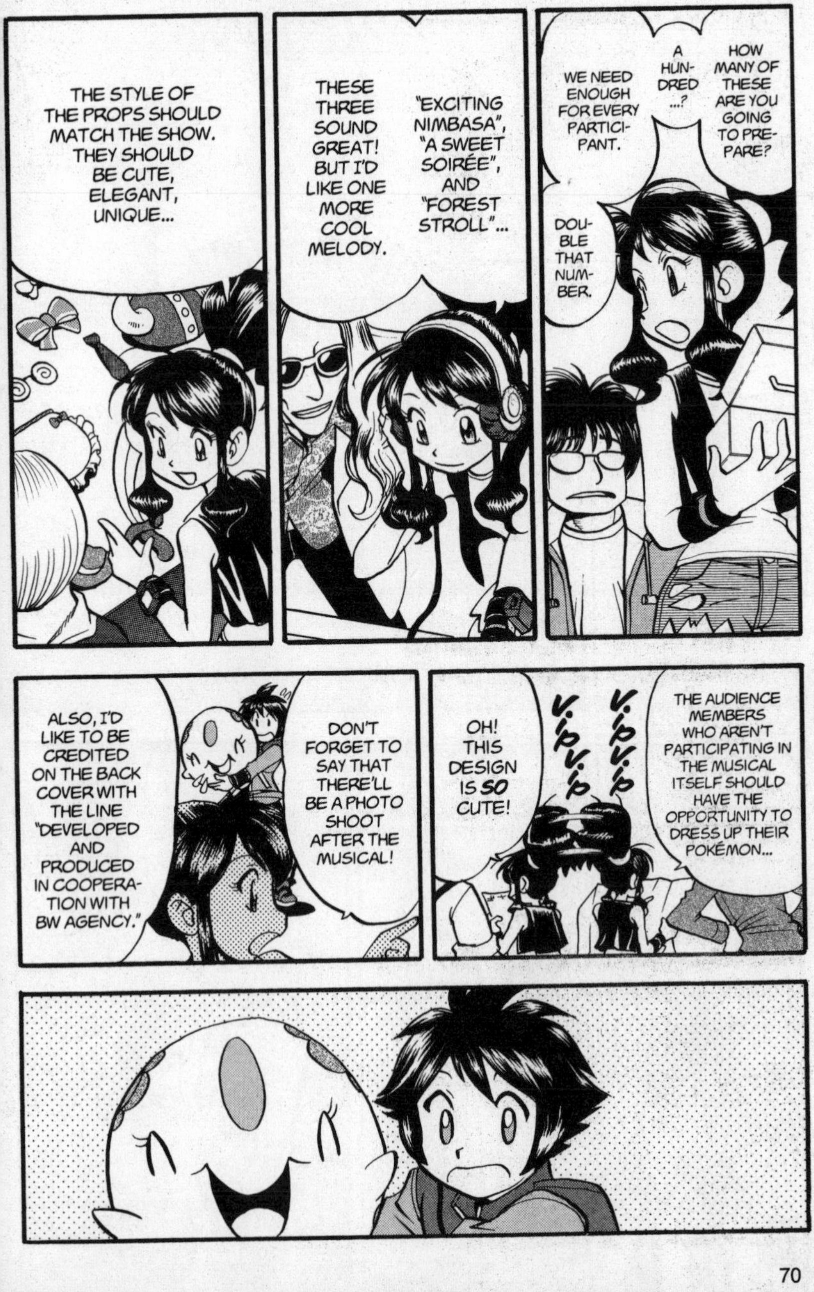
HOW MANY OF THESE ARE YOU GOING TO PREPARE?
A HUNDRED...?
WE NEED ENOUGH FOR EVERY PARTICIPANT.
DOUBLE THAT NUMBER.
"EXCITING NIMBASA", "A SWEET SOIRÉE", AND "FOREST STROLL"...
THESE THREE SOUND GREAT! BUT I'D LIKE ONE MORE COOL MELODY.
THE STYLE OF THE PROPS SHOULD MATCH THE SHOW. THEY SHOULD BE CUTE, ELEGANT, UNIQUE...
THE AUDIENCE MEMBERS WHO AREN'T PARTICIPATING IN THE MUSICAL ITSELF SHOULD HAVE THE OPPORTUNITY TO DRESS UP THEIR POKÉMON...
V.i.p V.i.p
V.i.p V.i.p
OH! THIS DESIGN IS ***SO*** CUTE!
DON'T FORGET TO SAY THAT THERE'LL BE A PHOTO SHOOT AFTER THE MUSICAL!
ALSO, I'D LIKE TO BE CREDITED ON THE BACK COVER WITH THE LINE "DEVELOPED AND PRODUCED IN COOPERATION WITH BW AGENCY."

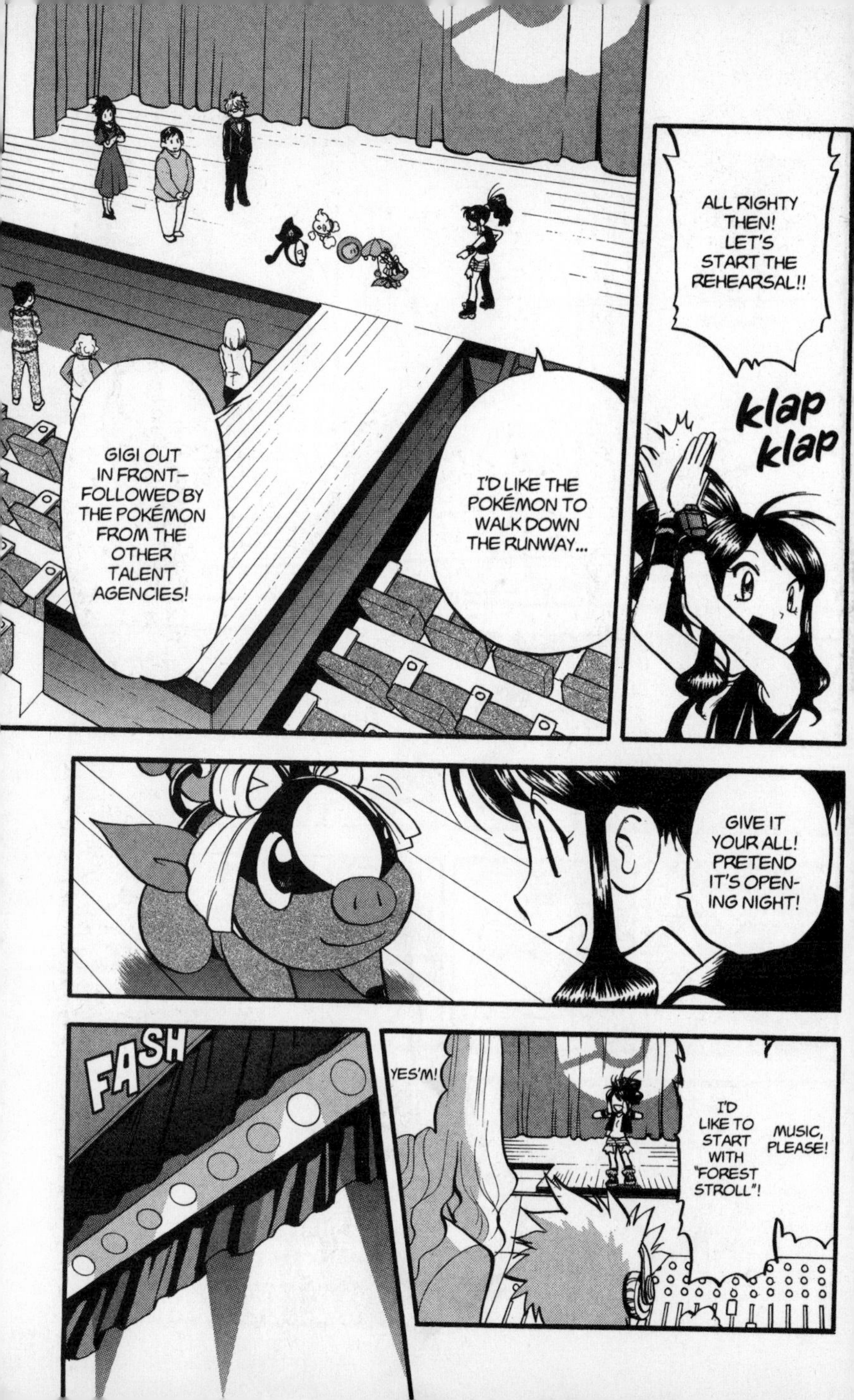
ALL RIGHTY THEN! LET'S START THE REHEARSAL!!
klap klap
I'D LIKE THE POKÉMON TO WALK DOWN THE RUNWAY...
GIGI OUT IN FRONT— FOLLOWED BY THE POKÉMON FROM THE OTHER TALENT AGENCIES!
GIVE IT YOUR ALL! PRETEND IT'S OPEN-ING NIGHT!
MUSIC, PLEASE!
I'D LIKE TO START WITH "FOREST STROLL"!
YES'M!
FASH

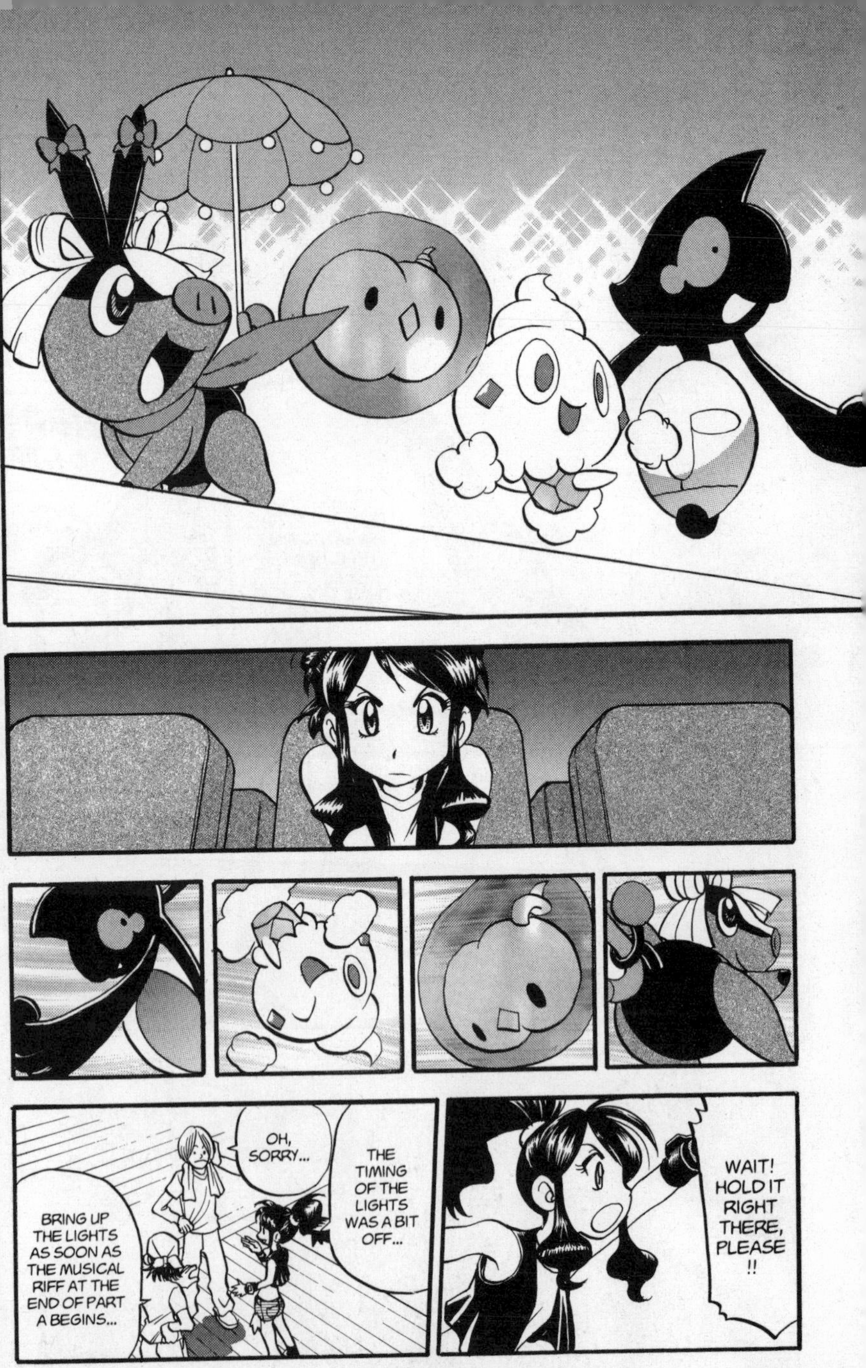
WAIT! HOLD IT RIGHT THERE, PLEASE!!
OH, SORRY...
THE TIMING OF THE LIGHTS WAS A BIT OFF...
BRING UP THE LIGHTS AS SOON AS THE MUSICAL RIFF AT THE END OF PART A BEGINS...

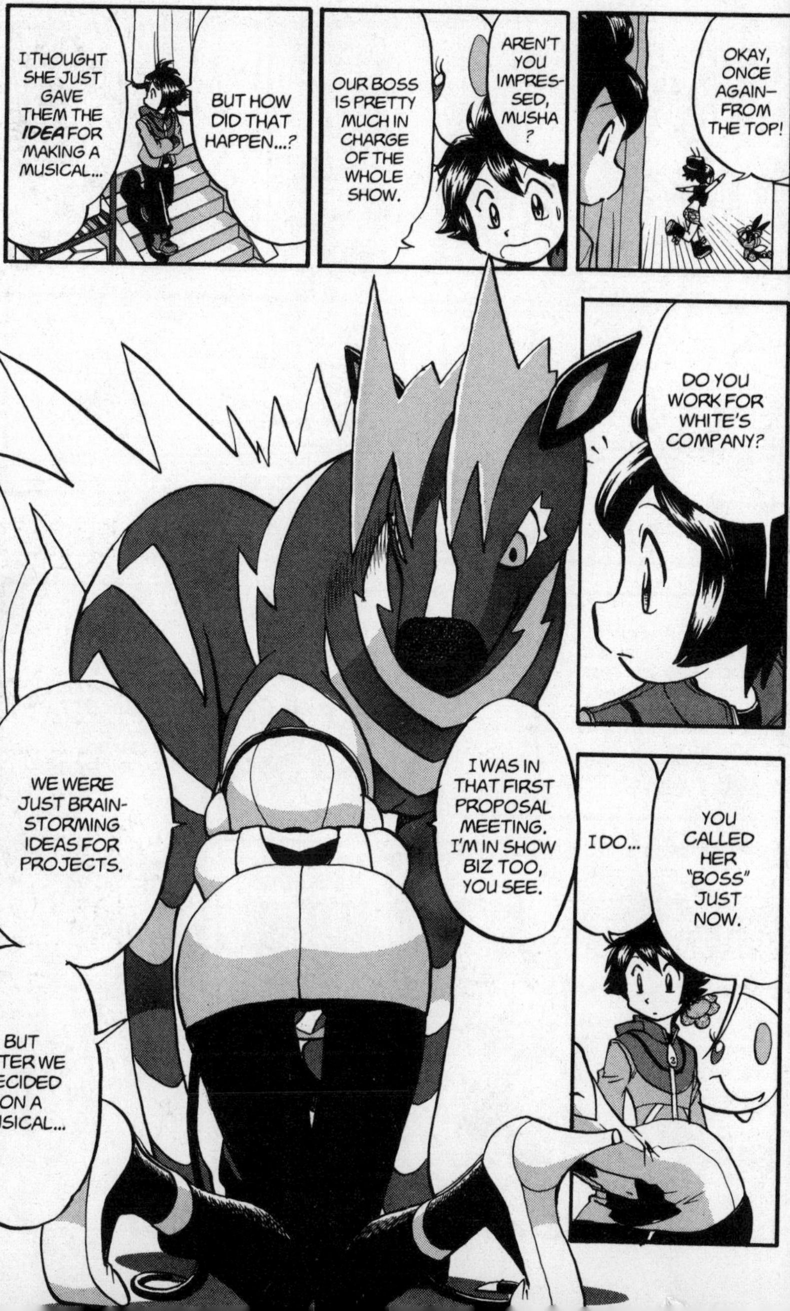
OKAY, ONCE AGAIN— FROM THE TOP!
AREN'T YOU IMPRES- SED, MUSHA ?
OUR BOSS IS PRETTY MUCH IN CHARGE OF THE WHOLE SHOW.
BUT HOW DID THAT HAPPEN...?
I THOUGHT SHE JUST GAVE THEM THE ***IDEA*** FOR MAKING A MUSICAL...
DO YOU WORK FOR WHITE'S COMPANY?
YOU CALLED HER "BOSS" JUST NOW.
I DO...
I WAS IN THAT FIRST PROPOSAL MEETING. I'M IN SHOW BIZ TOO, YOU SEE.
WE WERE JUST BRAIN- STORMING IDEAS FOR PROJECTS.
BUT AFTER WE DECIDED ON A MUSICAL...

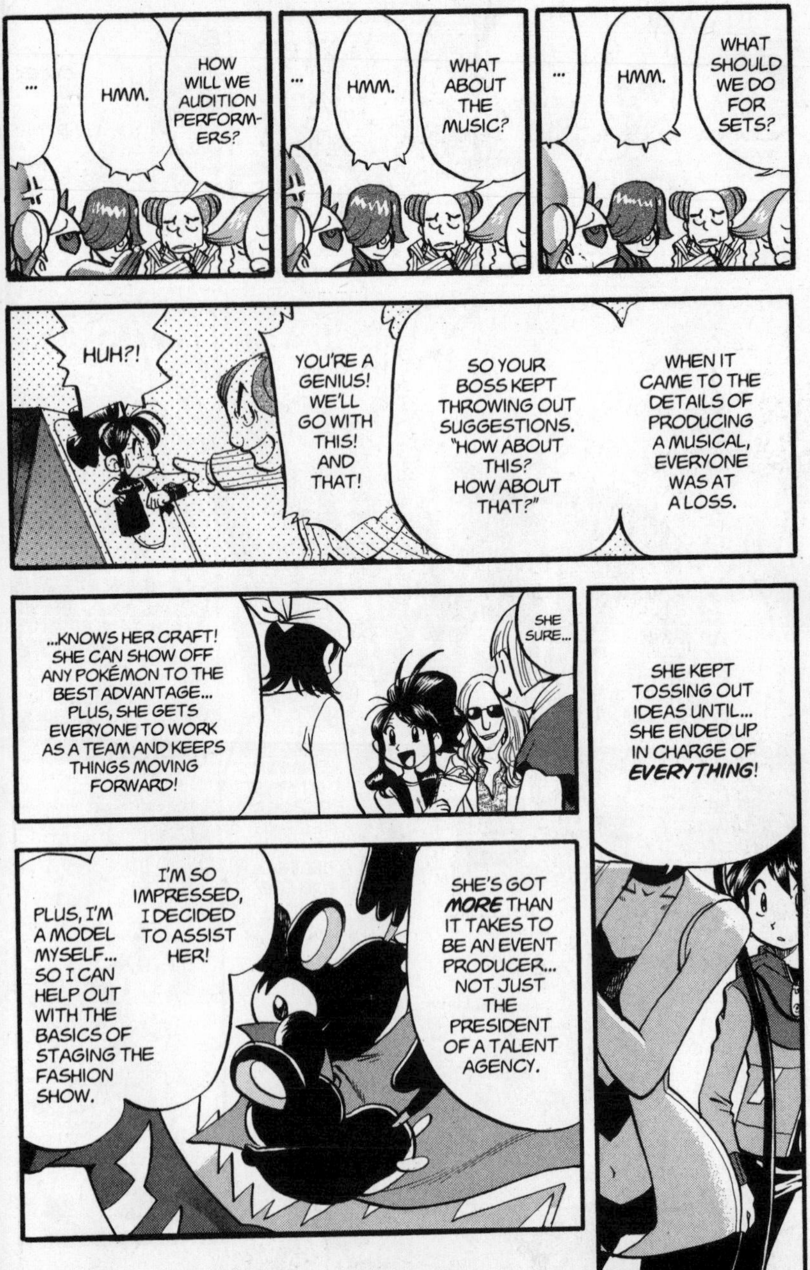
WHAT SHOULD WE DO FOR SETS?
HMM.
...
WHAT ABOUT THE MUSIC?
HMM.
...
HOW WILL WE AUDITION PERFORM-ERS?
HMM.
...
WHEN IT CAME TO THE DETAILS OF PRODUCING A MUSICAL, EVERYONE WAS AT A LOSS.
SO YOUR BOSS KEPT THROWING OUT SUGGESTIONS. "HOW ABOUT THIS? HOW ABOUT THAT?"
YOU'RE A GENIUS! WE'LL GO WITH THIS! AND THAT!
HUH?!
SHE KEPT TOSSING OUT IDEAS UNTIL... SHE ENDED UP IN CHARGE OF ***EVERYTHING***!
SHE SURE...
...KNOWS HER CRAFT! SHE CAN SHOW OFF ANY POKÉMON TO THE BEST ADVANTAGE... PLUS, SHE GETS EVERYONE TO WORK AS A TEAM AND KEEPS THINGS MOVING FORWARD!
SHE'S GOT ***MORE*** THAN IT TAKES TO BE AN EVENT PRODUCER... NOT JUST THE PRESIDENT OF A TALENT AGENCY.
I'M SO IMPRESSED, I DECIDED TO ASSIST HER!
PLUS, I'M A MODEL MYSELF... SO I CAN HELP OUT WITH THE BASICS OF STAGING THE FASHION SHOW.

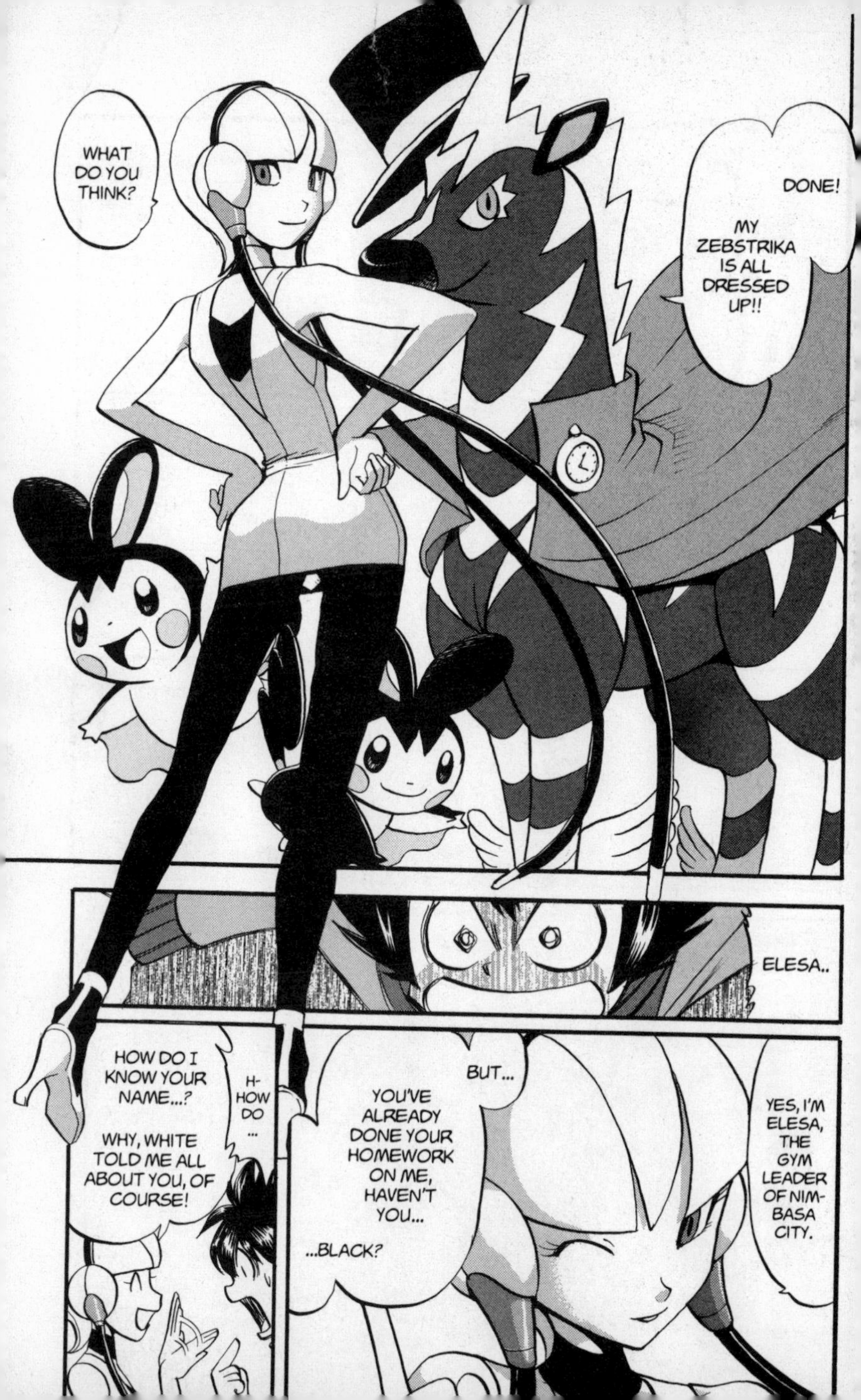
DONE!
MY ZEBSTRIKA IS ALL DRESSED UP!!
WHAT DO YOU THINK?
ELESA..
YES, I'M ELESA, THE GYM LEADER OF NIM-BASA CITY.
BUT...
YOU'VE ALREADY DONE YOUR HOMEWORK ON ME, HAVEN'T YOU...
...BLACK?
H-HOW DO...
HOW DO I KNOW YOUR NAME...?
WHY, WHITE TOLD ME ALL ABOUT YOU, OF COURSE!

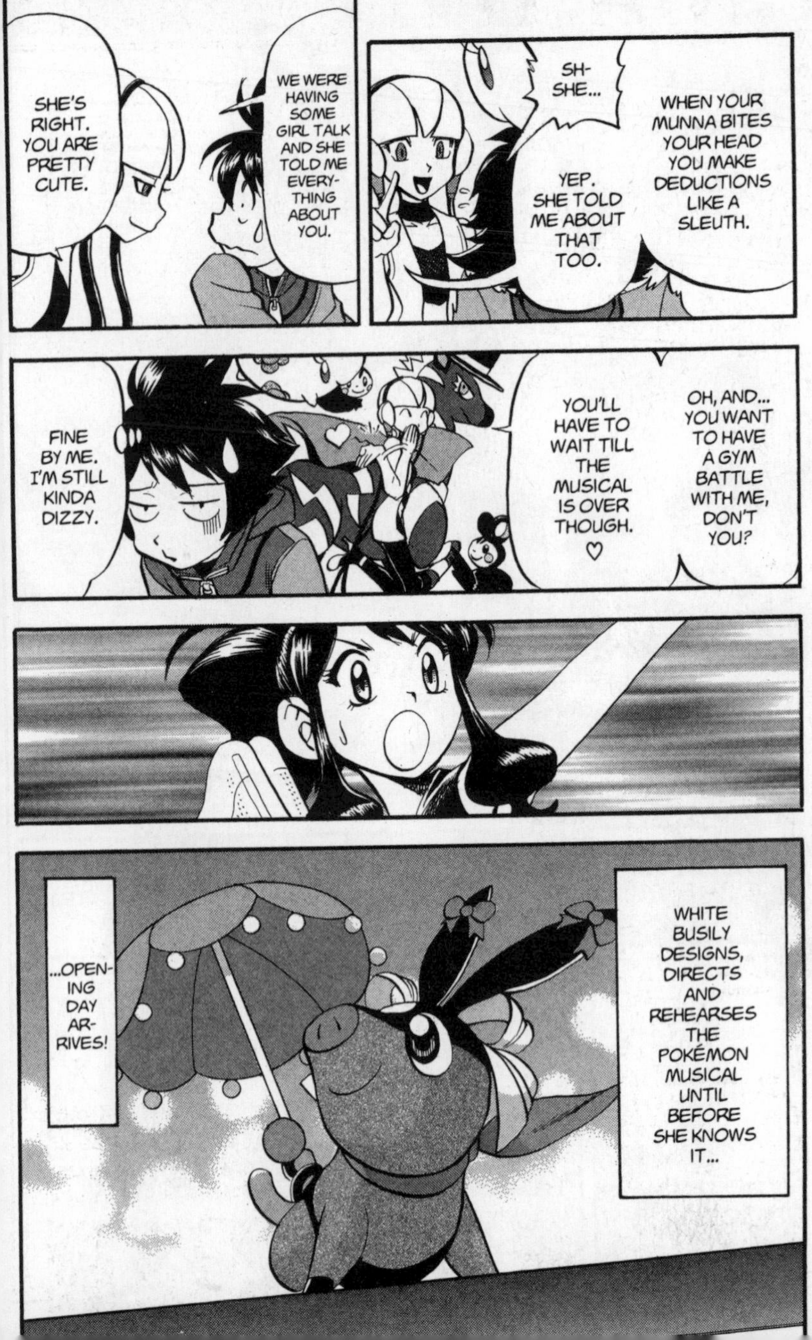
WHEN YOUR MUNNA BITES YOUR HEAD YOU MAKE DEDUCTIONS LIKE A SLEUTH.
SH- SHE...
YEP. SHE TOLD ME ABOUT THAT TOO.
WE WERE HAVING SOME GIRL TALK AND SHE TOLD ME EVERY-THING ABOUT YOU.
SHE'S RIGHT. YOU ARE PRETTY CUTE.
OH, AND... YOU WANT TO HAVE A GYM BATTLE WITH ME, DON'T YOU?
YOU'LL HAVE TO WAIT TILL THE MUSICAL IS OVER THOUGH. ♡
FINE BY ME. I'M STILL KINDA DIZZY.
WHITE BUSILY DESIGNS, DIRECTS AND REHEARSES THE POKÉMON MUSICAL UNTIL BEFORE SHE KNOWS IT...
...OPEN-ING DAY AR-RIVES!

ADVENTURE MAP

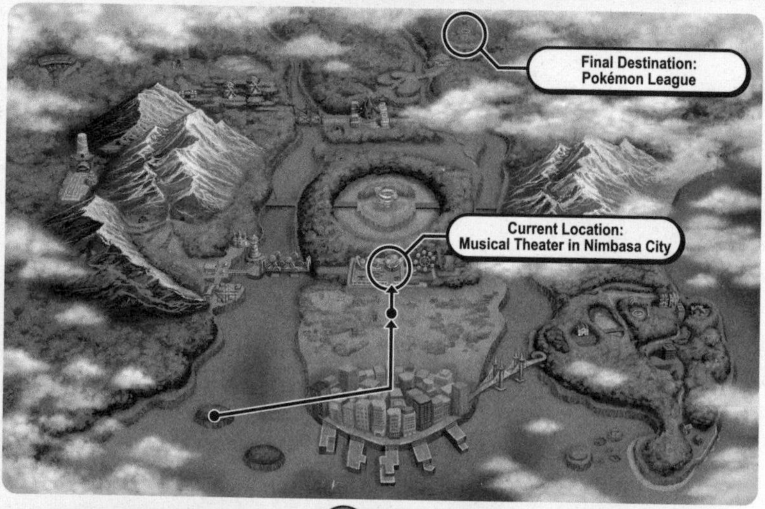

Final Destination: Pokémon League
Current Location: Musical Theater in Nimbasa City

Fire Pig Pokémon **Nite**
Pignite ♂ Fire Fighting
Lv.22 Ability: Blaze

Dream Eater Pokémon **Musha**
Munna ♂ Psychic
Lv.45 Ability: Forewarn

Valiant Pokémon **Brav**
Braviary ♂ Normal Flying
Lv.54 Ability: Sheer Force

EleSpider Pokémon **Tula**
Galvantula ♂ Bug Electric
Lv.47 Ability: Unnerve

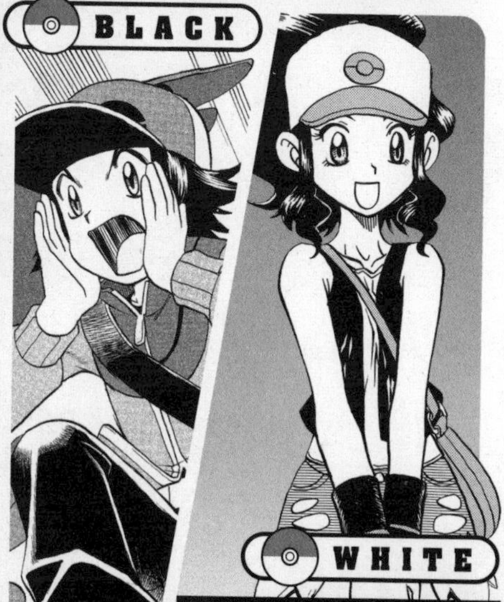

BLACK
WHITE

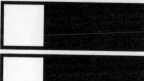

Fire Pig Pokémon **Gigi**
Tepig ♀ Fire
Lv.05 Ability: Blaze

TRIO BADGE · BASIC BADGE · INSECT BADGE · ? · ? · ? · ? · ?

Pokémon™ Adventures Black & White

EMOLGA

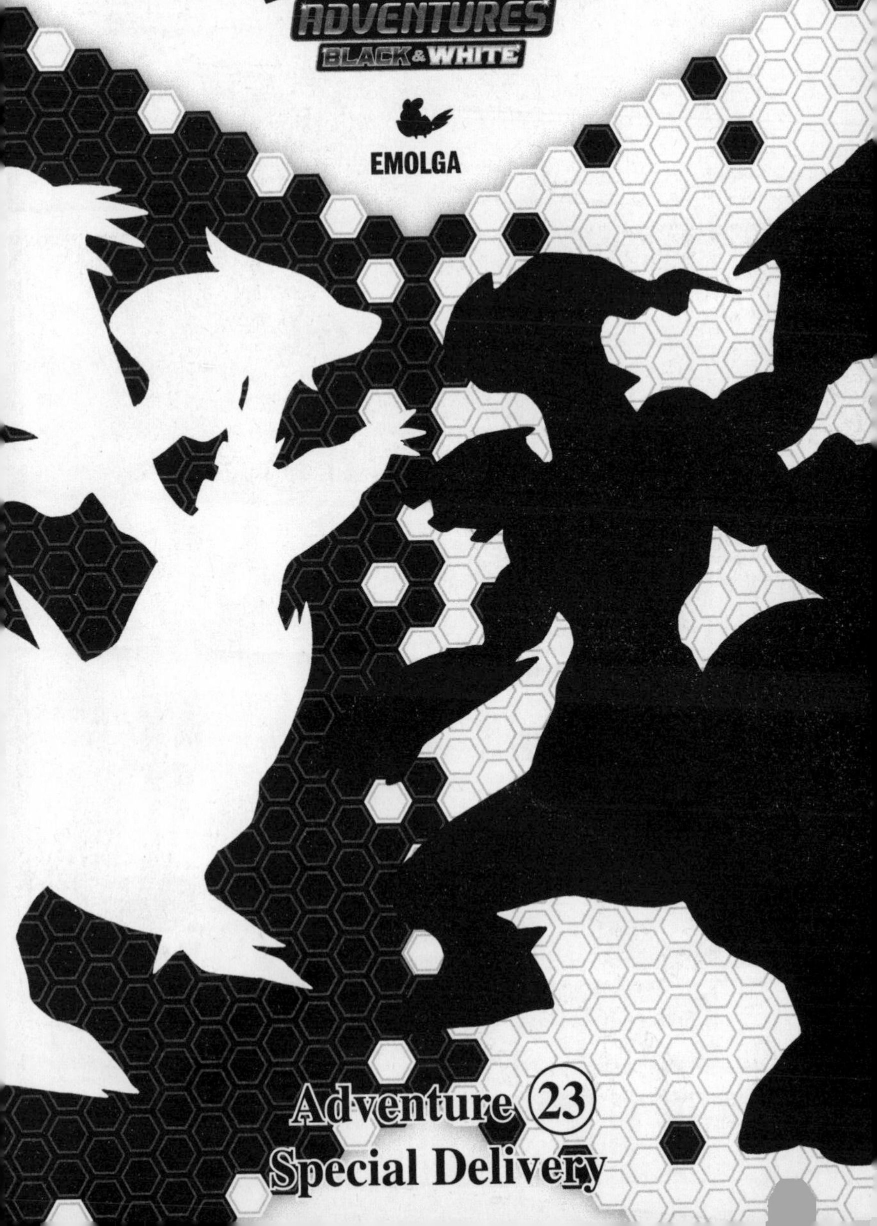

Adventure 23
Special Delivery

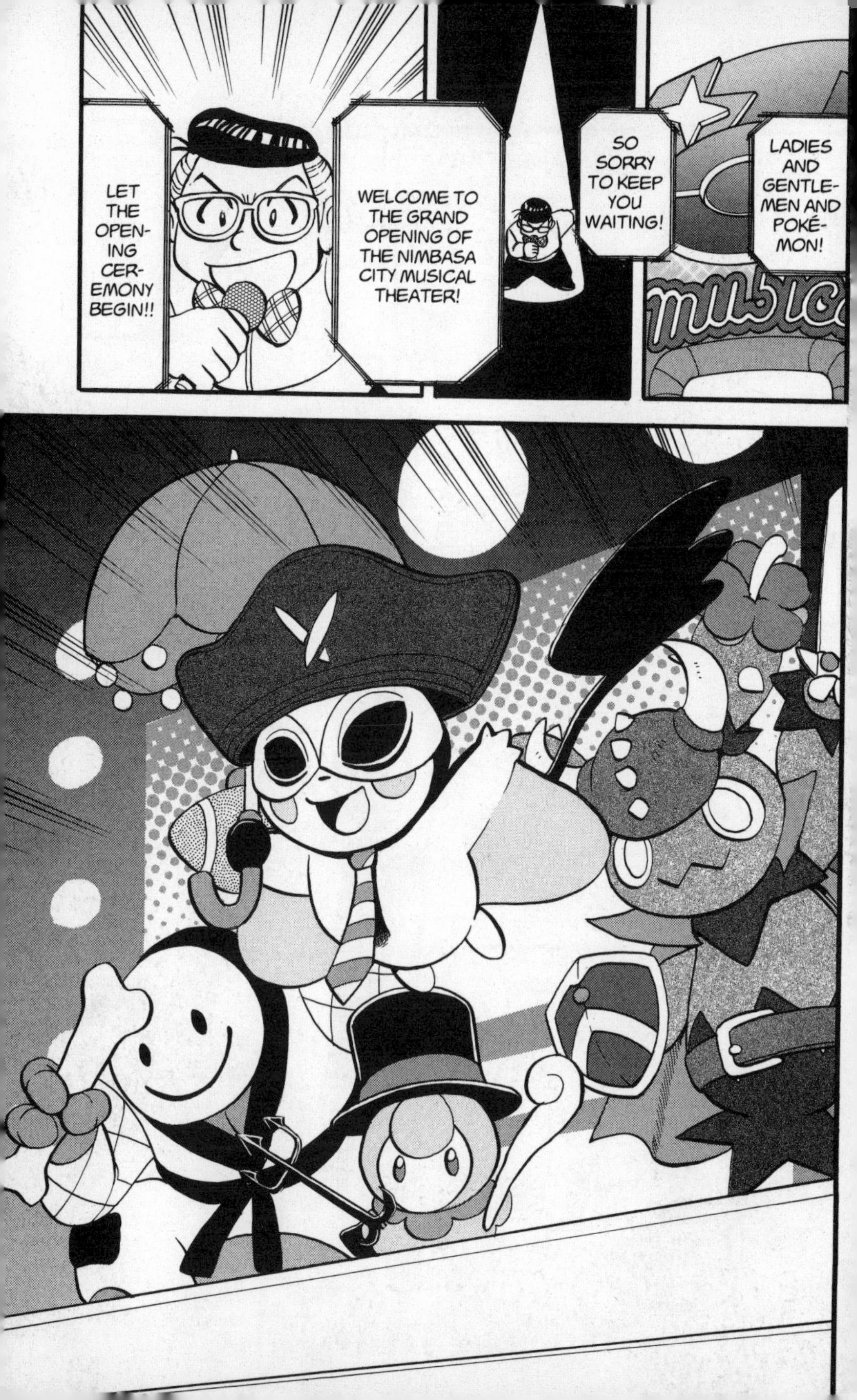
LADIES AND GENTLEMEN AND POKÉMON!
SO SORRY TO KEEP YOU WAITING!
WELCOME TO THE GRAND OPENING OF THE NIMBASA CITY MUSICAL THEATER!
LET THE OPENING CEREMONY BEGIN!!

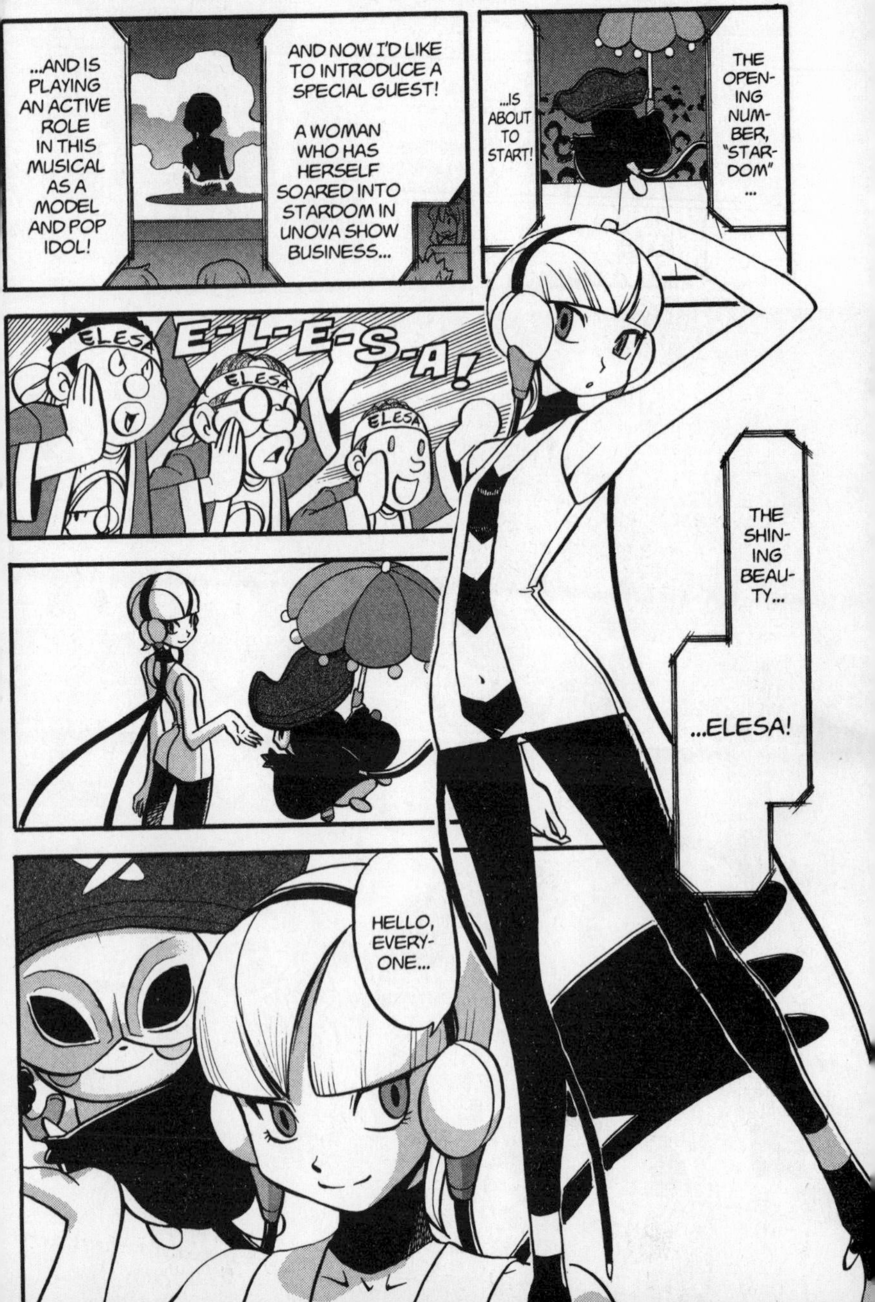
THE OPENING NUMBER, "STARDOM"...
...IS ABOUT TO START!
AND NOW I'D LIKE TO INTRODUCE A SPECIAL GUEST!
A WOMAN WHO HAS HERSELF SOARED INTO STARDOM IN UNOVA SHOW BUSINESS...
...AND IS PLAYING AN ACTIVE ROLE IN THIS MUSICAL AS A MODEL AND POP IDOL!
THE SHINING BEAUTY...
...ELESA!
E-L-E-S-A!
ELESA
ELESA
ELESA
HELLO, EVERYONE...

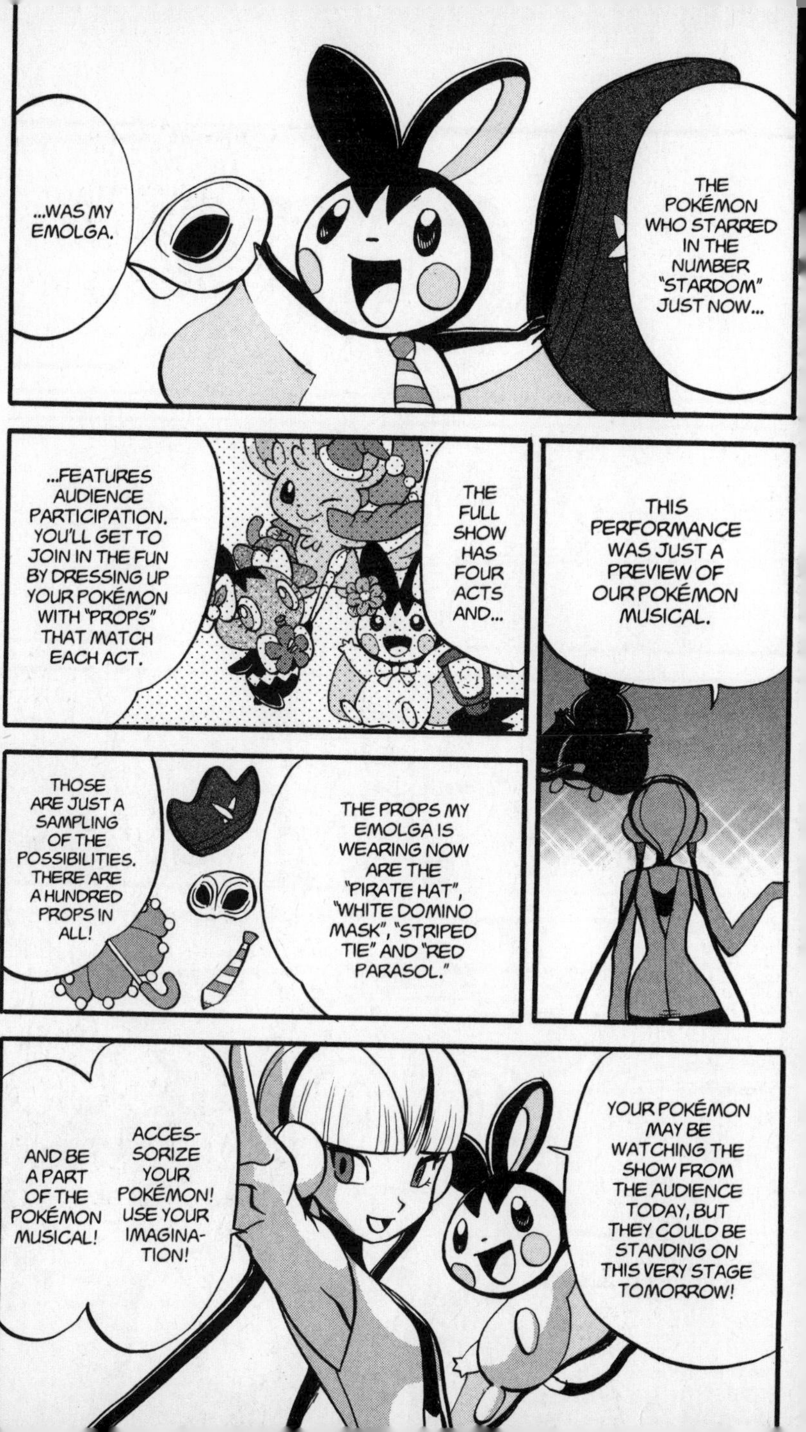

THE POKÉMON WHO STARRED IN THE NUMBER "STARDOM" JUST NOW...
...WAS MY EMOLGA.
THIS PERFORMANCE WAS JUST A PREVIEW OF OUR POKÉMON MUSICAL.
THE FULL SHOW HAS FOUR ACTS AND...
...FEATURES AUDIENCE PARTICIPATION. YOU'LL GET TO JOIN IN THE FUN BY DRESSING UP YOUR POKÉMON WITH "PROPS" THAT MATCH EACH ACT.
THE PROPS MY EMOLGA IS WEARING NOW ARE THE "PIRATE HAT", "WHITE DOMINO MASK", "STRIPED TIE" AND "RED PARASOL."
THOSE ARE JUST A SAMPLING OF THE POSSIBILITIES. THERE ARE A HUNDRED PROPS IN ALL!
YOUR POKÉMON MAY BE WATCHING THE SHOW FROM THE AUDIENCE TODAY, BUT THEY COULD BE STANDING ON THIS VERY STAGE TOMORROW!
ACCES-SORIZE YOUR POKÉMON! USE YOUR IMAGINA-TION!
AND BE A PART OF THE POKÉMON MUSICAL!

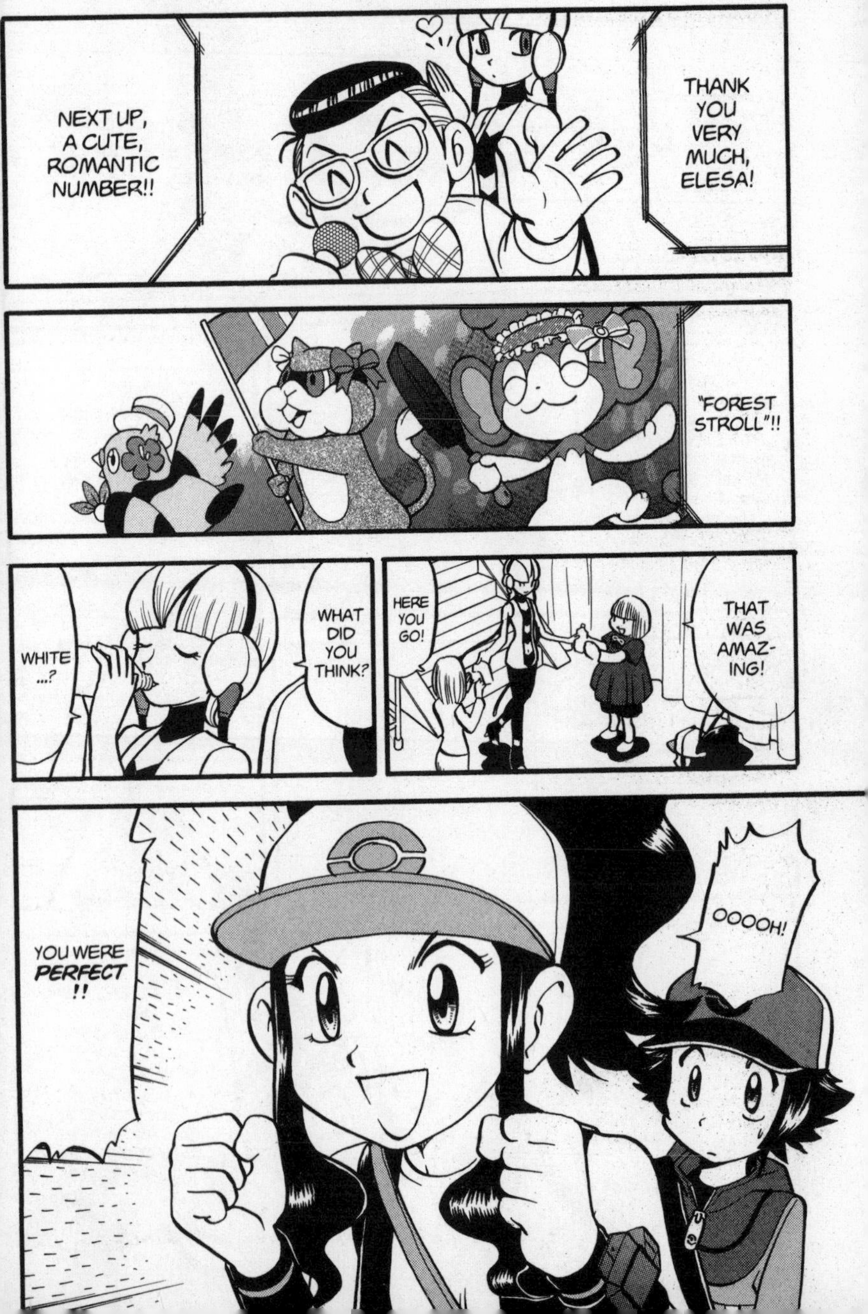
THANK YOU VERY MUCH, ELESA!
NEXT UP, A CUTE, ROMANTIC NUMBER!!
"FOREST STROLL"!!
THAT WAS AMAZ-ING!
HERE YOU GO!
WHAT DID YOU THINK?
WHITE ...?
OOOOH!
YOU WERE *PERFECT*!!

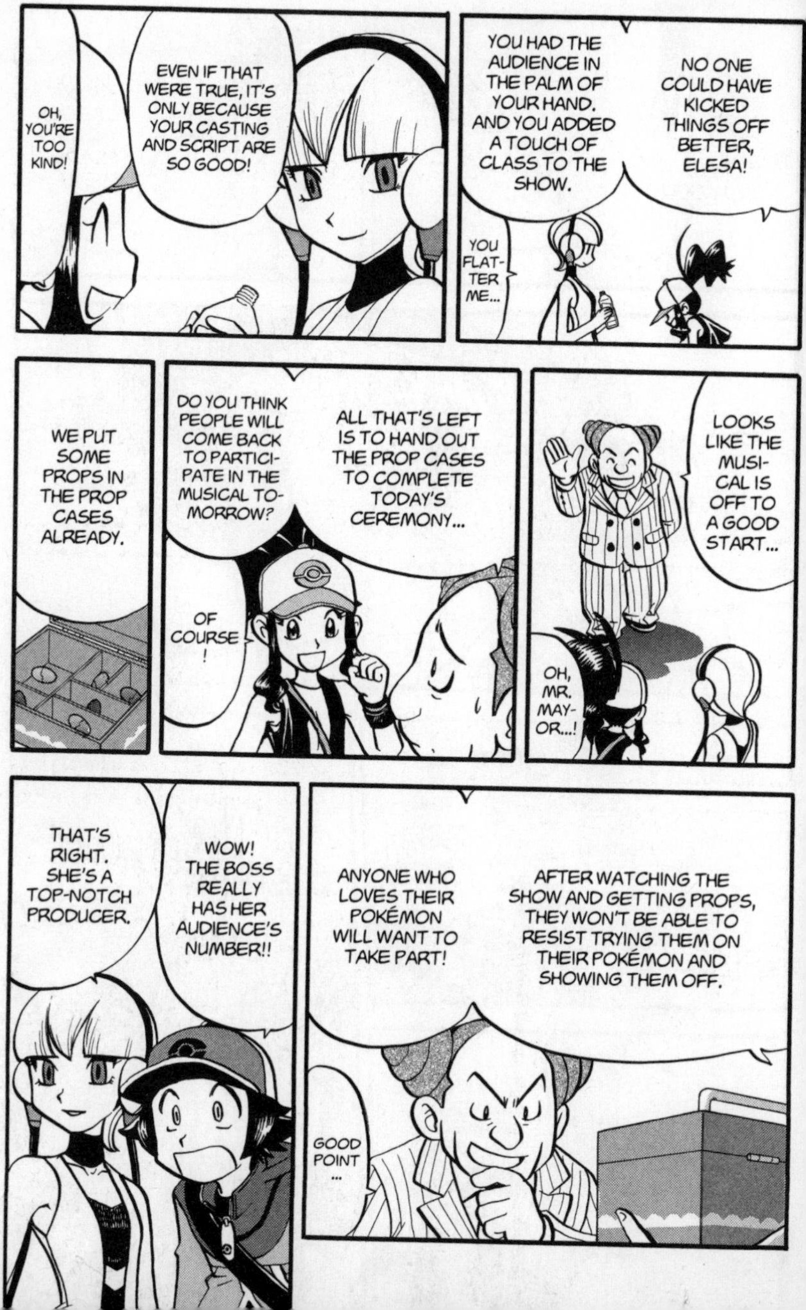
NO ONE COULD HAVE KICKED THINGS OFF BETTER, ELESA!
YOU HAD THE AUDIENCE IN THE PALM OF YOUR HAND. AND YOU ADDED A TOUCH OF CLASS TO THE SHOW.
YOU FLATTER ME...
EVEN IF THAT WERE TRUE, IT'S ONLY BECAUSE YOUR CASTING AND SCRIPT ARE SO GOOD!
OH, YOU'RE TOO KIND!
LOOKS LIKE THE MUSICAL IS OFF TO A GOOD START...
OH, MR. MAYOR...!
ALL THAT'S LEFT IS TO HAND OUT THE PROP CASES TO COMPLETE TODAY'S CEREMONY...
DO YOU THINK PEOPLE WILL COME BACK TO PARTICIPATE IN THE MUSICAL TOMORROW?
OF COURSE!
WE PUT SOME PROPS IN THE PROP CASES ALREADY.
AFTER WATCHING THE SHOW AND GETTING PROPS, THEY WON'T BE ABLE TO RESIST TRYING THEM ON THEIR POKÉMON AND SHOWING THEM OFF.
ANYONE WHO LOVES THEIR POKÉMON WILL WANT TO TAKE PART!
GOOD POINT...
WOW! THE BOSS REALLY HAS HER AUDIENCE'S NUMBER!!
THAT'S RIGHT. SHE'S A TOP-NOTCH PRODUCER.

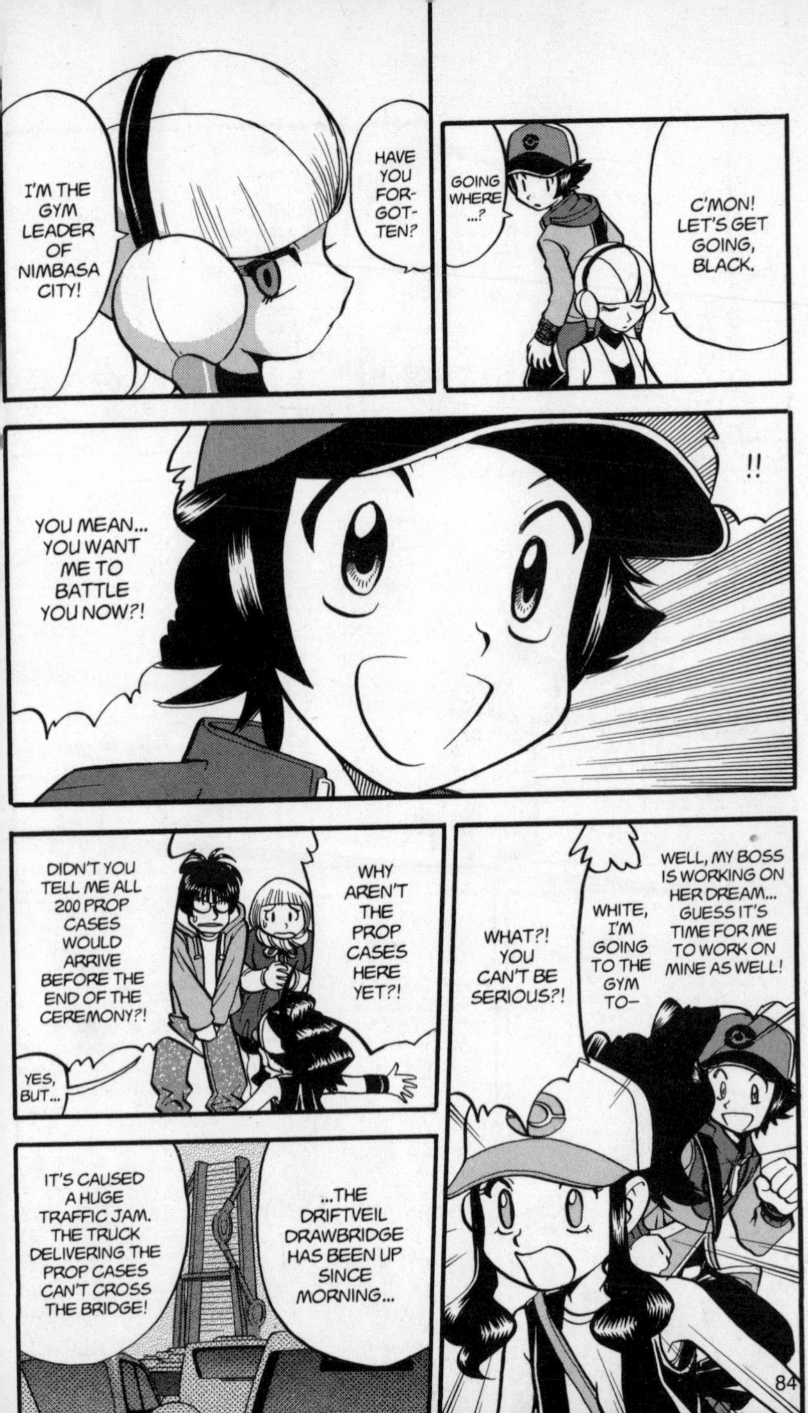
C'MON! LET'S GET GOING, BLACK.
GOING WHERE ...?
HAVE YOU FOR-GOT-TEN?
I'M THE GYM LEADER OF NIMBASA CITY!
!!
YOU MEAN... YOU WANT ME TO BATTLE YOU NOW?!
WELL, MY BOSS IS WORKING ON HER DREAM... GUESS IT'S TIME FOR ME TO WORK ON MINE AS WELL!
WHITE, I'M GOING TO THE GYM TO—
WHAT?! YOU CAN'T BE SERIOUS?!
WHY AREN'T THE PROP CASES HERE YET?!
DIDN'T YOU TELL ME ALL 200 PROP CASES WOULD ARRIVE BEFORE THE END OF THE CEREMONY?!
YES, BUT...
...THE DRIFTVEIL DRAWBRIDGE HAS BEEN UP SINCE MORNING...
IT'S CAUSED A HUGE TRAFFIC JAM. THE TRUCK DELIVERING THE PROP CASES CAN'T CROSS THE BRIDGE!

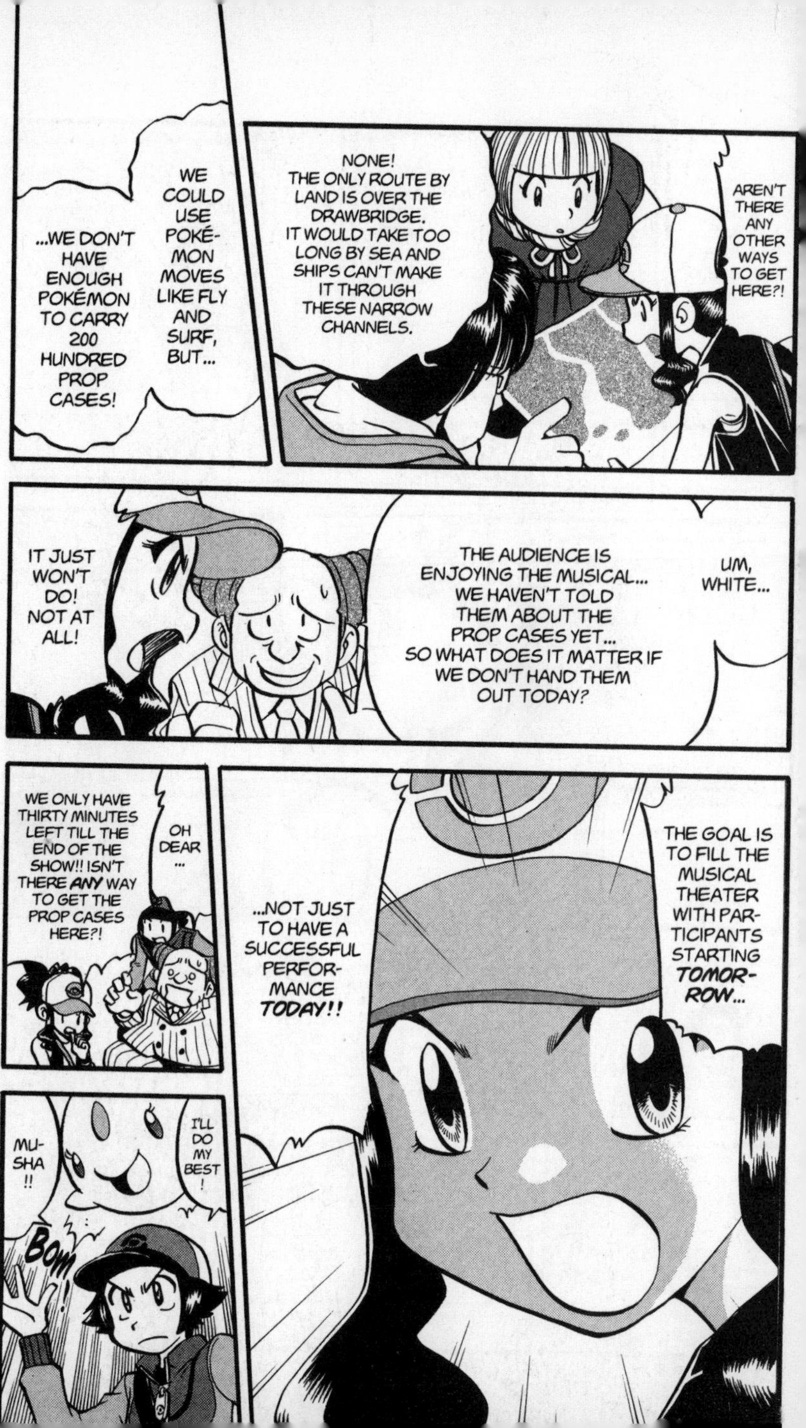

AREN'T THERE ANY OTHER WAYS TO GET HERE?!
NONE! THE ONLY ROUTE BY LAND IS OVER THE DRAWBRIDGE. IT WOULD TAKE TOO LONG BY SEA AND SHIPS CAN'T MAKE IT THROUGH THESE NARROW CHANNELS.
WE COULD USE POKÉMON MOVES LIKE FLY AND SURF, BUT...
...WE DON'T HAVE ENOUGH POKÉMON TO CARRY 200 HUNDRED PROP CASES!
UM, WHITE...
THE AUDIENCE IS ENJOYING THE MUSICAL... WE HAVEN'T TOLD THEM ABOUT THE PROP CASES YET... SO WHAT DOES IT MATTER IF WE DON'T HAND THEM OUT TODAY?
IT JUST WON'T DO! NOT AT ALL!
THE GOAL IS TO FILL THE MUSICAL THEATER WITH PARTICIPANTS STARTING ***TOMORROW***...
...NOT JUST TO HAVE A SUCCESSFUL PERFORMANCE ***TODAY!!***
OH DEAR...
WE ONLY HAVE THIRTY MINUTES LEFT TILL THE END OF THE SHOW!! ISN'T THERE ***ANY*** WAY TO GET THE PROP CASES HERE?!
I'LL DO MY BEST!
MU-SHA!!
BOM!

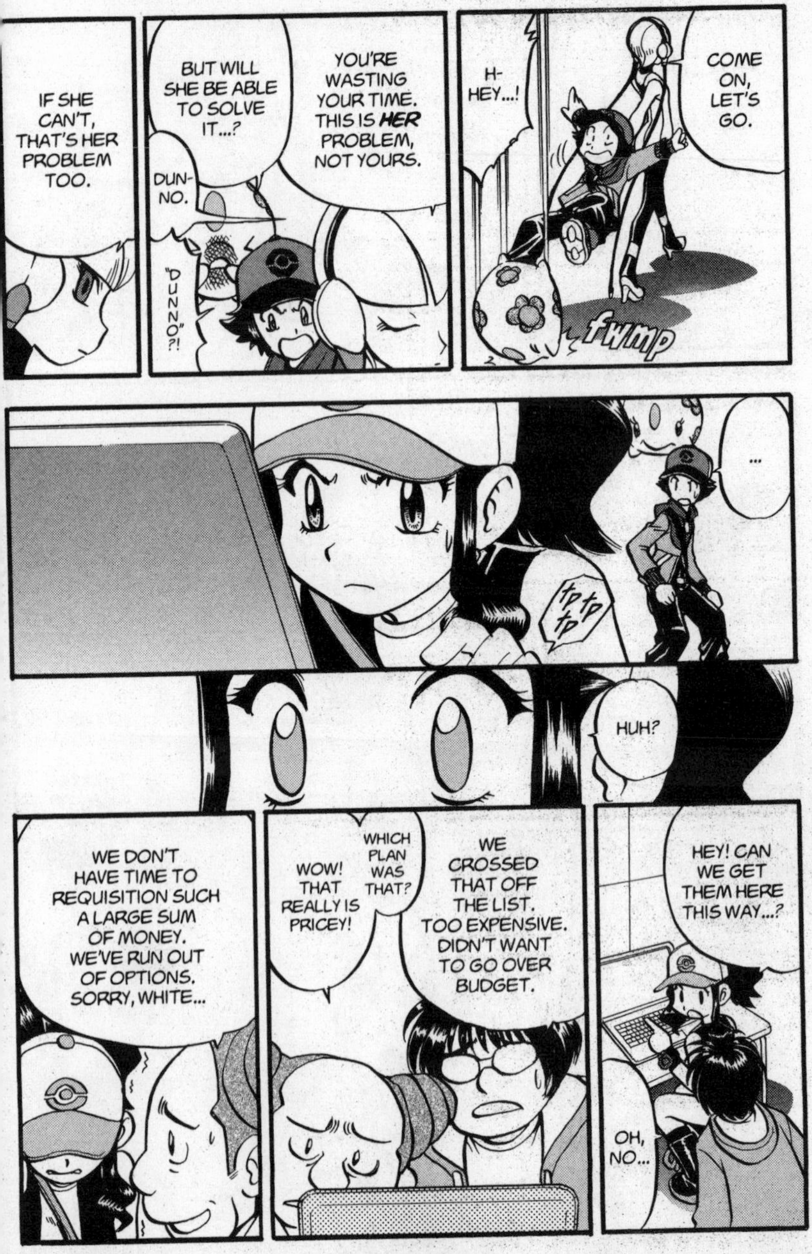
COME ON, LET'S GO.
H-HEY...!
fwmp
YOU'RE WASTING YOUR TIME. THIS IS **HER** PROBLEM, NOT YOURS.
BUT WILL SHE BE ABLE TO SOLVE IT...?
DUN-NO.
"DUNNO"?!
IF SHE CAN'T, THAT'S HER PROBLEM TOO.
...
tp tp tp
HUH?
HEY! CAN WE GET THEM HERE THIS WAY...?
OH, NO...
WE CROSSED THAT OFF THE LIST. TOO EXPENSIVE. DIDN'T WANT TO GO OVER BUDGET.
WHICH PLAN WAS THAT?
WOW! THAT REALLY IS PRICEY!
WE DON'T HAVE TIME TO REQUISITION SUCH A LARGE SUM OF MONEY. WE'VE RUN OUT OF OPTIONS. SORRY, WHITE...

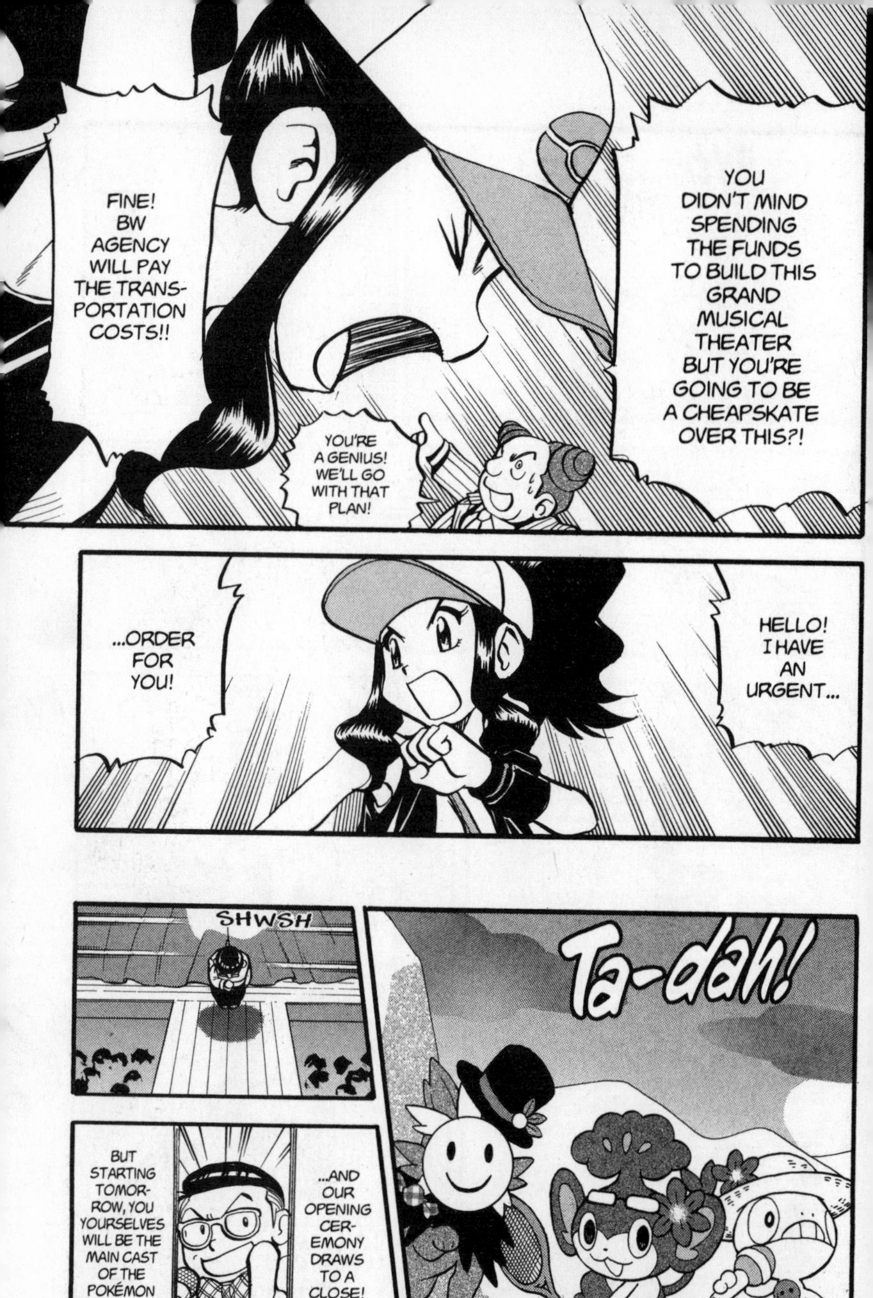
YOU DIDN'T MIND SPENDING THE FUNDS TO BUILD THIS GRAND MUSICAL THEATER BUT YOU'RE GOING TO BE A CHEAPSKATE OVER THIS?!
FINE! BW AGENCY WILL PAY THE TRANS-PORTATION COSTS!!
YOU'RE A GENIUS! WE'LL GO WITH THAT PLAN!
HELLO! I HAVE AN URGENT...
...ORDER FOR YOU!
Ta-dah!
SHWSH
...AND OUR OPENING CER-EMONY DRAWS TO A CLOSE!
BUT STARTING TOMOR-ROW, YOU YOURSELVES WILL BE THE MAIN CAST OF THE POKÉMON MUSICAL!!

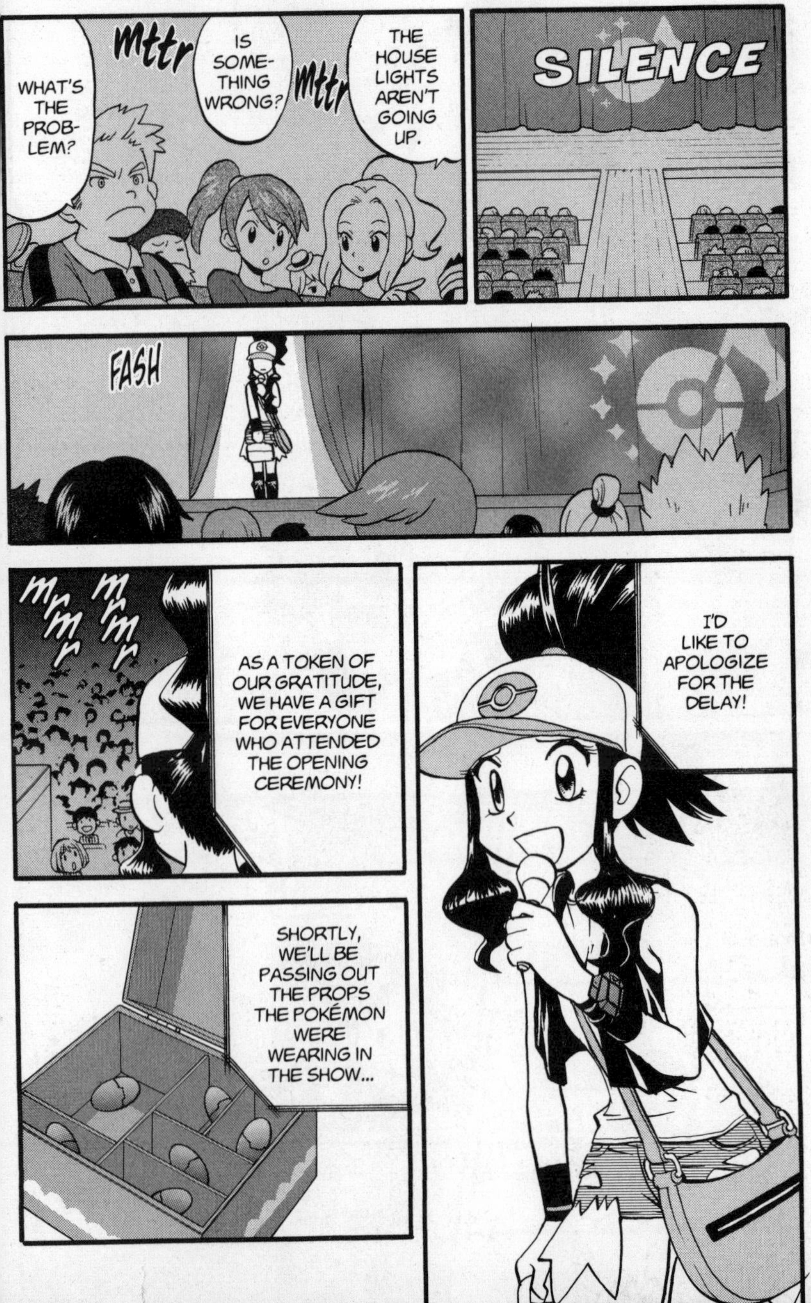
SILENCE
THE HOUSE LIGHTS AREN'T GOING UP.
mttr
IS SOME-THING WRONG?
mttr
WHAT'S THE PROB-LEM?
FASH
I'D LIKE TO APOLOGIZE FOR THE DELAY!
AS A TOKEN OF OUR GRATITUDE, WE HAVE A GIFT FOR EVERYONE WHO ATTENDED THE OPENING CEREMONY!
mrmr
mrmr
SHORTLY, WE'LL BE PASSING OUT THE PROPS THE POKÉMON WERE WEARING IN THE SHOW...

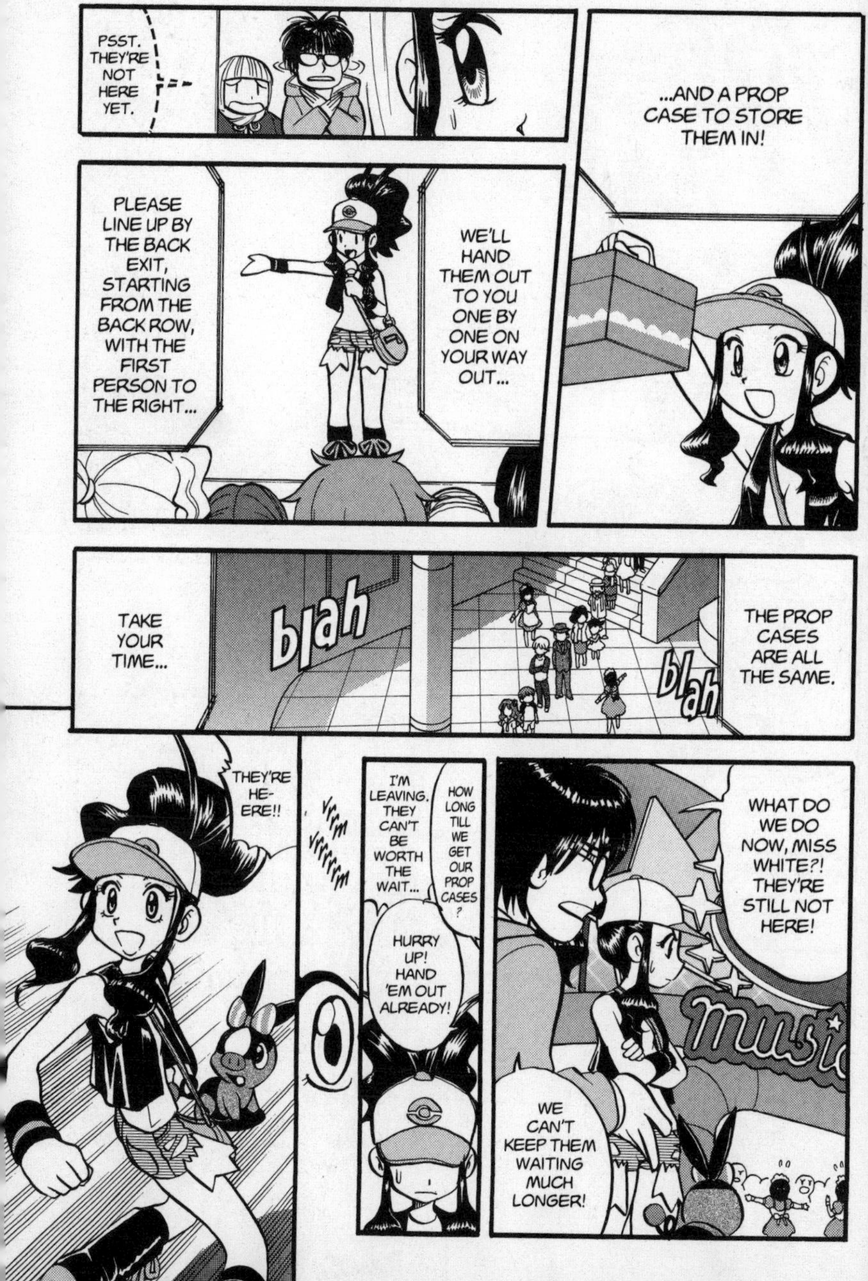
...AND A PROP CASE TO STORE THEM IN!
PSST. THEY'RE NOT HERE YET.
PLEASE LINE UP BY THE BACK EXIT, STARTING FROM THE BACK ROW, WITH THE FIRST PERSON TO THE RIGHT...
WE'LL HAND THEM OUT TO YOU ONE BY ONE ON YOUR WAY OUT...
THE PROP CASES ARE ALL THE SAME.
blah
blah
TAKE YOUR TIME...
WHAT DO WE DO NOW, MISS WHITE?! THEY'RE STILL NOT HERE!
WE CAN'T KEEP THEM WAITING MUCH LONGER!
HOW LONG TILL WE GET OUR PROP CASES?
I'M LEAVING. THEY CAN'T BE WORTH THE WAIT...
HURRY UP! HAND 'EM OUT ALREADY!
vrrm vrrrrrm
THEY'RE HE-ERE!!

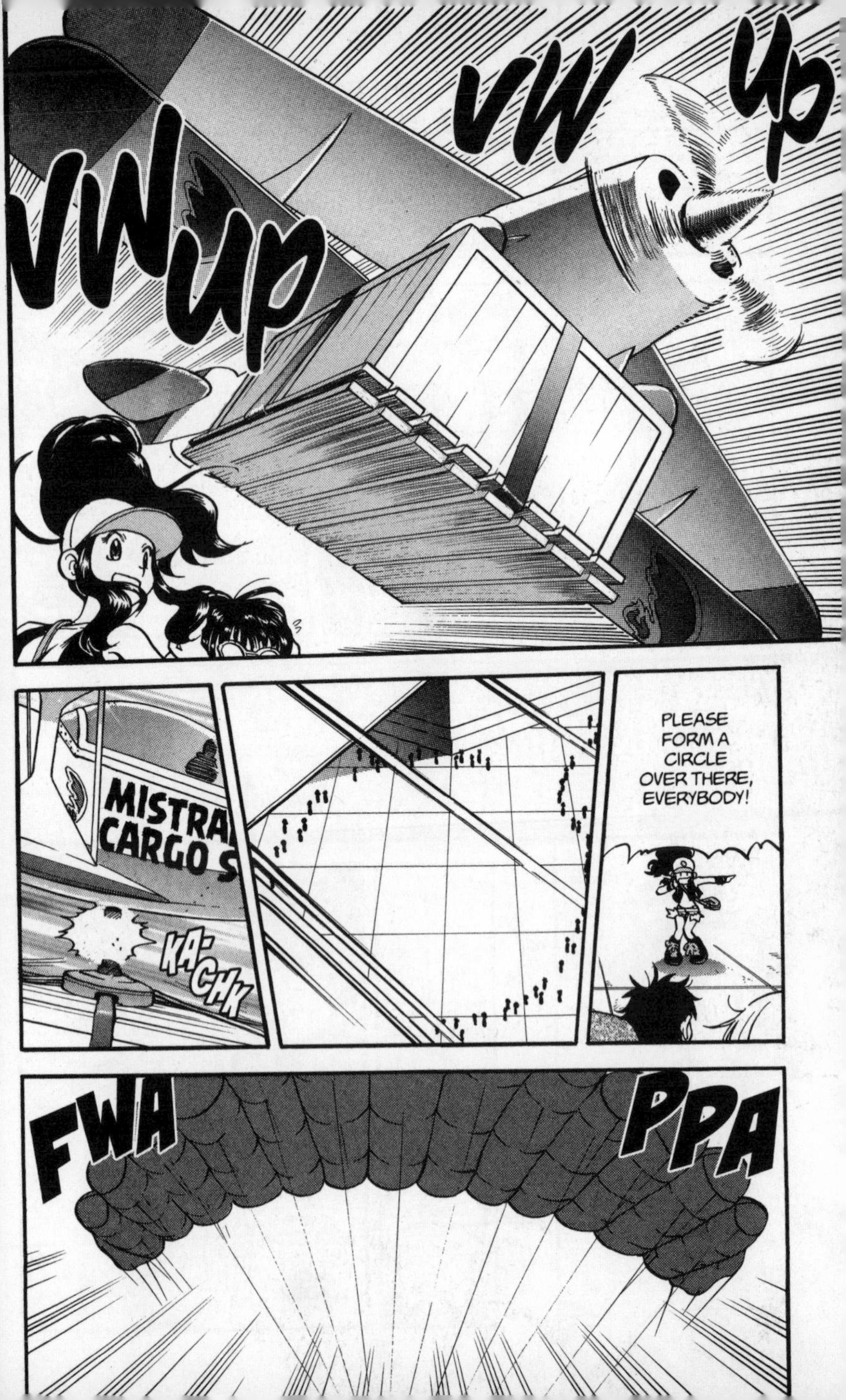
VWUP
VWUP
PLEASE FORM A CIRCLE OVER THERE, EVERYBODY!
MISTRA
CARGO S
KA-CHK
FWA PPA

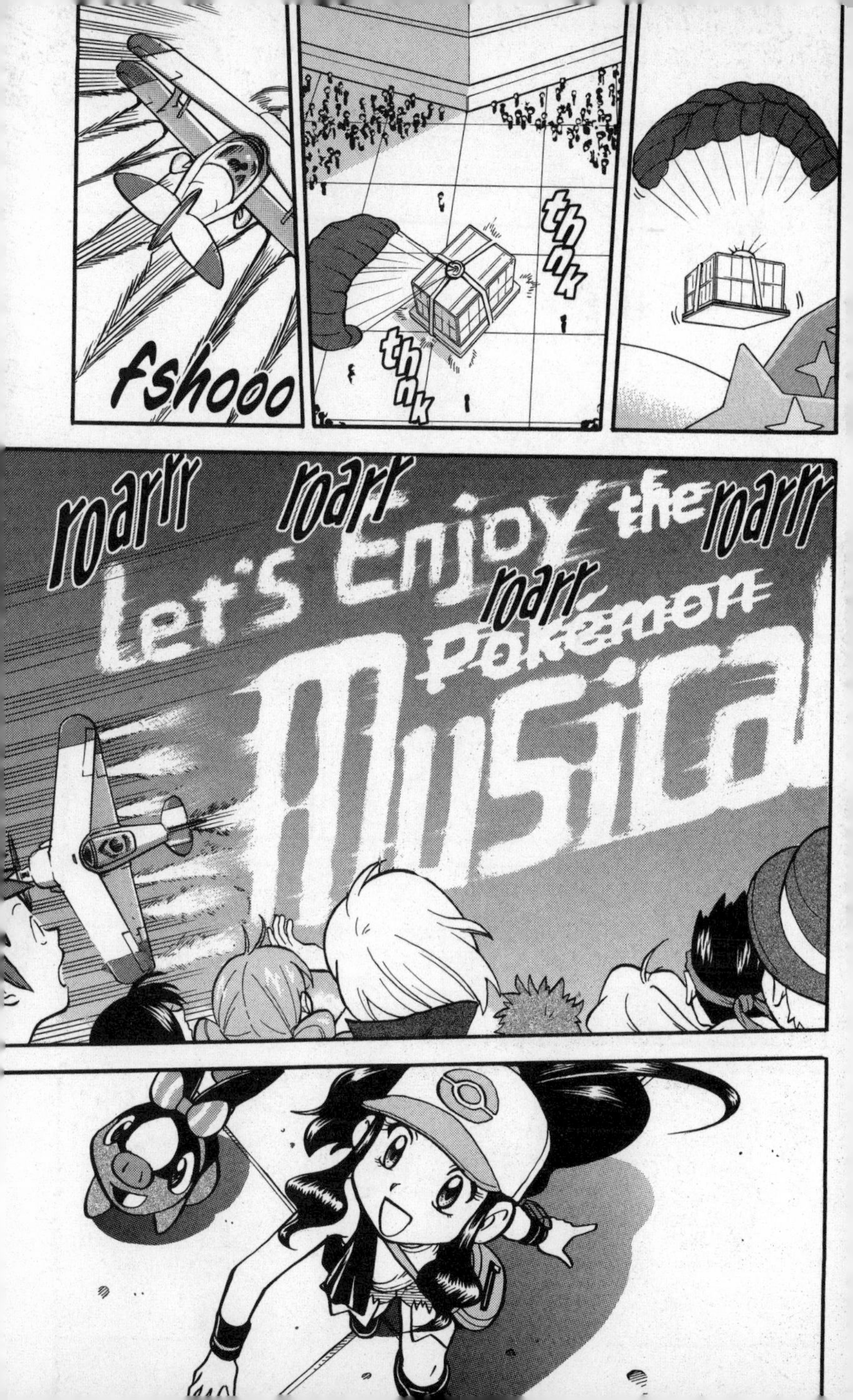
thnk
thnk
fshooo
roarrr
roarr
roarrr
let's enjoy the
roarr
Pokémon
Musica

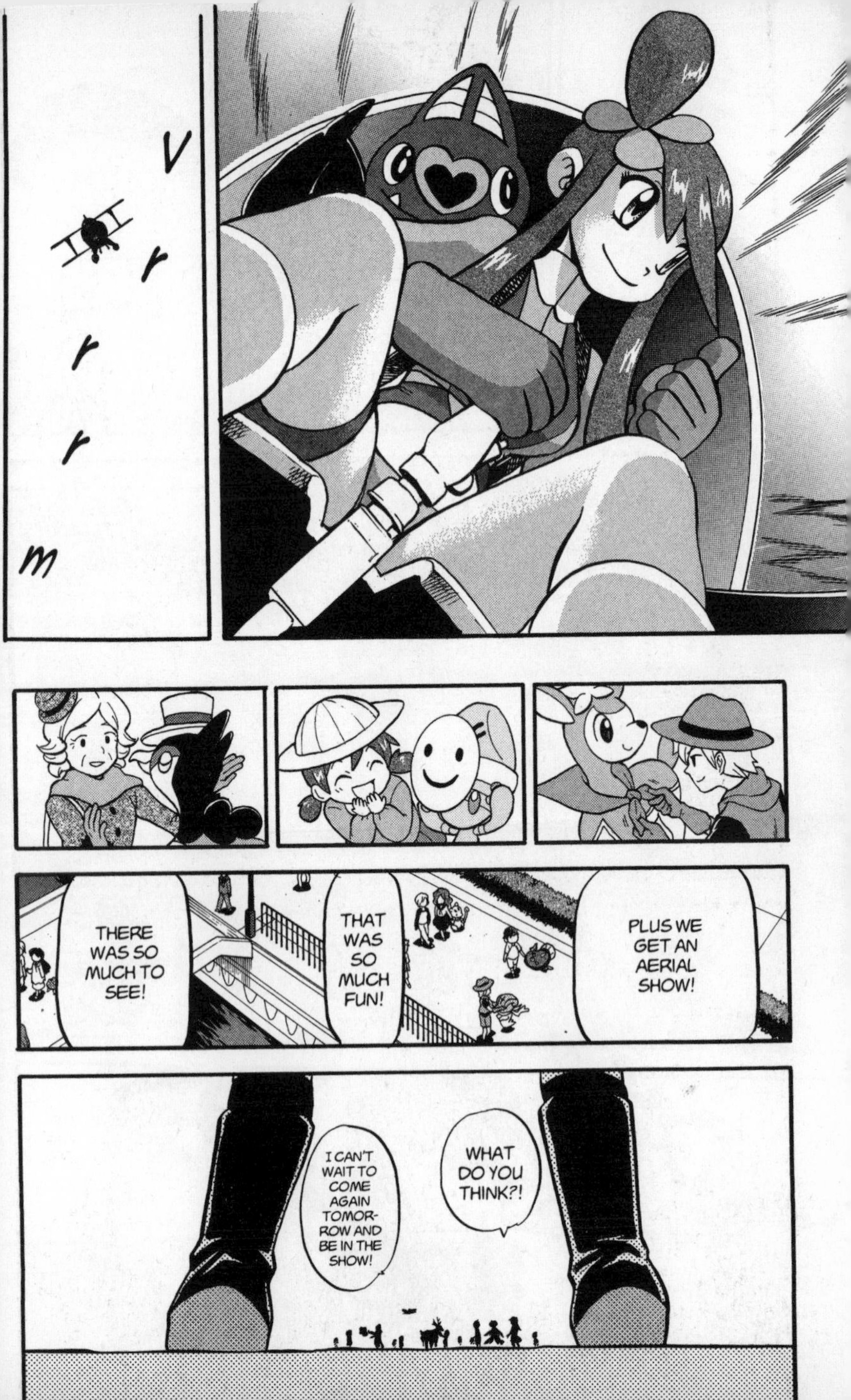
Vrrrm
PLUS WE GET AN AERIAL SHOW!
THAT WAS SO MUCH FUN!
THERE WAS SO MUCH TO SEE!
WHAT DO YOU THINK?!
I CAN'T WAIT TO COME AGAIN TOMORROW AND BE IN THE SHOW!

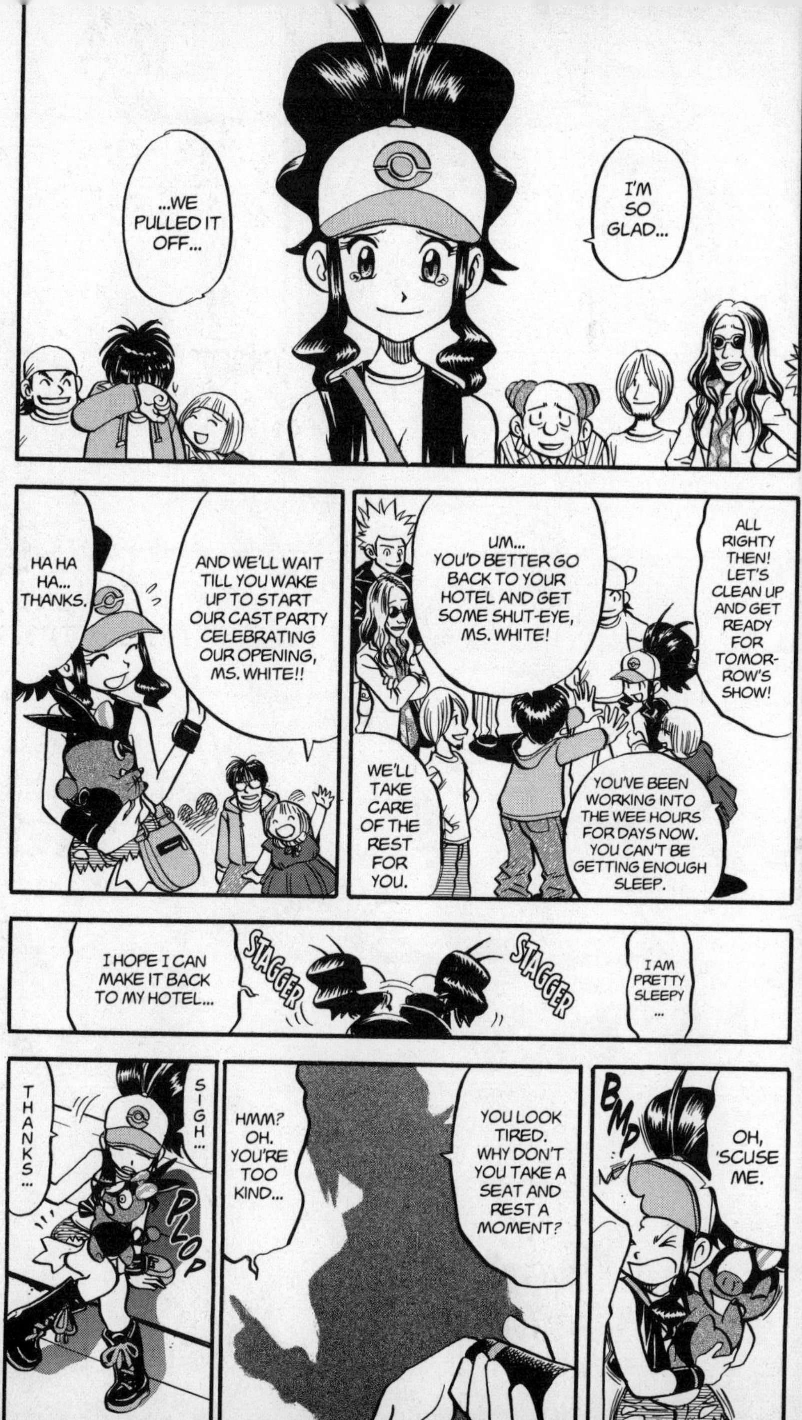
I'M SO GLAD...
...WE PULLED IT OFF...
ALL RIGHTY THEN! LET'S CLEAN UP AND GET READY FOR TOMORROW'S SHOW!
UM... YOU'D BETTER GO BACK TO YOUR HOTEL AND GET SOME SHUT-EYE, MS. WHITE!
YOU'VE BEEN WORKING INTO THE WEE HOURS FOR DAYS NOW. YOU CAN'T BE GETTING ENOUGH SLEEP.
WE'LL TAKE CARE OF THE REST FOR YOU.
AND WE'LL WAIT TILL YOU WAKE UP TO START OUR CAST PARTY CELEBRATING OUR OPENING, MS. WHITE!!
HA HA HA... THANKS.
I AM PRETTY SLEEPY...
STAGGER
STAGGER
I HOPE I CAN MAKE IT BACK TO MY HOTEL...
BMP
OH, 'SCUSE ME.
YOU LOOK TIRED. WHY DON'T YOU TAKE A SEAT AND REST A MOMENT?
HMM? OH. YOU'RE TOO KIND...
SIGH...
PLOP
THANKS...

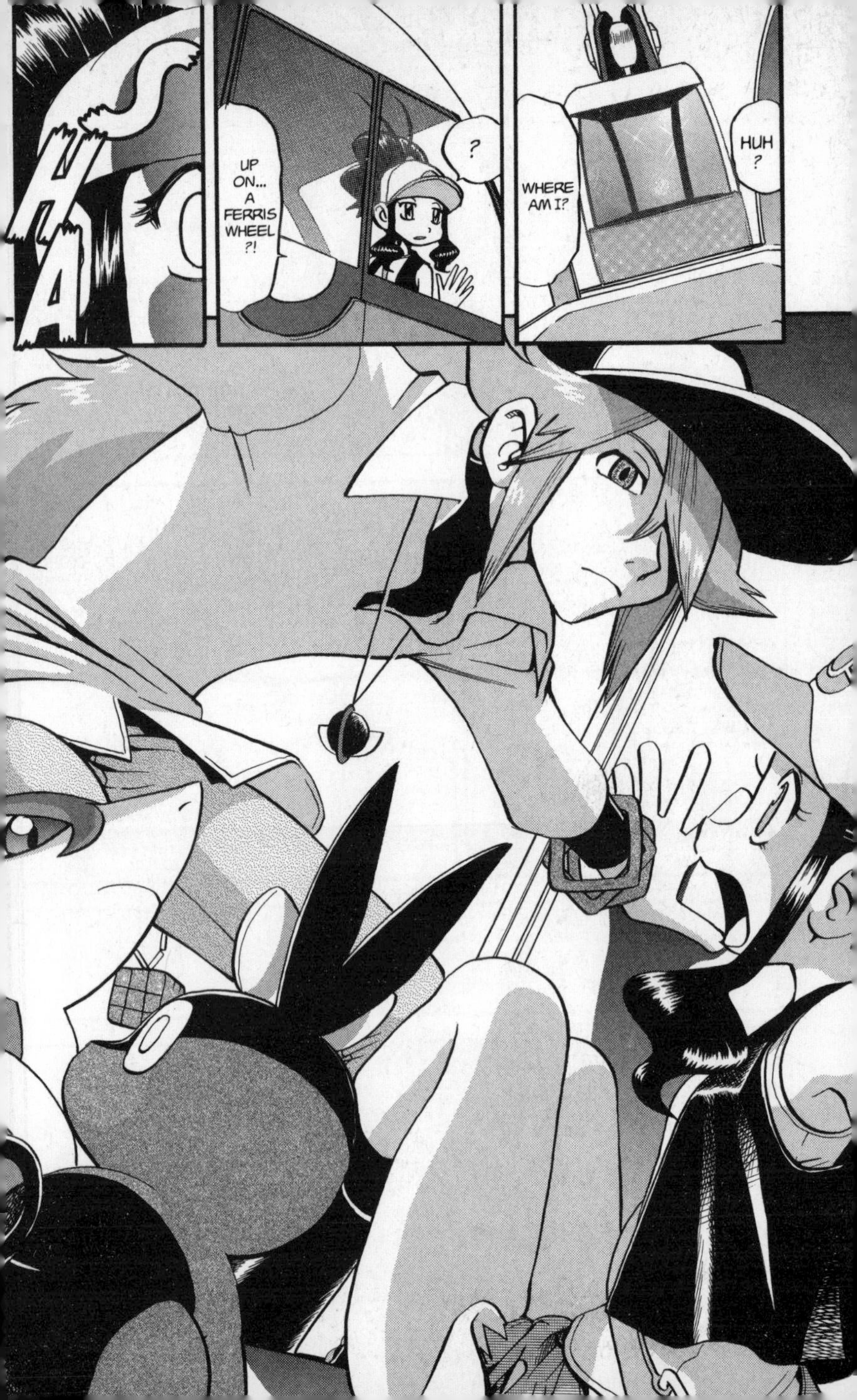
HUH ?
WHERE AM I?
?
UP ON... A FERRIS WHEEL ?!
HA

ADVENTURE MAP

Final Destination:
Pokémon League

Current Location:
Nimbasa City

	Fire Pig Pokémon **Nite**	
	Pignite ♂ Fire Fighting	
	Lv.23	Ability: Blaze

Dream Eater Pokémon **Musha**
Munna ♂ Psychic
Lv.46 Ability: Forewarn

Valiant Pokémon **Brav**
Braviary ♂ Normal Flying
Lv.54 Ability: Sheer Force

EleSpider Pokémon **Tula**
Galvantula ♂ Bug Electric
Lv.47 Ability: Unnerve

B L A C K

W H I T E

Fire Pig Pokémon **Gigi**
Tepig ♀ Fire
Lv.05 Ability: Blaze

TRIO BADGE BASIC BADGE INSECT BADGE   ? ? ? ? ?   ?

Pokémon™ Adventures Black & White

ZEBSTRIKA

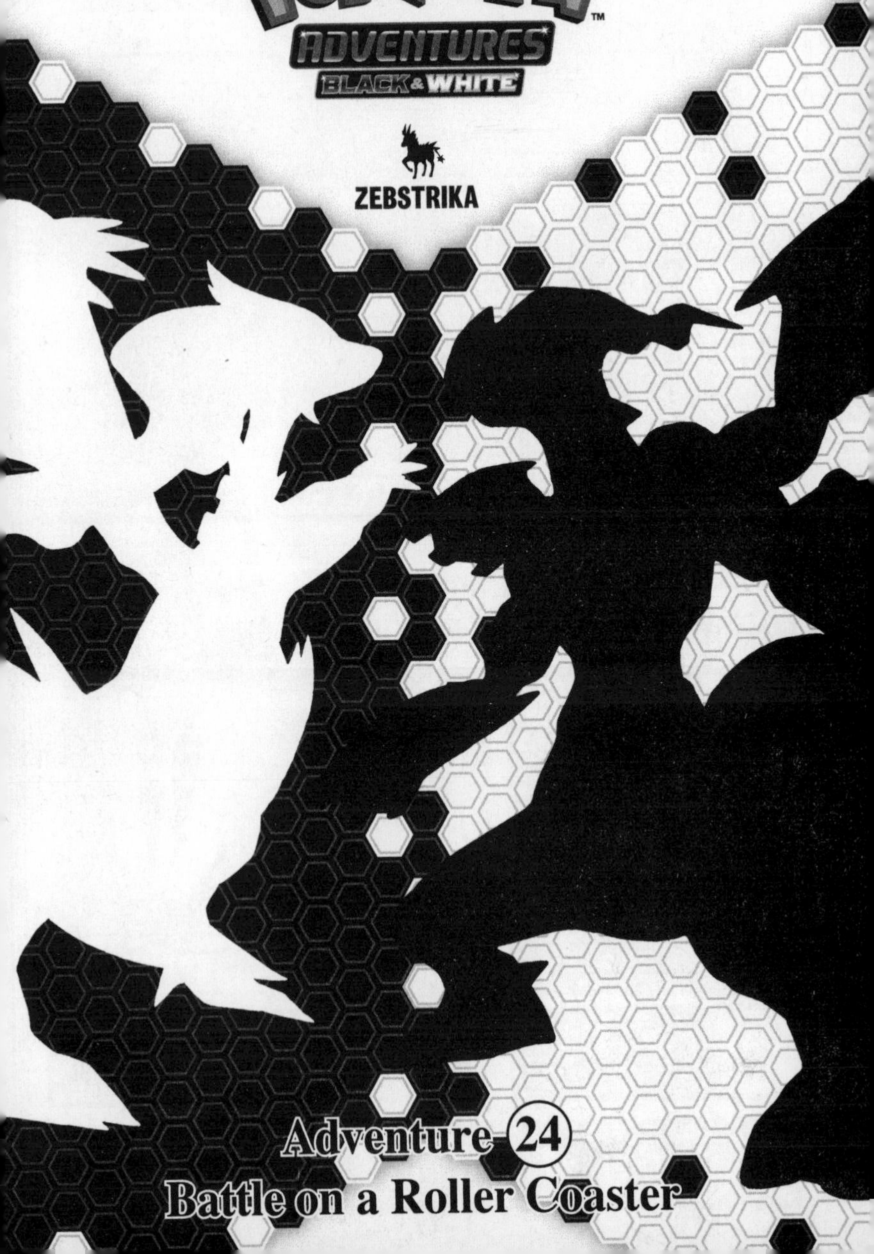

Adventure 24
Battle on a Roller Coaster

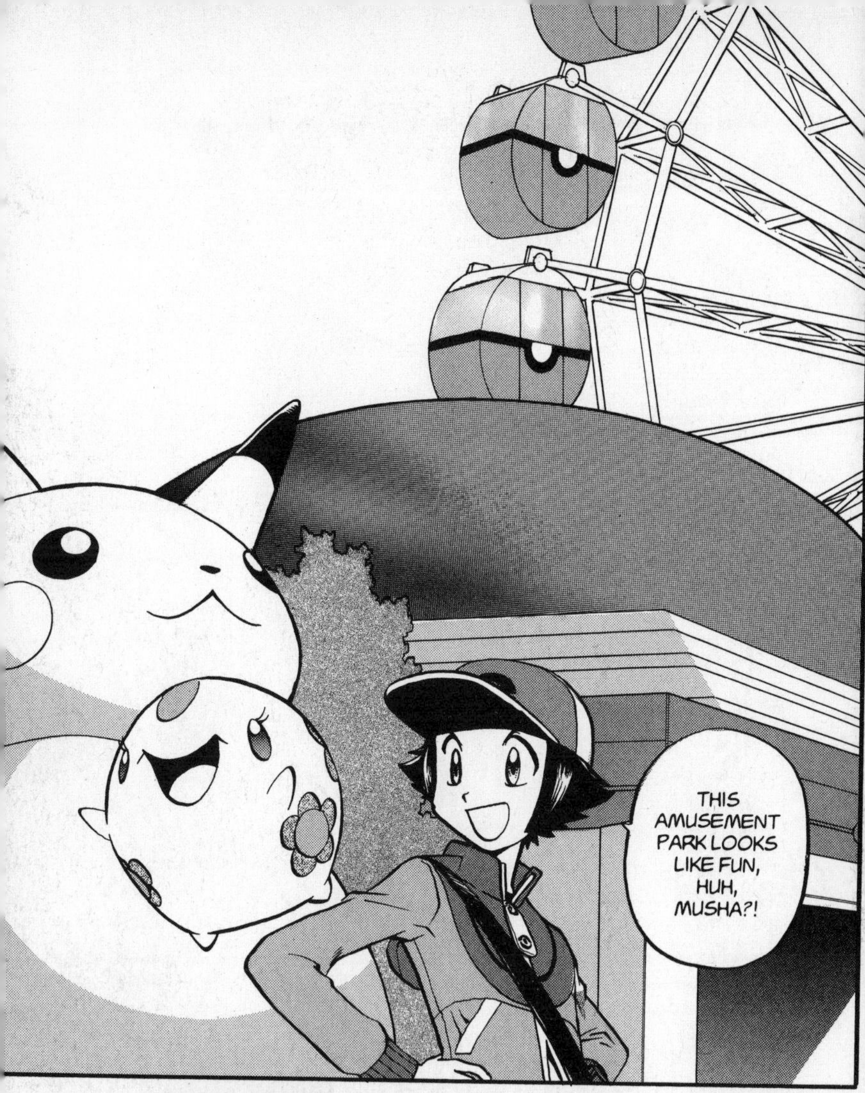
THIS AMUSEMENT PARK LOOKS LIKE FUN, HUH, MUSHA?!
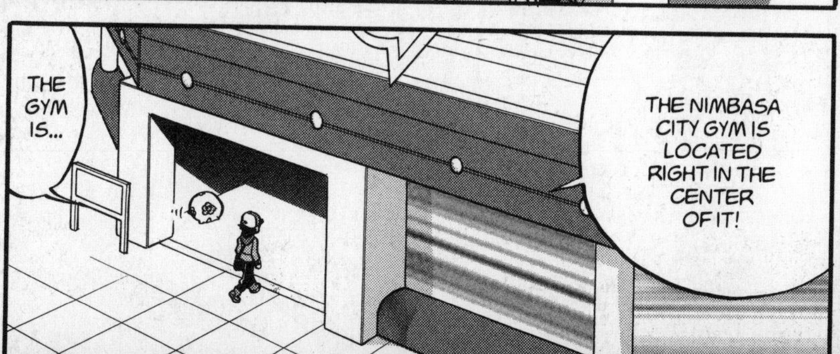
THE NIMBASA CITY GYM IS LOCATED RIGHT IN THE CENTER OF IT!
THE GYM IS...

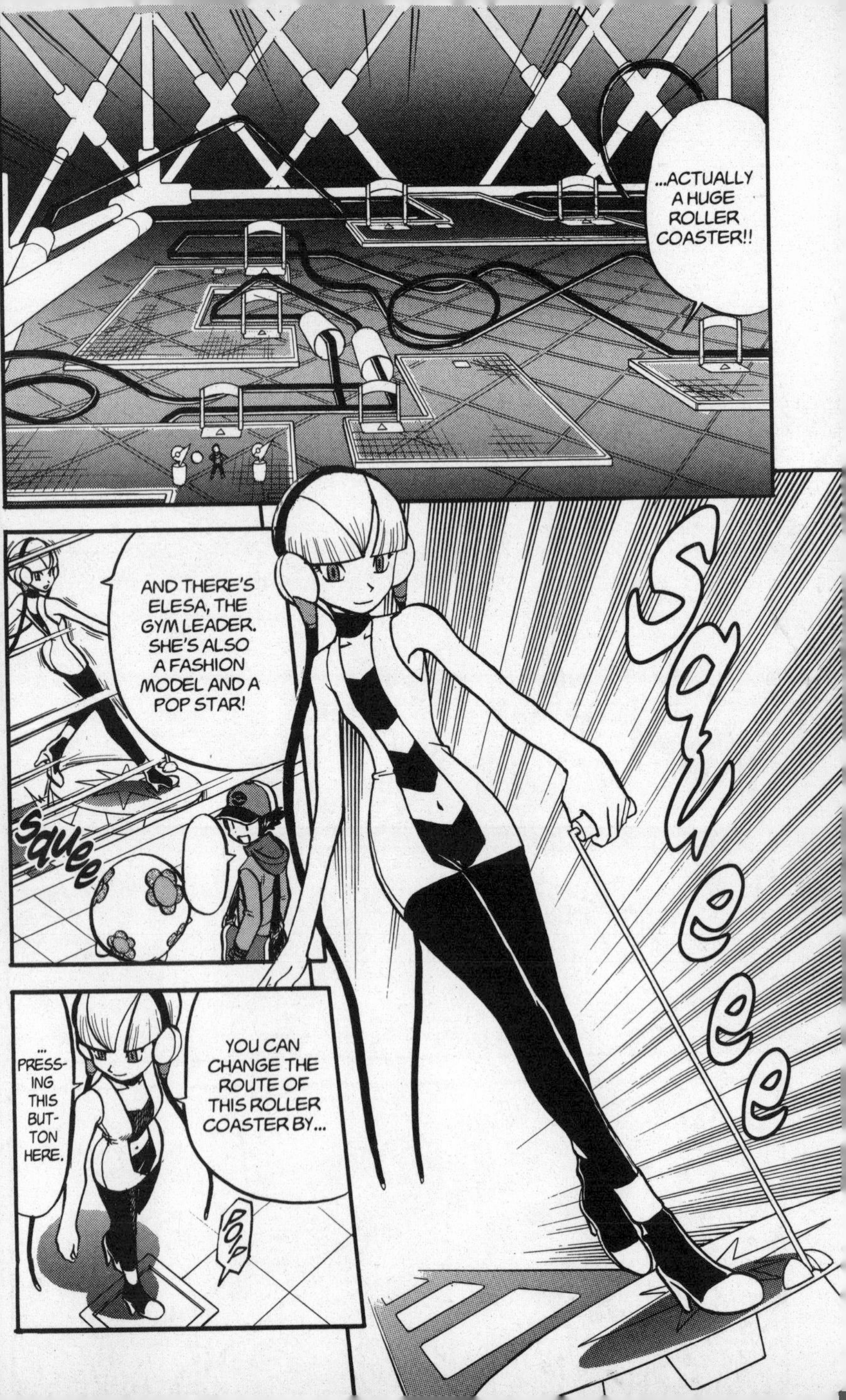
...ACTUALLY A HUGE ROLLER COASTER!!
Squeeeee
AND THERE'S ELESA, THE GYM LEADER. SHE'S ALSO A FASHION MODEL AND A POP STAR!
squee
YOU CAN CHANGE THE ROUTE OF THIS ROLLER COASTER BY...
...PRESSING THIS BUTTON HERE.
POP

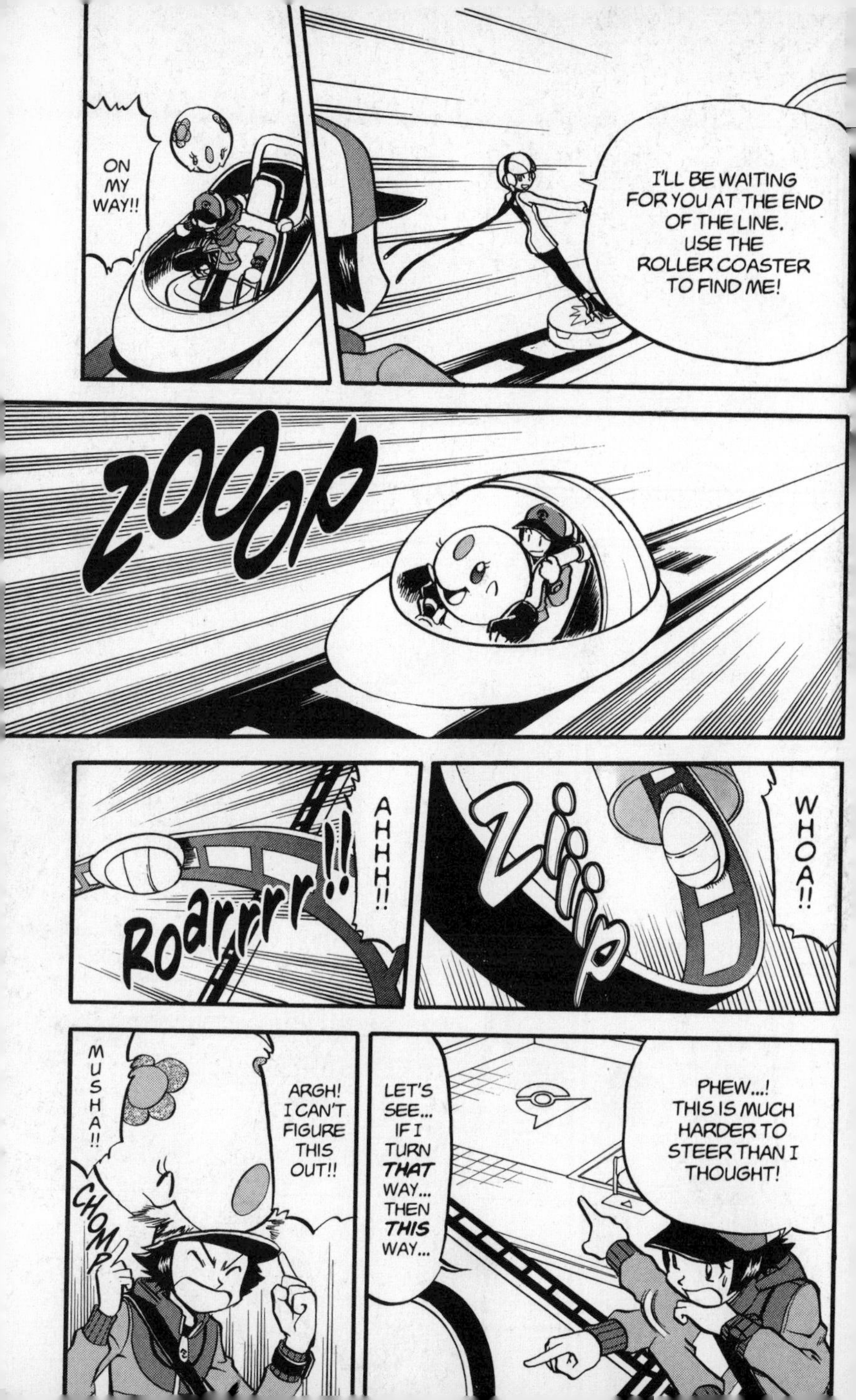
I'LL BE WAITING FOR YOU AT THE END OF THE LINE. USE THE ROLLER COASTER TO FIND ME!
ON MY WAY!!
ZOOOP
WHOA!!
Ziiip
AHHHH!!
Roarrrr!!
PHEW...! THIS IS MUCH HARDER TO STEER THAN I THOUGHT!
LET'S SEE... IF I TURN THAT WAY... THEN THIS WAY...
ARGH! I CAN'T FIGURE THIS OUT!!
MUSHA!!
CHOMP

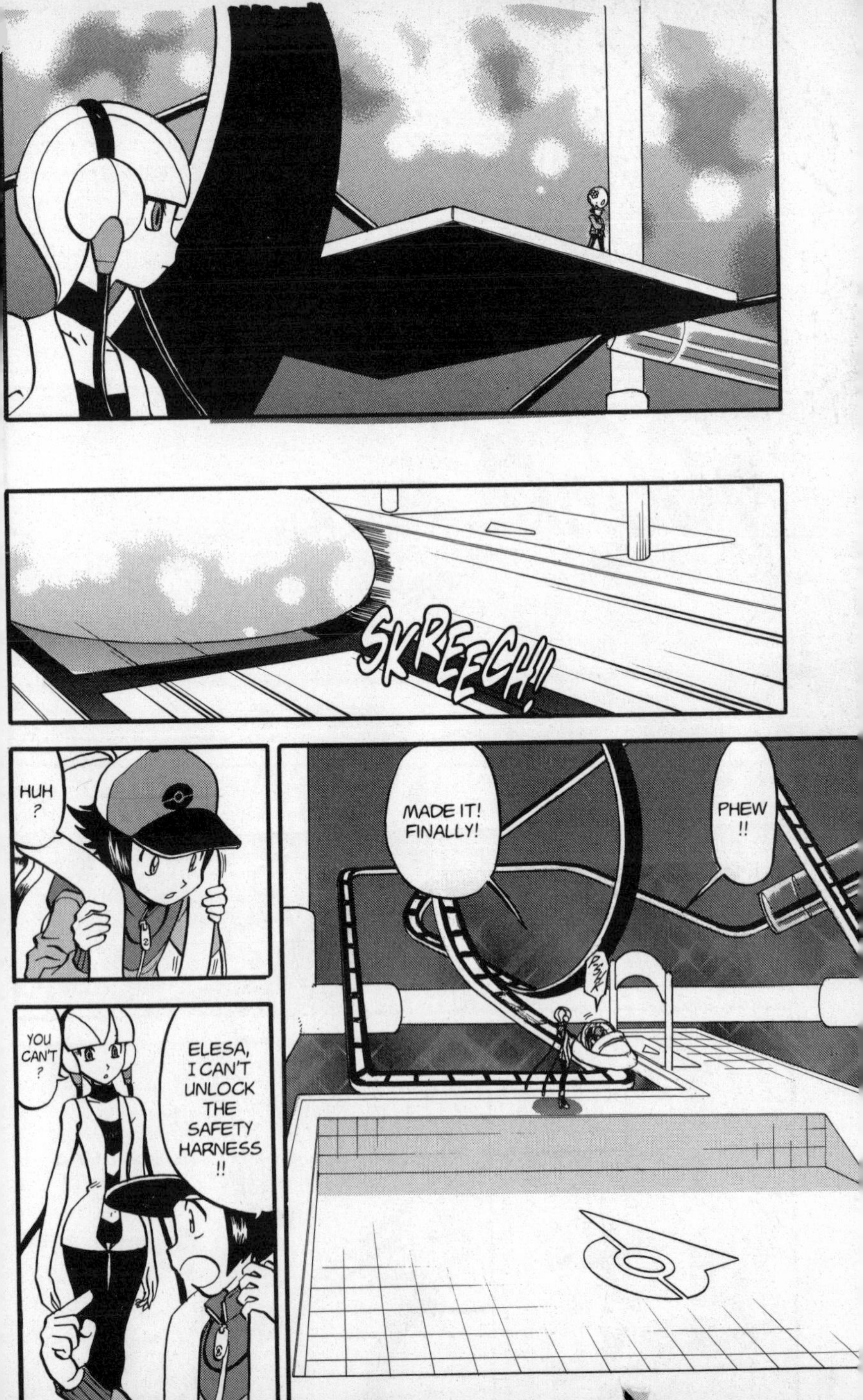
SKREECH!!
PHEW!!
MADE IT! FINALLY!
HUH?
ELESA, I CAN'T UNLOCK THE SAFETY HARNESS!!
YOU CAN'T?

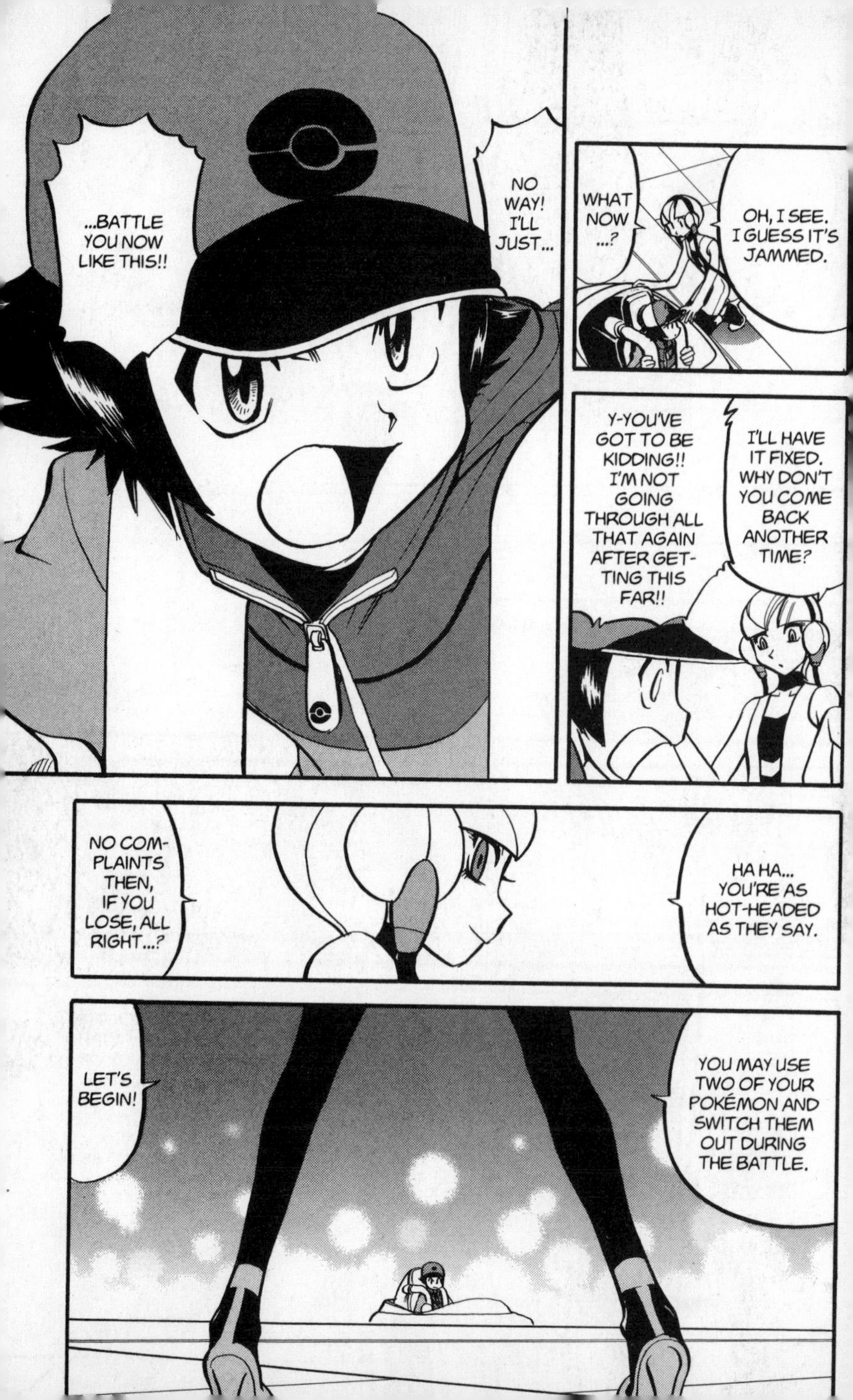
OH, I SEE. I GUESS IT'S JAMMED.
WHAT NOW ...?
I'LL HAVE IT FIXED. WHY DON'T YOU COME BACK ANOTHER TIME?
Y-YOU'VE GOT TO BE KIDDING!! I'M NOT GOING THROUGH ALL THAT AGAIN AFTER GET-TING THIS FAR!!
NO WAY! I'LL JUST...
...BATTLE YOU NOW LIKE THIS!!
HA HA... YOU'RE AS HOT-HEADED AS THEY SAY.
NO COM-PLAINTS THEN, IF YOU LOSE, ALL RIGHT...?
YOU MAY USE TWO OF YOUR POKÉMON AND SWITCH THEM OUT DURING THE BATTLE.
LET'S BEGIN!

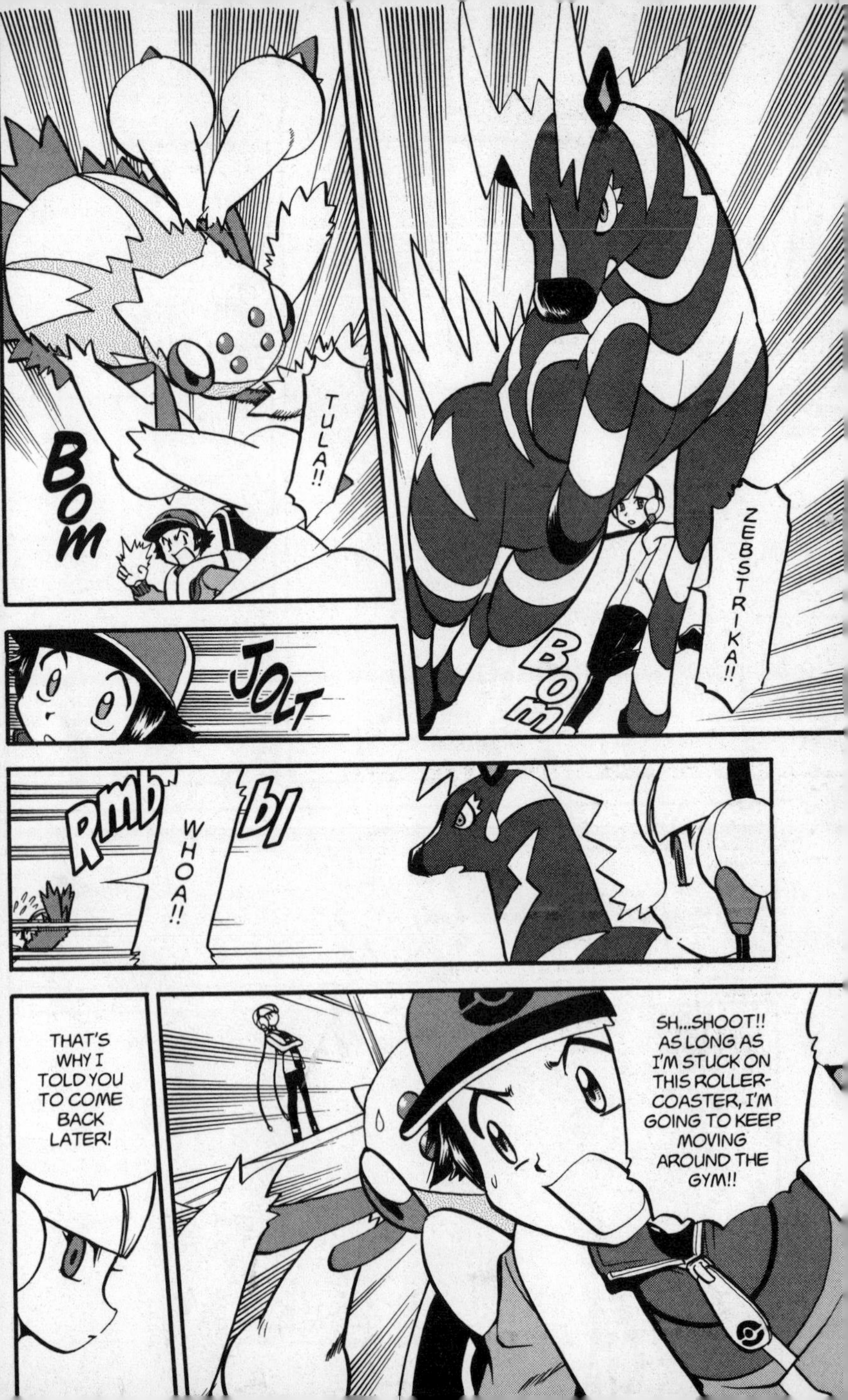
ZEBSTRIKA!!
BOM
TULA!!
BOM
JOLT
Rmb
bl
WHOA!!
SH...SHOOT!! AS LONG AS I'M STUCK ON THIS ROLLER-COASTER, I'M GOING TO KEEP MOVING AROUND THE GYM!!
THAT'S WHY I TOLD YOU TO COME BACK LATER!

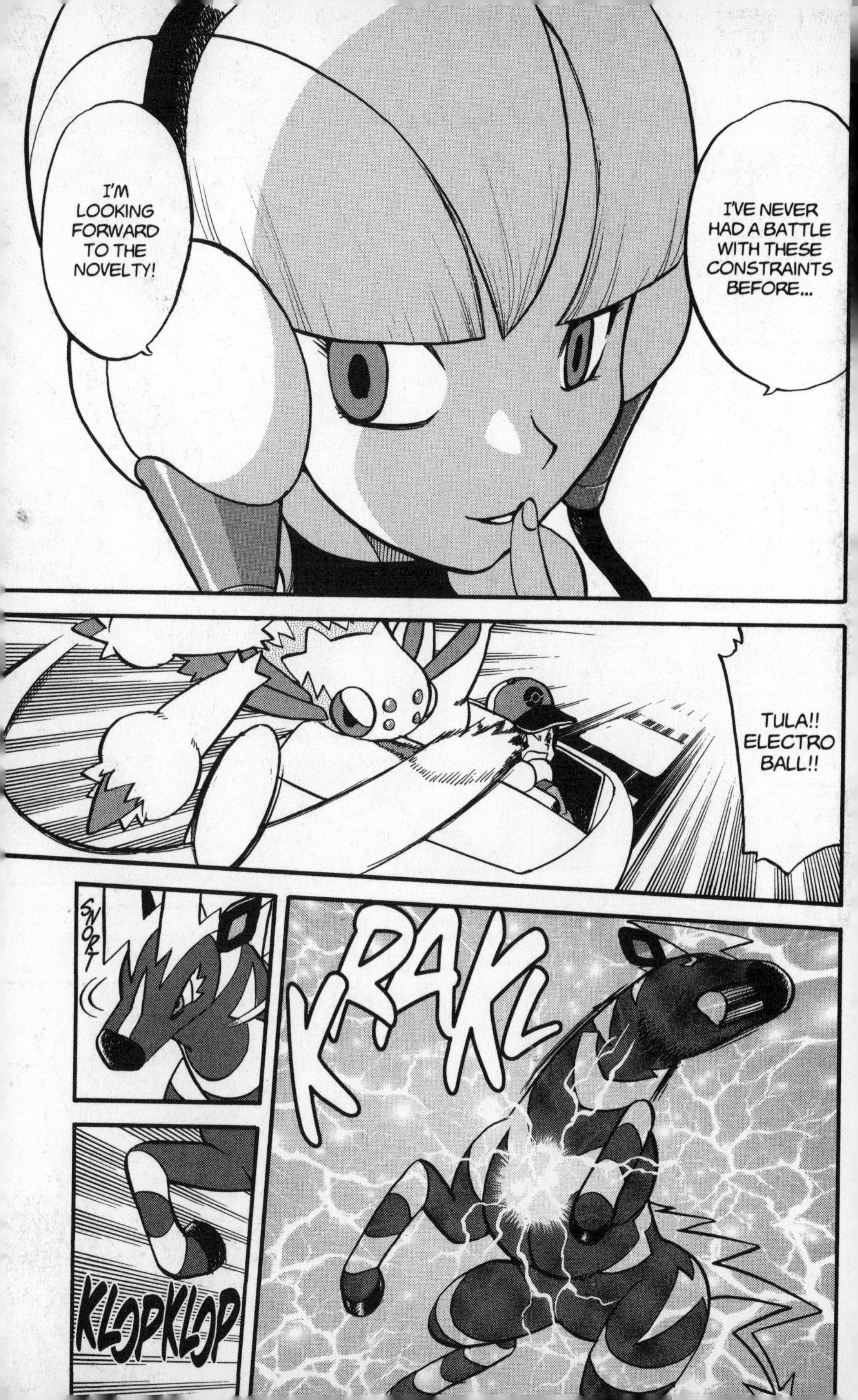
I'VE NEVER HAD A BATTLE WITH THESE CONSTRAINTS BEFORE...
I'M LOOKING FORWARD TO THE NOVELTY!
TULA!! ELECTRO BALL!!
KRAKL
SNORT
KLOPKLOP

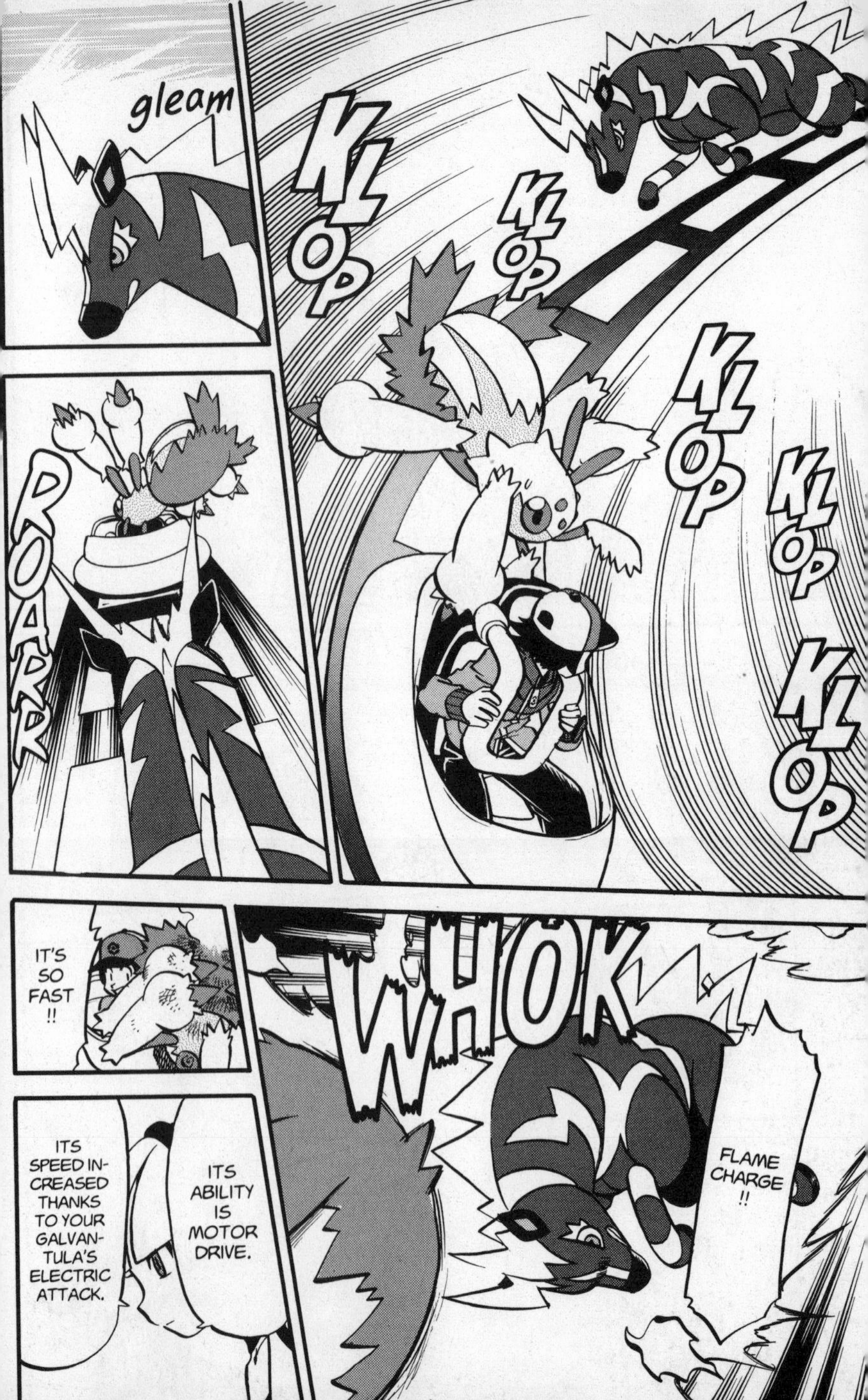
KLOP
KLOP
KLOP
KLOP
KLOP
gleam
ROARR
WHOK
FLAME CHARGE !!
IT'S SO FAST !!
ITS ABILITY IS MOTOR DRIVE.
ITS SPEED IN-CREASED THANKS TO YOUR GALVAN-TULA'S ELECTRIC ATTACK.

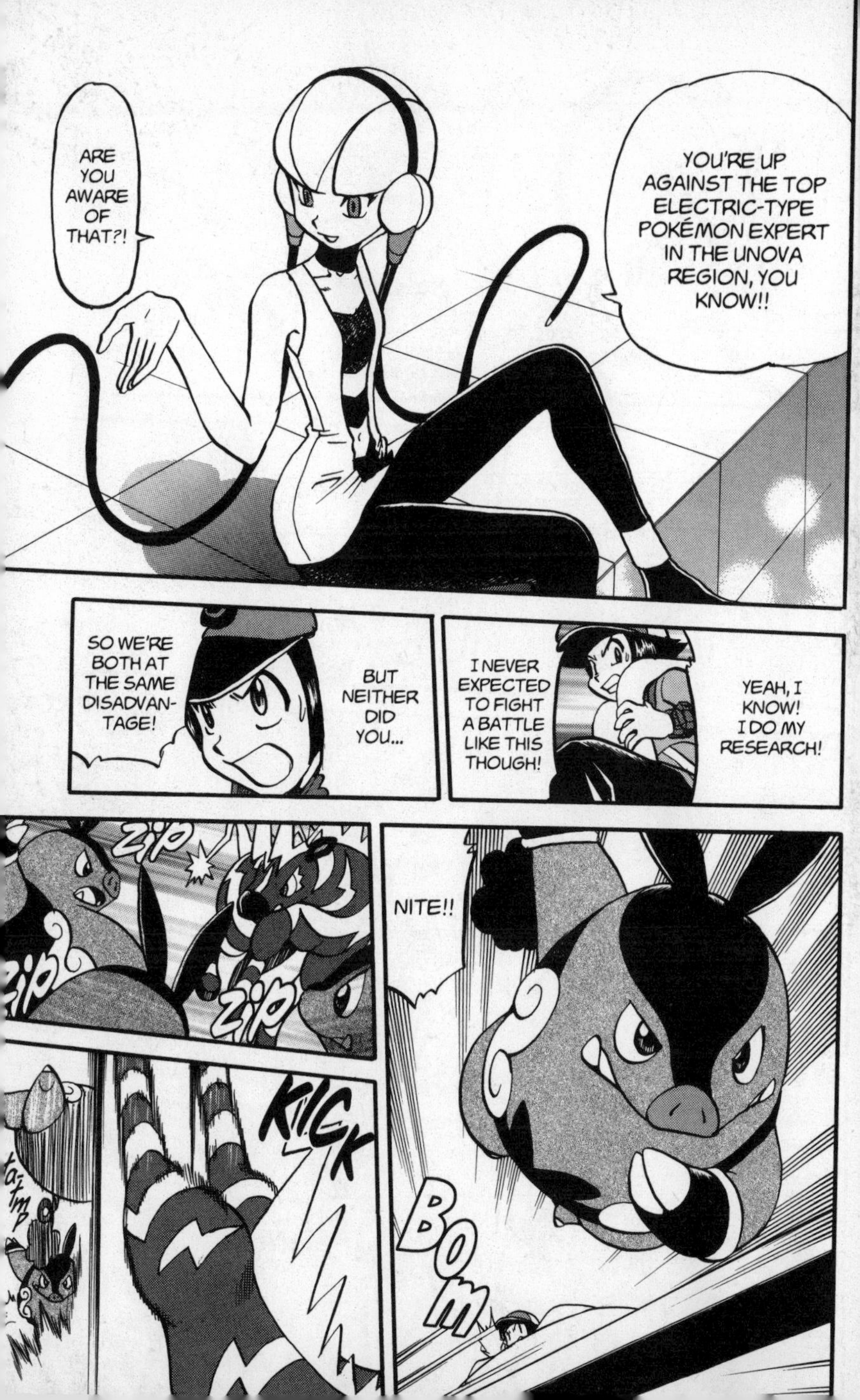
YOU'RE UP AGAINST THE TOP ELECTRIC-TYPE POKÉMON EXPERT IN THE UNOVA REGION, YOU KNOW!!
ARE YOU AWARE OF THAT?!
YEAH, I KNOW! I DO MY RESEARCH!
I NEVER EXPECTED TO FIGHT A BATTLE LIKE THIS THOUGH!
BUT NEITHER DID YOU...
SO WE'RE BOTH AT THE SAME DISADVANTAGE!
NITE!!
BOM
zip
zip
zip
KICK

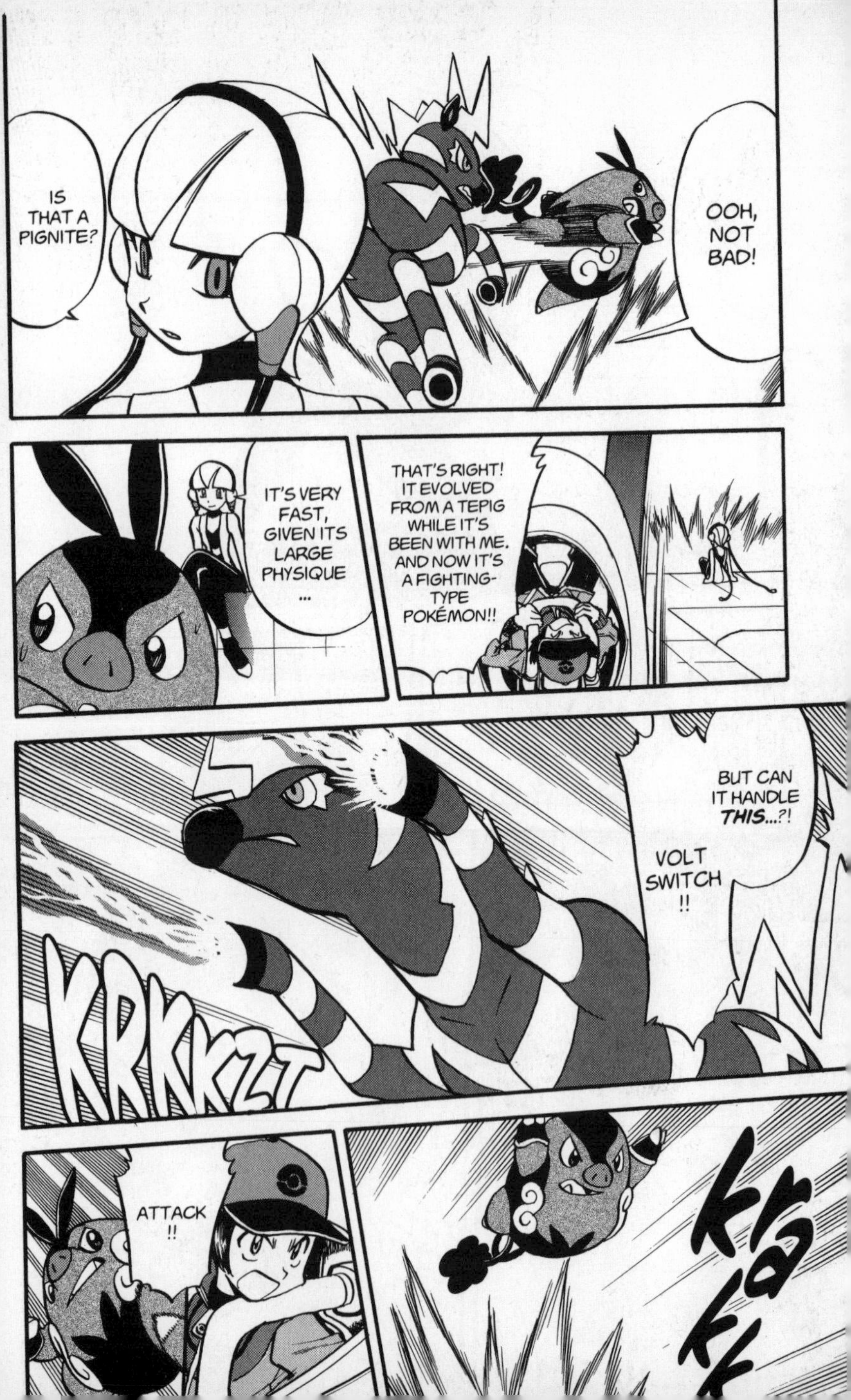
OOH, NOT BAD!
IS THAT A PIGNITE?
THAT'S RIGHT! IT EVOLVED FROM A TEPIG WHILE IT'S BEEN WITH ME. AND NOW IT'S A FIGHTING-TYPE POKÉMON!!
IT'S VERY FAST, GIVEN ITS LARGE PHYSIQUE ...
BUT CAN IT HANDLE *THIS*...?!
VOLT SWITCH !!
KRKKZZT
krakk
ATTACK !!

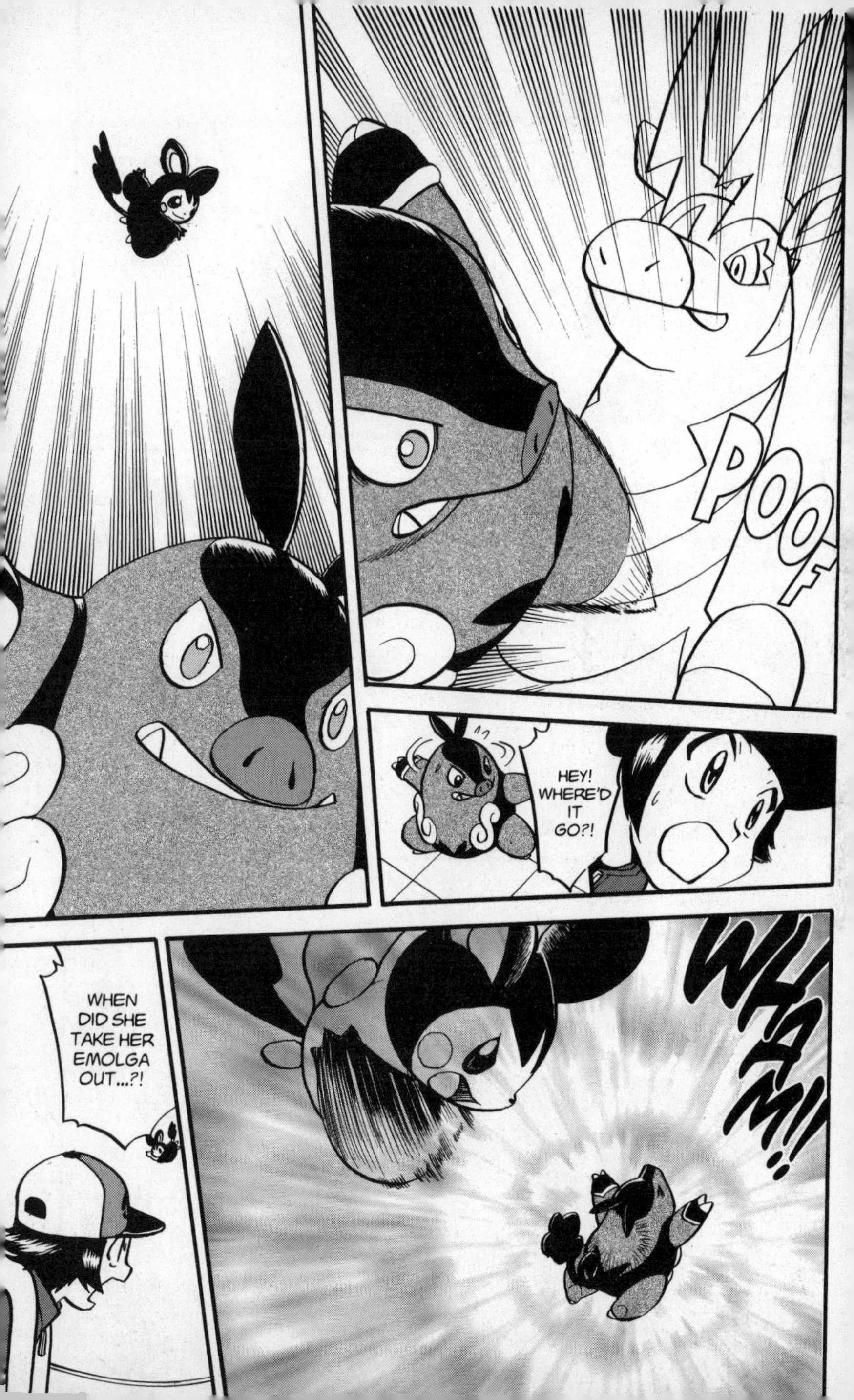
POOF
HEY! WHERE'D IT GO?!
WHAM!!
WHEN DID SHE TAKE HER EMOLGA OUT...?!

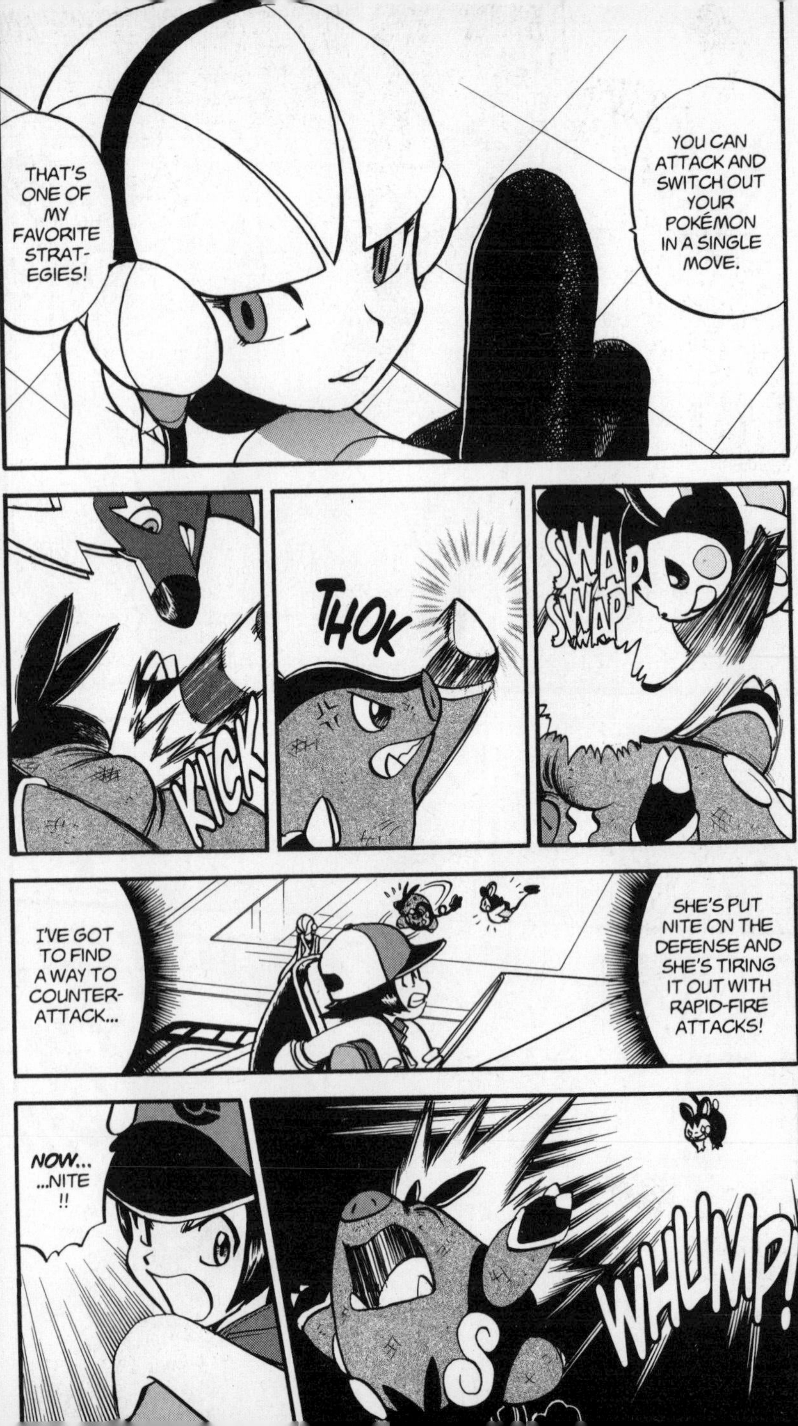
YOU CAN ATTACK AND SWITCH OUT YOUR POKÉMON IN A SINGLE MOVE.
THAT'S ONE OF MY FAVORITE STRAT-EGIES!
SWAP SWAP
THOK
KICK
SHE'S PUT NITE ON THE DEFENSE AND SHE'S TIRING IT OUT WITH RAPID-FIRE ATTACKS!
I'VE GOT TO FIND A WAY TO COUNTER-ATTACK...
WHUMP!
NOW... ...NITE !!

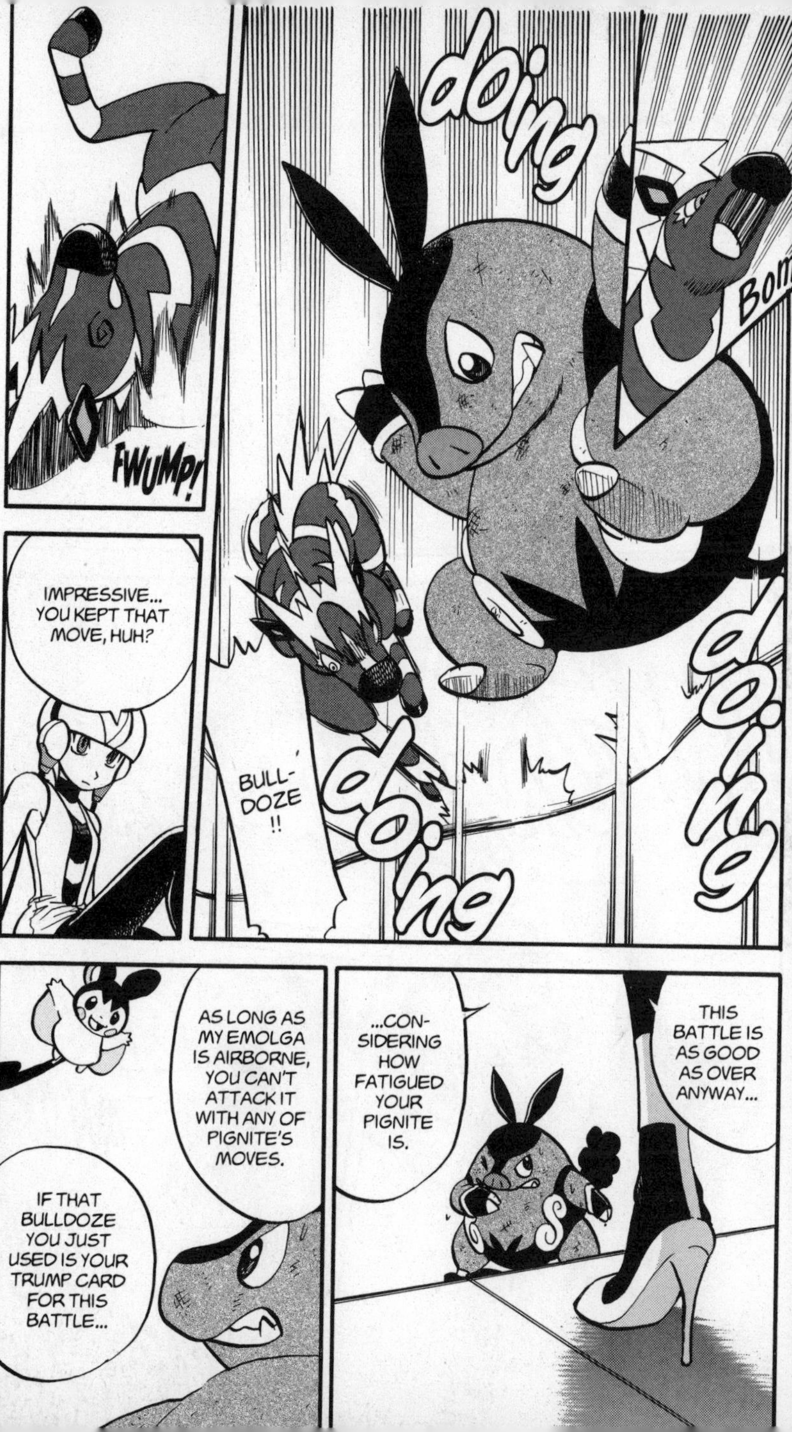
doing
Bom
doing
BULL-DOZE!!
doing
FWUMP!
IMPRESSIVE... YOU KEPT THAT MOVE, HUH?
THIS BATTLE IS AS GOOD AS OVER ANYWAY...
...CON-SIDERING HOW FATIGUED YOUR PIGNITE IS.
AS LONG AS MY EMOLGA IS AIRBORNE, YOU CAN'T ATTACK IT WITH ANY OF PIGNITE'S MOVES.
IF THAT BULLDOZE YOU JUST USED IS YOUR TRUMP CARD FOR THIS BATTLE...

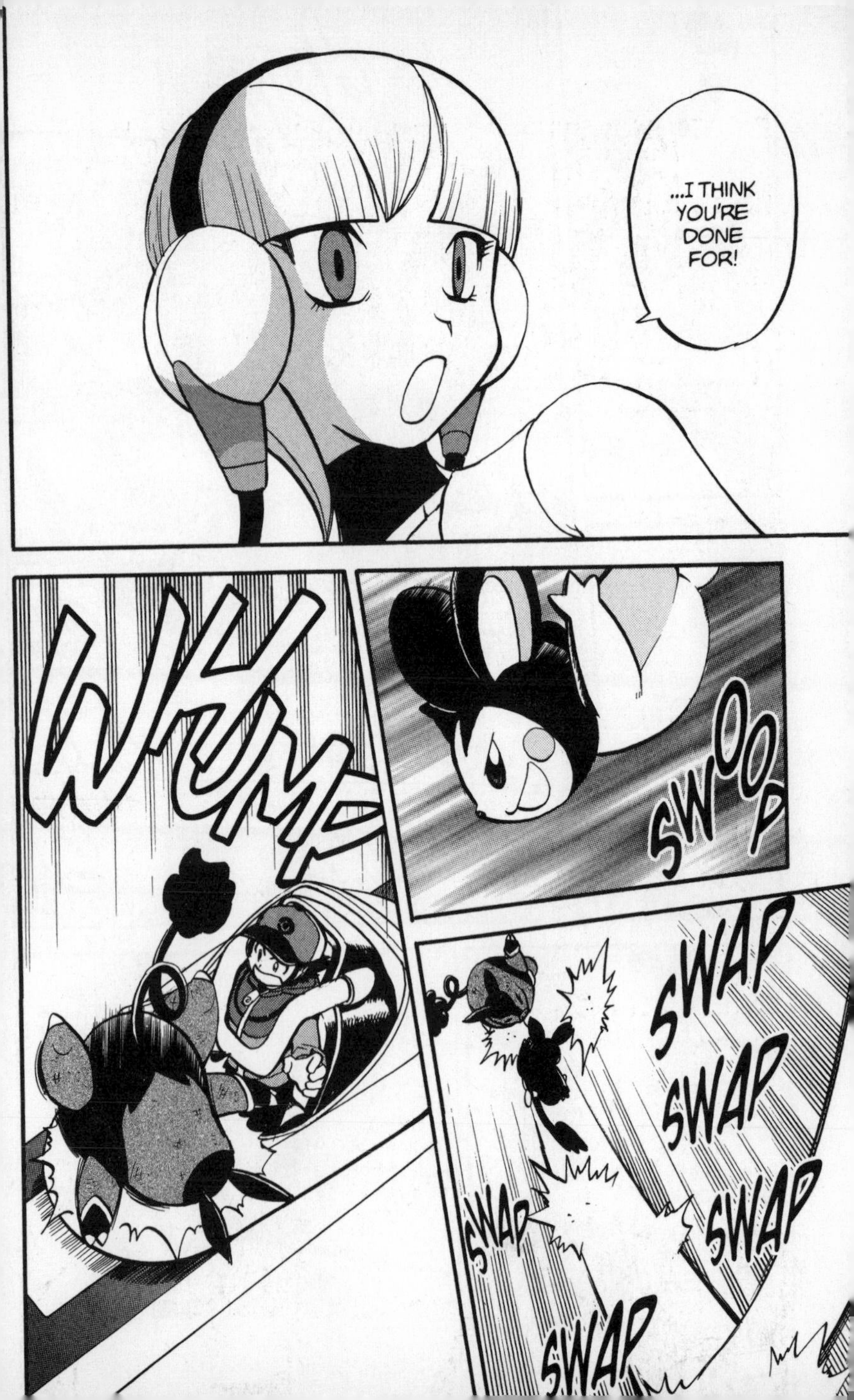
...I THINK YOU'RE DONE FOR!
SWOOP
SWAP
SWAP
SWAP
SWAP
SWAP
WUMP

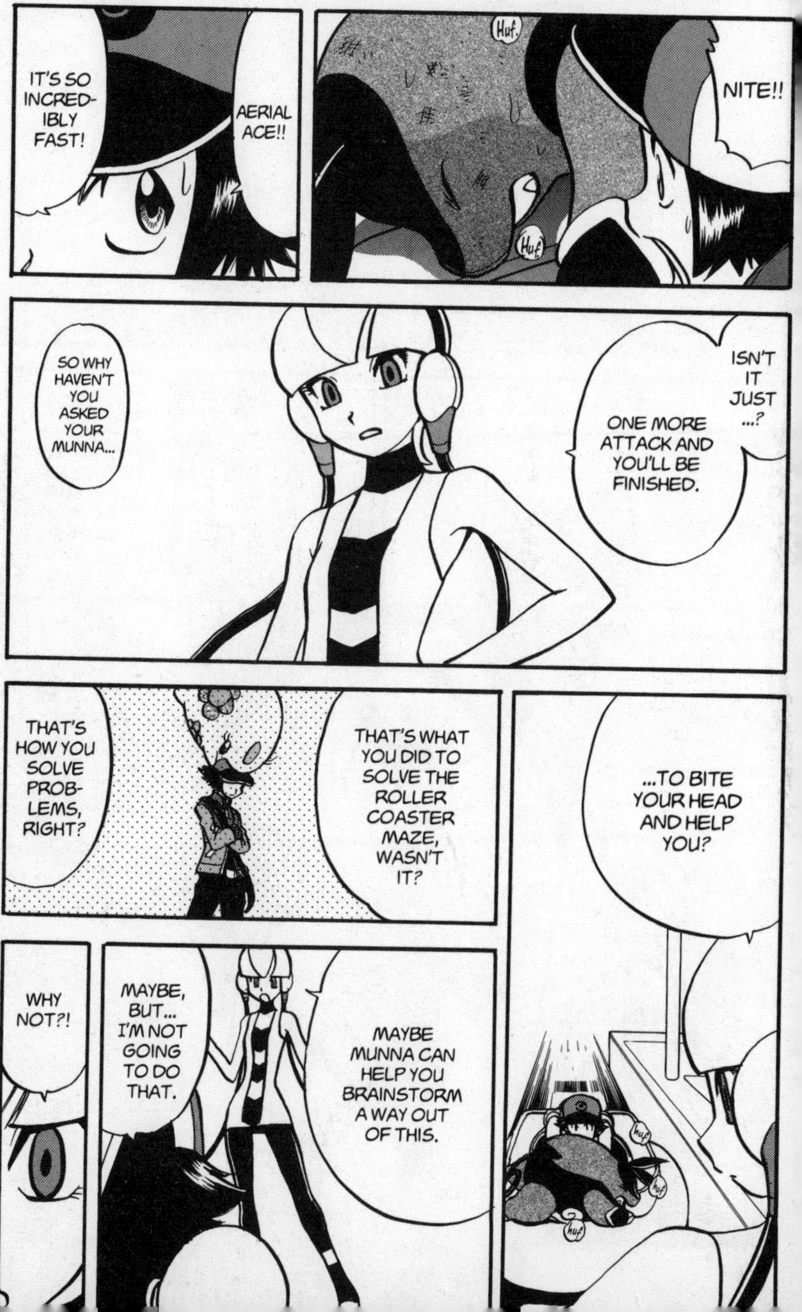
Huf
NITE!!
Huf
AERIAL ACE!!
IT'S SO INCREDIBLY FAST!
ISN'T IT JUST ...?
ONE MORE ATTACK AND YOU'LL BE FINISHED.
SO WHY HAVEN'T YOU ASKED YOUR MUNNA...
...TO BITE YOUR HEAD AND HELP YOU?
huf
huf
huf
THAT'S WHAT YOU DID TO SOLVE THE ROLLER COASTER MAZE, WASN'T IT?
THAT'S HOW YOU SOLVE PROBLEMS, RIGHT?
MAYBE MUNNA CAN HELP YOU BRAINSTORM A WAY OUT OF THIS.
MAYBE, BUT... I'M NOT GOING TO DO THAT.
WHY NOT?!

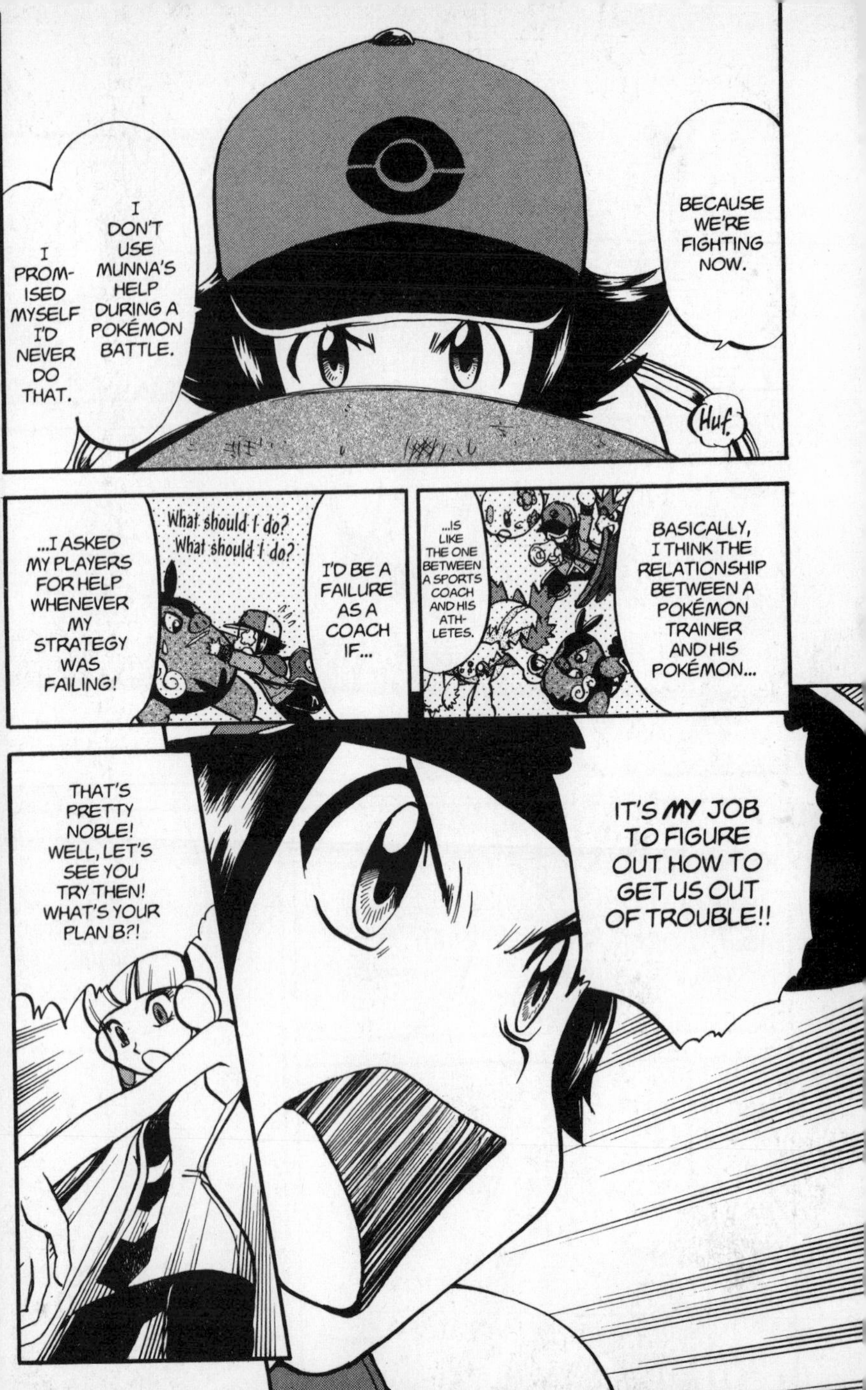
BECAUSE WE'RE FIGHTING NOW.
Huf.
I DON'T USE MUNNA'S HELP DURING A POKÉMON BATTLE.
I PROMISED MYSELF I'D NEVER DO THAT.
BASICALLY, I THINK THE RELATIONSHIP BETWEEN A POKÉMON TRAINER AND HIS POKÉMON...
...IS LIKE THE ONE BETWEEN A SPORTS COACH AND HIS ATHLETES.
I'D BE A FAILURE AS A COACH IF...
What should I do? What should I do?
...I ASKED MY PLAYERS FOR HELP WHENEVER MY STRATEGY WAS FAILING!
IT'S *MY* JOB TO FIGURE OUT HOW TO GET US OUT OF TROUBLE!!
THAT'S PRETTY NOBLE! WELL, LET'S SEE YOU TRY THEN! WHAT'S YOUR PLAN B?!

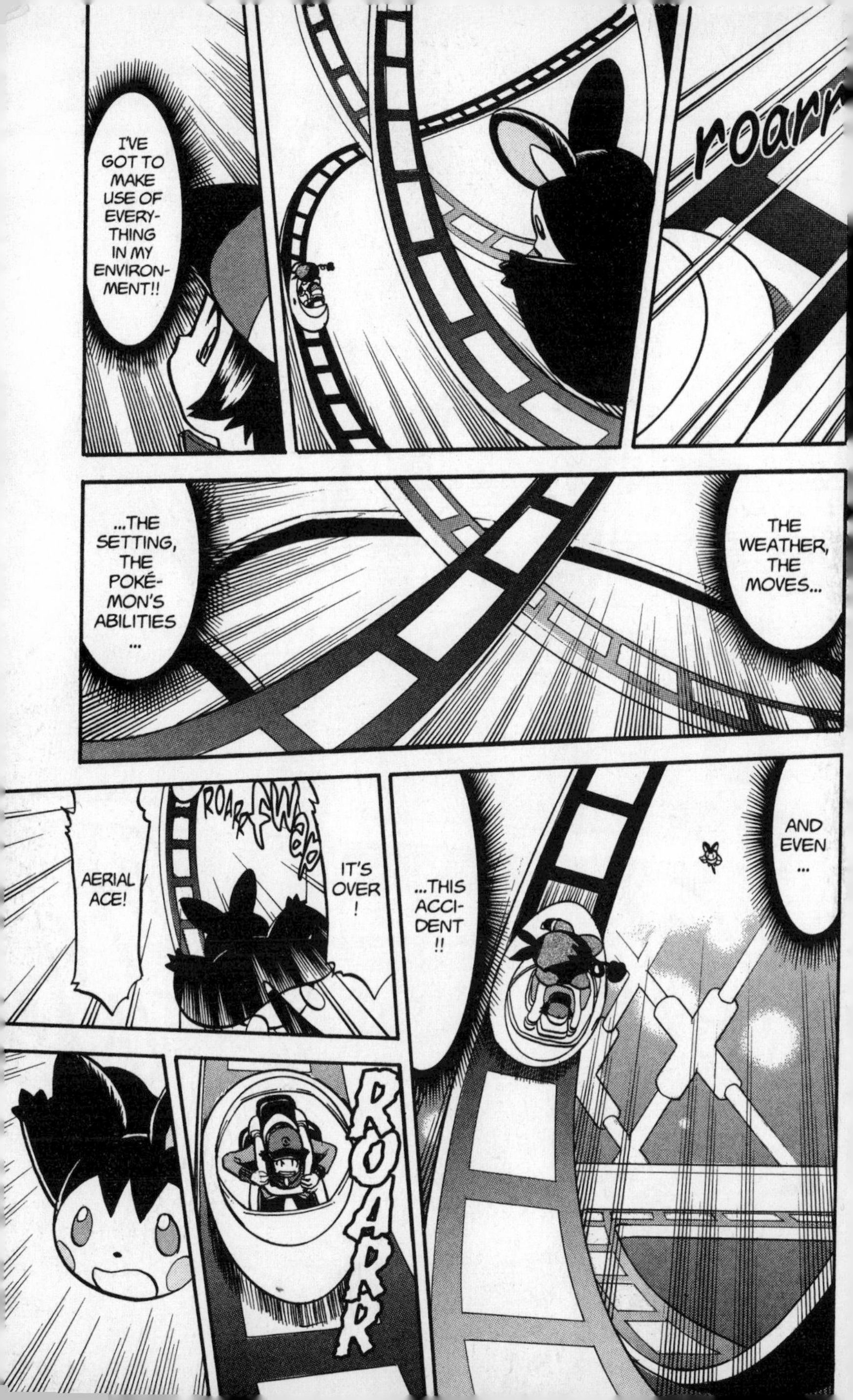
roarr
I'VE GOT TO MAKE USE OF EVERYTHING IN MY ENVIRONMENT!!
THE WEATHER, THE MOVES...
...THE SETTING, THE POKÉMON'S ABILITIES ...
AND EVEN ...
...THIS ACCIDENT !!
IT'S OVER !
ROARR
FWOOP
AERIAL ACE!
ROARR

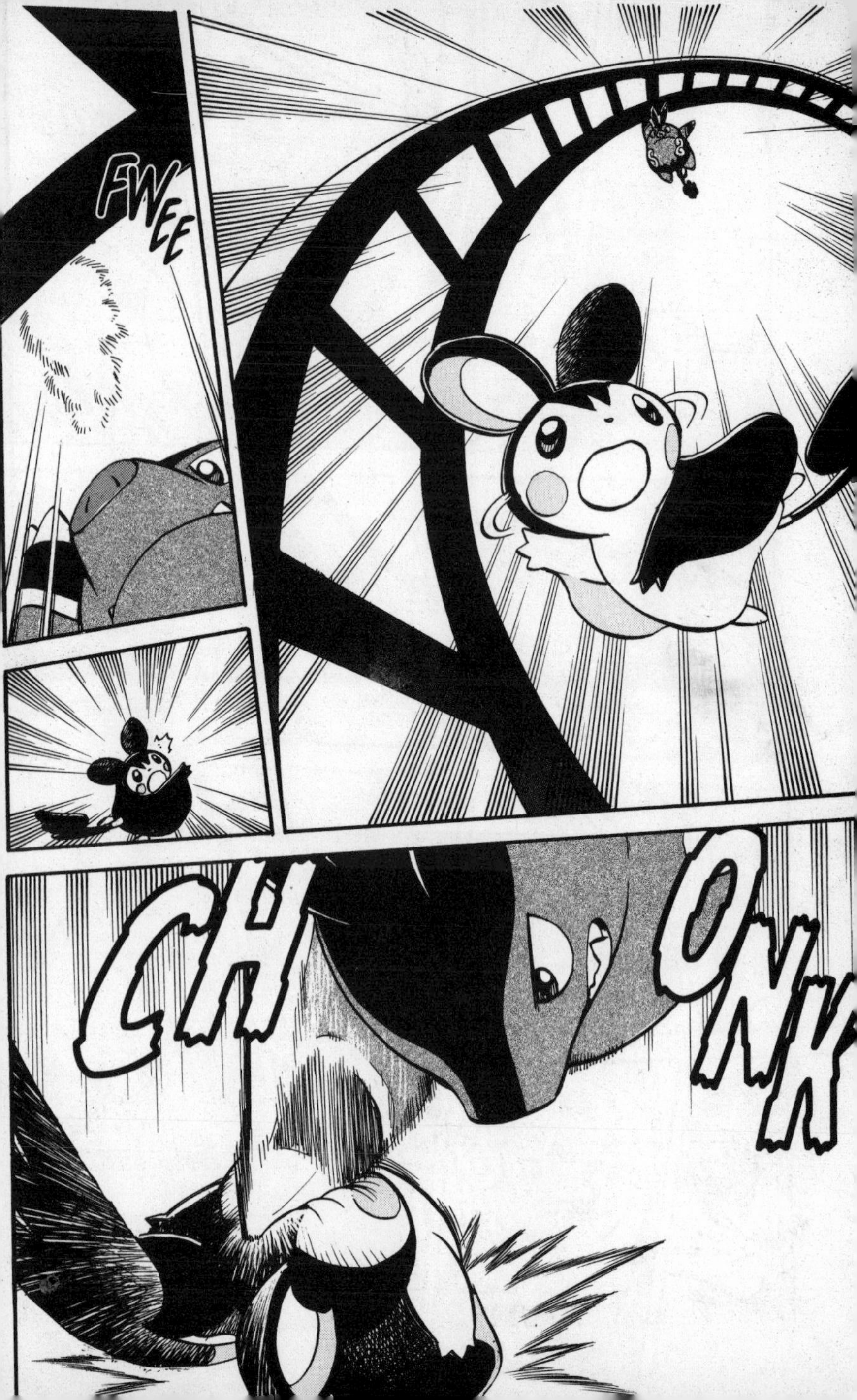
FWEE
CHONK

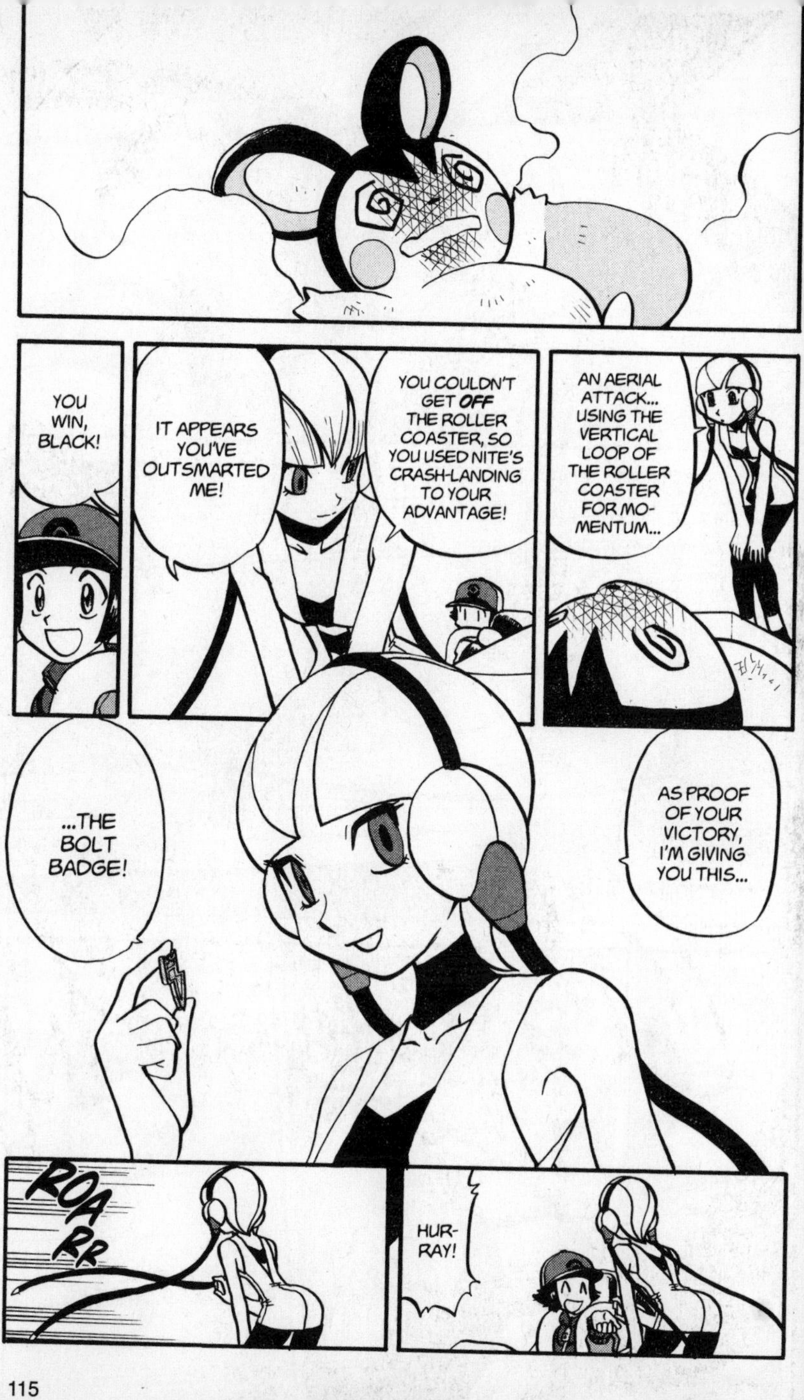
AN AERIAL ATTACK... USING THE VERTICAL LOOP OF THE ROLLER COASTER FOR MOMENTUM...
YOU COULDN'T GET **OFF** THE ROLLER COASTER, SO YOU USED NITE'S CRASH-LANDING TO YOUR ADVANTAGE!
IT APPEARS YOU'VE OUTSMARTED ME!
YOU WIN, BLACK!
AS PROOF OF YOUR VICTORY, I'M GIVING YOU THIS...
...THE BOLT BADGE!
HUR-RAY!
ROARRR

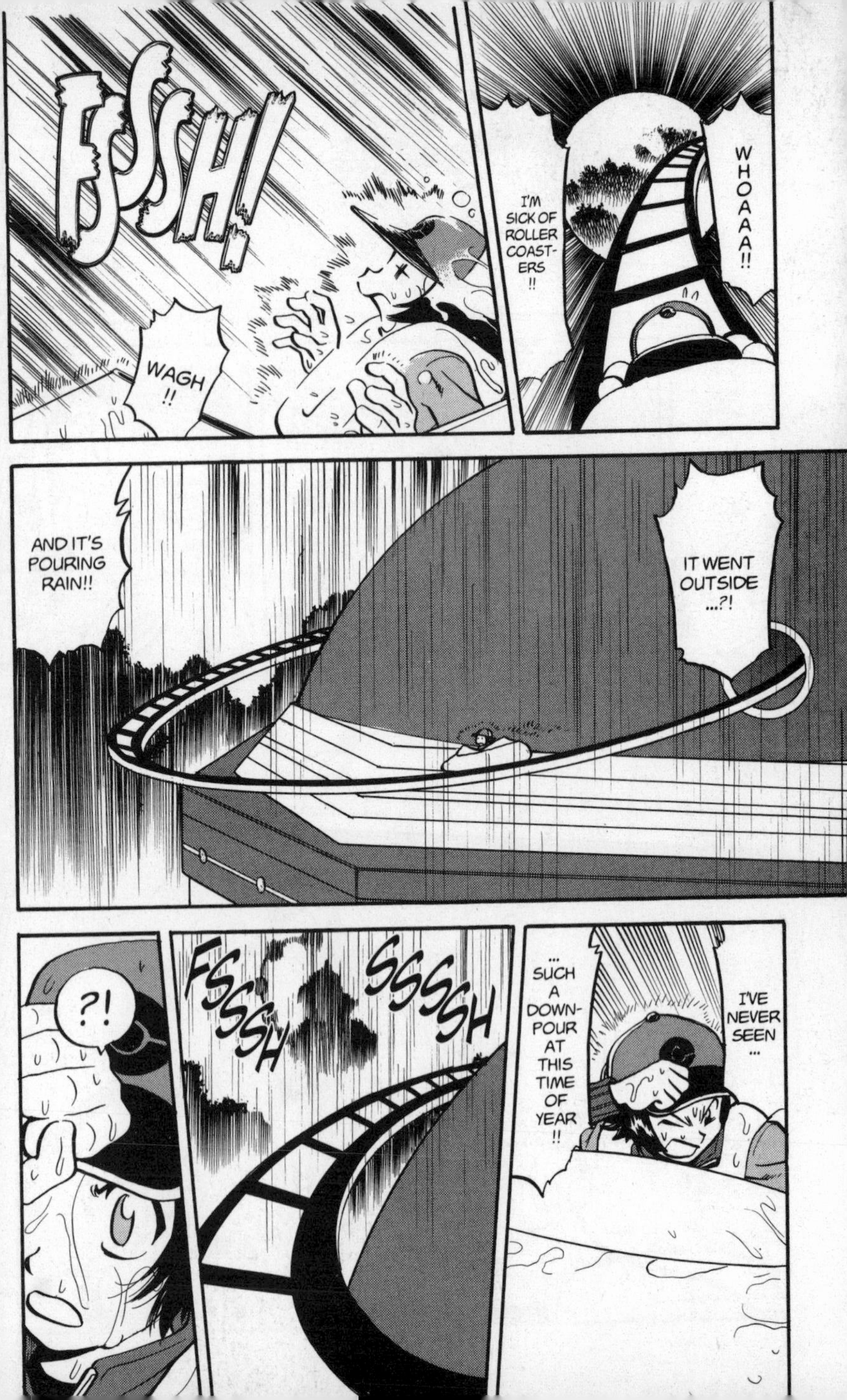
WHOAAA!!
I'M SICK OF ROLLER COASTERS!!
ESSH!
WAGH!!
IT WENT OUTSIDE ...?!
AND IT'S POURING RAIN!!
I'VE NEVER SEEN ...
... SUCH A DOWNPOUR AT THIS TIME OF YEAR!!
SSSSH
FSSSH
?!

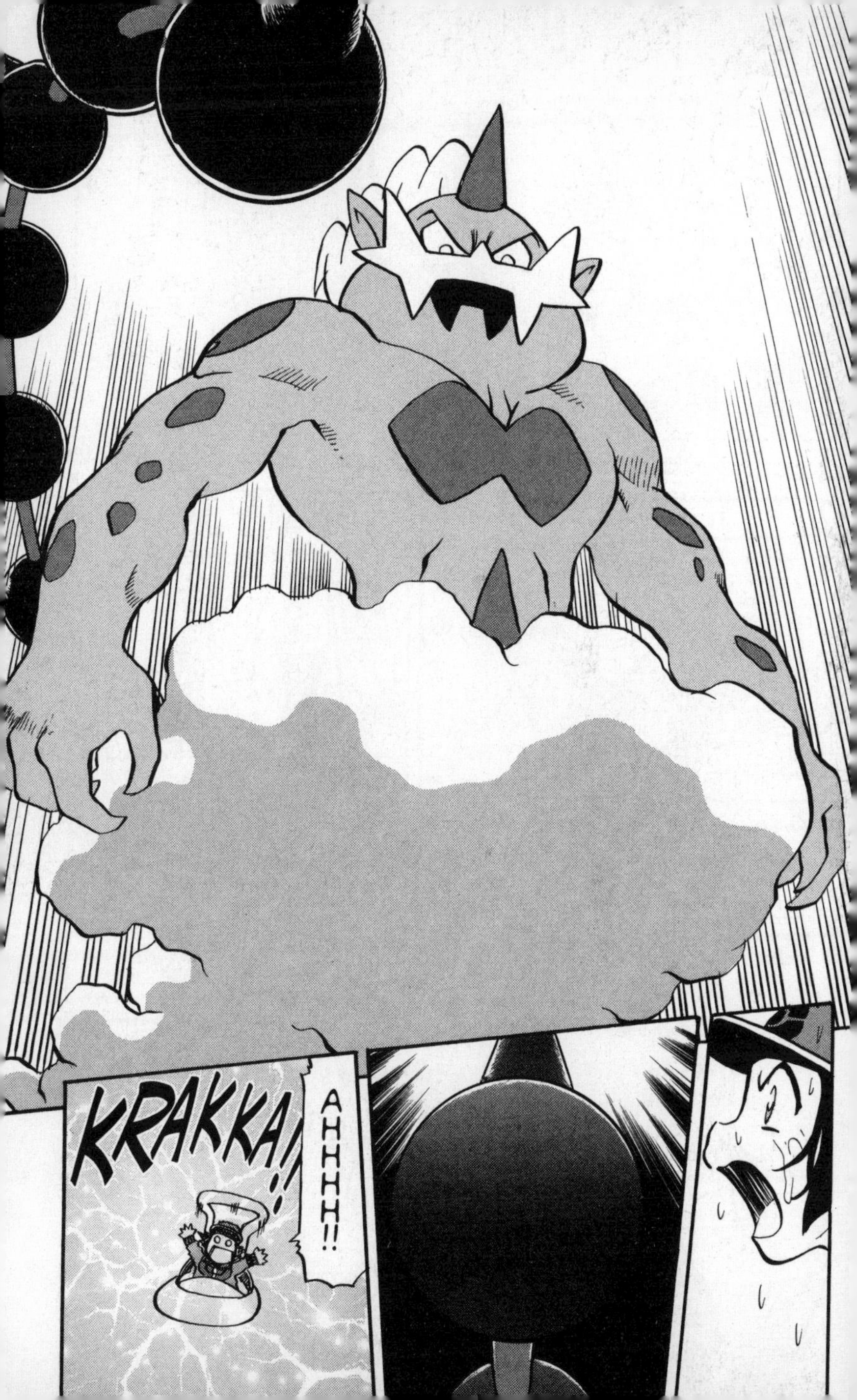
KRAKKA!!
AHHHH!!

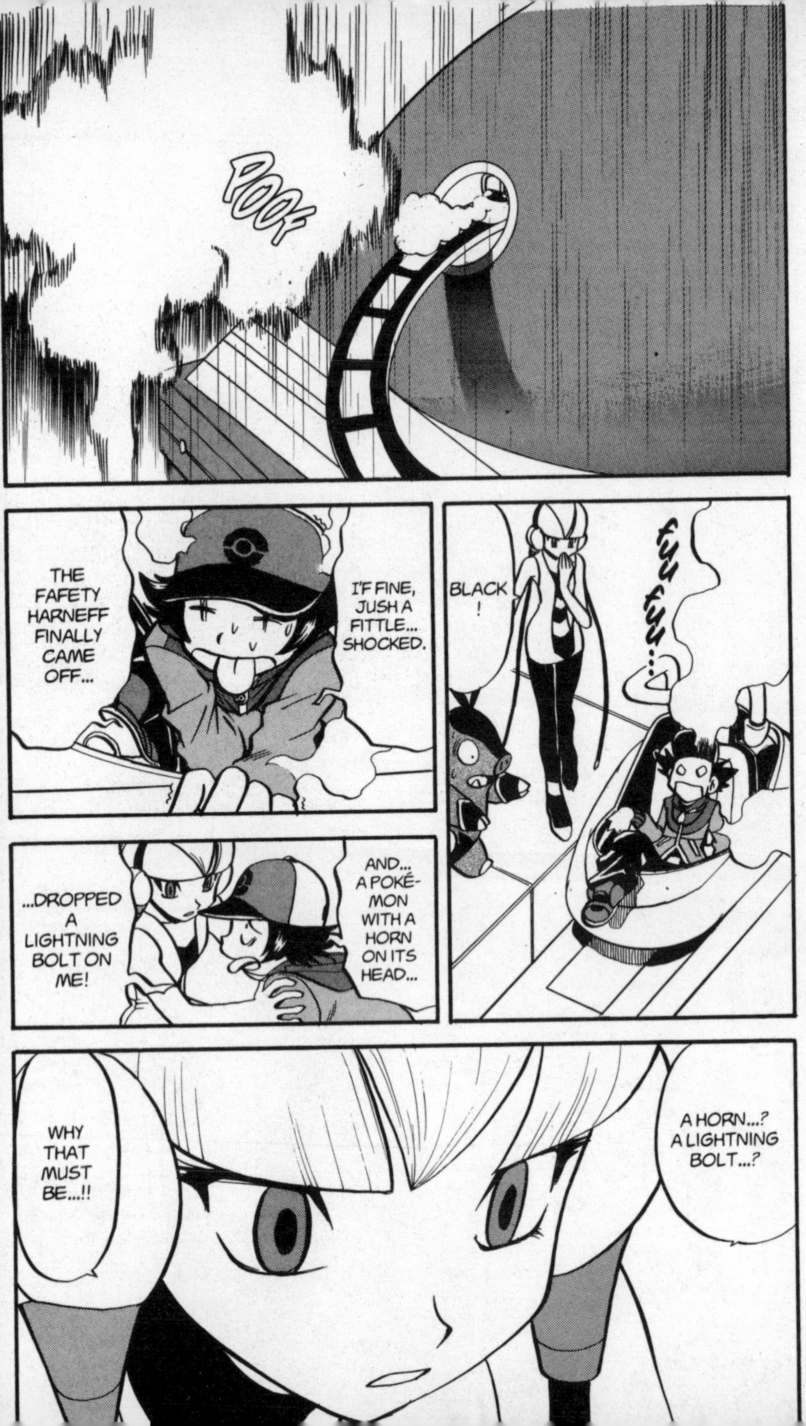
POOF
FUFU FUFU...
BLACK!
I'F FINE, JUSH A FITTLE... SHOCKED.
THE FAFETY HARNEFF FINALLY CAME OFF...
AND... A POKÉMON WITH A HORN ON ITS HEAD...
...DROPPED A LIGHTNING BOLT ON ME!
A HORN...? A LIGHTNING BOLT...?
WHY THAT MUST BE...!!

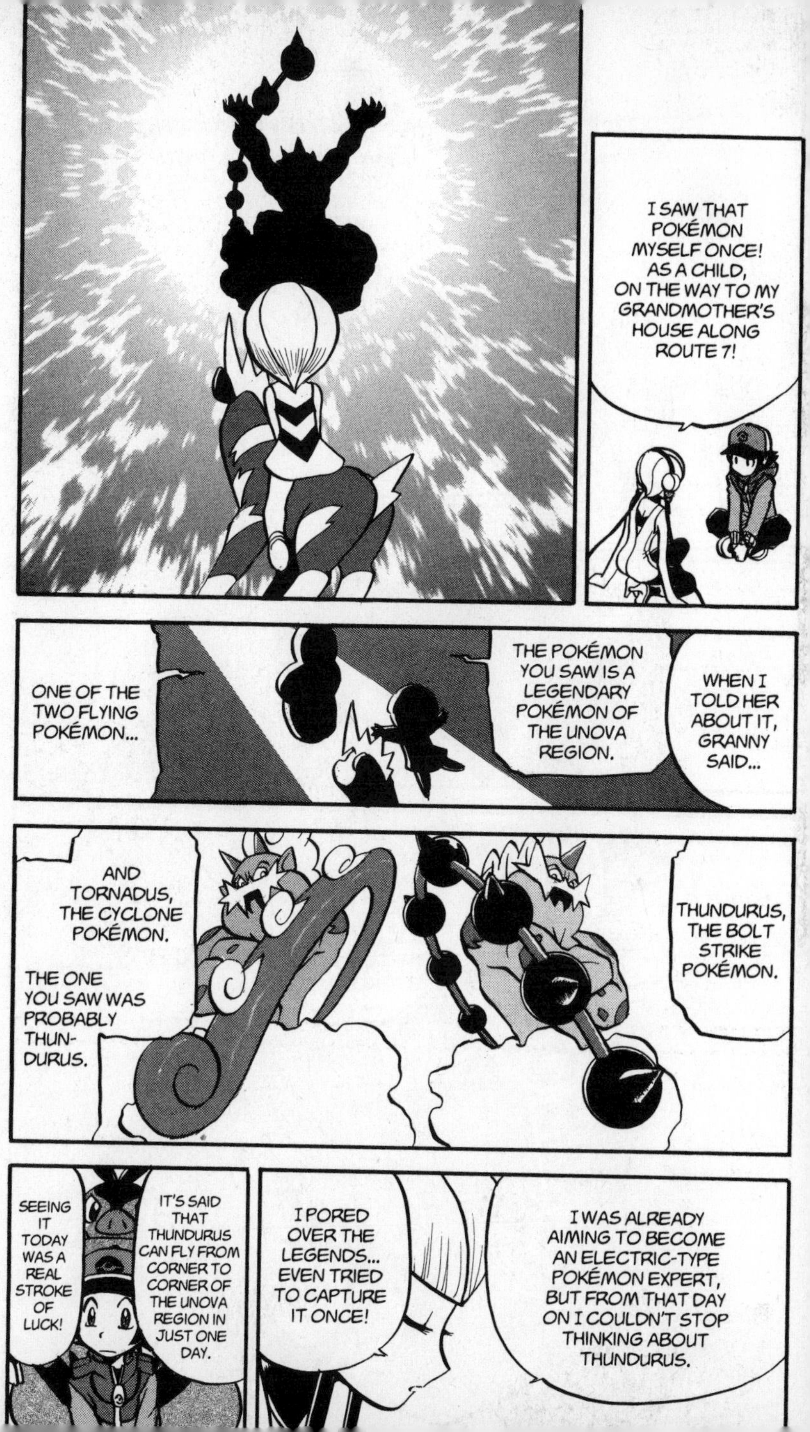
I SAW THAT POKÉMON MYSELF ONCE! AS A CHILD, ON THE WAY TO MY GRANDMOTHER'S HOUSE ALONG ROUTE 7!
WHEN I TOLD HER ABOUT IT, GRANNY SAID...
THE POKÉMON YOU SAW IS A LEGENDARY POKÉMON OF THE UNOVA REGION.
ONE OF THE TWO FLYING POKÉMON...
THUNDURUS, THE BOLT STRIKE POKÉMON.
AND TORNADUS, THE CYCLONE POKÉMON.
THE ONE YOU SAW WAS PROBABLY THUN-DURUS.
I WAS ALREADY AIMING TO BECOME AN ELECTRIC-TYPE POKÉMON EXPERT, BUT FROM THAT DAY ON I COULDN'T STOP THINKING ABOUT THUNDURUS.
I PORED OVER THE LEGENDS... EVEN TRIED TO CAPTURE IT ONCE!
IT'S SAID THAT THUNDURUS CAN FLY FROM CORNER TO CORNER OF THE UNOVA REGION IN JUST ONE DAY.
SEEING IT TODAY WAS A REAL STROKE OF LUCK!

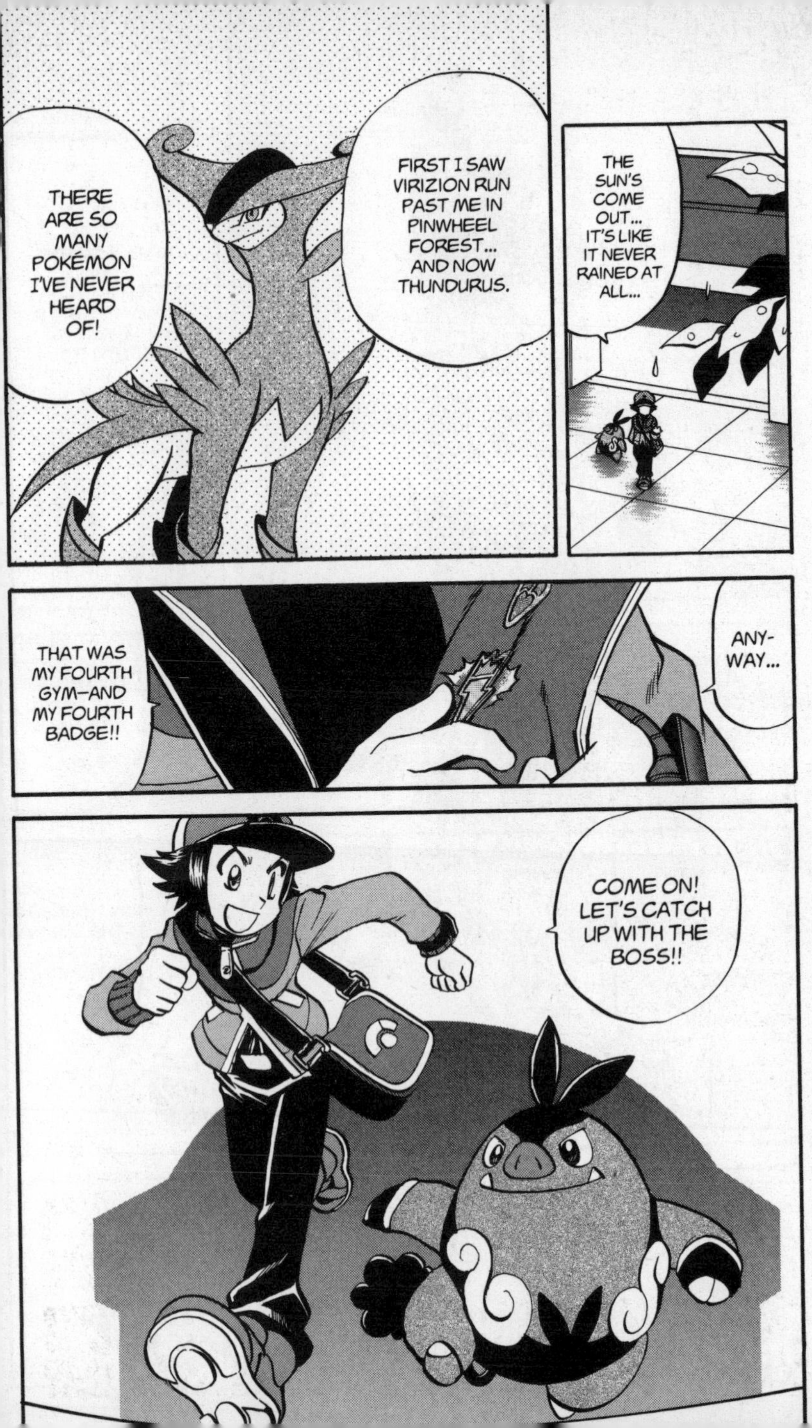
THE SUN'S COME OUT... IT'S LIKE IT NEVER RAINED AT ALL...
FIRST I SAW VIRIZION RUN PAST ME IN PINWHEEL FOREST... AND NOW THUNDURUS.
THERE ARE SO MANY POKÉMON I'VE NEVER HEARD OF!
ANY-WAY...
THAT WAS MY FOURTH GYM—AND MY FOURTH BADGE!!
COME ON! LET'S CATCH UP WITH THE BOSS!!

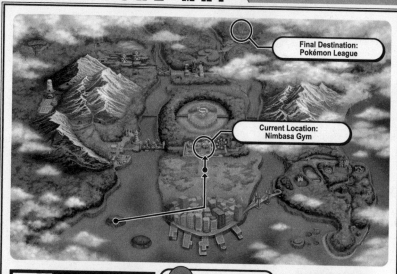

Final Destination:
Pokémon League

Current Location:
Nimbasa Gym

BLACK

Fire Pig Pokémon **Nite**
Pignite ♂ | Fire | Fighting
Lv.25 Ability: Blaze

Dream Eater Pokémon **Musha**
Munna ♂ | Psychic
Lv.46 Ability: Forewarn

Valiant Pokémon **Brav**
Braviary ♂ | Normal | Flying
Lv.54 Ability: Sheer Force

EleSpider Pokémon **Tula**
Galvantula ♂ | Bug | Electric
Lv.49 Ability: Unnerve

WHITE

Fire Pig Pokémon **Gigi**
Tepig ♀ | Fire
Lv.05 Ability: Blaze

TRIO BADGE | BASIC BADGE | INSECT BADGE | BOLT BADGE | ? | ? | ? | ?

Pokémon™
Adventures
Black & White

SERVINE

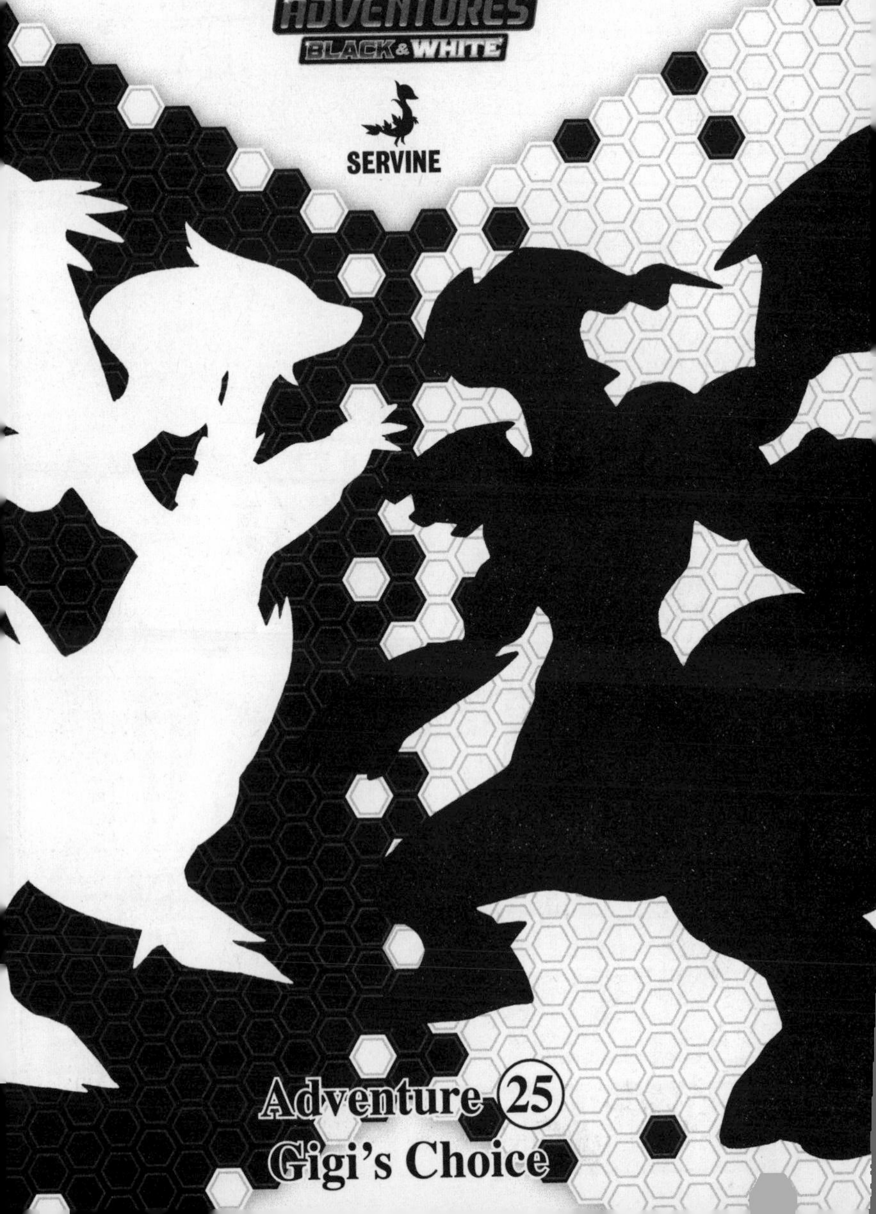

Adventure 25
Gigi's Choice

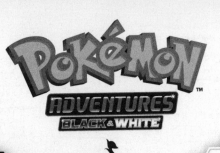

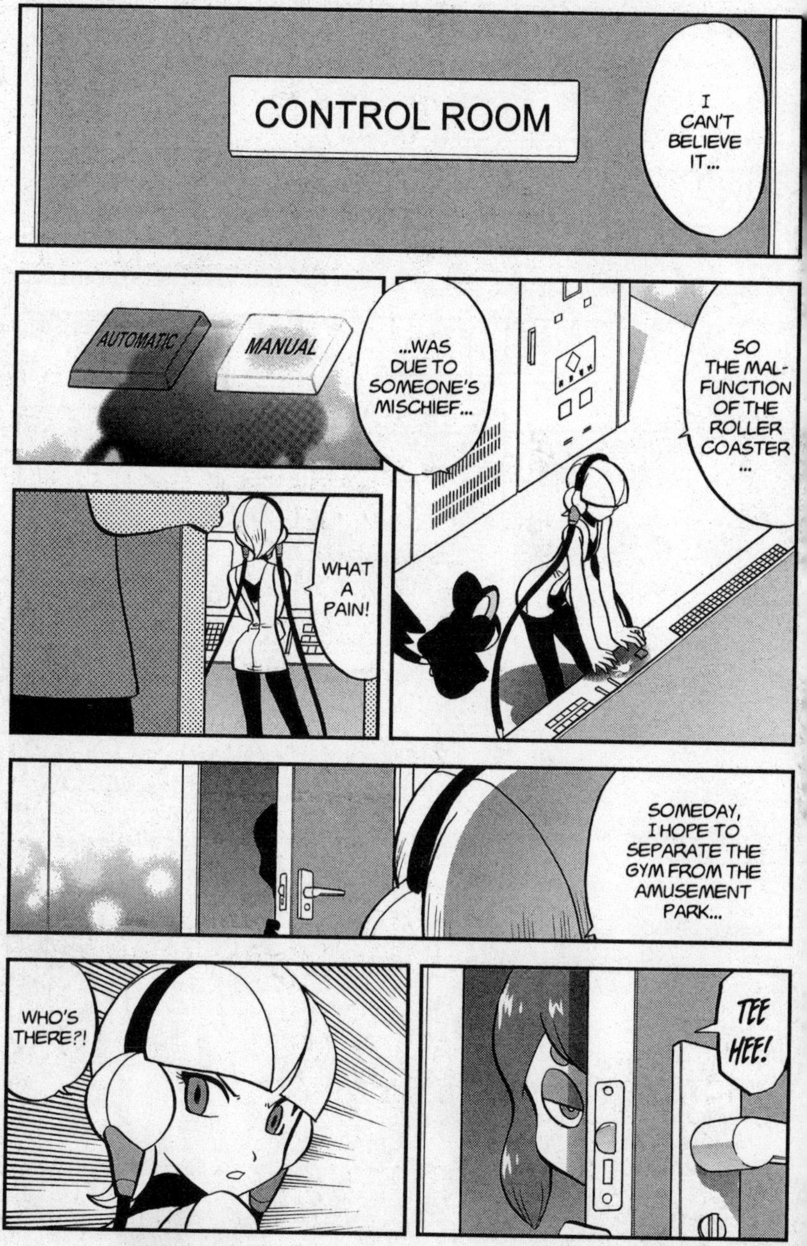
I CAN'T BELIEVE IT...
CONTROL ROOM
SO THE MAL-FUNCTION OF THE ROLLER COASTER...
...WAS DUE TO SOMEONE'S MISCHIEF...
AUTOMATIC
MANUAL
WHAT A PAIN!
SOMEDAY, I HOPE TO SEPARATE THE GYM FROM THE AMUSEMENT PARK...
TEE HEE!
WHO'S THERE?!

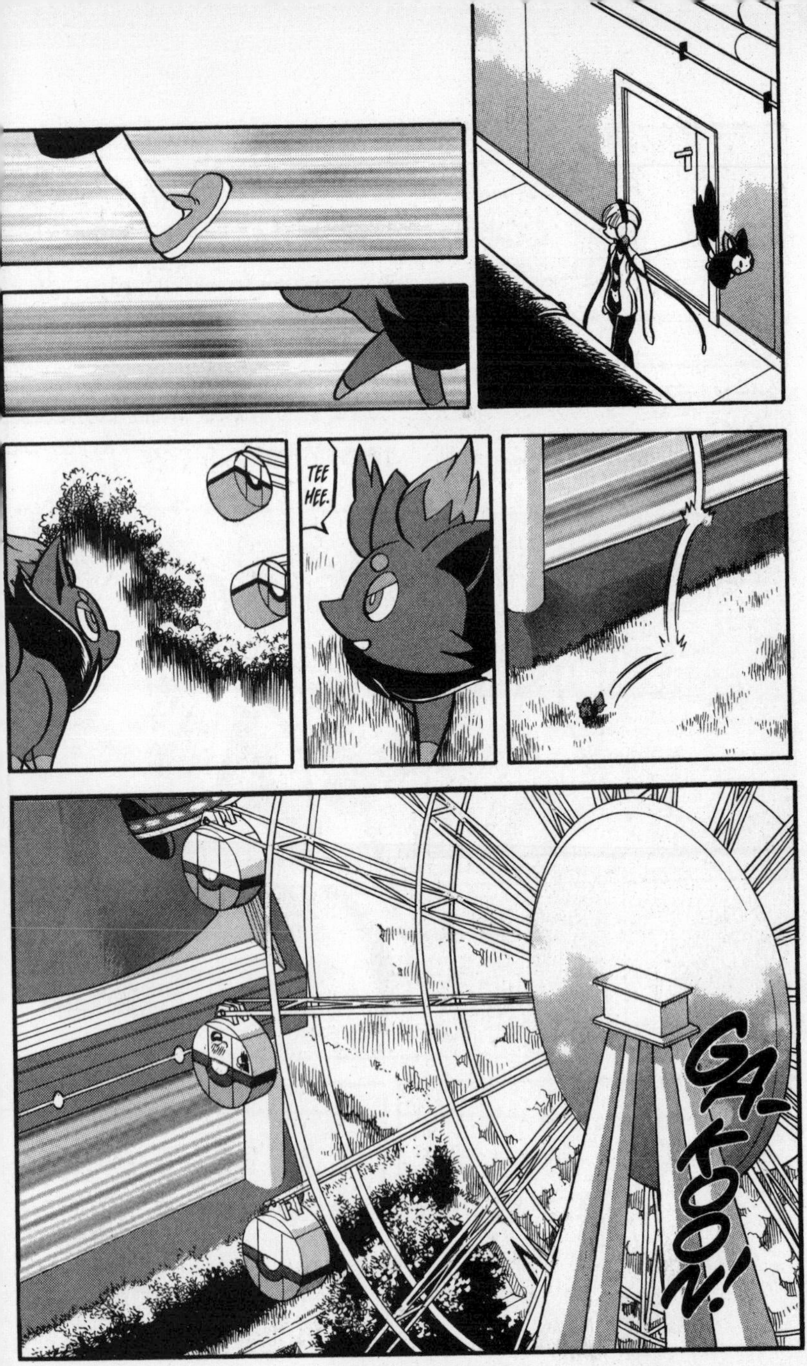
TEE HEE.
GA-KOON!

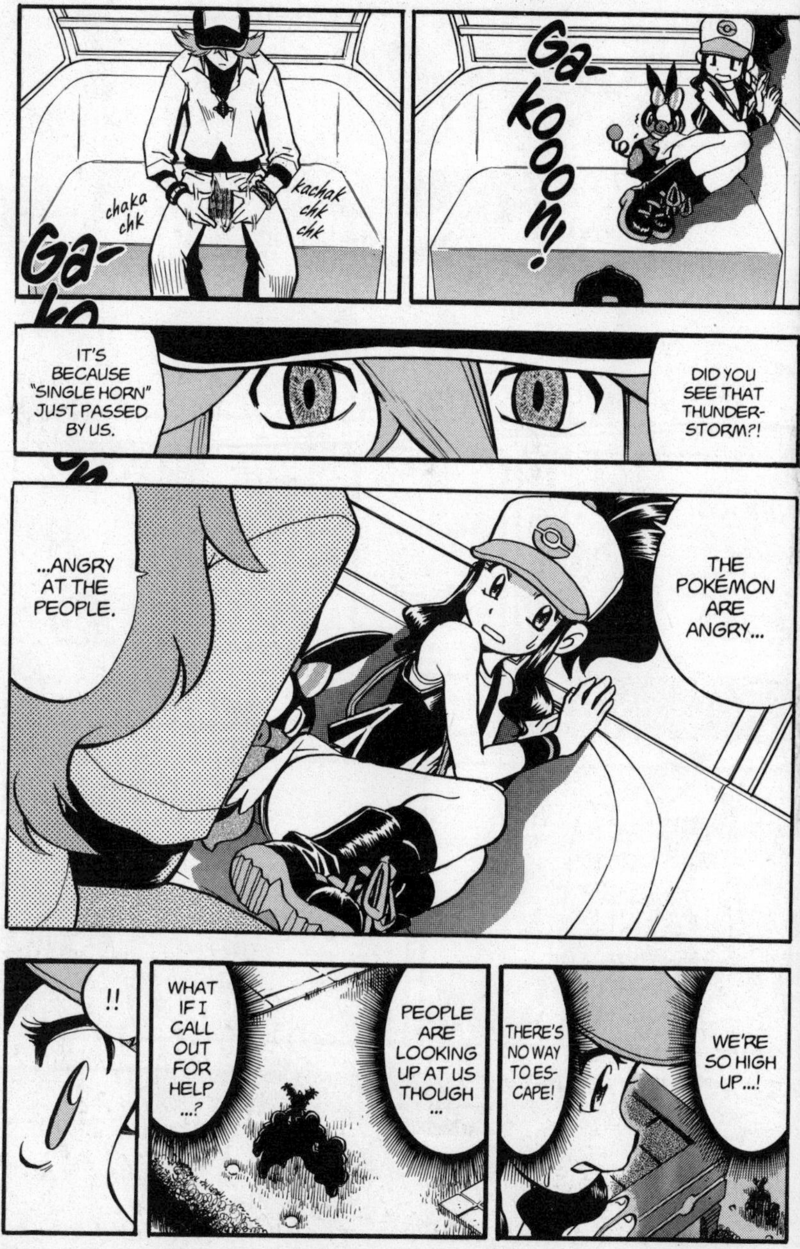
Ga-kooon!!
kachak chk chk
chaka chk
Ga-
DID YOU SEE THAT THUNDER-STORM?!
IT'S BECAUSE "SINGLE HORN" JUST PASSED BY US.
THE POKÉMON ARE ANGRY...
...ANGRY AT THE PEOPLE.
WE'RE SO HIGH UP...!
THERE'S NO WAY TO ES-CAPE!
PEOPLE ARE LOOKING UP AT US THOUGH ...
WHAT IF I CALL OUT FOR HELP ...?
!!

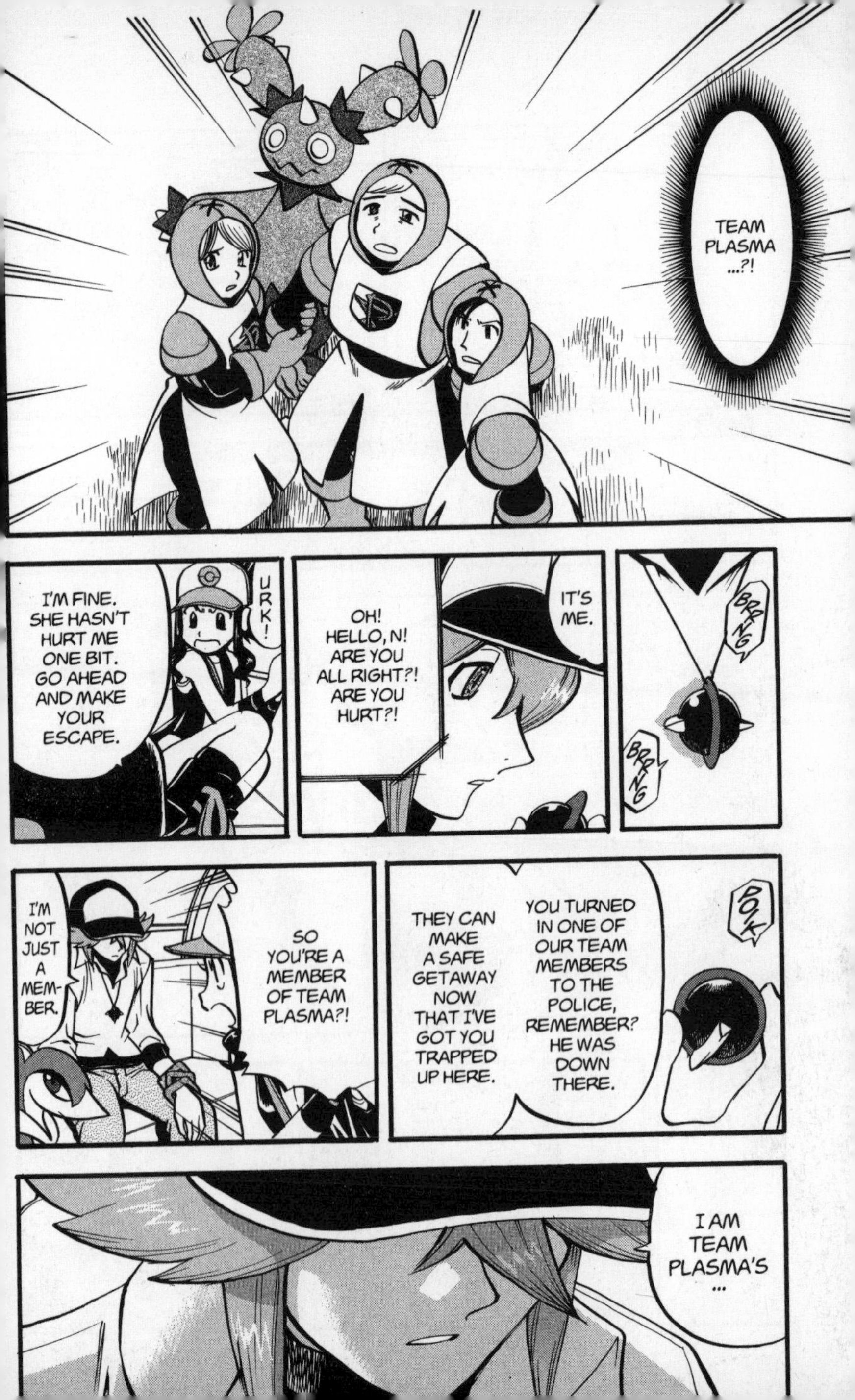
TEAM PLASMA ...?!
BRRING
BRRING
IT'S ME.
OH! HELLO, N! ARE YOU ALL RIGHT?! ARE YOU HURT?!
URK!
I'M FINE. SHE HASN'T HURT ME ONE BIT. GO AHEAD AND MAKE YOUR ESCAPE.
POIK
YOU TURNED IN ONE OF OUR TEAM MEMBERS TO THE POLICE, REMEMBER? HE WAS DOWN THERE.
THEY CAN MAKE A SAFE GETAWAY NOW THAT I'VE GOT YOU TRAPPED UP HERE.
SO YOU'RE A MEMBER OF TEAM PLASMA?!
I'M NOT JUST A MEM-BER.
I AM TEAM PLASMA'S ...

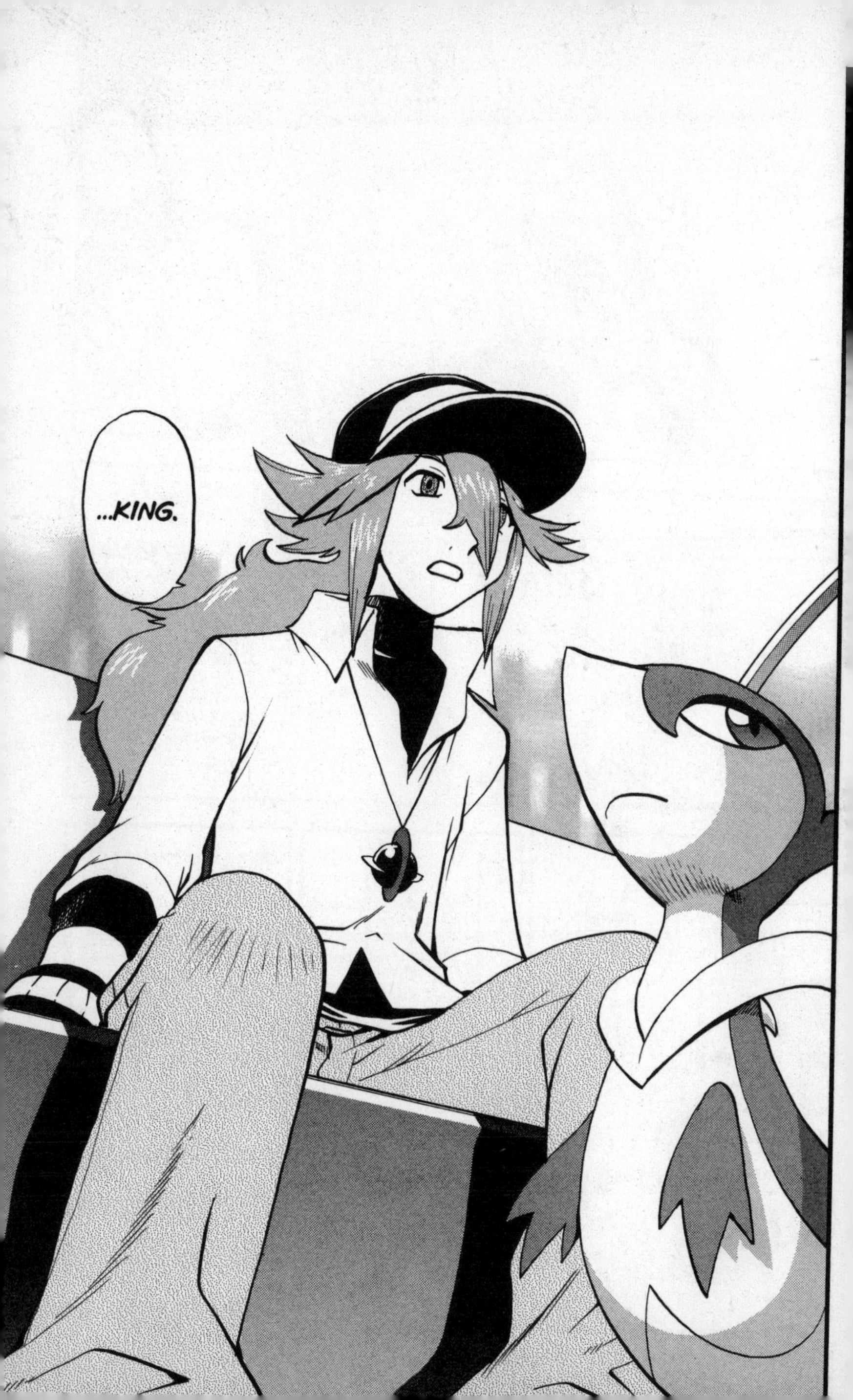
...KING.

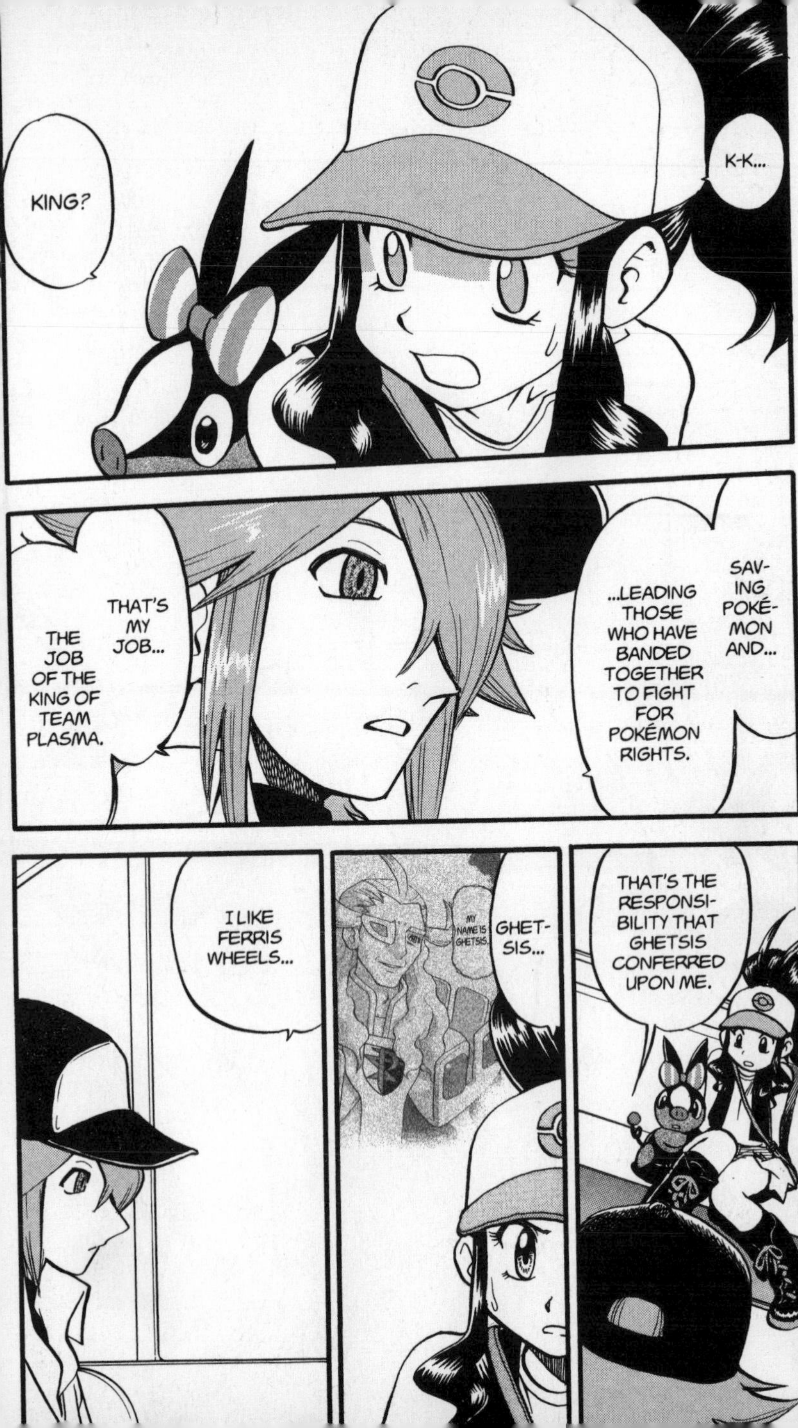
K-K...
KING?
SAV-ING POKÉ-MON AND...
...LEADING THOSE WHO HAVE BANDED TOGETHER TO FIGHT FOR POKÉMON RIGHTS.
THAT'S MY JOB...
THE JOB OF THE KING OF TEAM PLASMA.
THAT'S THE RESPONSI-BILITY THAT GHETSIS CONFERRED UPON ME.
GHET-SIS...
MY NAME IS GHETSIS.
I LIKE FERRIS WHEELS...

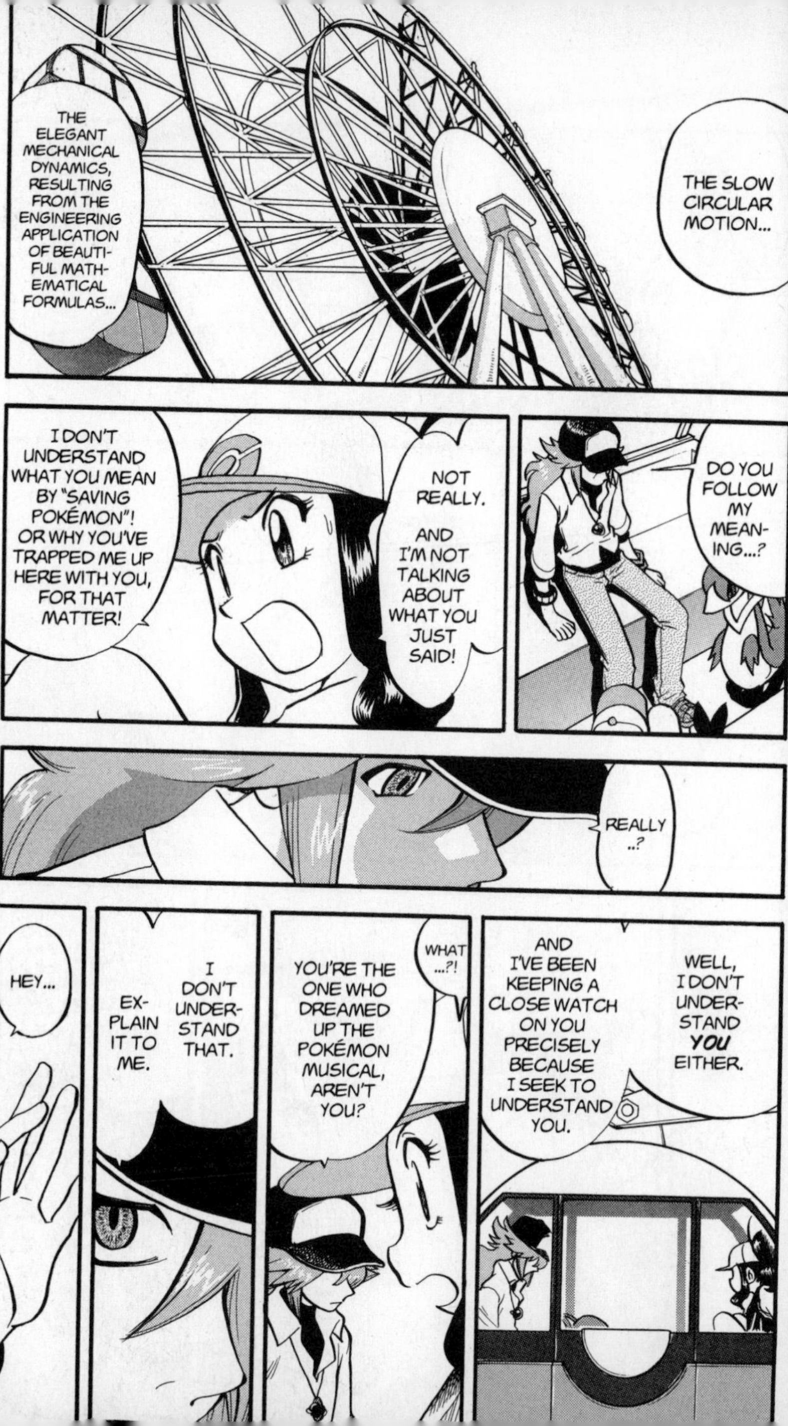

THE SLOW CIRCULAR MOTION...
THE ELEGANT MECHANICAL DYNAMICS, RESULTING FROM THE ENGINEERING APPLICATION OF BEAUTIFUL MATHEMATICAL FORMULAS...
DO YOU FOLLOW MY MEANING...?
NOT REALLY.
AND I'M NOT TALKING ABOUT WHAT YOU JUST SAID!
I DON'T UNDERSTAND WHAT YOU MEAN BY "SAVING POKÉMON"! OR WHY YOU'VE TRAPPED ME UP HERE WITH YOU, FOR THAT MATTER!
REALLY ..?
WELL, I DON'T UNDERSTAND ***YOU*** EITHER.
AND I'VE BEEN KEEPING A CLOSE WATCH ON YOU PRECISELY BECAUSE I SEEK TO UNDERSTAND YOU.
WHAT ...?!
YOU'RE THE ONE WHO DREAMED UP THE POKÉMON MUSICAL, AREN'T YOU?
I DON'T UNDERSTAND THAT.
EXPLAIN IT TO ME.
HEY...

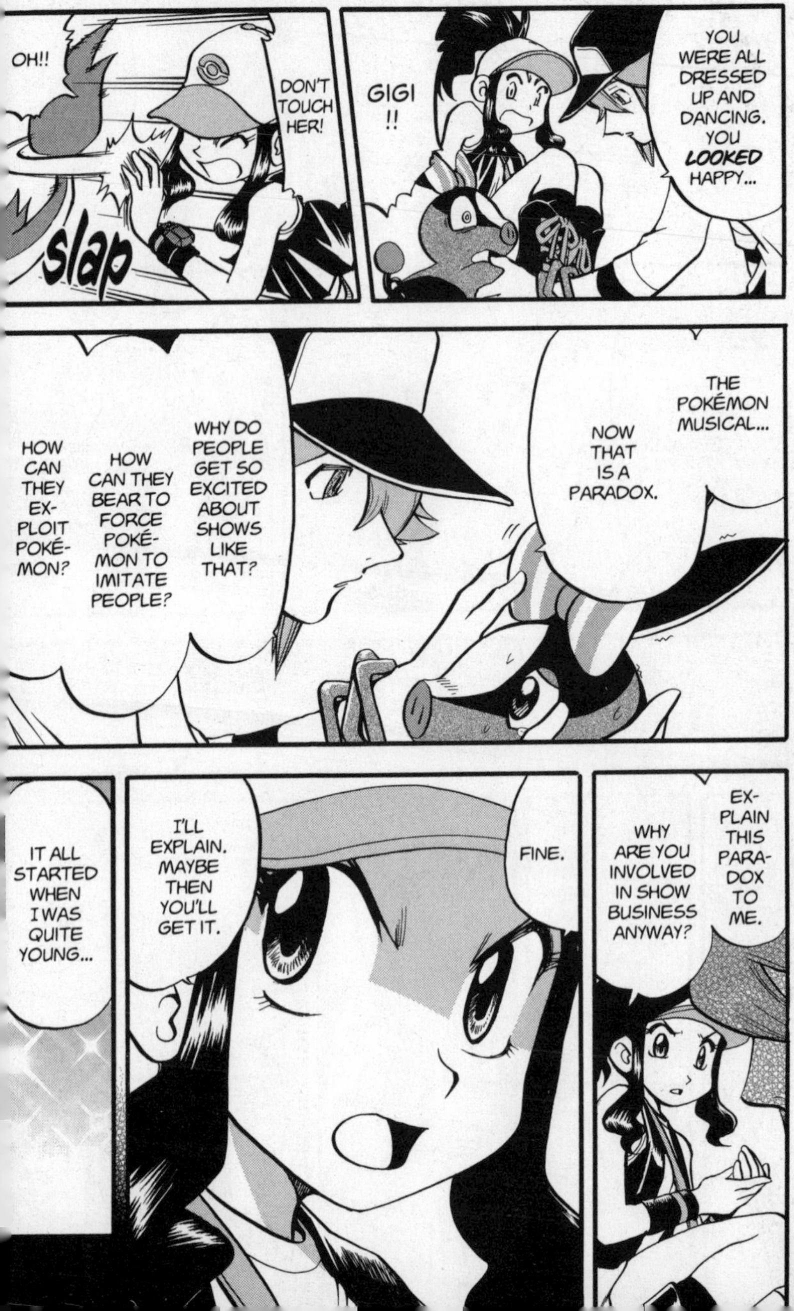
YOU WERE ALL DRESSED UP AND DANCING. YOU **LOOKED** HAPPY...
GIGI !!
DON'T TOUCH HER!
OH!!
slap
THE POKÉMON MUSICAL...
NOW THAT IS A PARADOX.
WHY DO PEOPLE GET SO EXCITED ABOUT SHOWS LIKE THAT?
HOW CAN THEY BEAR TO FORCE POKÉMON TO IMITATE PEOPLE?
HOW CAN THEY EXPLOIT POKÉMON?
EXPLAIN THIS PARADOX TO ME.
WHY ARE YOU INVOLVED IN SHOW BUSINESS ANYWAY?
FINE.
I'LL EXPLAIN. MAYBE THEN YOU'LL GET IT.
IT ALL STARTED WHEN I WAS QUITE YOUNG...

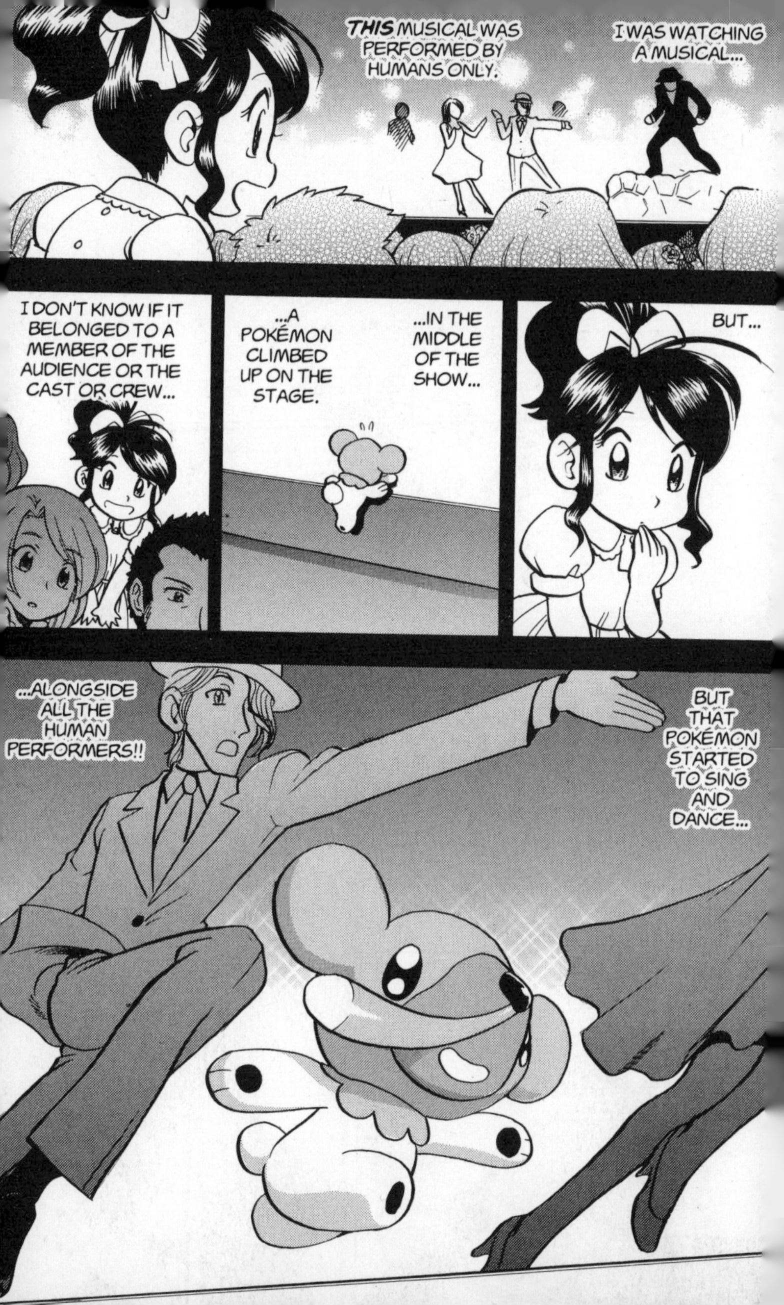
I WAS WATCHING A MUSICAL...
THIS MUSICAL WAS PERFORMED BY HUMANS ONLY.
BUT...
...IN THE MIDDLE OF THE SHOW...
...A POKÉMON CLIMBED UP ON THE STAGE.
I DON'T KNOW IF IT BELONGED TO A MEMBER OF THE AUDIENCE OR THE CAST OR CREW...
BUT THAT POKÉMON STARTED TO SING AND DANCE...
...ALONGSIDE ALL THE HUMAN PERFORMERS!!

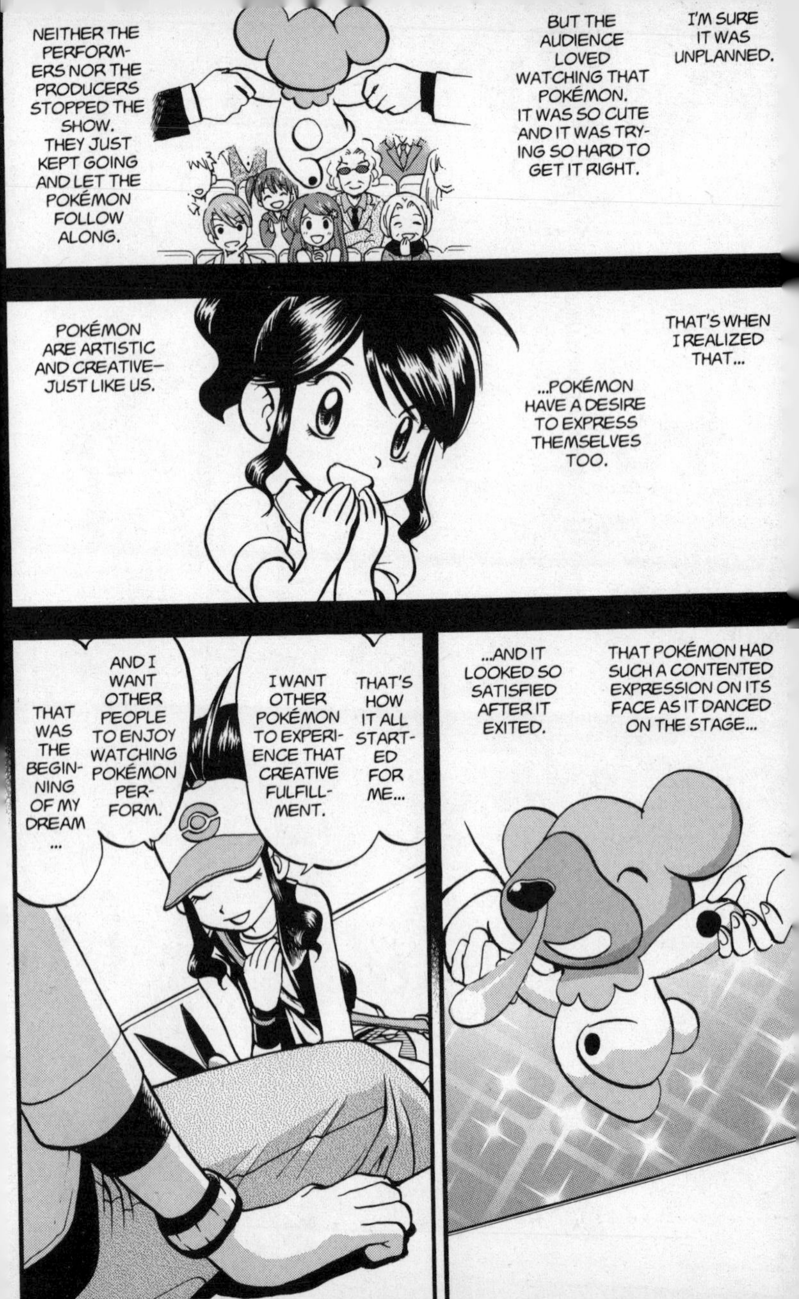
I'M SURE IT WAS UNPLANNED.
BUT THE AUDIENCE LOVED WATCHING THAT POKÉMON. IT WAS SO CUTE AND IT WAS TRYING SO HARD TO GET IT RIGHT.
NEITHER THE PERFORMERS NOR THE PRODUCERS STOPPED THE SHOW. THEY JUST KEPT GOING AND LET THE POKÉMON FOLLOW ALONG.
THAT'S WHEN I REALIZED THAT...
...POKÉMON HAVE A DESIRE TO EXPRESS THEMSELVES TOO.
POKÉMON ARE ARTISTIC AND CREATIVE—JUST LIKE US.
THAT POKÉMON HAD SUCH A CONTENTED EXPRESSION ON ITS FACE AS IT DANCED ON THE STAGE...
...AND IT LOOKED SO SATISFIED AFTER IT EXITED.
THAT'S HOW IT ALL STARTED FOR ME...
I WANT OTHER POKÉMON TO EXPERIENCE THAT CREATIVE FULFILLMENT.
AND I WANT OTHER PEOPLE TO ENJOY WATCHING POKÉMON PERFORM.
THAT WAS THE BEGINNING OF MY DREAM...

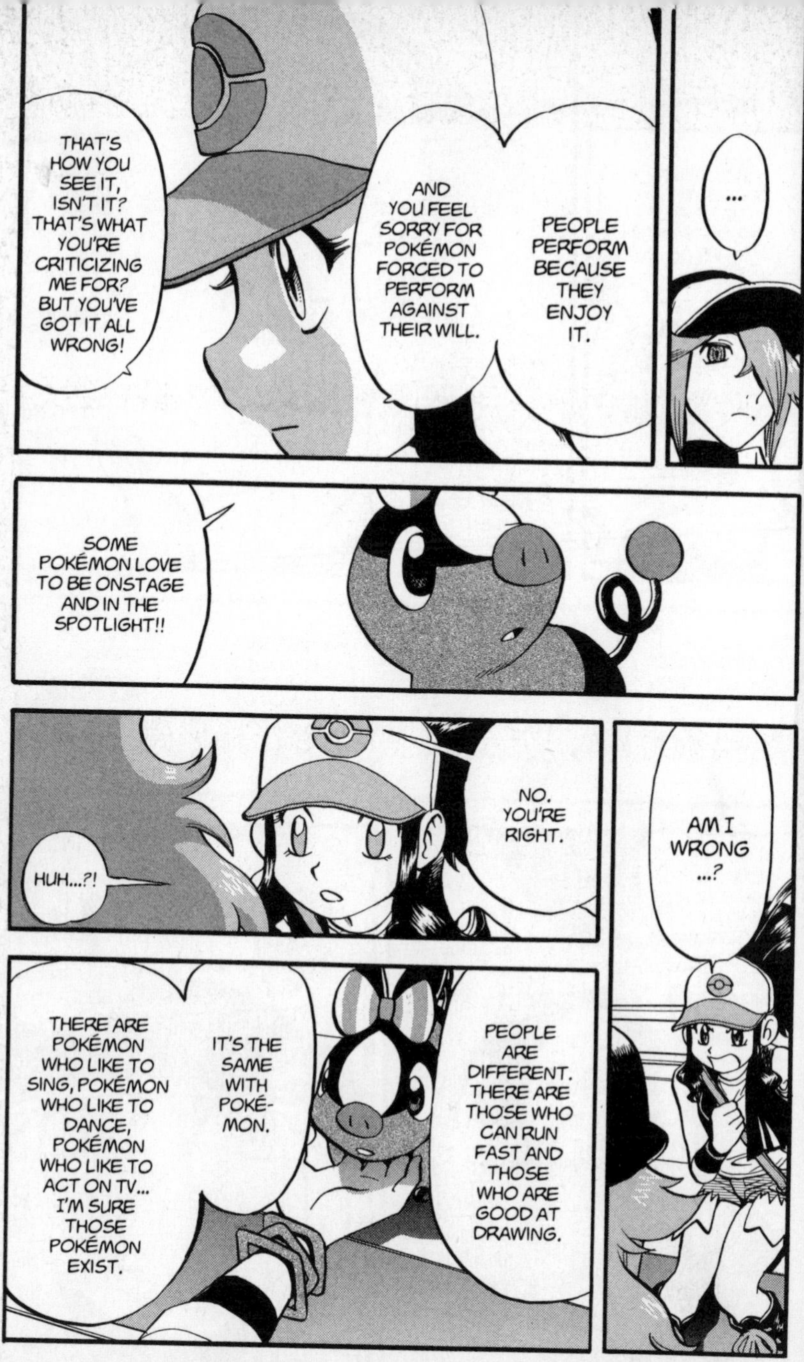
...
PEOPLE PERFORM BECAUSE THEY ENJOY IT.
AND YOU FEEL SORRY FOR POKÉMON FORCED TO PERFORM AGAINST THEIR WILL.
THAT'S HOW YOU SEE IT, ISN'T IT? THAT'S WHAT YOU'RE CRITICIZING ME FOR? BUT YOU'VE GOT IT ALL WRONG!
SOME POKÉMON LOVE TO BE ONSTAGE AND IN THE SPOTLIGHT!!
AM I WRONG ...?
NO. YOU'RE RIGHT.
HUH...?!
PEOPLE ARE DIFFERENT. THERE ARE THOSE WHO CAN RUN FAST AND THOSE WHO ARE GOOD AT DRAWING.
IT'S THE SAME WITH POKÉ-MON.
THERE ARE POKÉMON WHO LIKE TO SING, POKÉMON WHO LIKE TO DANCE, POKÉMON WHO LIKE TO ACT ON TV... I'M SURE THOSE POKÉMON EXIST.

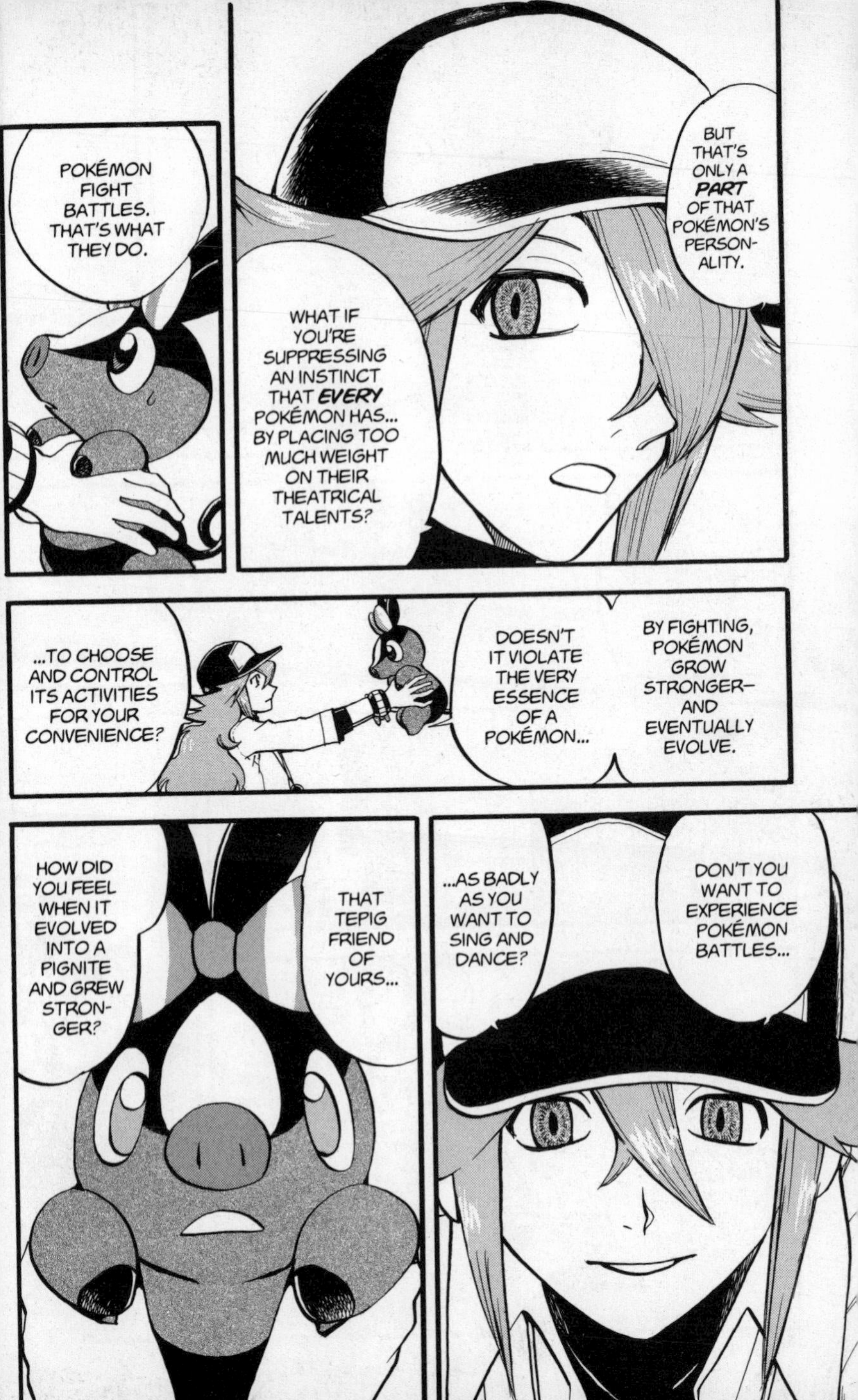
BUT THAT'S ONLY A **PART** OF THAT POKÉMON'S PERSON-ALITY.
WHAT IF YOU'RE SUPPRESSING AN INSTINCT THAT **EVERY** POKÉMON HAS... BY PLACING TOO MUCH WEIGHT ON THEIR THEATRICAL TALENTS?
POKÉMON FIGHT BATTLES. THAT'S WHAT THEY DO.
BY FIGHTING, POKÉMON GROW STRONGER—AND EVENTUALLY EVOLVE.
DOESN'T IT VIOLATE THE VERY ESSENCE OF A POKÉMON...
...TO CHOOSE AND CONTROL ITS ACTIVITIES FOR YOUR CONVENIENCE?
DON'T YOU WANT TO EXPERIENCE POKÉMON BATTLES...
...AS BADLY AS YOU WANT TO SING AND DANCE?
THAT TEPIG FRIEND OF YOURS...
HOW DID YOU FEEL WHEN IT EVOLVED INTO A PIGNITE AND GREW STRONGER-GER?

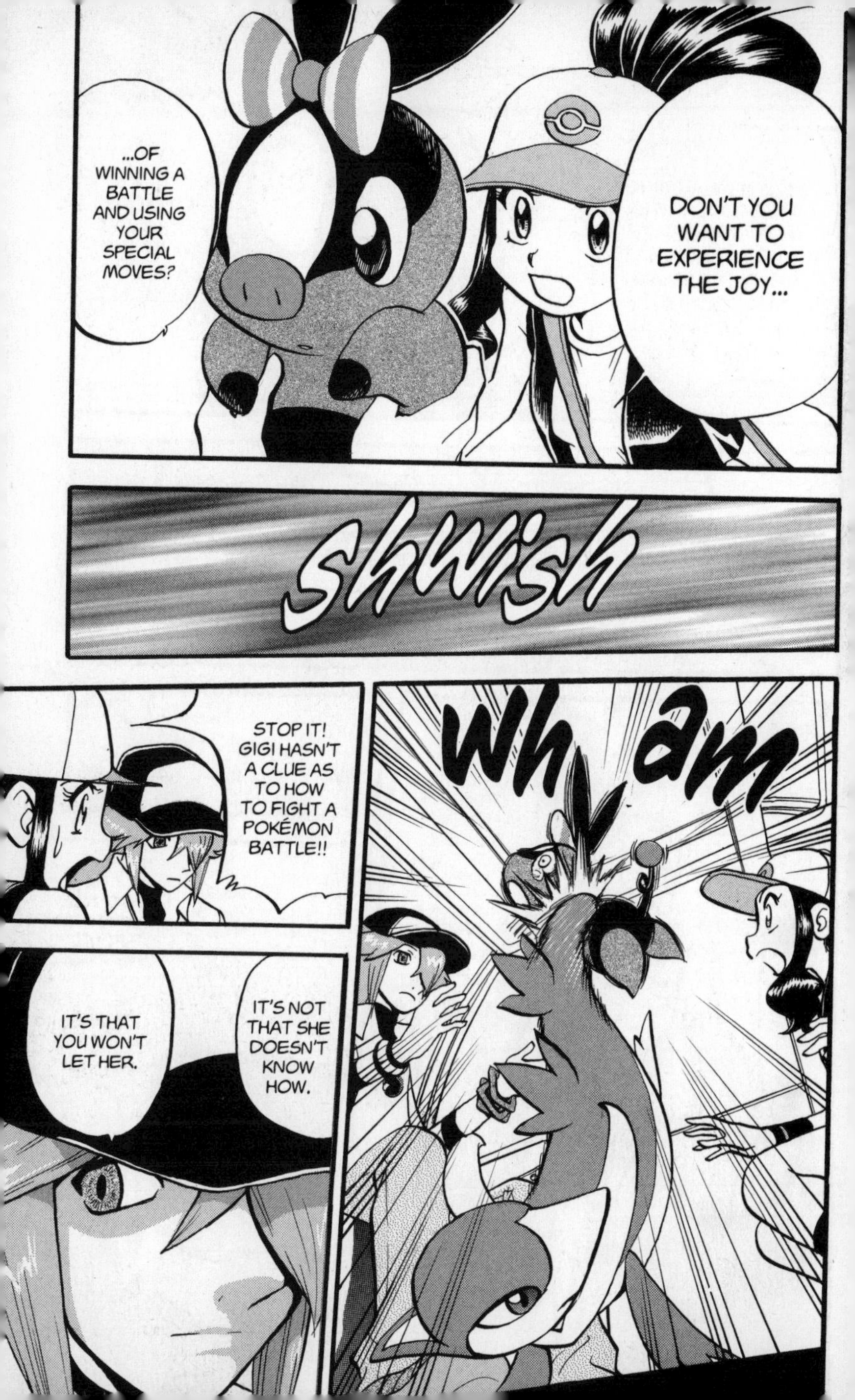
DON'T YOU WANT TO EXPERIENCE THE JOY...
...OF WINNING A BATTLE AND USING YOUR SPECIAL MOVES?
shwish
wham
STOP IT! GIGI HASN'T A CLUE AS TO HOW TO FIGHT A POKÉMON BATTLE!!
IT'S NOT THAT SHE DOESN'T KNOW HOW.
IT'S THAT YOU WON'T LET HER.

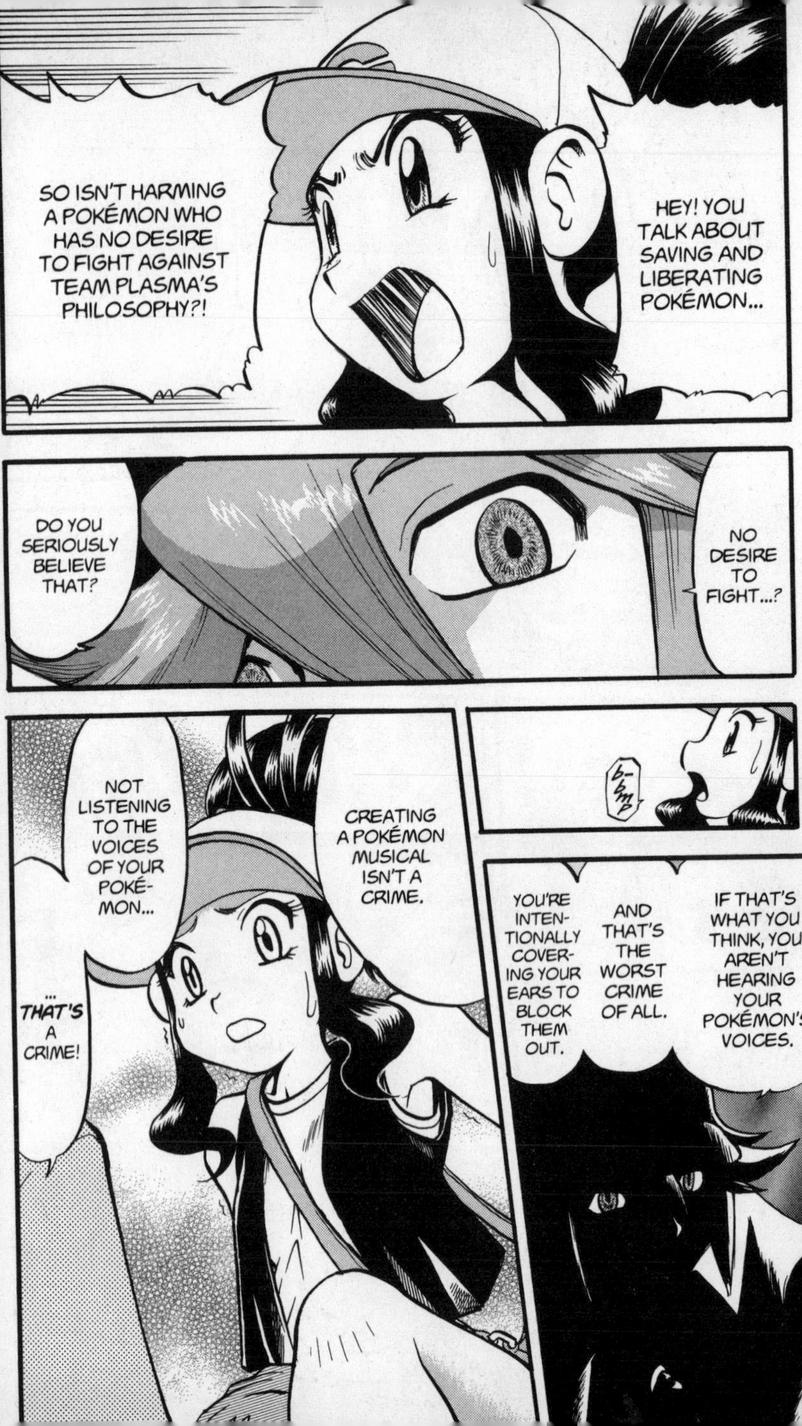
HEY! YOU TALK ABOUT SAVING AND LIBERATING POKÉMON...
SO ISN'T HARMING A POKÉMON WHO HAS NO DESIRE TO FIGHT AGAINST TEAM PLASMA'S PHILOSOPHY?!
NO DESIRE TO FIGHT...?
DO YOU SERIOUSLY BELIEVE THAT?
b-bmp
IF THAT'S WHAT YOU THINK, YOU AREN'T HEARING YOUR POKÉMON'S VOICES.
AND THAT'S THE WORST CRIME OF ALL.
YOU'RE INTENTIONALLY COVERING YOUR EARS TO BLOCK THEM OUT.
CREATING A POKÉMON MUSICAL ISN'T A CRIME.
NOT LISTENING TO THE VOICES OF YOUR POKÉMON...
...THAT'S A CRIME!

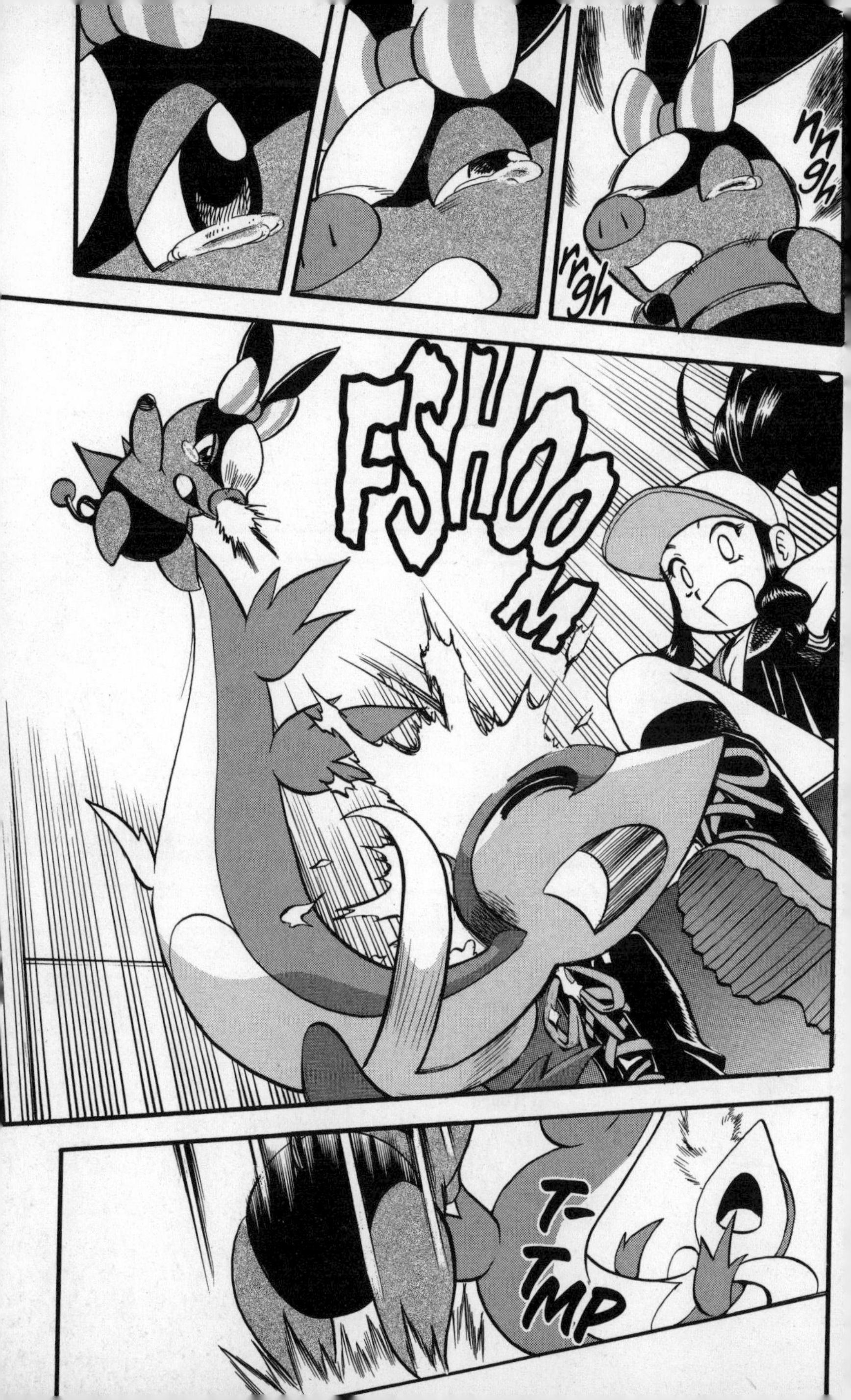
nngh
rrgh
FSHOOM
T-TMP

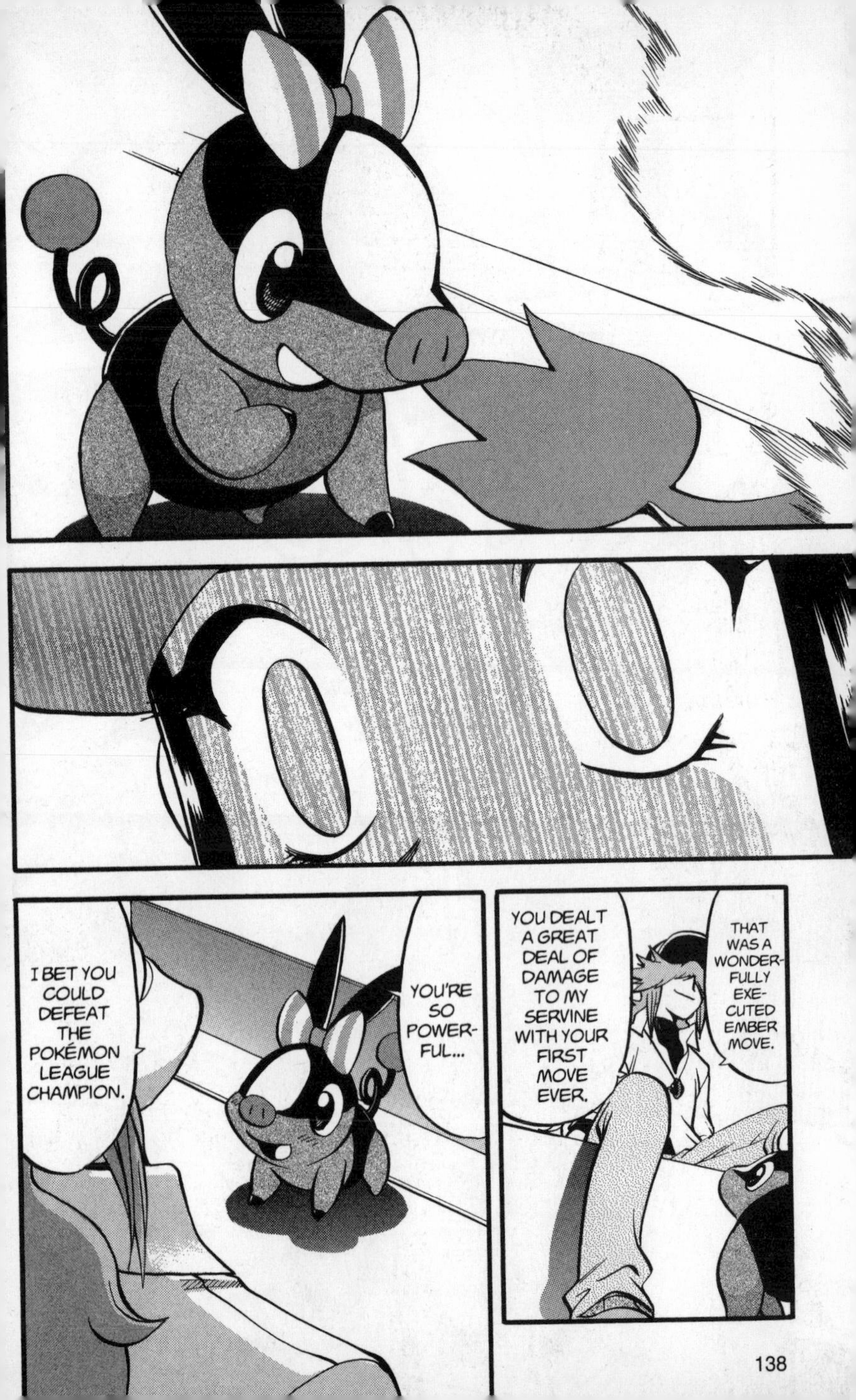
THAT WAS A WONDERFULLY EXECUTED EMBER MOVE.
YOU DEALT A GREAT DEAL OF DAMAGE TO MY SERVINE WITH YOUR FIRST MOVE EVER.
YOU'RE SO POWERFUL...
I BET YOU COULD DEFEAT THE POKÉMON LEAGUE CHAMPION.

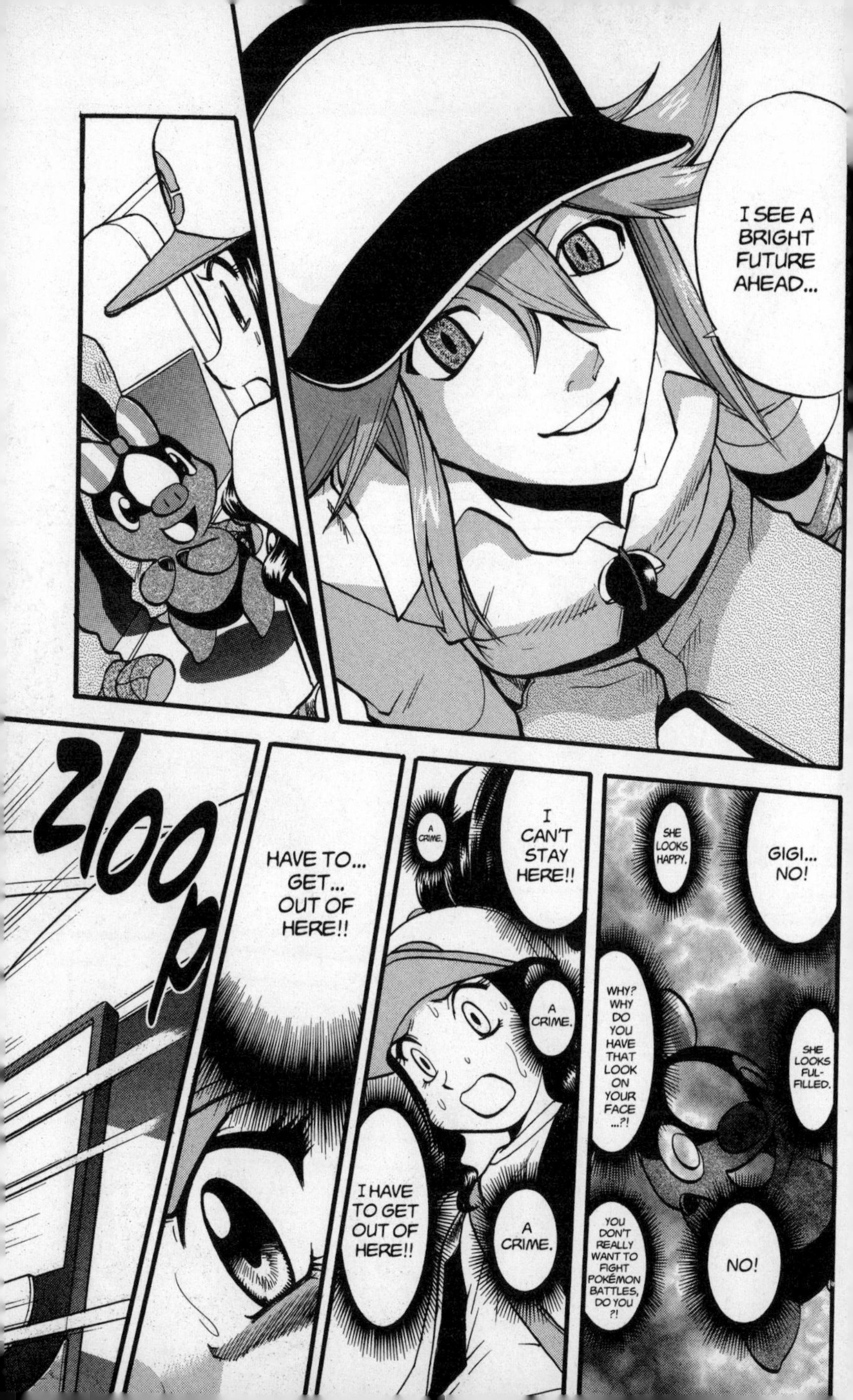
I SEE A BRIGHT FUTURE AHEAD...
GIGI... NO!
SHE LOOKS HAPPY.
SHE LOOKS FUL-FILLED.
WHY? WHY DO YOU HAVE THAT LOOK ON YOUR FACE ...?!
NO!
YOU DON'T REALLY WANT TO FIGHT POKÉMON BATTLES, DO YOU ?!
I CAN'T STAY HERE!!
A CRIME.
A CRIME.
A CRIME.
I HAVE TO GET OUT OF HERE!!
HAVE TO... GET... OUT OF HERE!!
ZLOOP

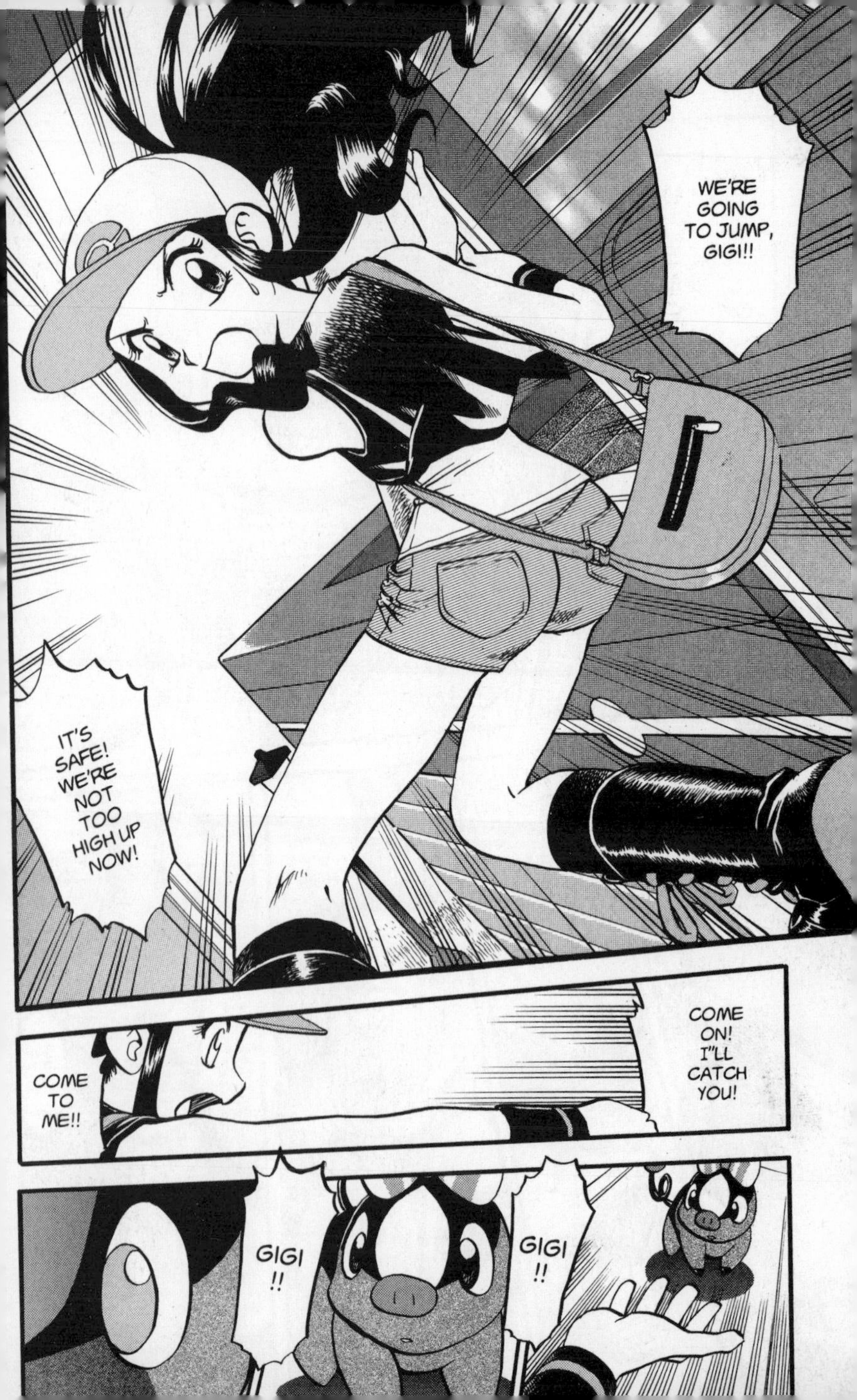
WE'RE GOING TO JUMP, GIGI!!
IT'S SAFE! WE'RE NOT TOO HIGH UP NOW!
COME ON! I'LL CATCH YOU!
COME TO ME!!
GIGI !!
GIGI !!

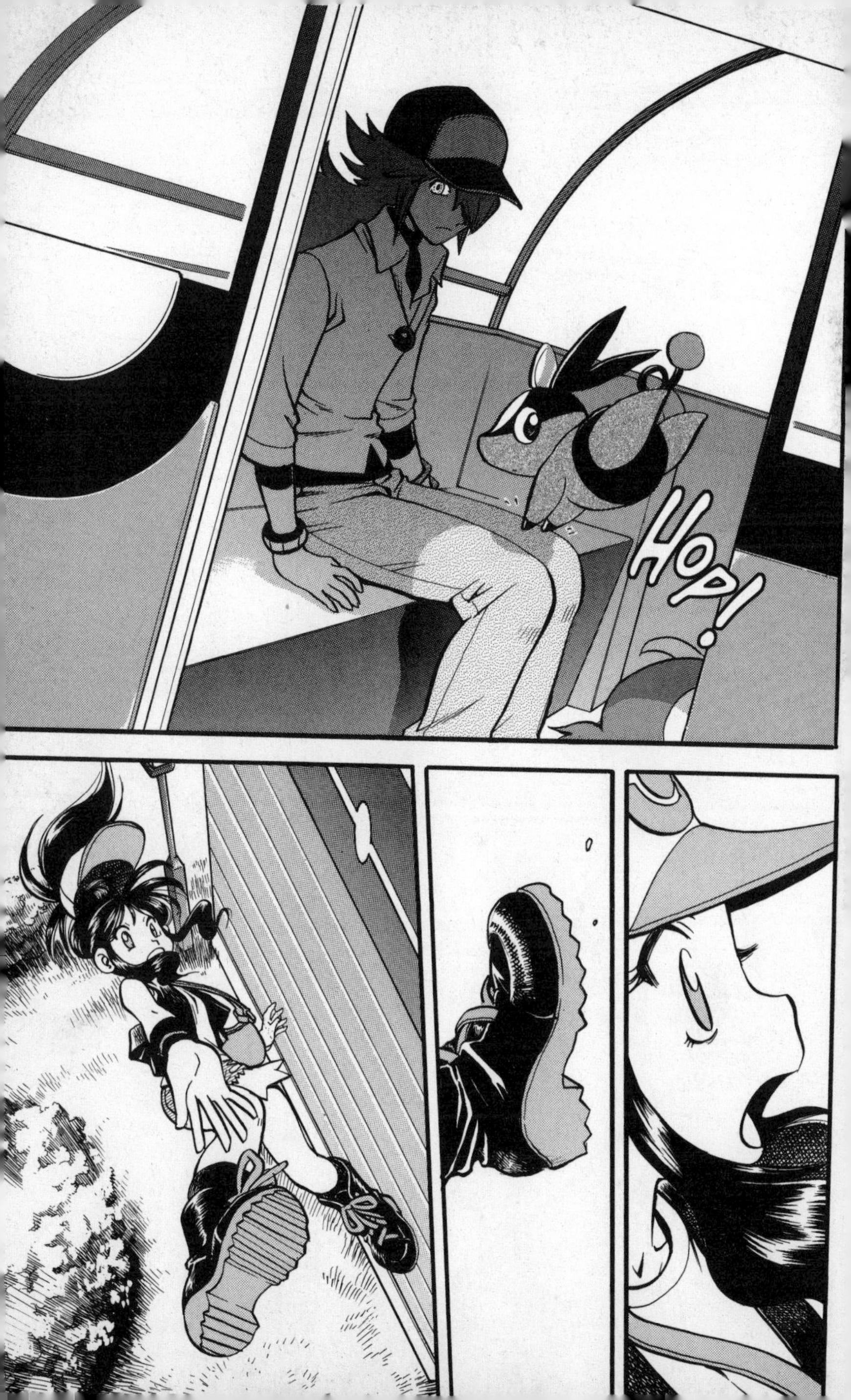
HOP!

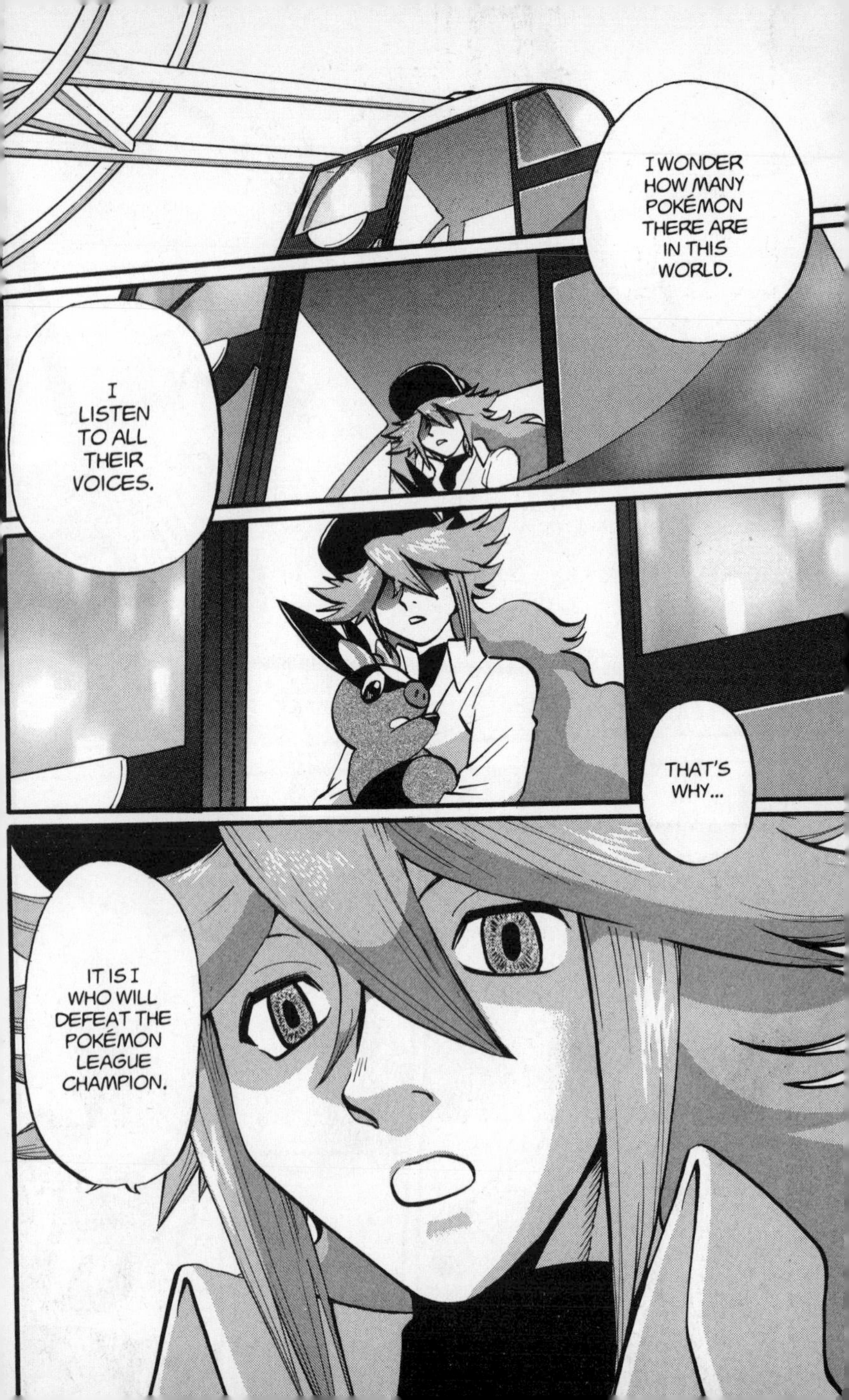
I WONDER HOW MANY POKÉMON THERE ARE IN THIS WORLD.
I LISTEN TO ALL THEIR VOICES.
THAT'S WHY...
IT IS I WHO WILL DEFEAT THE POKÉMON LEAGUE CHAMPION.

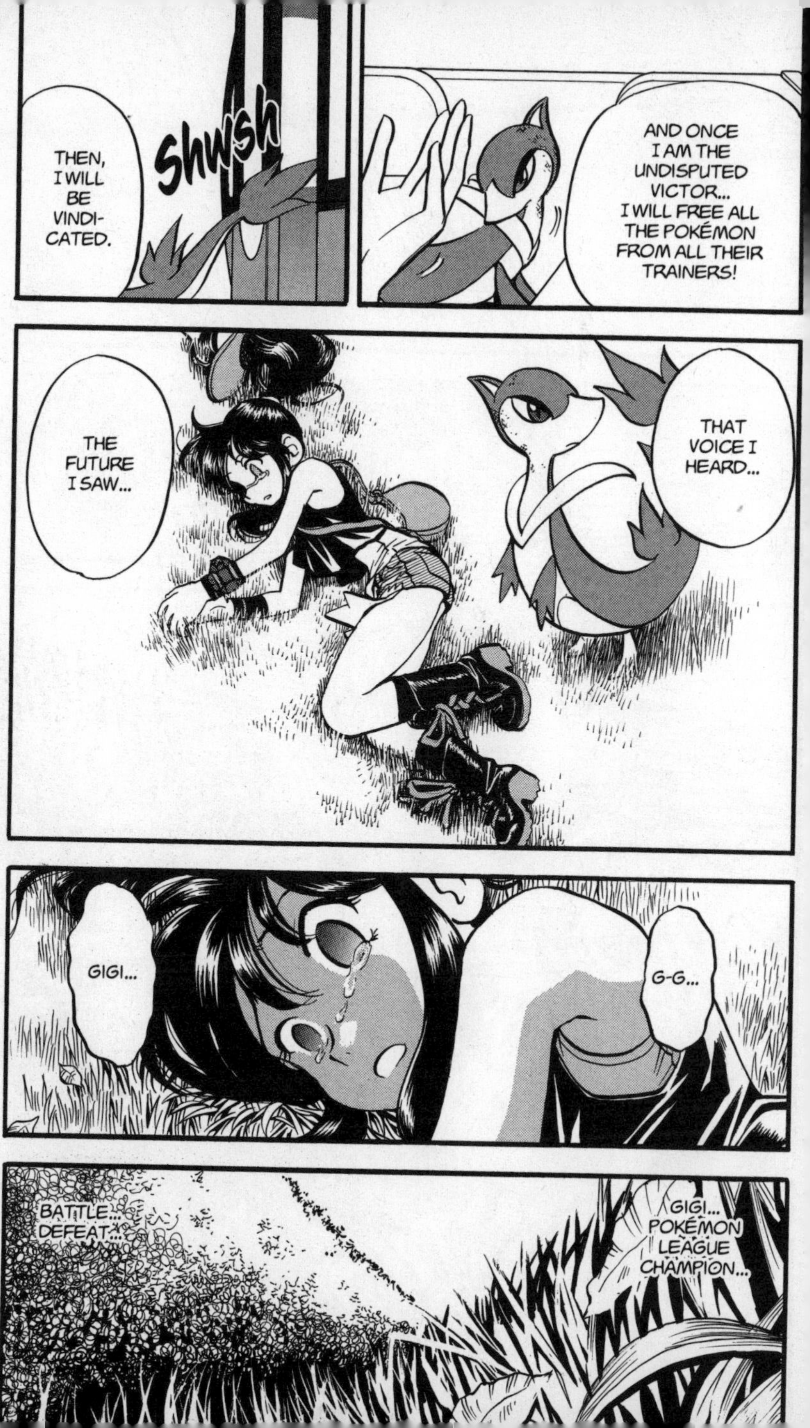
AND ONCE I AM THE UNDISPUTED VICTOR... I WILL FREE ALL THE POKÉMON FROM ALL THEIR TRAINERS!
Shwsh
THEN, I WILL BE VINDI-CATED.
THAT VOICE I HEARD...
THE FUTURE I SAW...
G-G...
GIGI...
GIGI... POKÉMON LEAGUE CHAMPION...
BATTLE... DEFEAT...

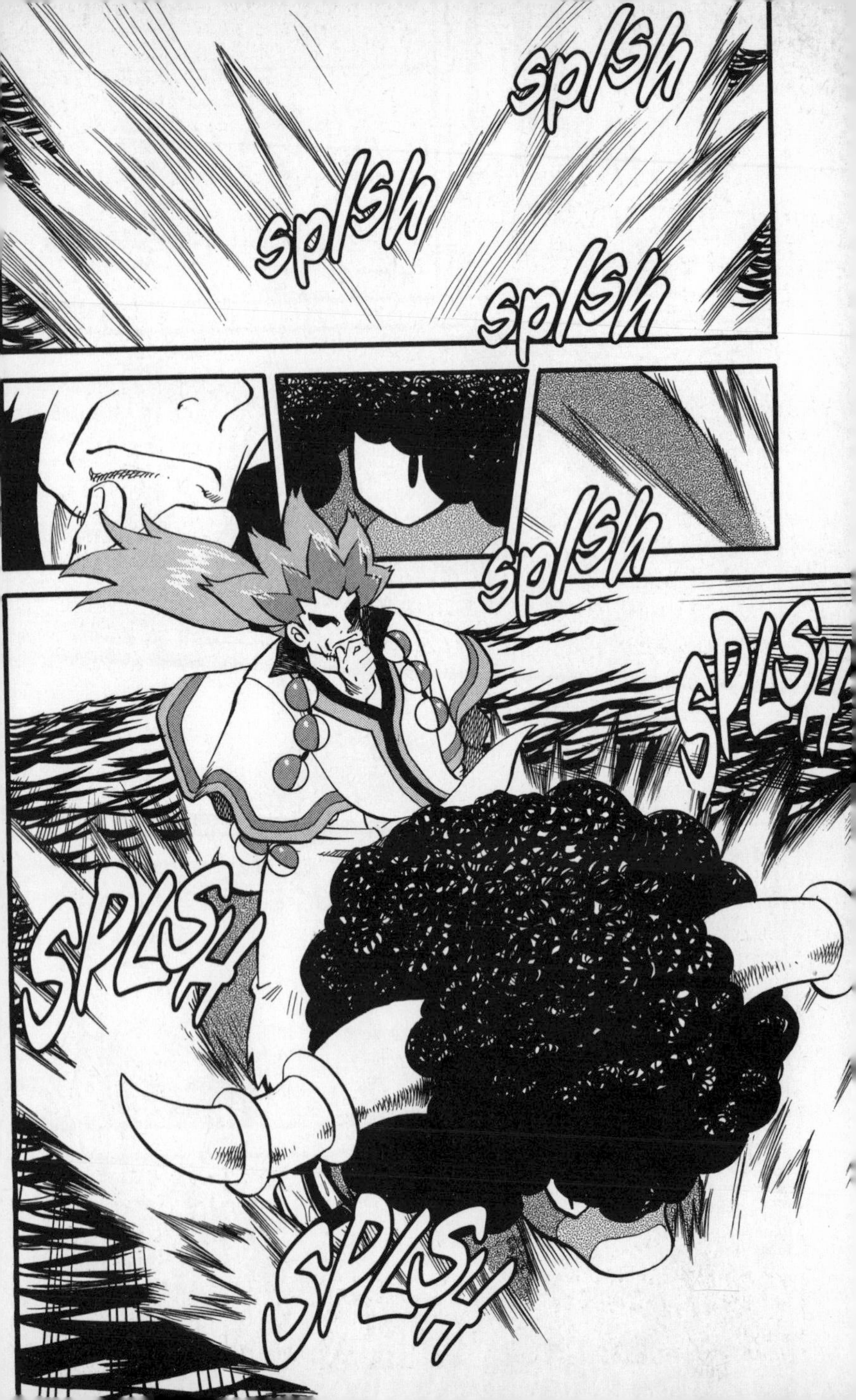
splsh
splsh
splsh
splsh
SPLSH
SPLSH
SPLSH

Final Destination:
Pokémon League

Current Location:
Nimbasa City

Fire Pig Pokémon **Nite**
Pignite ♂ | Fire | Fighting |
Lv.26 Ability: Blaze

Dream Eater Pokémon **Musha**
Munna ♂ | Psychic |
Lv.46 Ability: Forewarn

Valiant Pokémon **Brav**
Braviary ♂ | Normal | Flying |
Lv.54 Ability: Sheer Force

EleSpider Pokémon **Tula**
Galvantula ♂ | Bug | Electric |
Lv.49 Ability: Unnerve

BLACK

WHITE

Grass Snake Pokémon **Servine**
Servine ♀ | Grass |
Lv.18 Ability: Overgrow

TRIO BADGE | BASIC BADGE | INSECT BADGE | BOLT BADGE | ? | ? | ? | ? | ?

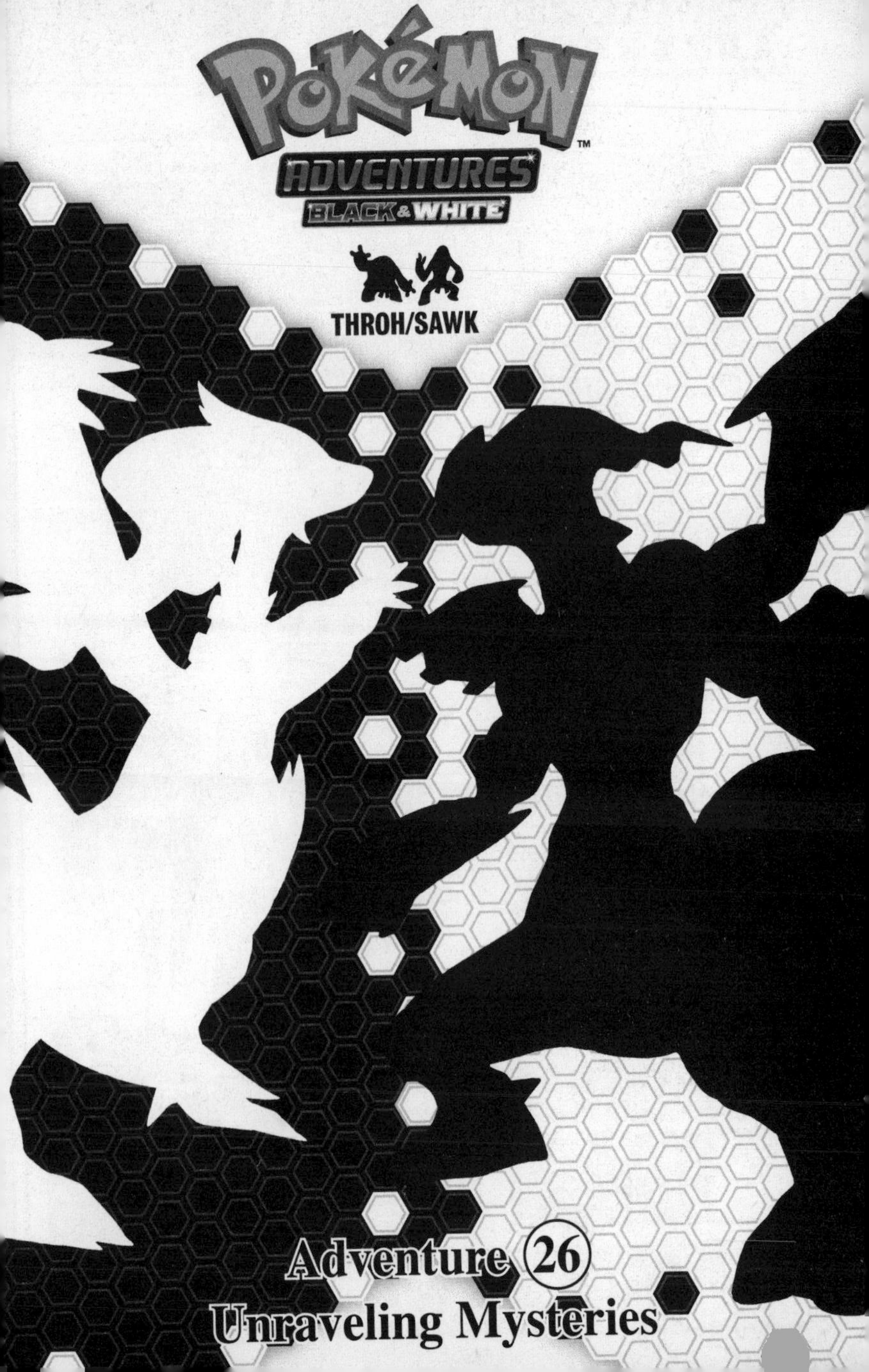
Pokémon™
ADVENTURES
BLACK & WHITE
THROH/SAWK
Adventure 26
Unraveling Mysteries

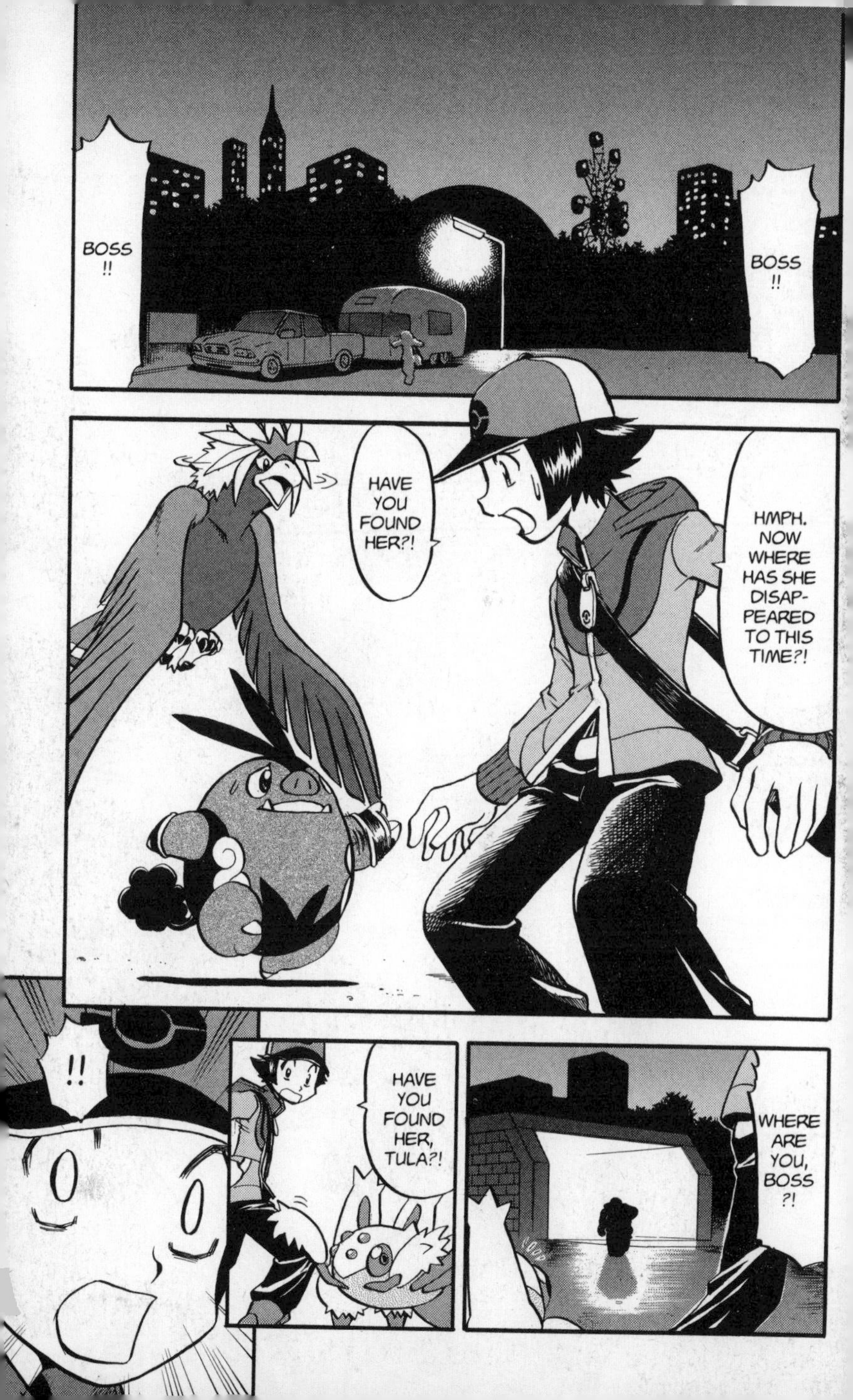
BOSS !!
BOSS !!
HMPH. NOW WHERE HAS SHE DISAP-PEARED TO THIS TIME?!
HAVE YOU FOUND HER?!
WHERE ARE YOU, BOSS ?!
HAVE YOU FOUND HER, TULA?!
!!

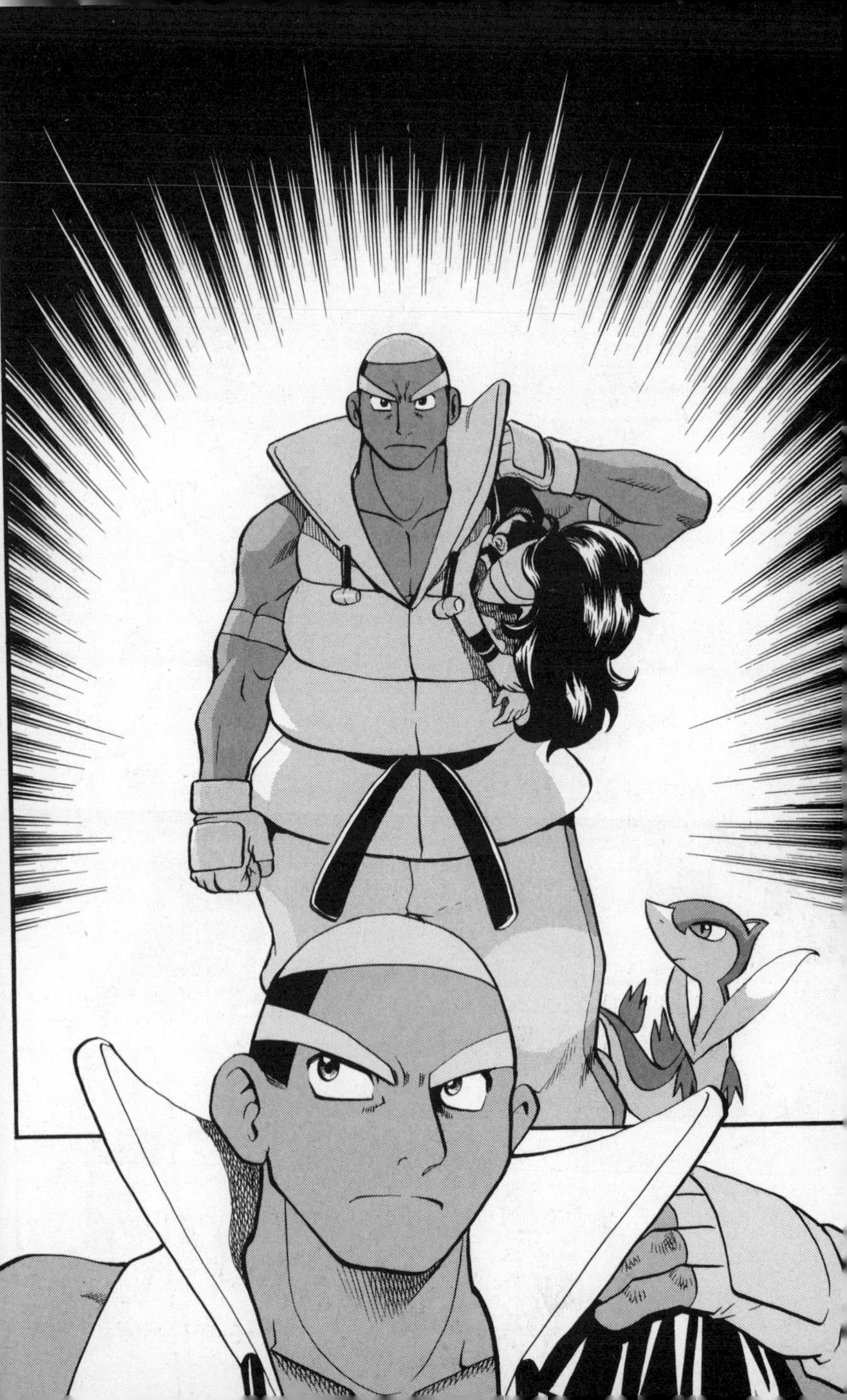

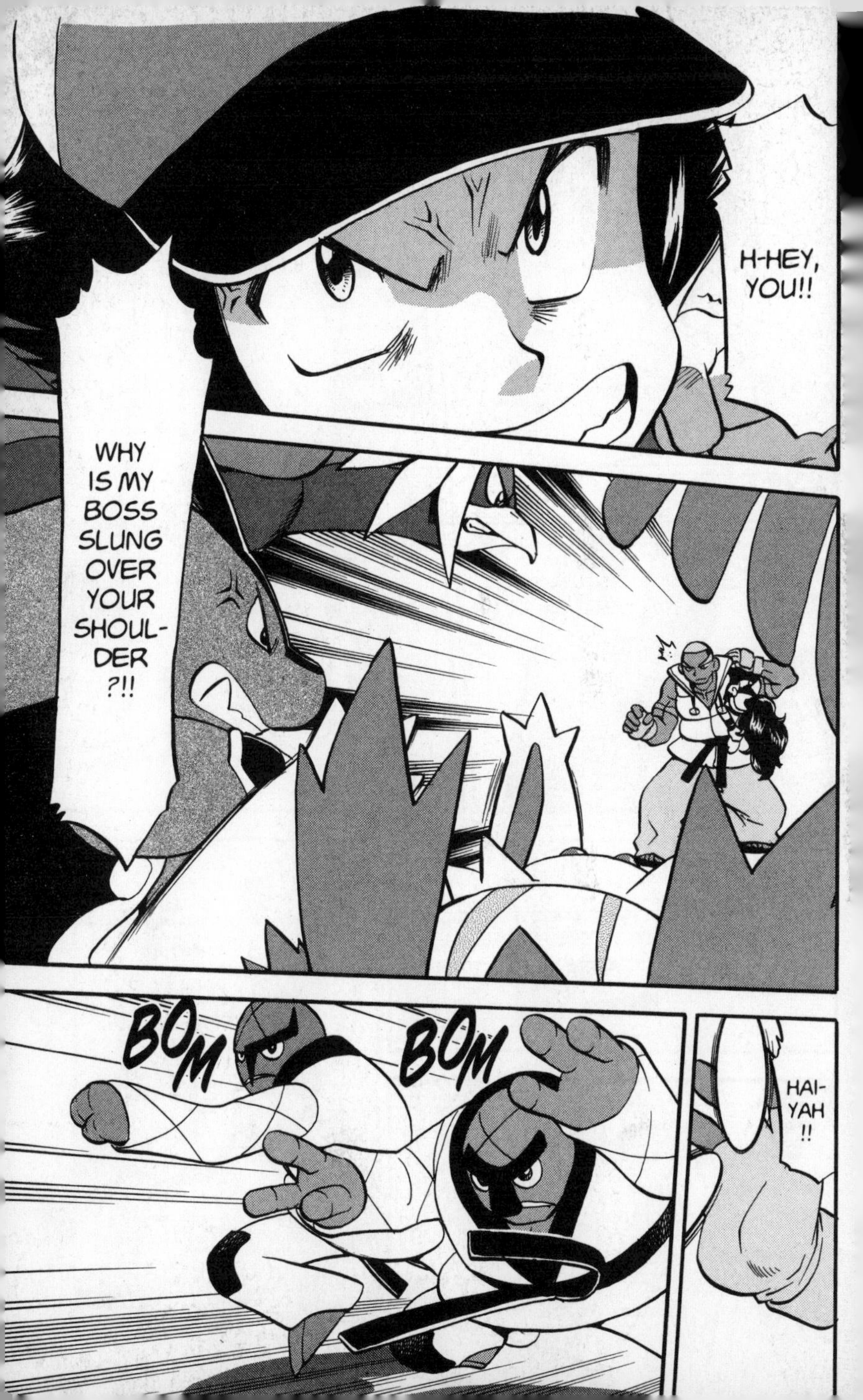
H-HEY, YOU!!
WHY IS MY BOSS SLUNG OVER YOUR SHOUL-DER ?!!
HAI-YAH !!
BOM
BOM

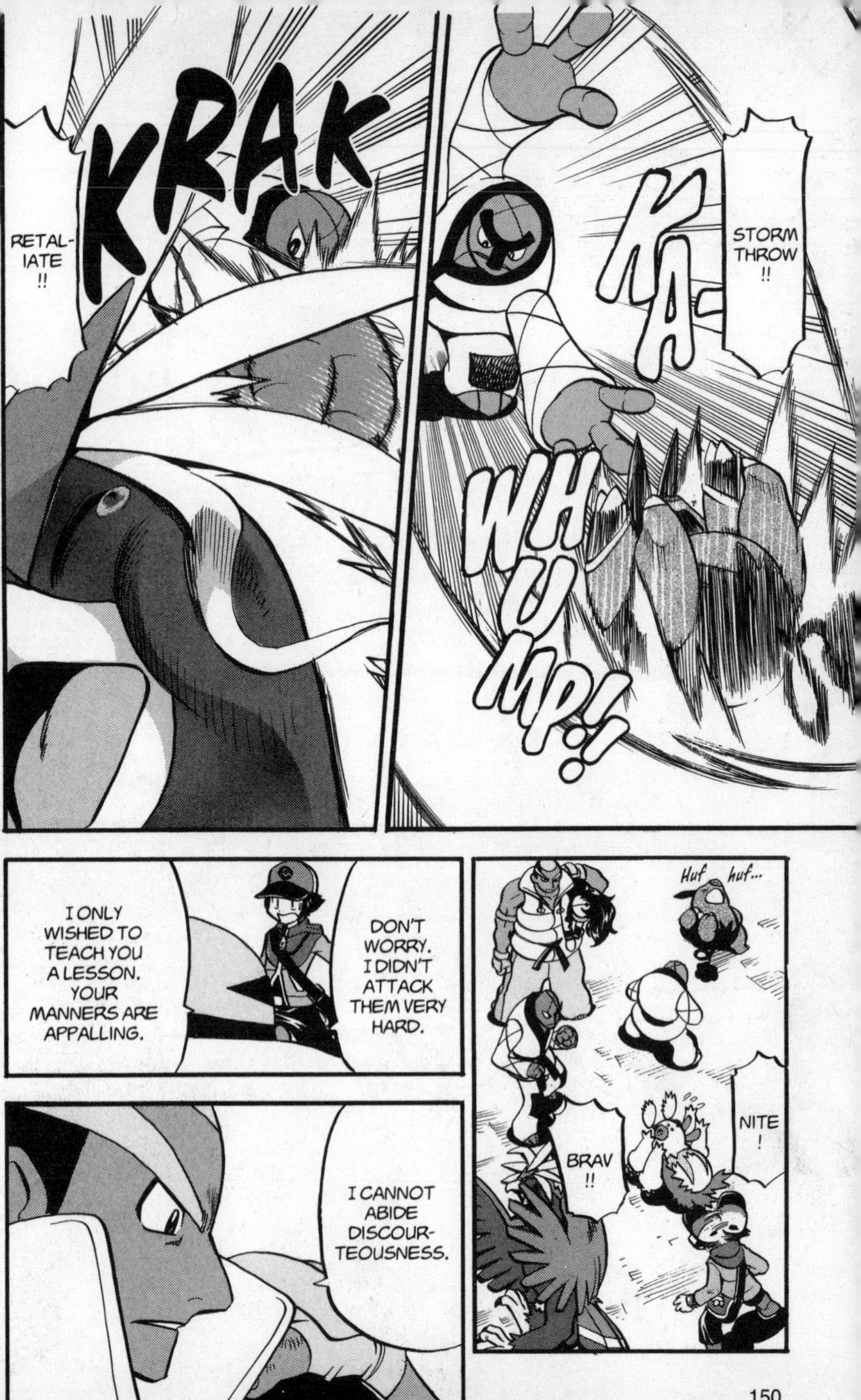
STORM THROW !!
KA-
WHUMP!!
KRAK
RETAL- IATE !!
Huf huf...
NITE !
BRAV !!
DON'T WORRY. I DIDN'T ATTACK THEM VERY HARD.
I ONLY WISHED TO TEACH YOU A LESSON. YOUR MANNERS ARE APPALLING.
I CANNOT ABIDE DISCOUR- TEOUSNESS.

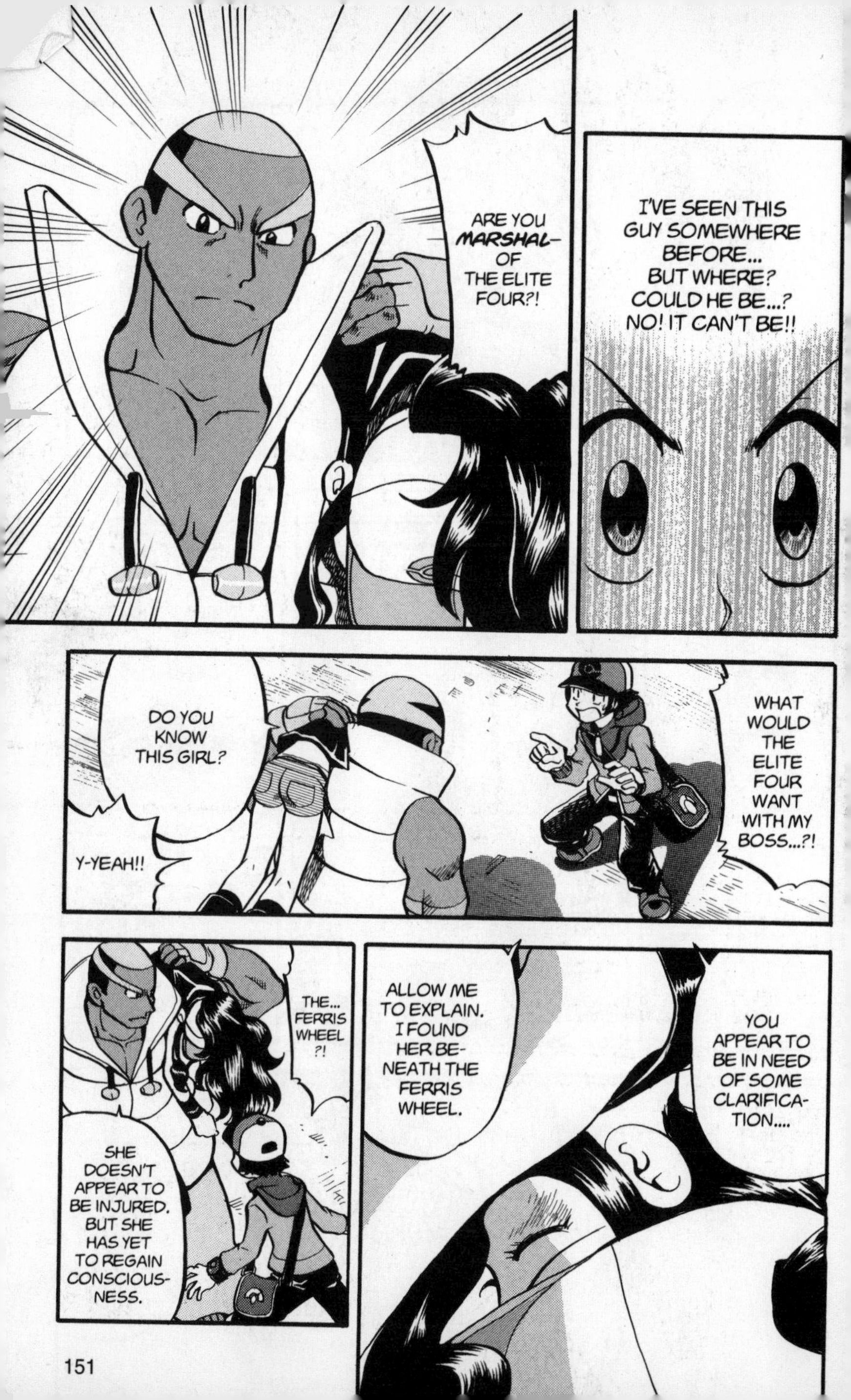
I'VE SEEN THIS GUY SOMEWHERE BEFORE... BUT WHERE? COULD HE BE...? NO! IT CAN'T BE!!
ARE YOU *MARSHAL*— OF THE ELITE FOUR?!
WHAT WOULD THE ELITE FOUR WANT WITH MY BOSS...?!
DO YOU KNOW THIS GIRL?
Y-YEAH!!
YOU APPEAR TO BE IN NEED OF SOME CLARIFICATION....
ALLOW ME TO EXPLAIN. I FOUND HER BENEATH THE FERRIS WHEEL.
THE... FERRIS WHEEL ?!
SHE DOESN'T APPEAR TO BE INJURED. BUT SHE HAS YET TO REGAIN CONSCIOUSNESS.

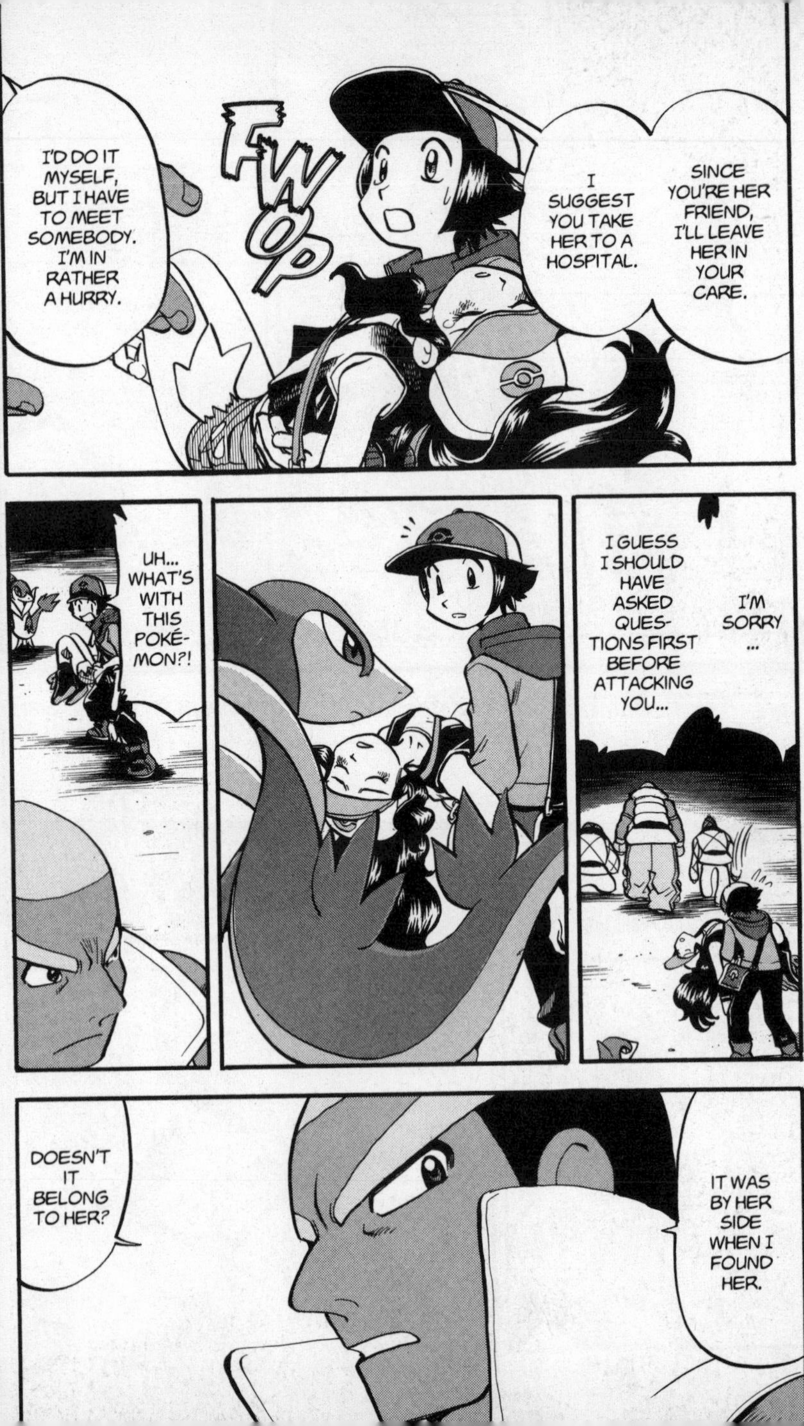
SINCE YOU'RE HER FRIEND, I'LL LEAVE HER IN YOUR CARE.
I SUGGEST YOU TAKE HER TO A HOSPITAL.
FWOP
I'D DO IT MYSELF, BUT I HAVE TO MEET SOMEBODY. I'M IN RATHER A HURRY.
I'M SORRY...
I GUESS I SHOULD HAVE ASKED QUES-TIONS FIRST BEFORE ATTACKING YOU...
UH... WHAT'S WITH THIS POKÉ-MON?!
IT WAS BY HER SIDE WHEN I FOUND HER.
DOESN'T IT BELONG TO HER?

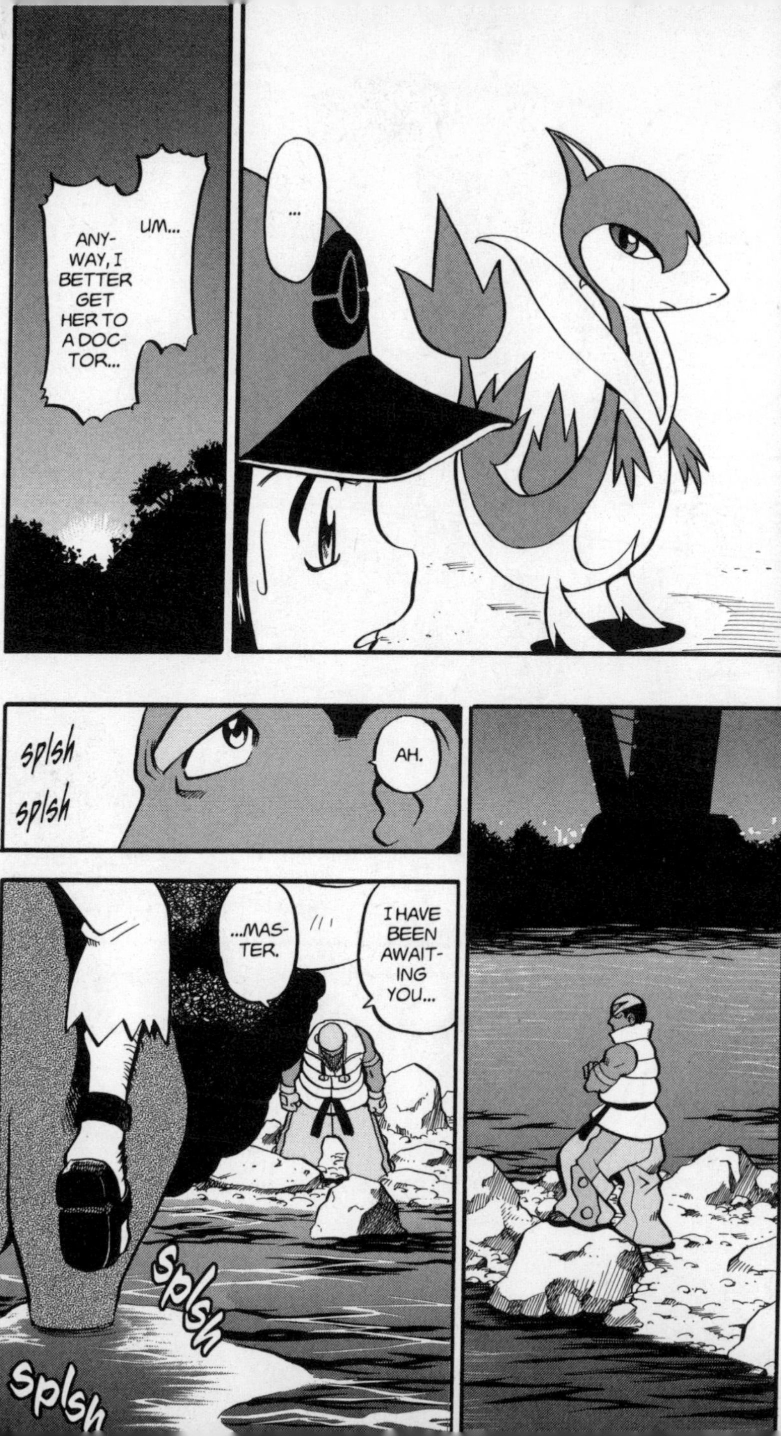
...
UM...
ANYWAY, I BETTER GET HER TO A DOCTOR...
AH.
splsh
splsh
I HAVE BEEN AWAITING YOU...
...MASTER.
splsh
splsh

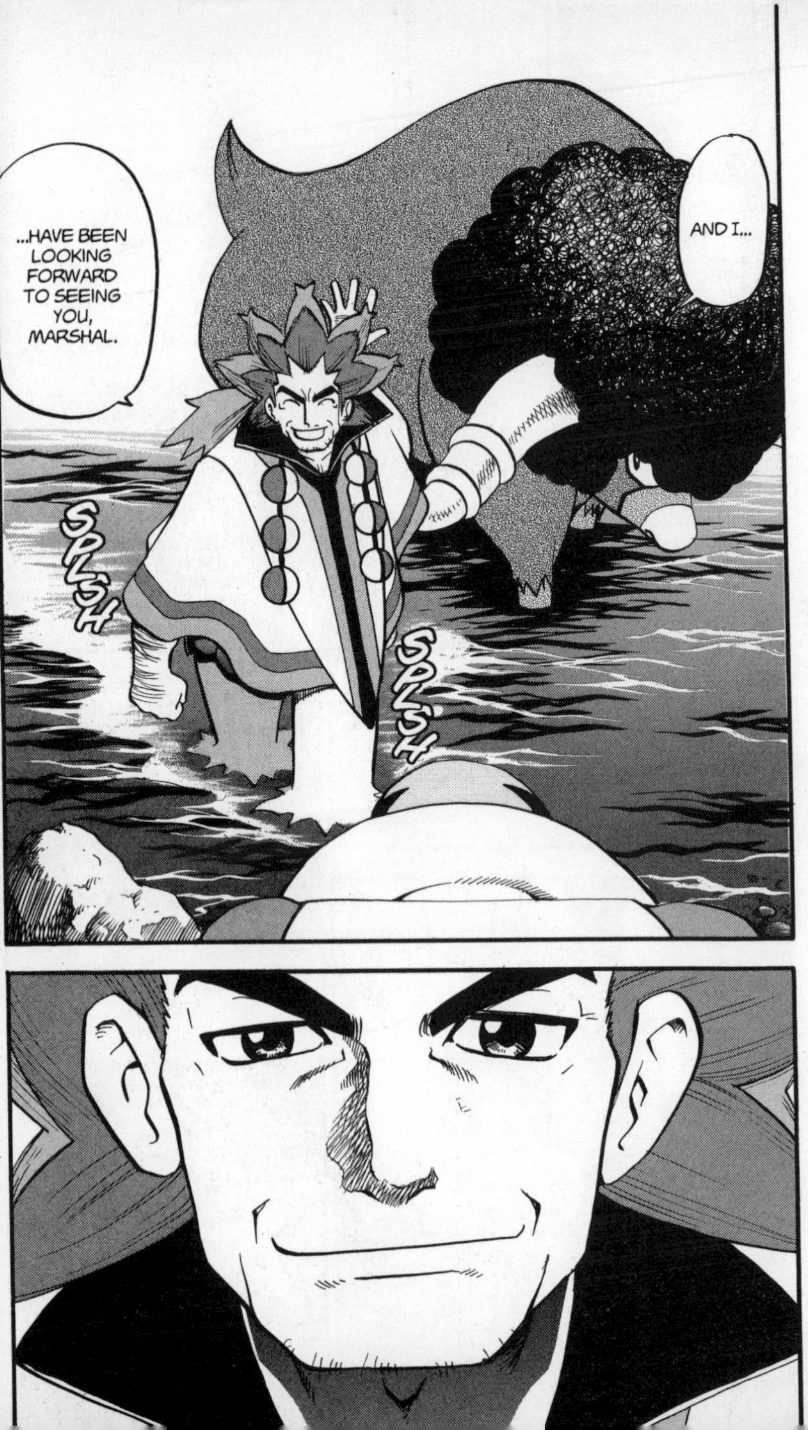
AND I...
...HAVE BEEN LOOKING FORWARD TO SEEING YOU, MARSHAL.
SPLSH
SPLSH

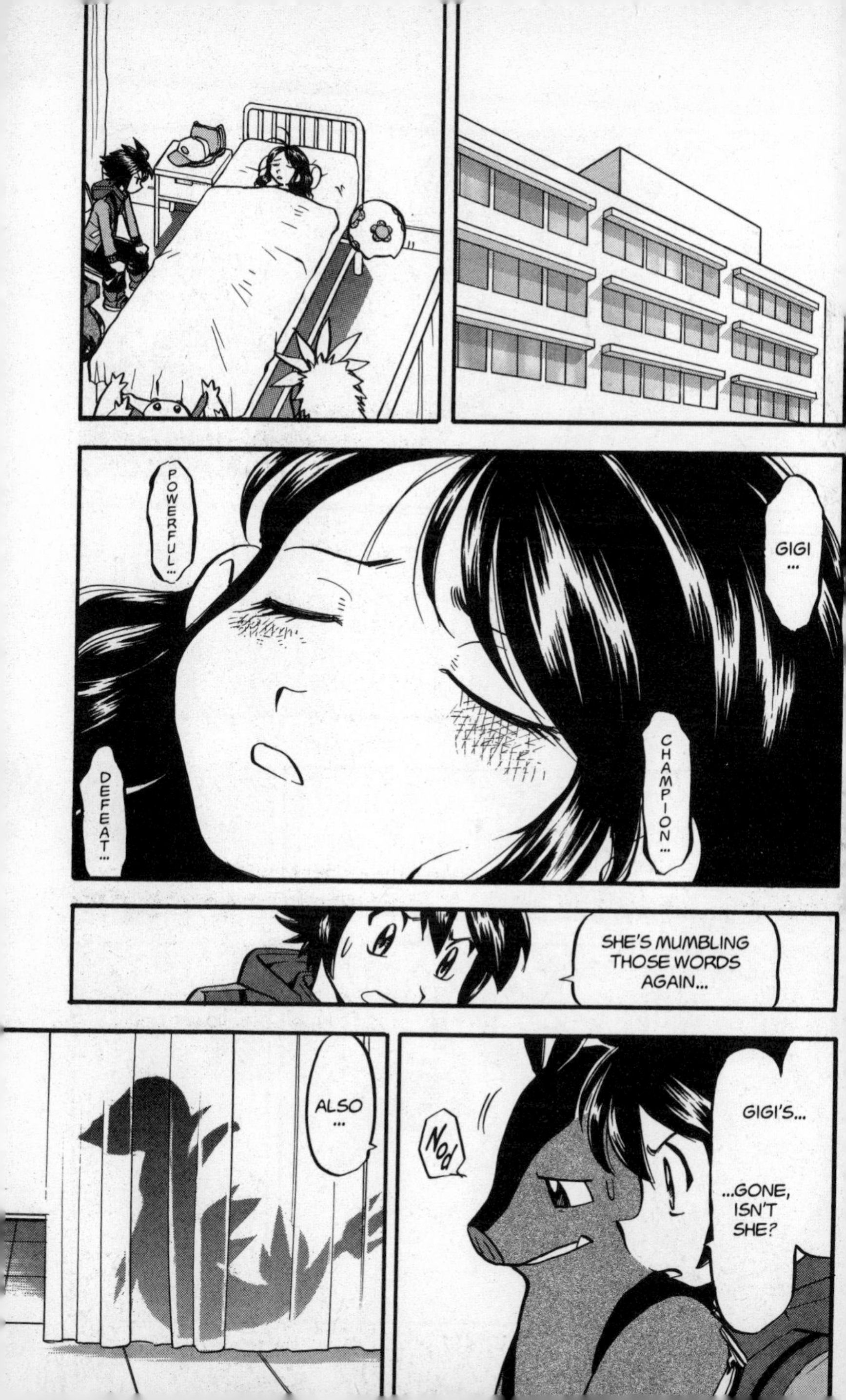
GIGI...
POWERFUL...
CHAMPION...
DEFEAT...
SHE'S MUMBLING THOSE WORDS AGAIN...
GIGI'S...
...GONE, ISN'T SHE?
Nod
ALSO...

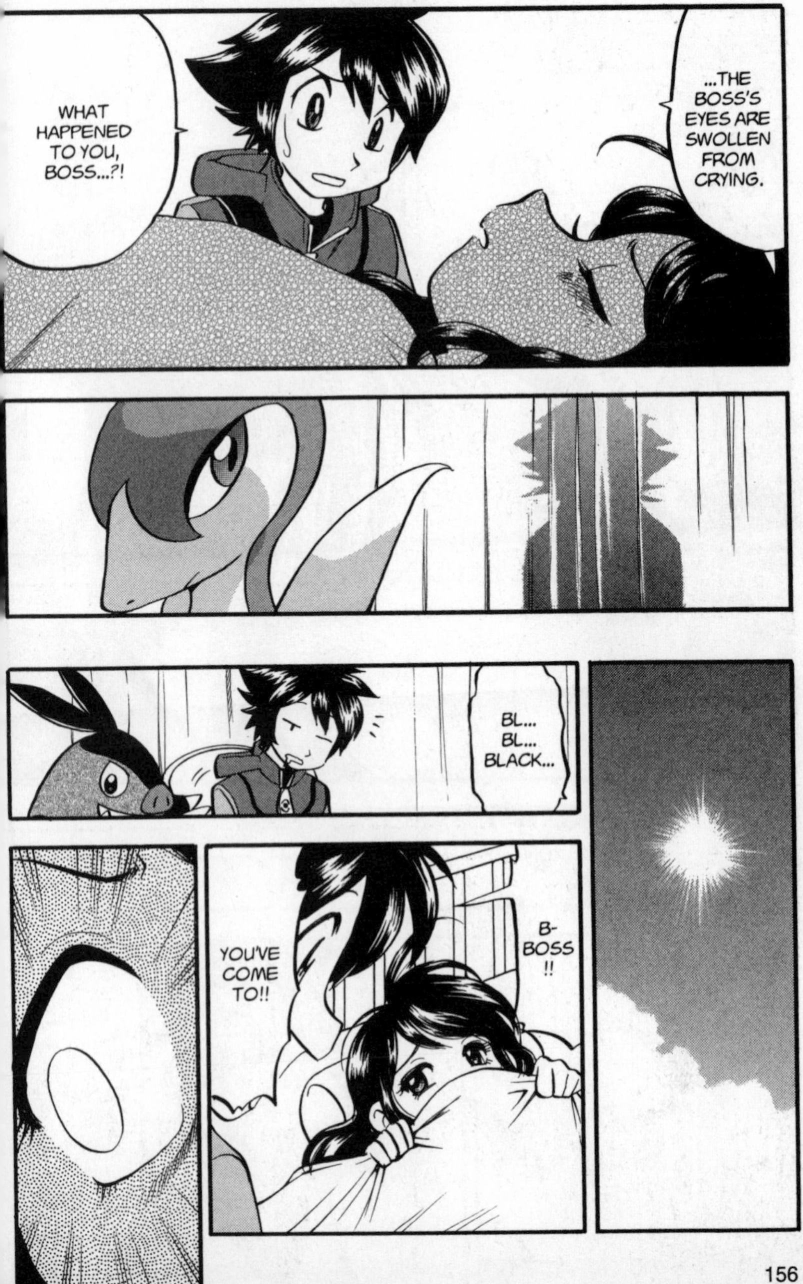
...THE BOSS'S EYES ARE SWOLLEN FROM CRYING.
WHAT HAPPENED TO YOU, BOSS...?!
BL... BL... BLACK...
B-BOSS!!
YOU'VE COME TO!!

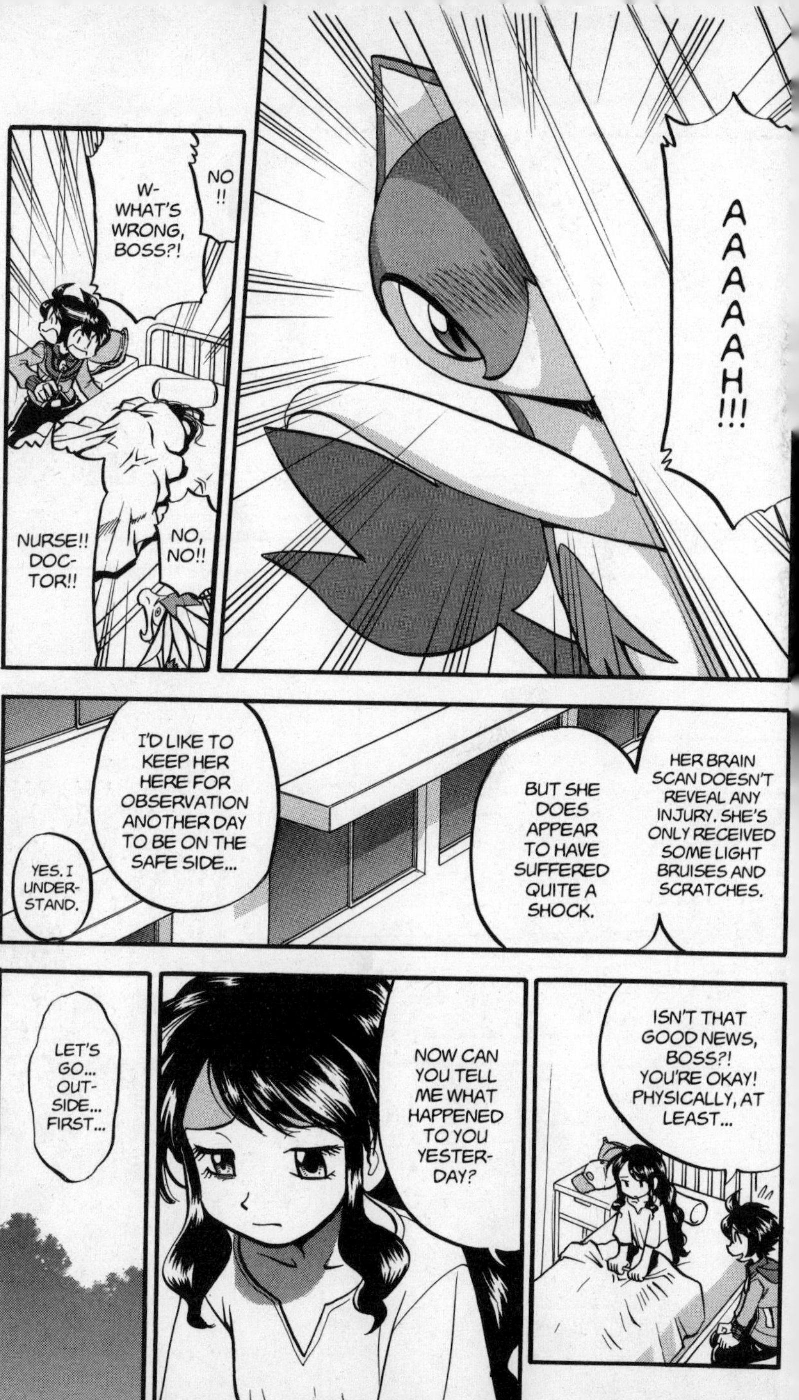
AAAAAAH!!!
NO!!
W-WHAT'S WRONG, BOSS?!
NO, NO!!
NURSE!! DOCTOR!!
HER BRAIN SCAN DOESN'T REVEAL ANY INJURY. SHE'S ONLY RECEIVED SOME LIGHT BRUISES AND SCRATCHES.
BUT SHE DOES APPEAR TO HAVE SUFFERED QUITE A SHOCK.
I'D LIKE TO KEEP HER HERE FOR OBSERVATION ANOTHER DAY TO BE ON THE SAFE SIDE...
YES. I UNDERSTAND.
ISN'T THAT GOOD NEWS, BOSS?! YOU'RE OKAY! PHYSICALLY, AT LEAST...
NOW CAN YOU TELL ME WHAT HAPPENED TO YOU YESTERDAY?
LET'S GO... OUTSIDE... FIRST...

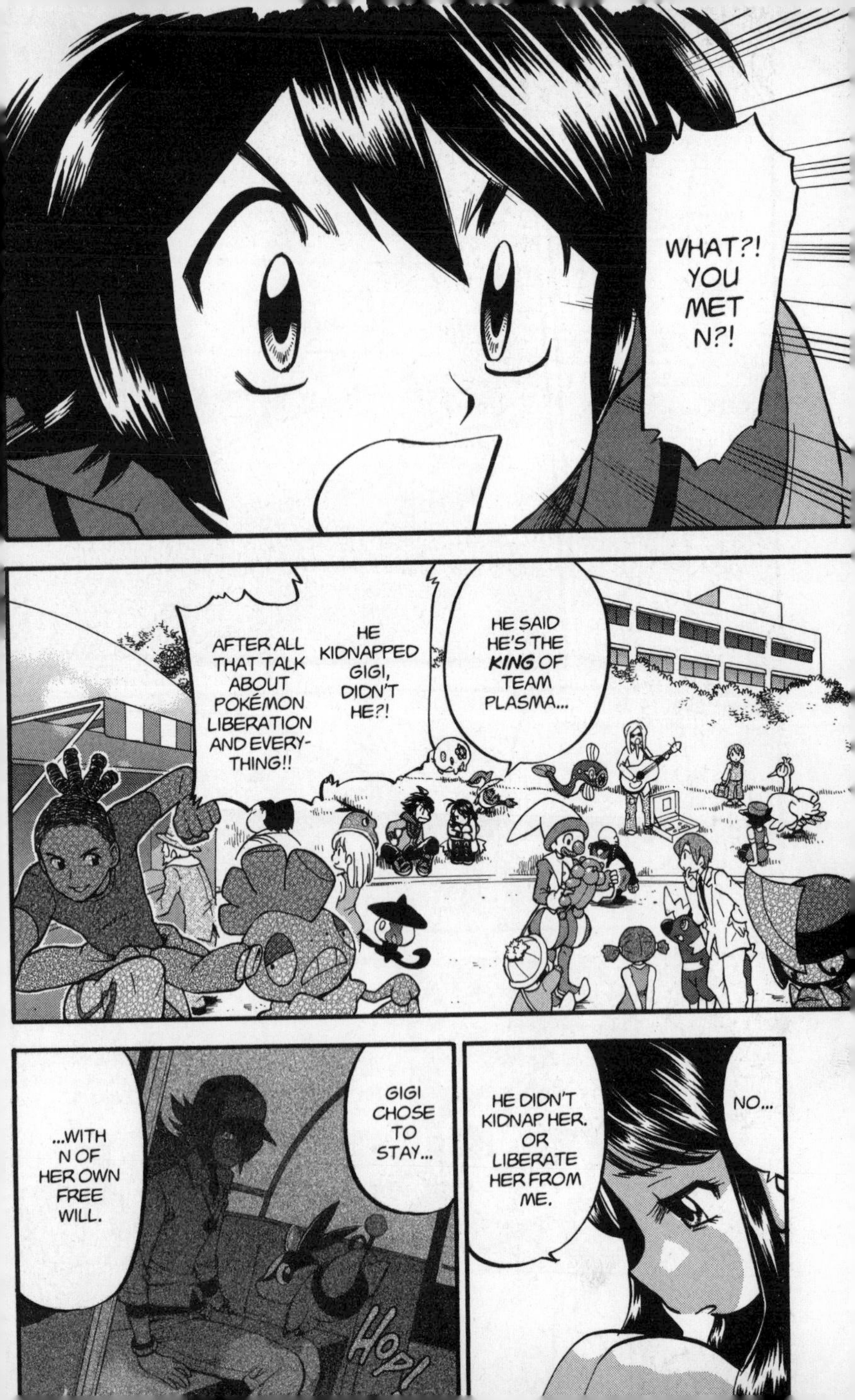
WHAT?! YOU MET N?!
HE SAID HE'S THE **KING** OF TEAM PLASMA...
HE KIDNAPPED GIGI, DIDN'T HE?!
AFTER ALL THAT TALK ABOUT POKÉMON LIBERATION AND EVERY-THING!!
NO...
HE DIDN'T KIDNAP HER. OR LIBERATE HER FROM ME.
GIGI CHOSE TO STAY...
...WITH N OF HER OWN FREE WILL.
HOP!

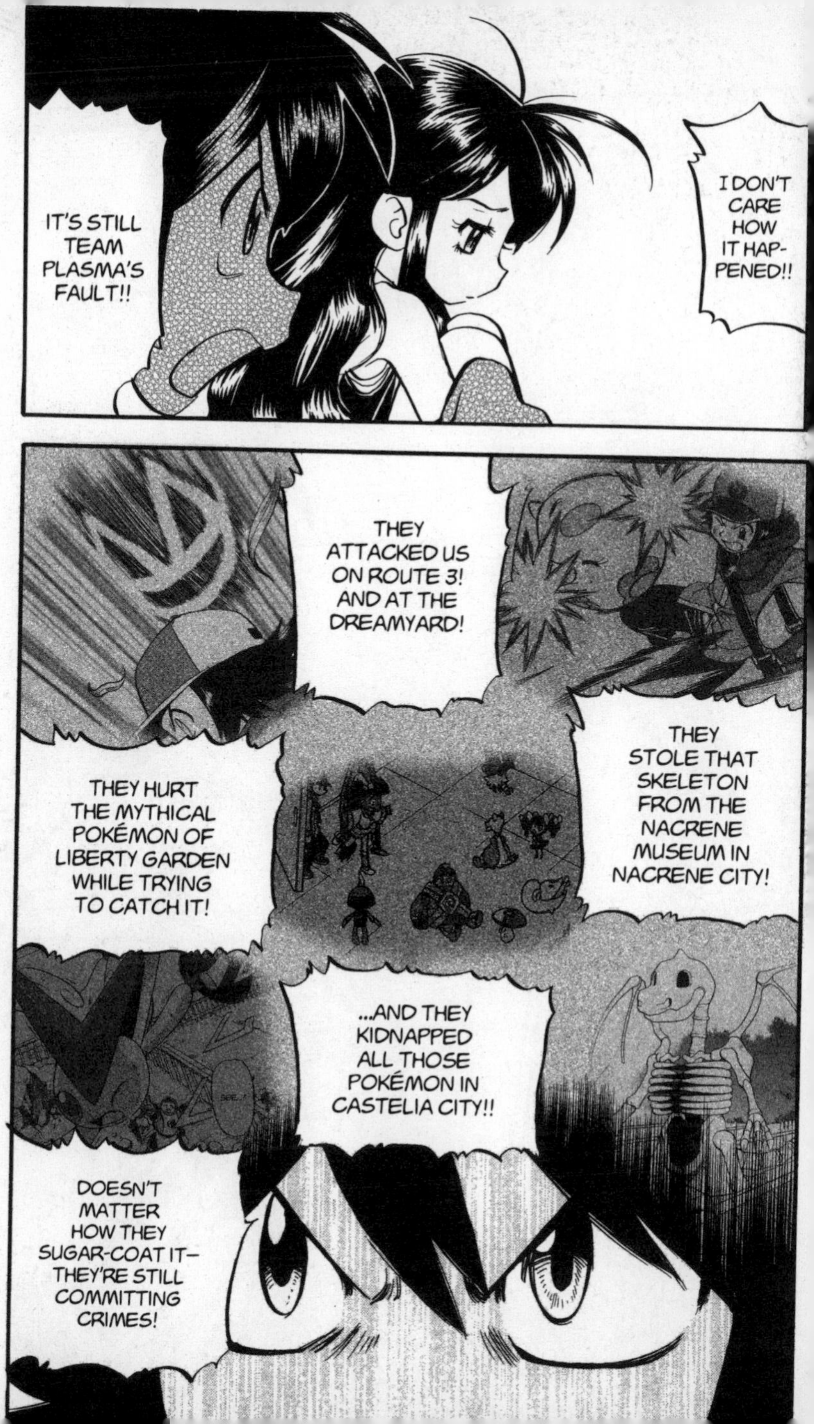
I DON'T CARE HOW IT HAPPENED!!
IT'S STILL TEAM PLASMA'S FAULT!!
THEY ATTACKED US ON ROUTE 3! AND AT THE DREAMYARD!
THEY STOLE THAT SKELETON FROM THE NACRENE MUSEUM IN NACRENE CITY!
THEY HURT THE MYTHICAL POKÉMON OF LIBERTY GARDEN WHILE TRYING TO CATCH IT!
...AND THEY KIDNAPPED ALL THOSE POKÉMON IN CASTELIA CITY!!
DOESN'T MATTER HOW THEY SUGAR-COAT IT— THEY'RE STILL COMMITTING CRIMES!

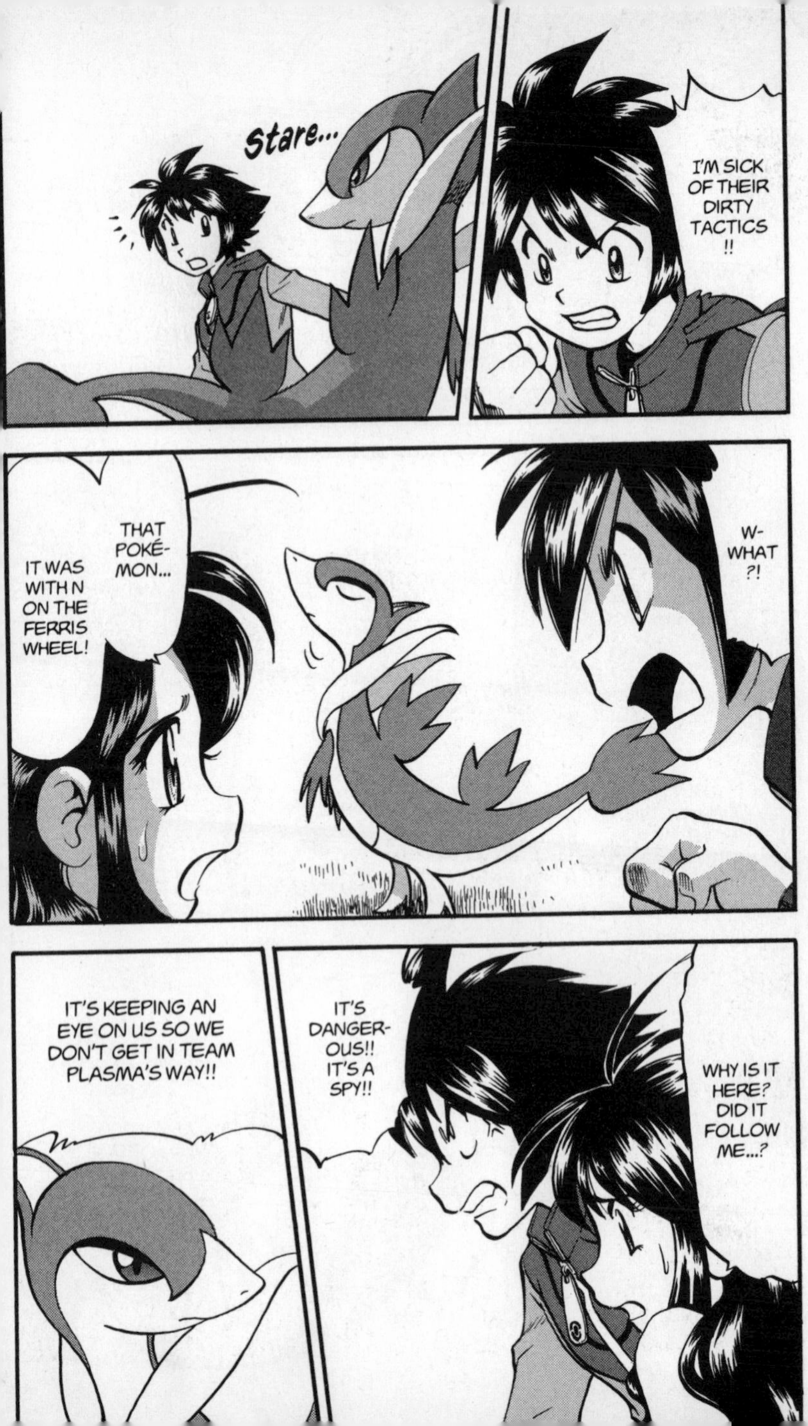
I'M SICK OF THEIR DIRTY TACTICS !!
Stare...
W-WHAT ?!
THAT POKÉMON...
IT WAS WITH N ON THE FERRIS WHEEL!
WHY IS IT HERE? DID IT FOLLOW ME...?
IT'S DANGEROUS!! IT'S A SPY!!
IT'S KEEPING AN EYE ON US SO WE DON'T GET IN TEAM PLASMA'S WAY!!

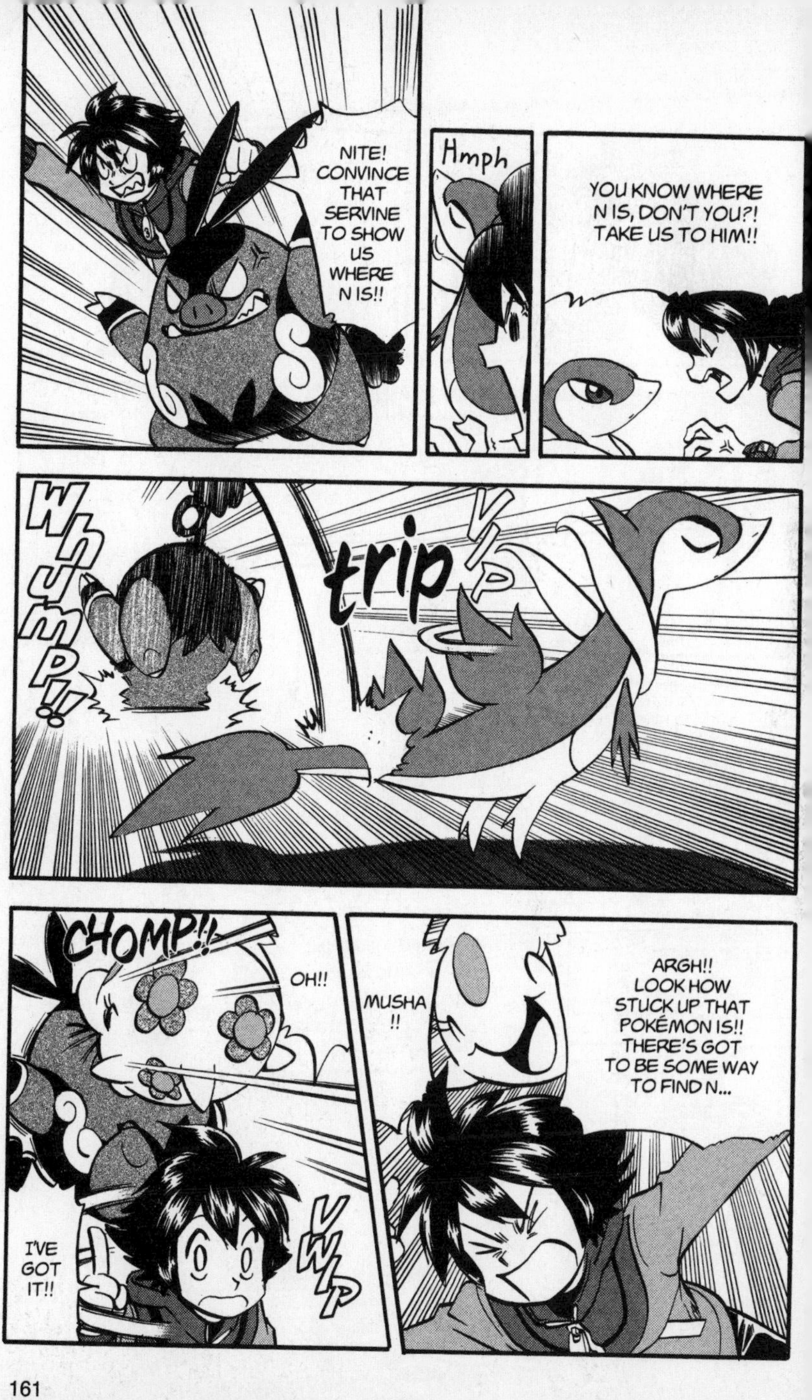
YOU KNOW WHERE N IS, DON'T YOU?! TAKE US TO HIM!!
Hmph
NITE! CONVINCE THAT SERVINE TO SHOW US WHERE N IS!!
YIP
trip
WHUMP!!
ARGH!! LOOK HOW STUCK UP THAT POKÉMON IS!! THERE'S GOT TO BE SOME WAY TO FIND N...
MUSHA !!
CHOMP!!
OH!!
VWIP
I'VE GOT IT!!

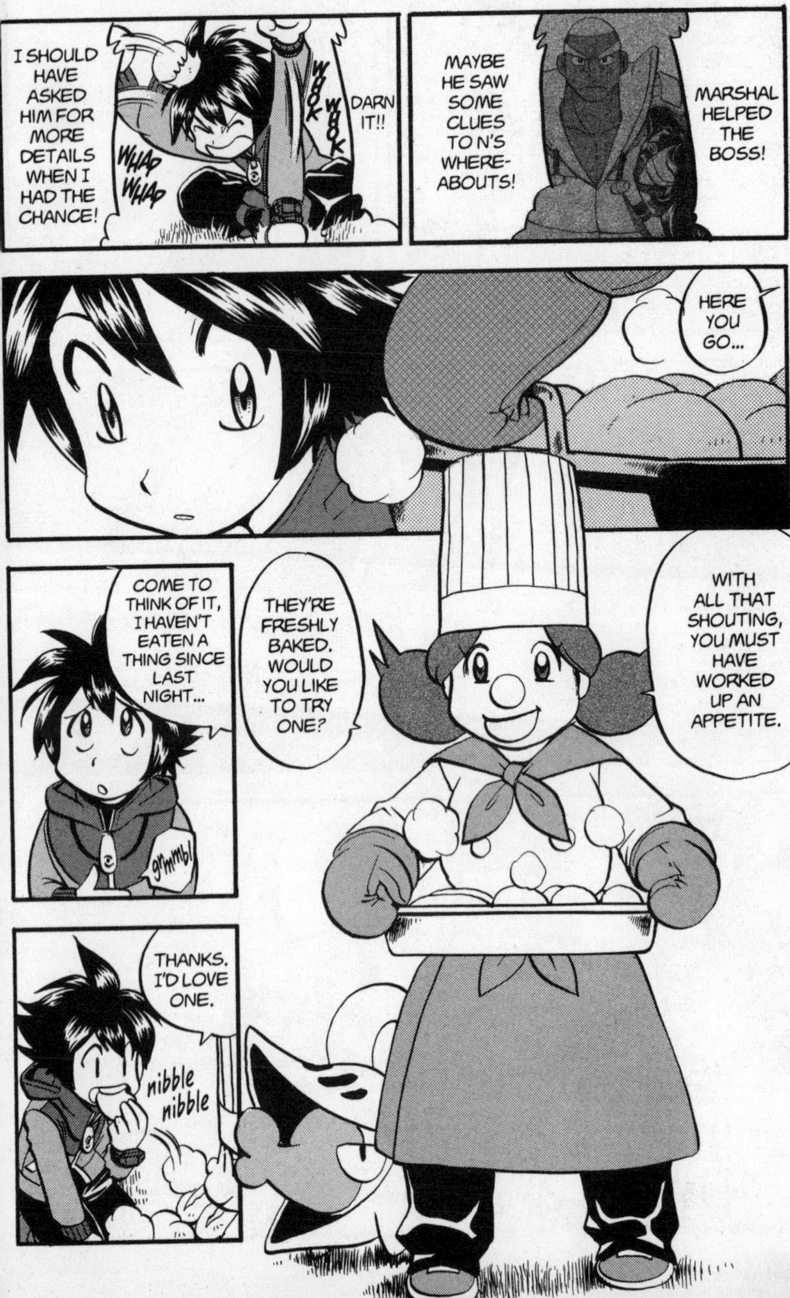
MARSHAL HELPED THE BOSS!
MAYBE HE SAW SOME CLUES TO N'S WHERE-ABOUTS!
DARN IT!!
WHOK WHOK
WHAP WHAP
I SHOULD HAVE ASKED HIM FOR MORE DETAILS WHEN I HAD THE CHANCE!
HERE YOU GO...
WITH ALL THAT SHOUTING, YOU MUST HAVE WORKED UP AN APPETITE.
THEY'RE FRESHLY BAKED. WOULD YOU LIKE TO TRY ONE?
COME TO THINK OF IT, I HAVEN'T EATEN A THING SINCE LAST NIGHT...
grmmbl
THANKS. I'D LOVE ONE.
nibble nibble

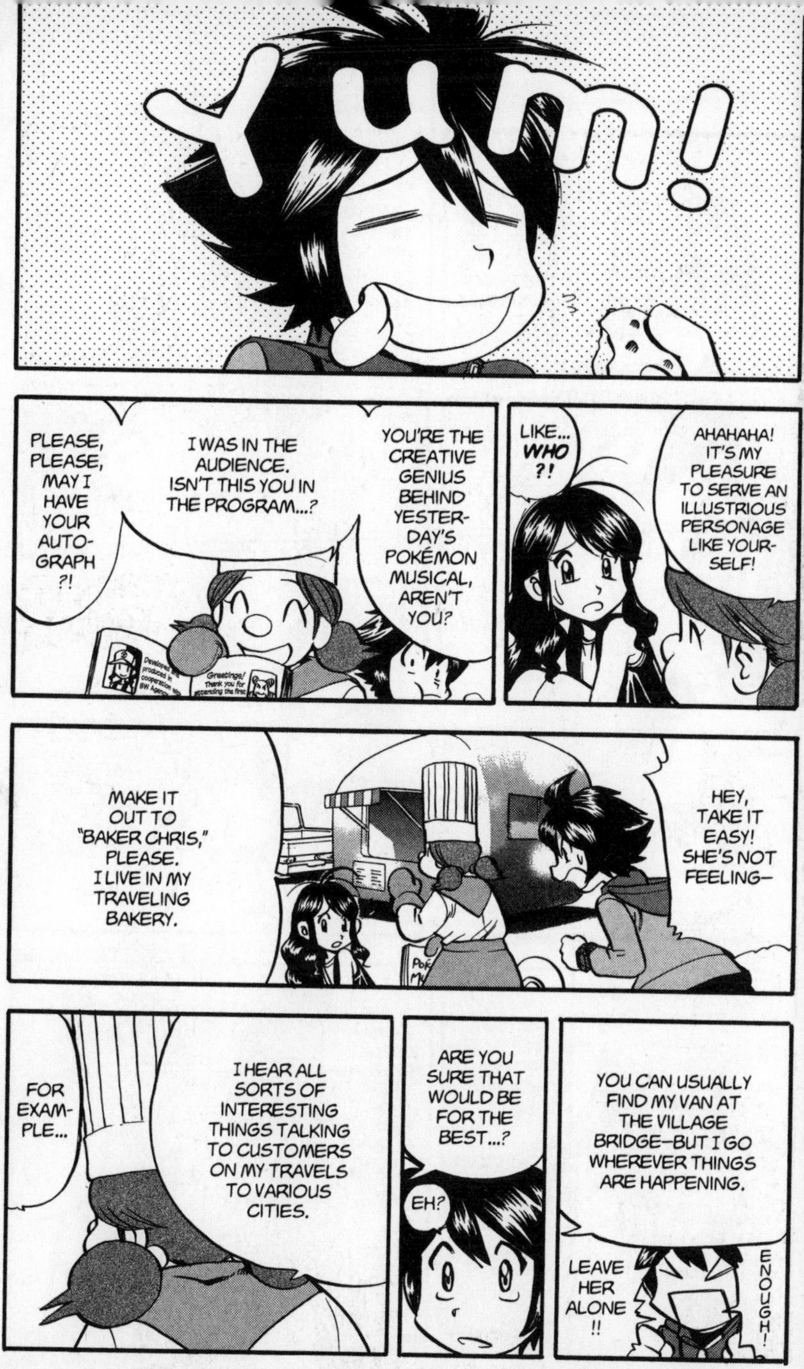
Yum!
AHAHAHA! IT'S MY PLEASURE TO SERVE AN ILLUSTRIOUS PERSONAGE LIKE YOURSELF!
LIKE... **WHO**?!
YOU'RE THE CREATIVE GENIUS BEHIND YESTERDAY'S POKÉMON MUSICAL, AREN'T YOU?
I WAS IN THE AUDIENCE. ISN'T THIS YOU IN THE PROGRAM...?
PLEASE, PLEASE, MAY I HAVE YOUR AUTOGRAPH?!
HEY, TAKE IT EASY! SHE'S NOT FEELING—
MAKE IT OUT TO "BAKER CHRIS," PLEASE. I LIVE IN MY TRAVELING BAKERY.
YOU CAN USUALLY FIND MY VAN AT THE VILLAGE BRIDGE—BUT I GO WHEREVER THINGS ARE HAPPENING.
ENOUGH!
LEAVE HER ALONE!!
ARE YOU SURE THAT WOULD BE FOR THE BEST...?
EH?
I HEAR ALL SORTS OF INTERESTING THINGS TALKING TO CUSTOMERS ON MY TRAVELS TO VARIOUS CITIES.
FOR EXAMPLE...

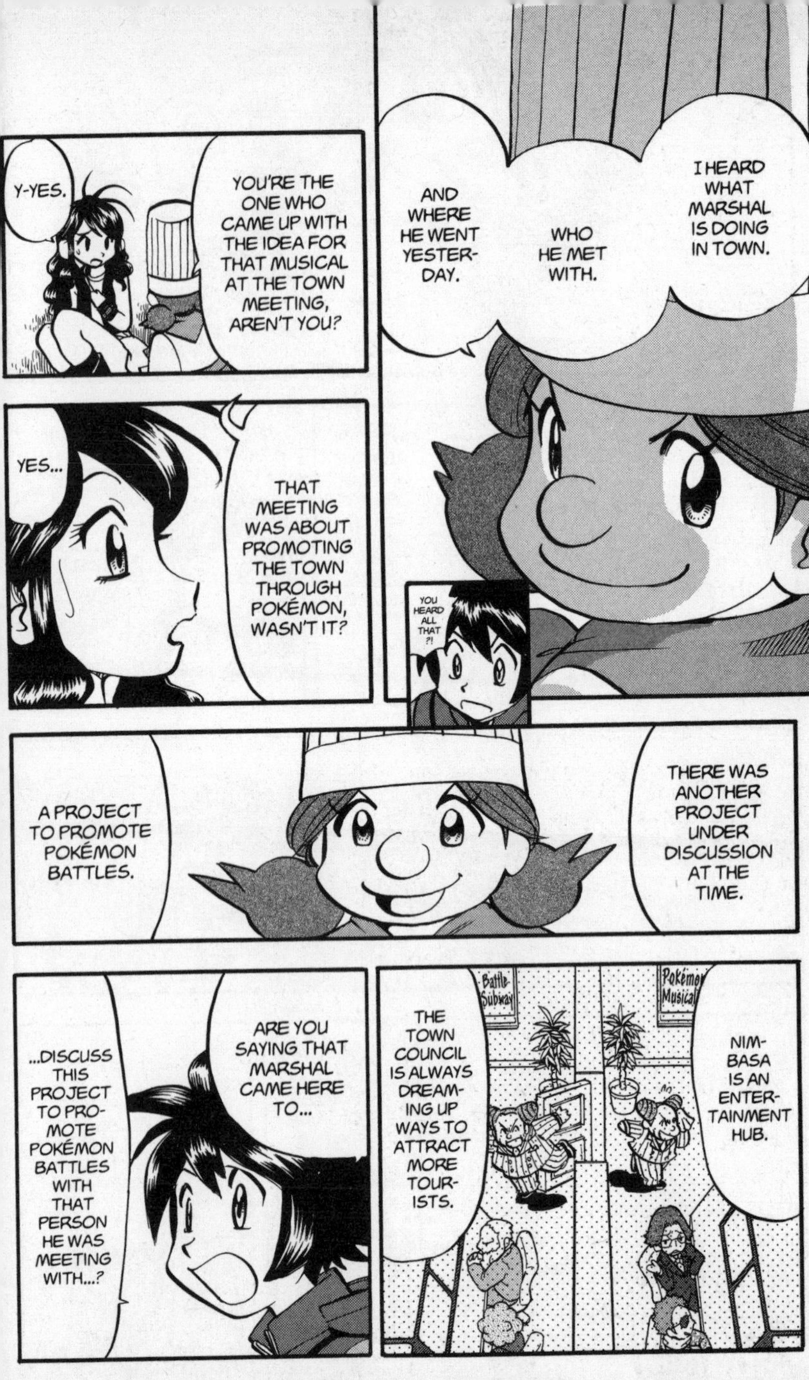
I HEARD WHAT MARSHAL IS DOING IN TOWN.
WHO HE MET WITH.
AND WHERE HE WENT YESTER-DAY.
YOU HEARD ALL THAT ?!
YOU'RE THE ONE WHO CAME UP WITH THE IDEA FOR THAT MUSICAL AT THE TOWN MEETING, AREN'T YOU?
Y-YES.
THAT MEETING WAS ABOUT PROMOTING THE TOWN THROUGH POKÉMON, WASN'T IT?
YES...
THERE WAS ANOTHER PROJECT UNDER DISCUSSION AT THE TIME.
A PROJECT TO PROMOTE POKÉMON BATTLES.
Pokémon Musical
Battle Subway
NIM-BASA IS AN ENTER-TAINMENT HUB.
THE TOWN COUNCIL IS ALWAYS DREAM-ING UP WAYS TO ATTRACT MORE TOUR-ISTS.
ARE YOU SAYING THAT MARSHAL CAME HERE TO...
...DISCUSS THIS PROJECT TO PRO-MOTE POKÉMON BATTLES WITH THAT PERSON HE WAS MEETING WITH...?

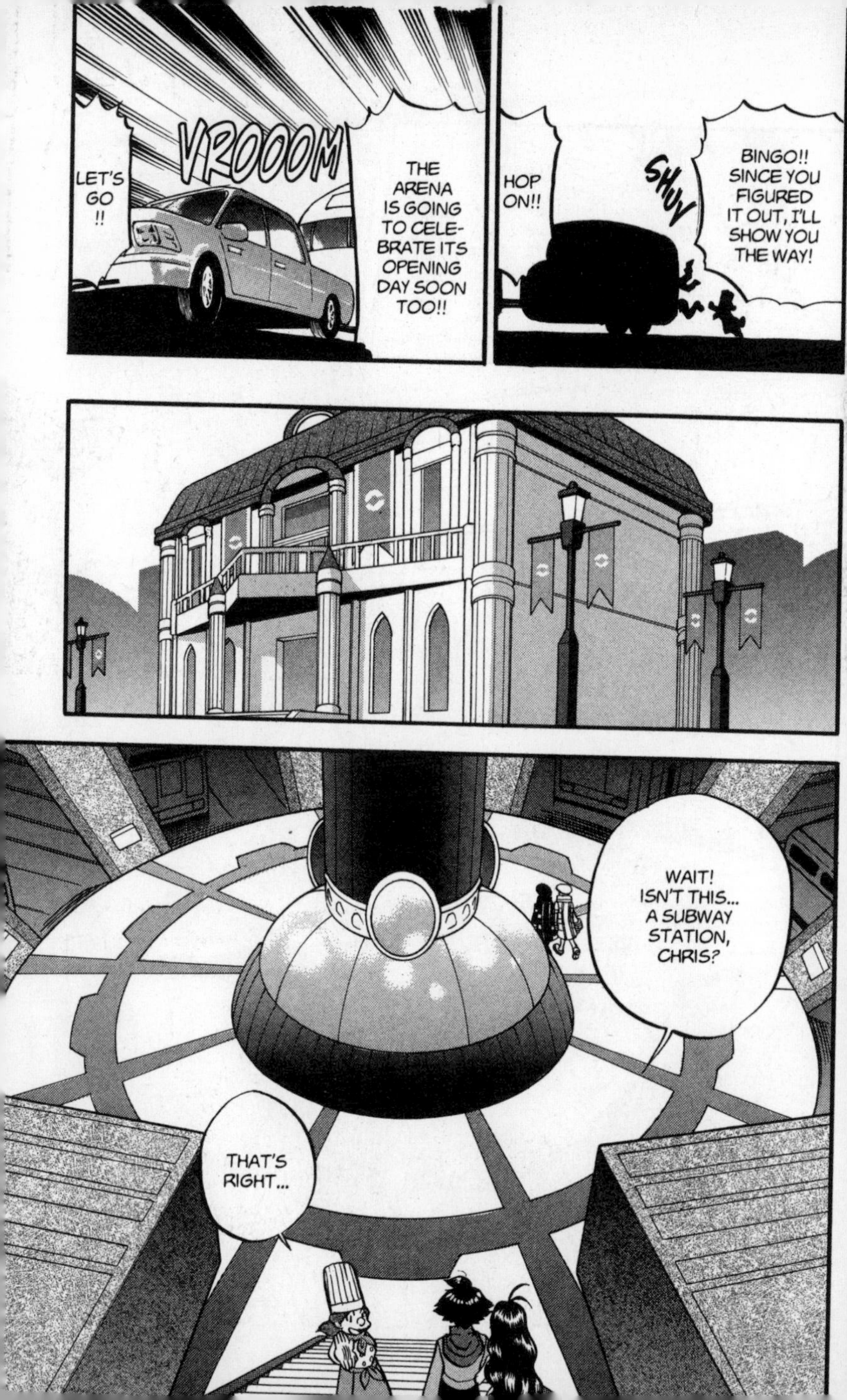
BINGO!! SINCE YOU FIGURED IT OUT, I'LL SHOW YOU THE WAY!
SHUV
HOP ON!!
THE ARENA IS GOING TO CELEBRATE ITS OPENING DAY SOON TOO!!
VROOOM
LET'S GO !!
WAIT! ISN'T THIS... A SUBWAY STATION, CHRIS?
THAT'S RIGHT...

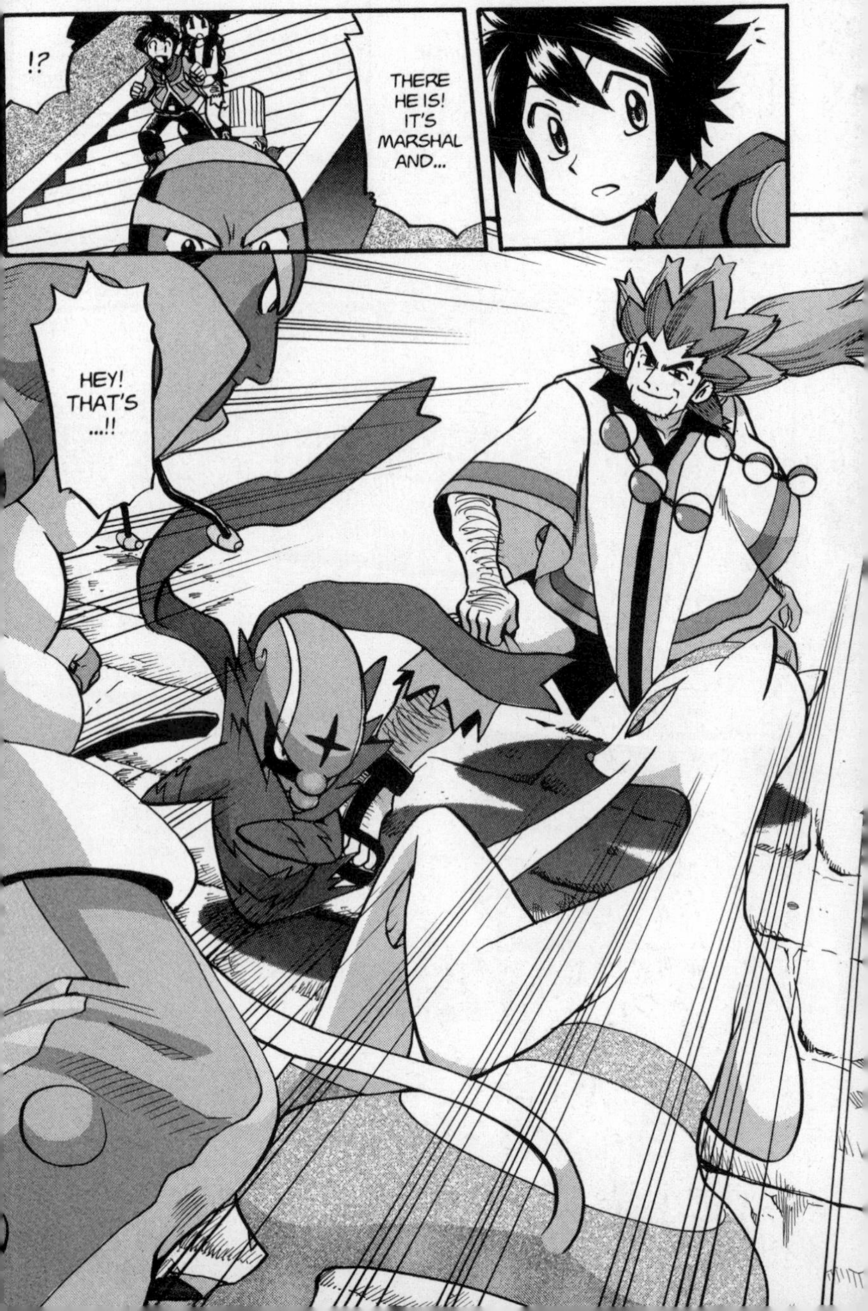
THERE HE IS! IT'S MARSHAL AND...
!?
HEY! THAT'S ...!!

ADVENTURE MAP

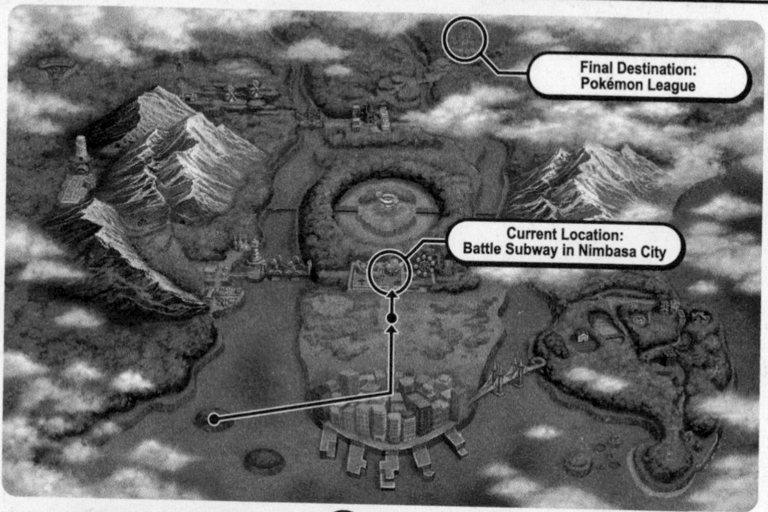

Final Destination:
Pokémon League
Current Location:
Battle Subway in Nimbasa City

Fire Pig Pokémon **Nite**
Pignite ♂ Fire Fighting
Lv.27 Ability: Blaze

Dream Eater Pokémon **Musha**
Munna ♂ Psychic
Lv.47 Ability: Forewarn

Valiant Pokémon **Brav**
Braviary ♂ Normal Flying
Lv.54 Ability: Sheer Force

EleSpider Pokémon **Tula**
Galvantula ♂ Bug Electric
Lv.50 Ability: Unnerve

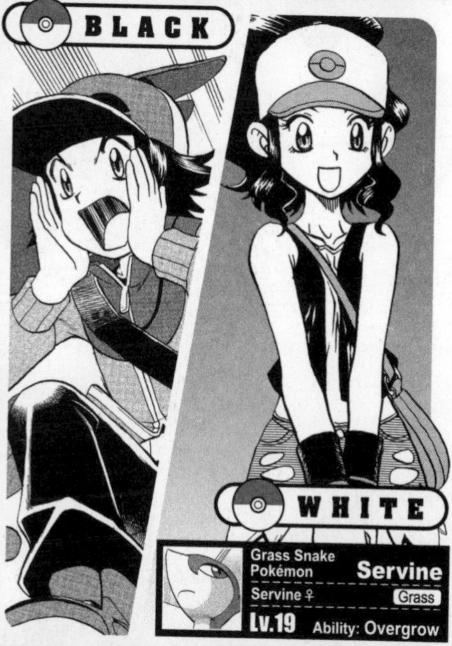

BLACK
WHITE

Grass Snake Pokémon **Servine**
Servine ♀ Grass
Lv.19 Ability: Overgrow

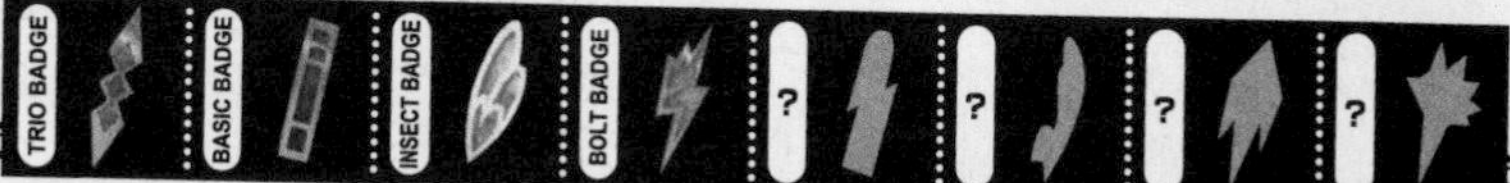

TRIO BADGE
BASIC BADGE
INSECT BADGE
BOLT BADGE
?
?
?
?

Pokémon™ Adventures Black & White

DEERLING

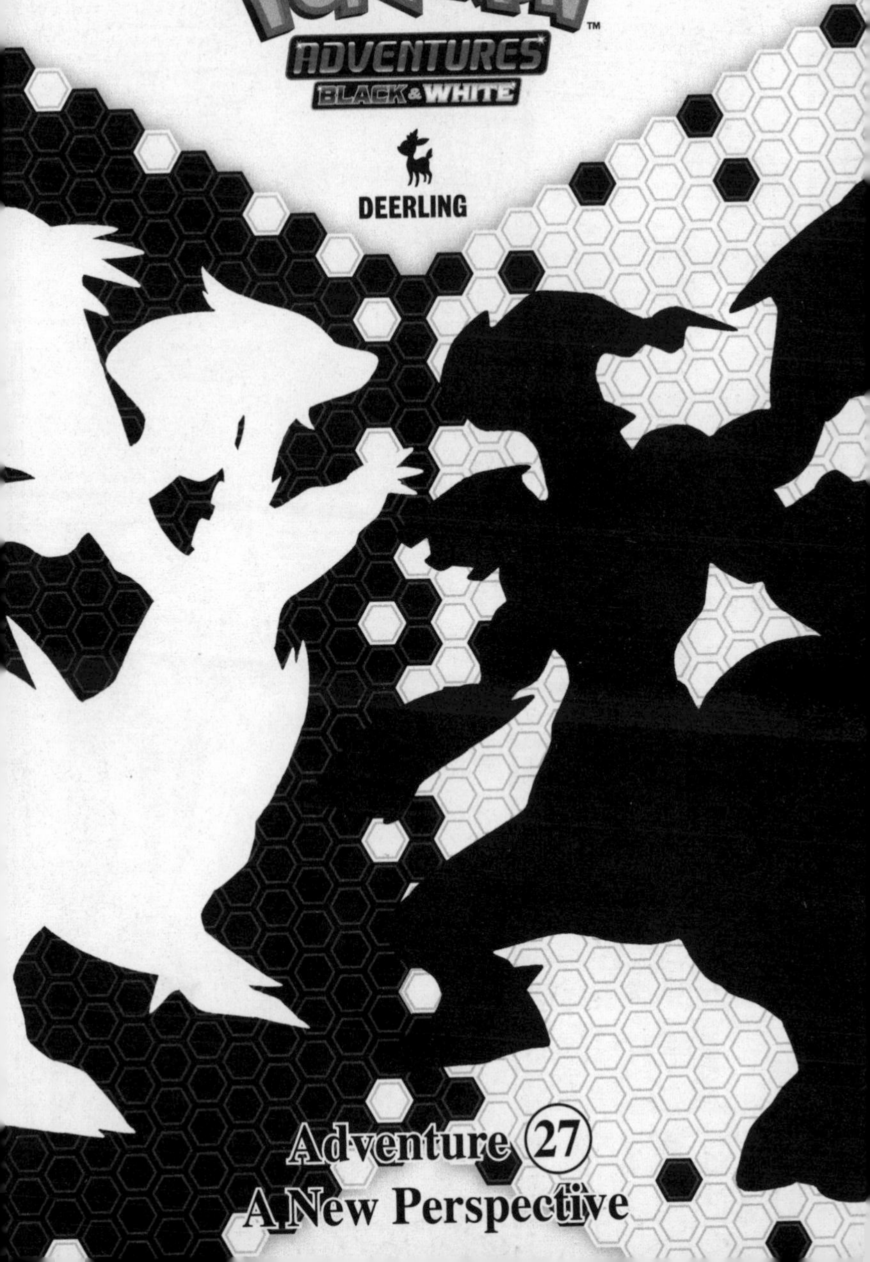

Adventure 27
A New Perspective

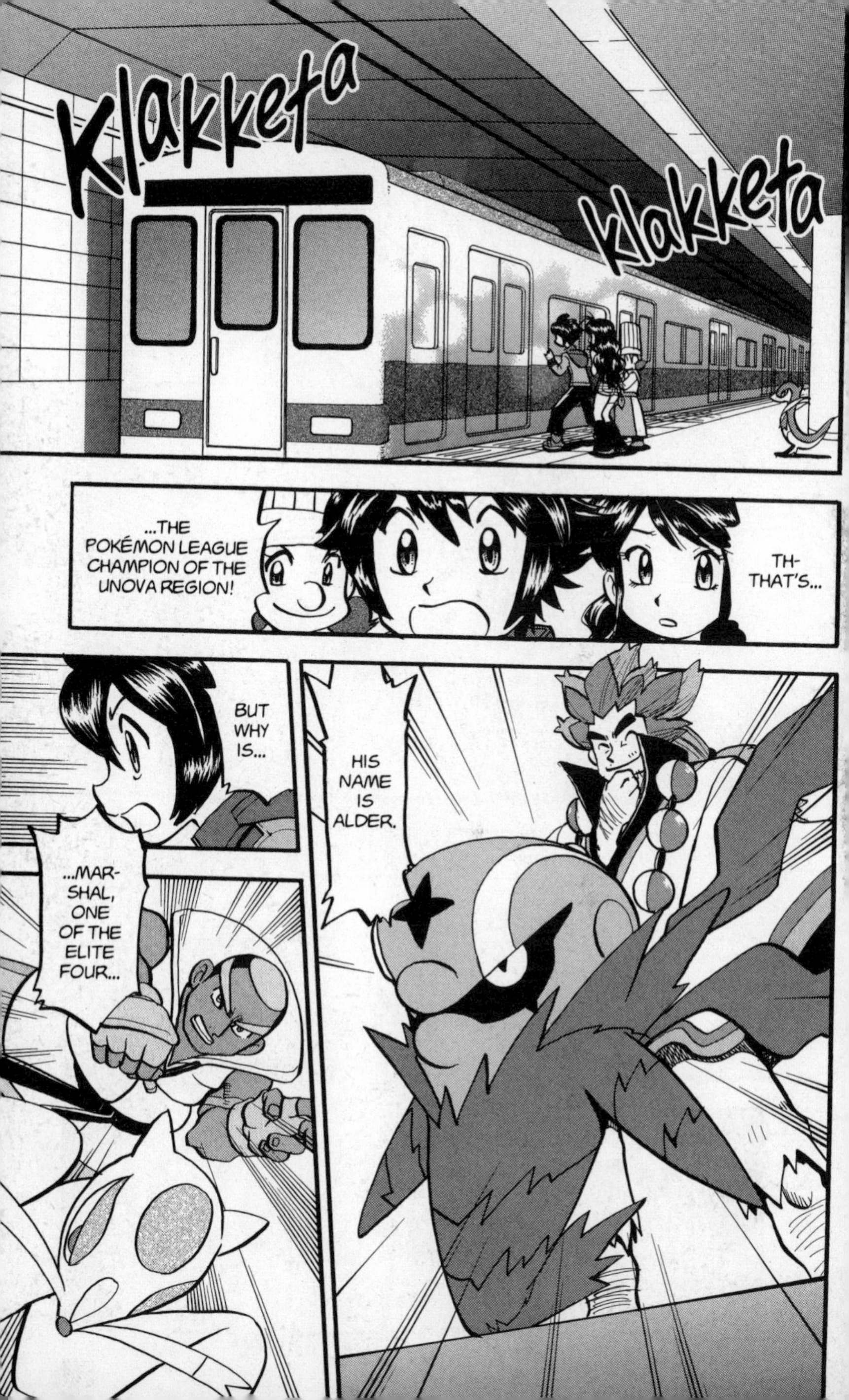
Klakketa
klakketa
TH- THAT'S...
...THE POKÉMON LEAGUE CHAMPION OF THE UNOVA REGION!
HIS NAME IS ALDER.
BUT WHY IS...
...MAR-SHAL, ONE OF THE ELITE FOUR...

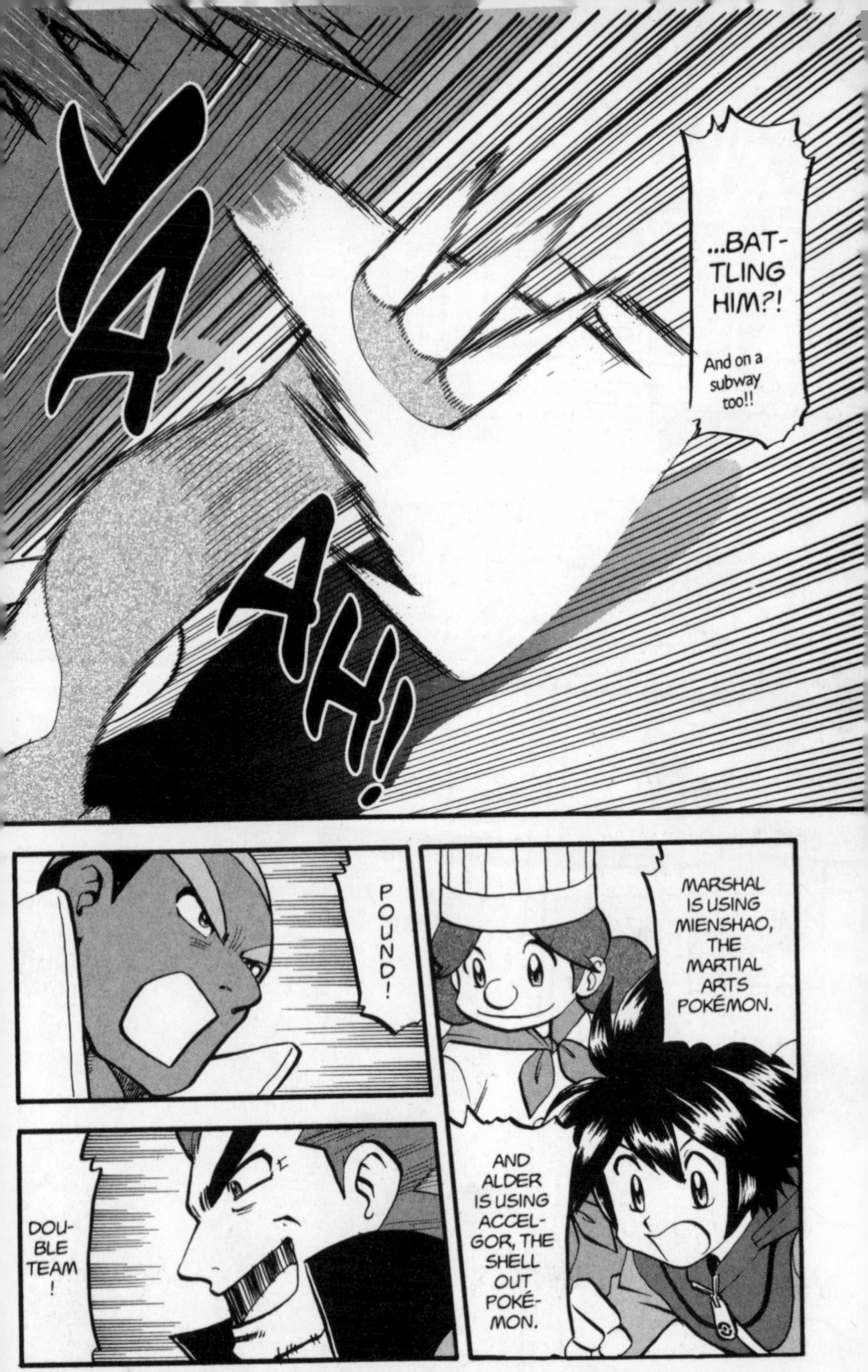
...BATTLING HIM?!
And on a subway too!!
YA
AH!
MARSHAL IS USING MIENSHAO, THE MARTIAL ARTS POKÉMON.
AND ALDER IS USING ACCELGOR, THE SHELL OUT POKÉMON.
POUND!
DOUBLE TEAM!

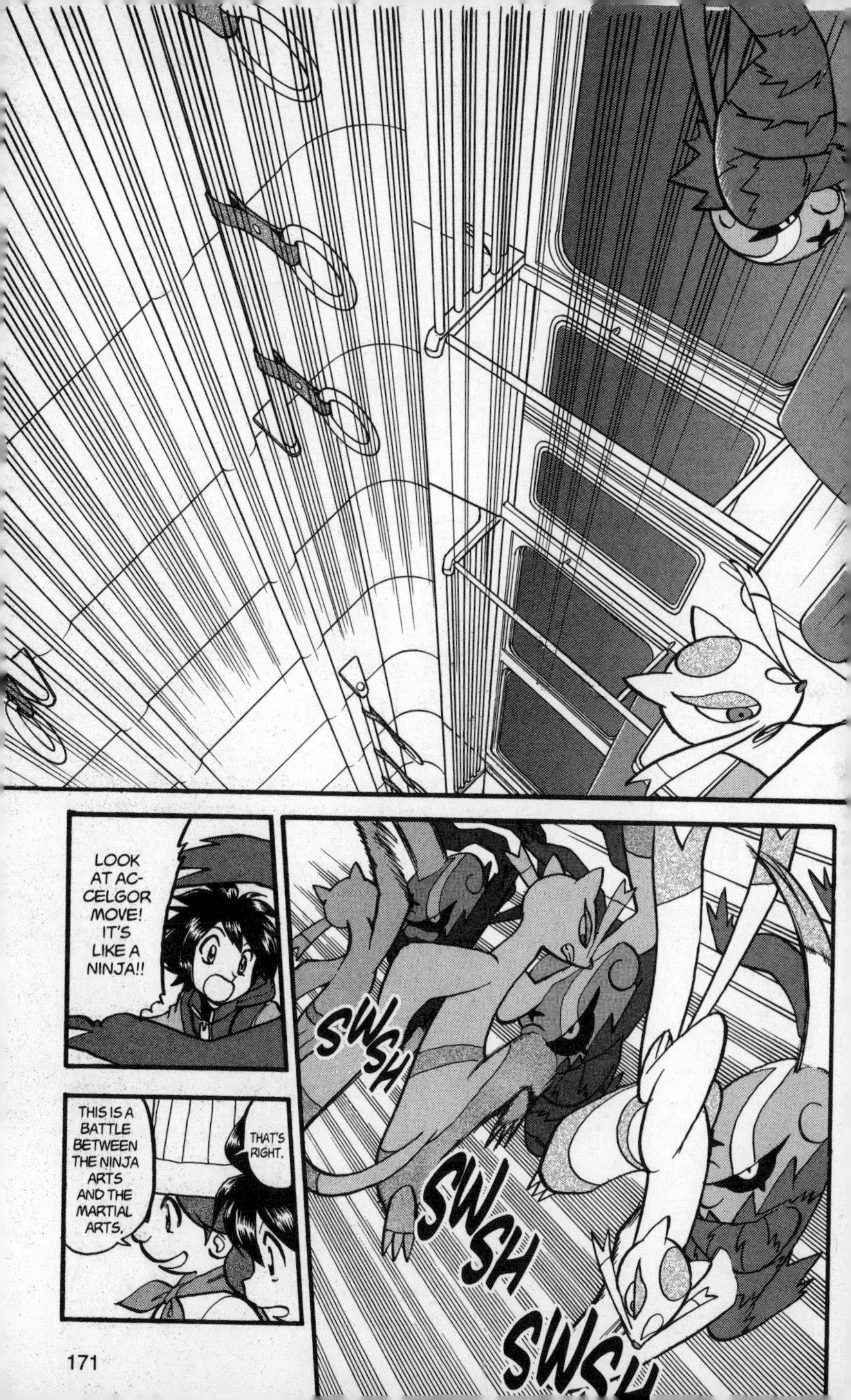
SWSH
SWSH
SWSH
LOOK AT ACCELGOR MOVE! IT'S LIKE A NINJA!!
THIS IS A BATTLE BETWEEN THE NINJA ARTS AND THE MARTIAL ARTS.
THAT'S RIGHT.

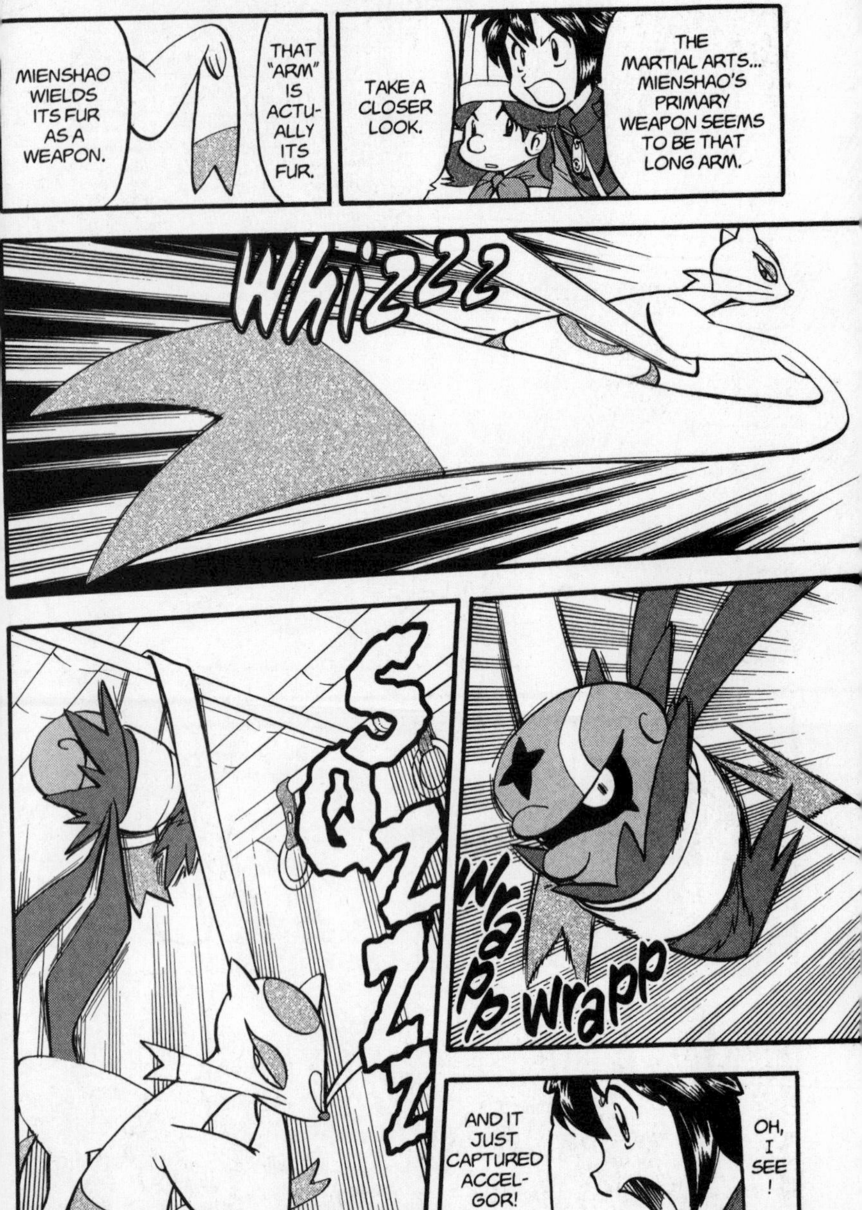
THE MARTIAL ARTS... MIENSHAO'S PRIMARY WEAPON SEEMS TO BE THAT LONG ARM.
TAKE A CLOSER LOOK.
THAT "ARM" IS ACTUALLY ITS FUR.
MIENSHAO WIELDS ITS FUR AS A WEAPON.
WHIZZZ
WRAPP WRAPP
OH, I SEE!
AND IT JUST CAPTURED ACCELGOR!
SQZZZ

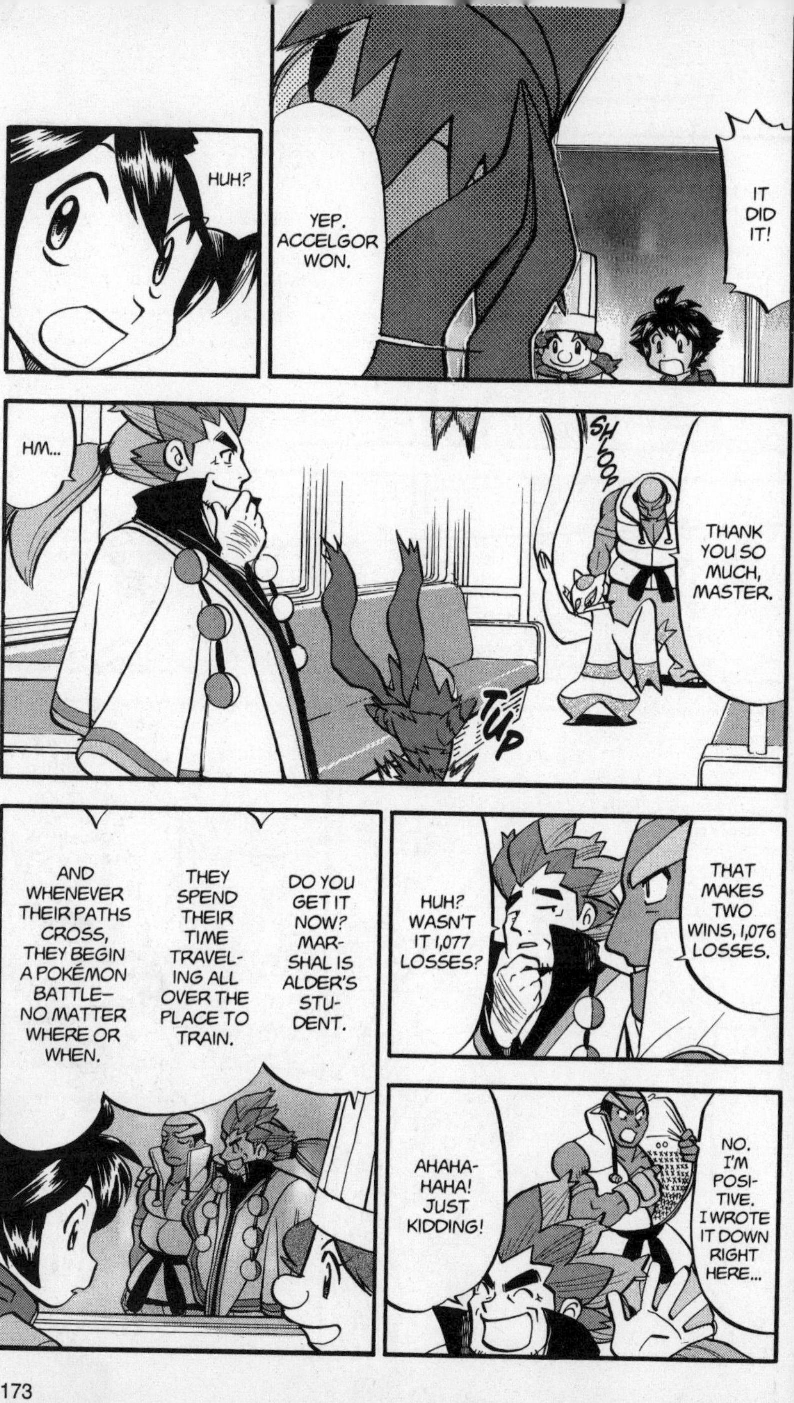
IT DID IT!
YEP. ACCELGOR WON.
HUH?
THANK YOU SO MUCH, MASTER.
SHLOOP
HM...
TUP
THAT MAKES TWO WINS, 1,076 LOSSES.
HUH? WASN'T IT 1,077 LOSSES?
NO. I'M POSITIVE. I WROTE IT DOWN RIGHT HERE...
AHAHAHAHA! JUST KIDDING!
DO YOU GET IT NOW? MARSHAL IS ALDER'S STUDENT.
THEY SPEND THEIR TIME TRAVELING ALL OVER THE PLACE TO TRAIN.
AND WHENEVER THEIR PATHS CROSS, THEY BEGIN A POKÉMON BATTLE—NO MATTER WHERE OR WHEN.

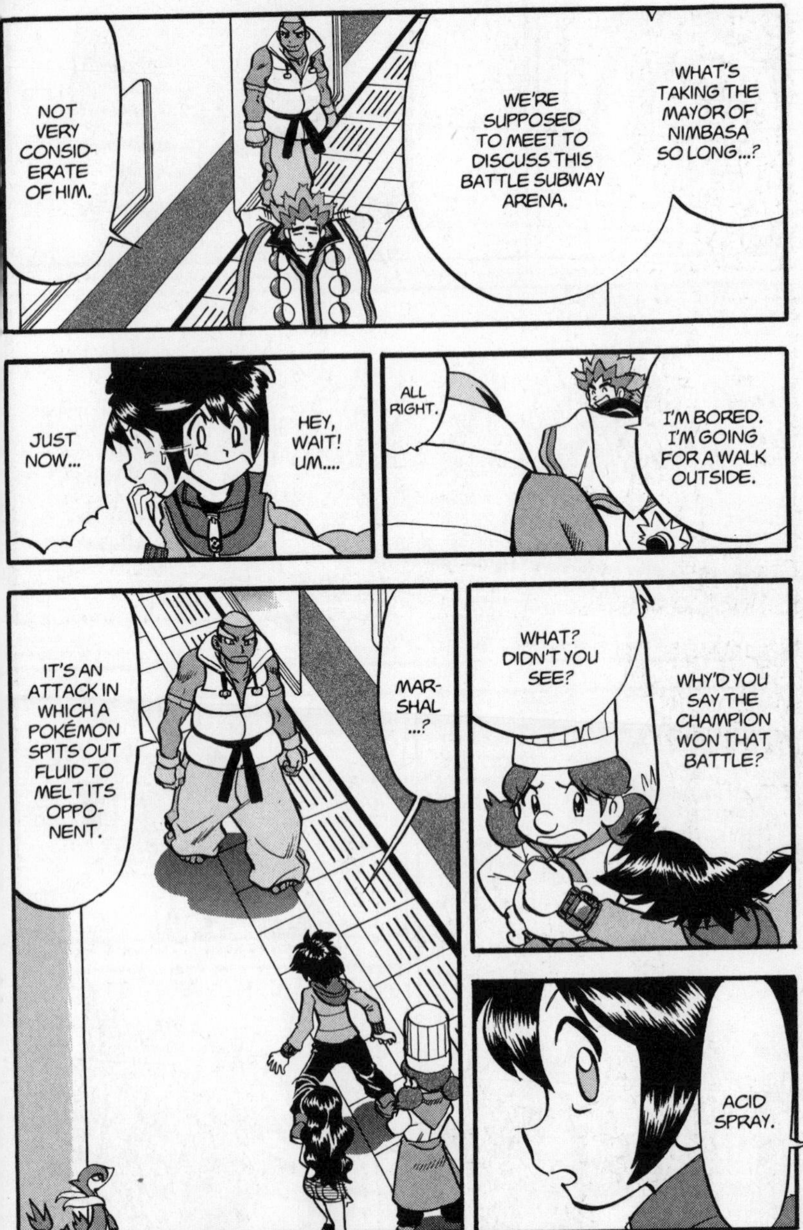
WHAT'S TAKING THE MAYOR OF NIMBASA SO LONG...?
WE'RE SUPPOSED TO MEET TO DISCUSS THIS BATTLE SUBWAY ARENA.
NOT VERY CONSIDERATE OF HIM.
I'M BORED. I'M GOING FOR A WALK OUTSIDE.
ALL RIGHT.
HEY, WAIT! UM....
JUST NOW...
WHY'D YOU SAY THE CHAMPION WON THAT BATTLE?
WHAT? DIDN'T YOU SEE?
ACID SPRAY.
MARSHAL...?
IT'S AN ATTACK IN WHICH A POKÉMON SPITS OUT FLUID TO MELT ITS OPPONENT.

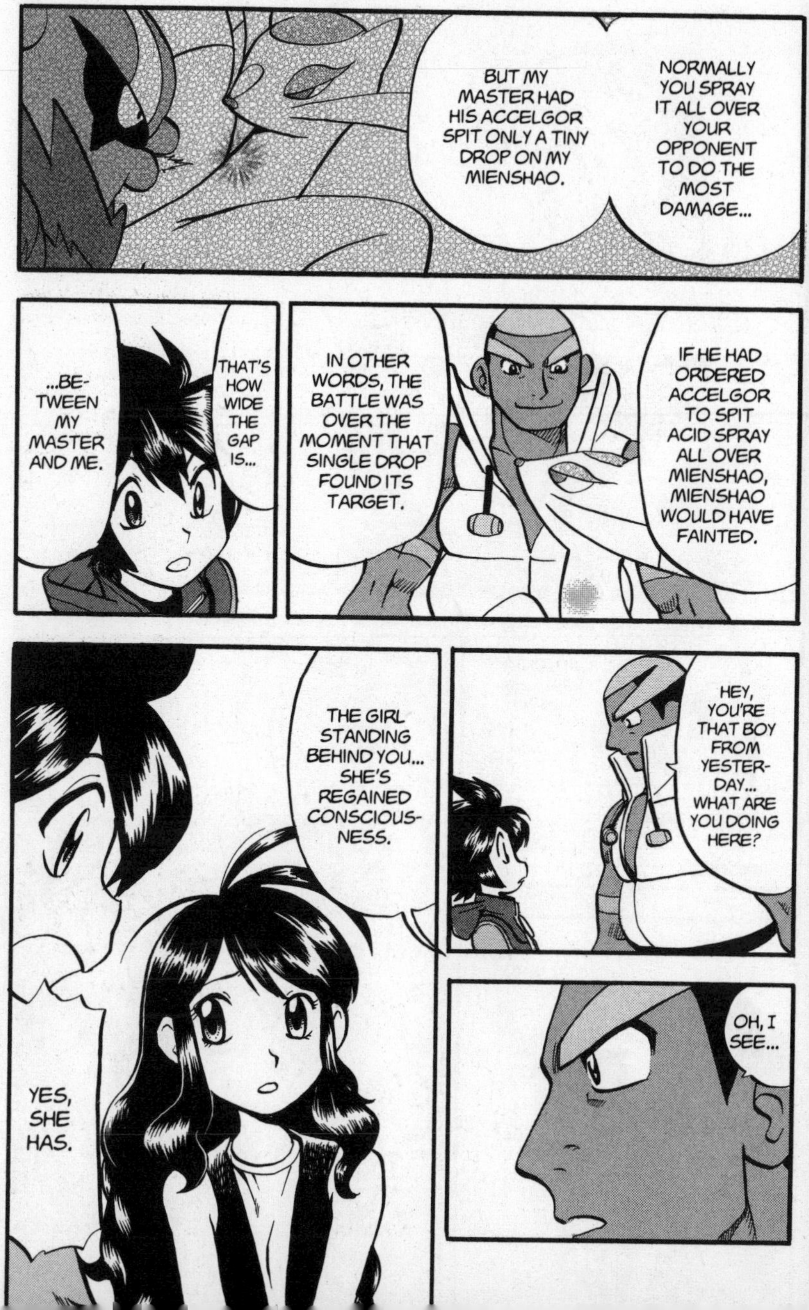
NORMALLY YOU SPRAY IT ALL OVER YOUR OPPONENT TO DO THE MOST DAMAGE...
BUT MY MASTER HAD HIS ACCELGOR SPIT ONLY A TINY DROP ON MY MIENSHAO.
IF HE HAD ORDERED ACCELGOR TO SPIT ACID SPRAY ALL OVER MIENSHAO, MIENSHAO WOULD HAVE FAINTED.
IN OTHER WORDS, THE BATTLE WAS OVER THE MOMENT THAT SINGLE DROP FOUND ITS TARGET.
THAT'S HOW WIDE THE GAP IS...
...BETWEEN MY MASTER AND ME.
HEY, YOU'RE THAT BOY FROM YESTERDAY... WHAT ARE YOU DOING HERE?
OH, I SEE...
THE GIRL STANDING BEHIND YOU... SHE'S REGAINED CONSCIOUSNESS.
YES, SHE HAS.

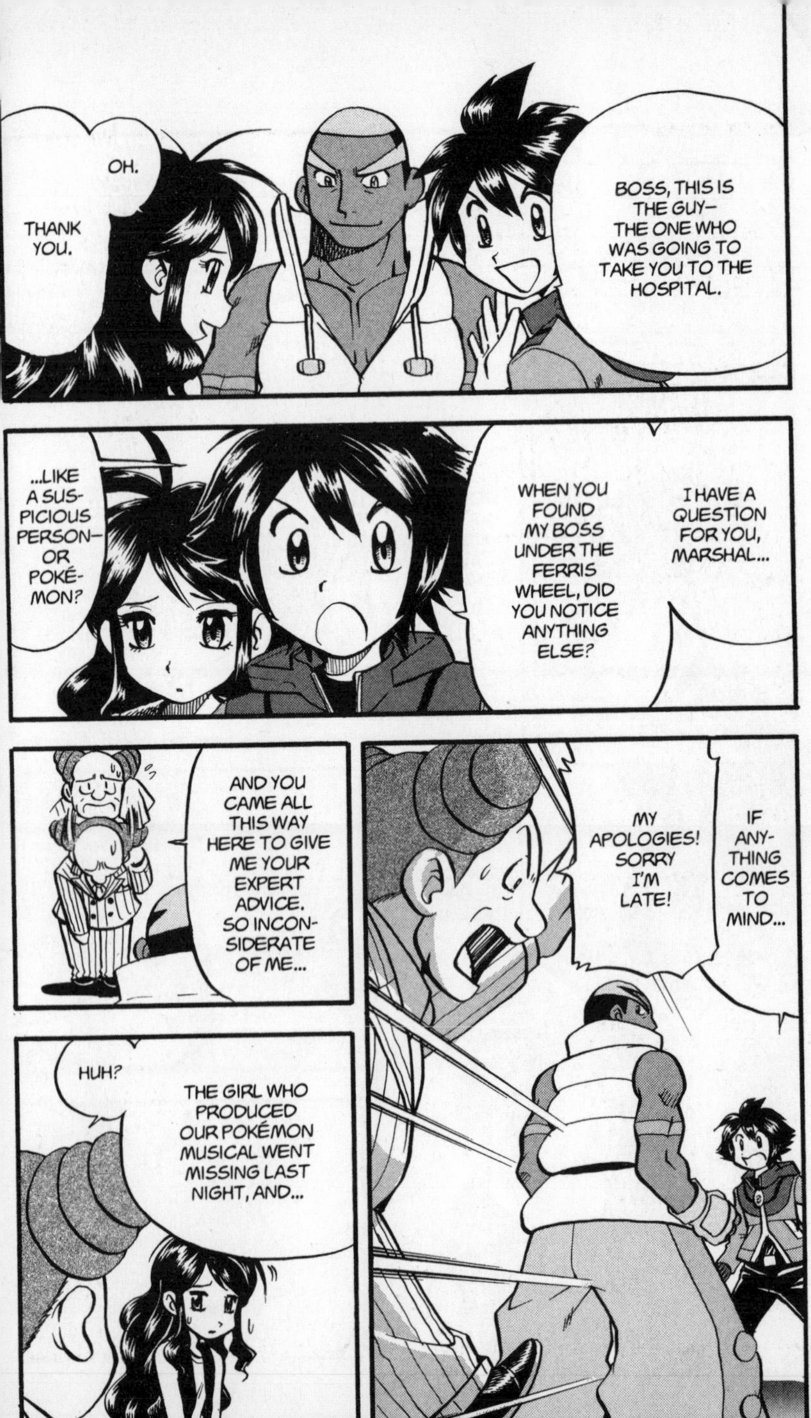
BOSS, THIS IS THE GUY— THE ONE WHO WAS GOING TO TAKE YOU TO THE HOSPITAL.
OH.
THANK YOU.
I HAVE A QUESTION FOR YOU, MARSHAL...
WHEN YOU FOUND MY BOSS UNDER THE FERRIS WHEEL, DID YOU NOTICE ANYTHING ELSE?
...LIKE A SUSPICIOUS PERSON—OR POKÉMON?
IF ANYTHING COMES TO MIND...
MY APOLOGIES! SORRY I'M LATE!
AND YOU CAME ALL THIS WAY HERE TO GIVE ME YOUR EXPERT ADVICE. SO INCONSIDERATE OF ME...
HUH?
THE GIRL WHO PRODUCED OUR POKÉMON MUSICAL WENT MISSING LAST NIGHT, AND...

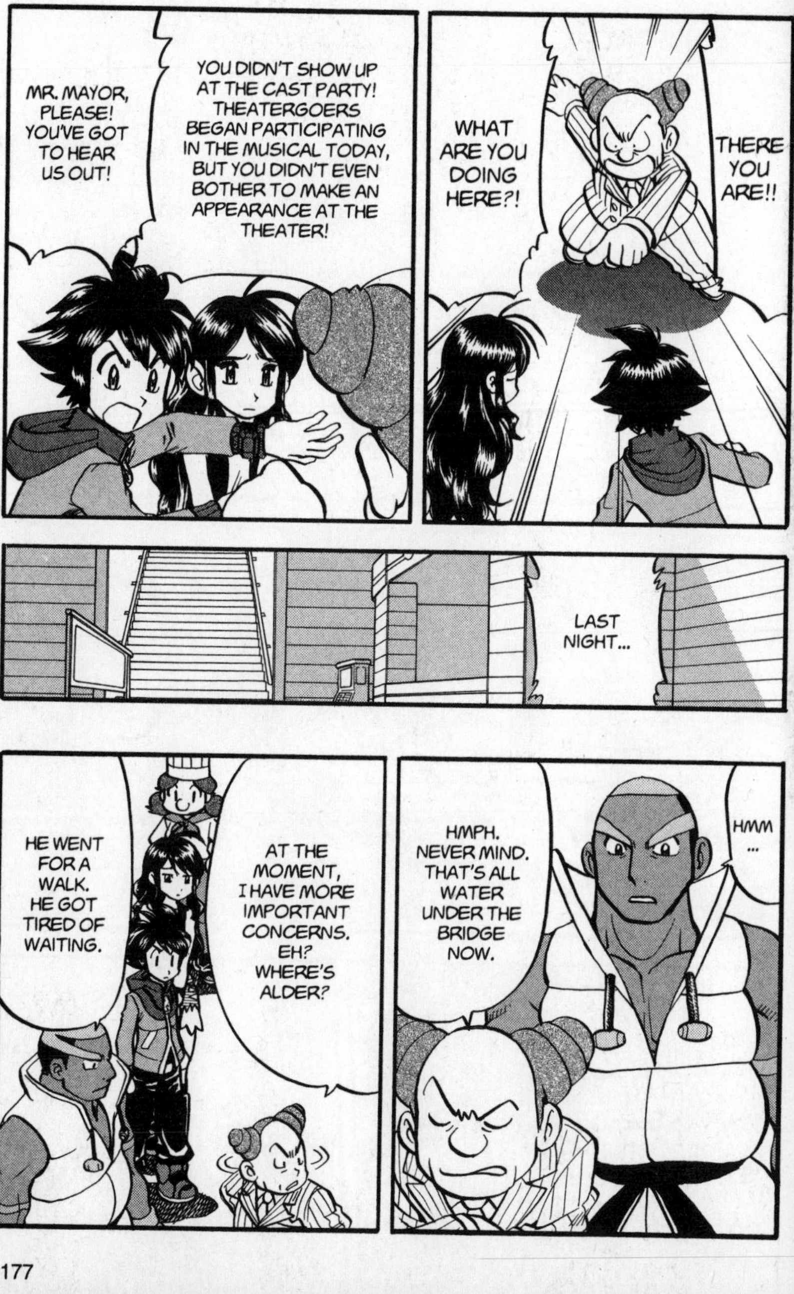
THERE YOU ARE!!
WHAT ARE YOU DOING HERE?!
YOU DIDN'T SHOW UP AT THE CAST PARTY! THEATERGOERS BEGAN PARTICIPATING IN THE MUSICAL TODAY, BUT YOU DIDN'T EVEN BOTHER TO MAKE AN APPEARANCE AT THE THEATER!
MR. MAYOR, PLEASE! YOU'VE GOT TO HEAR US OUT!
LAST NIGHT...
HMM ...
HMPH. NEVER MIND. THAT'S ALL WATER UNDER THE BRIDGE NOW.
AT THE MOMENT, I HAVE MORE IMPORTANT CONCERNS. EH? WHERE'S ALDER?
HE WENT FOR A WALK. HE GOT TIRED OF WAITING.

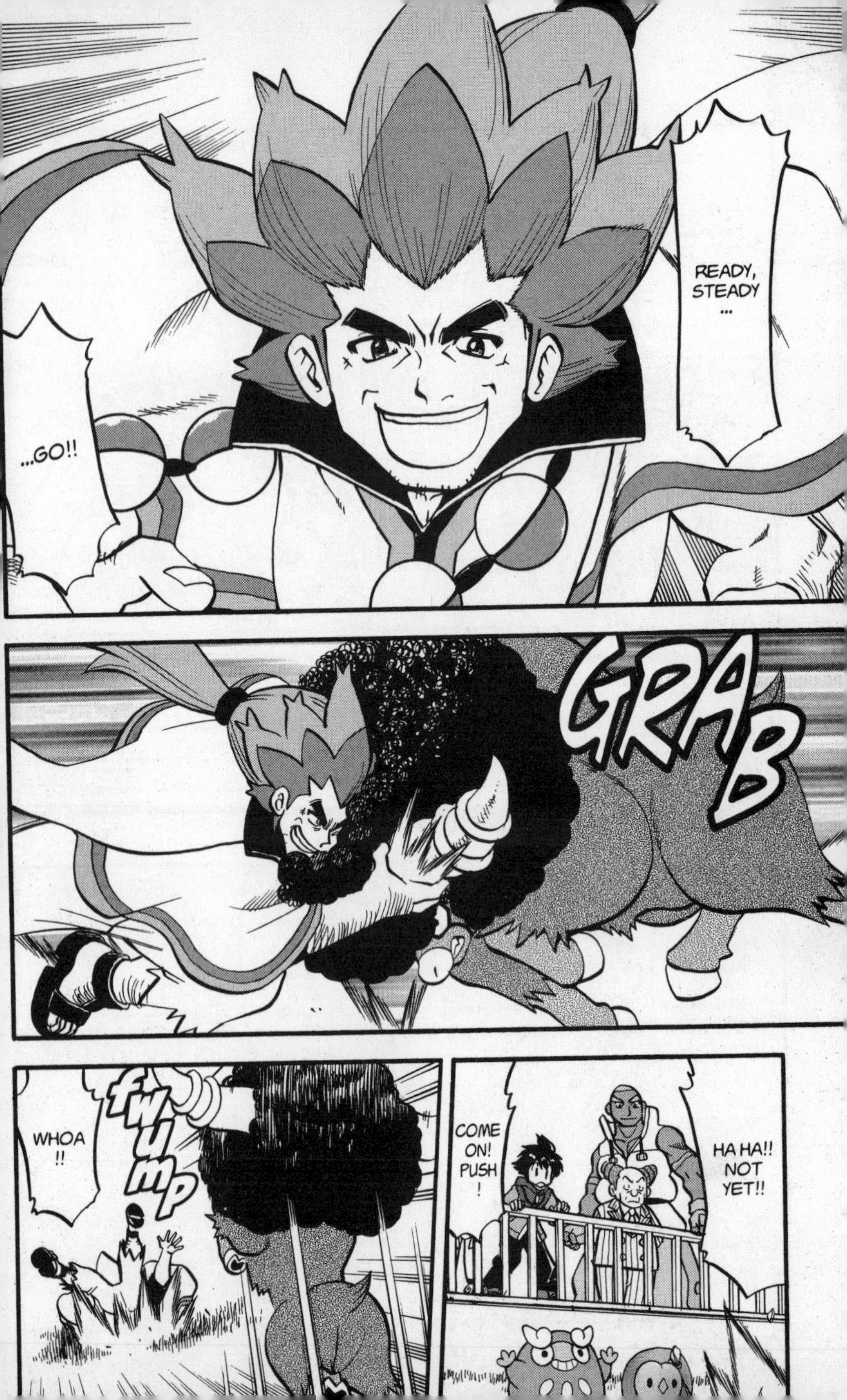
READY, STEADY ...
...GO!!
GRAB
HA HA!! NOT YET!!
COME ON! PUSH!
fwump
WHOA!!

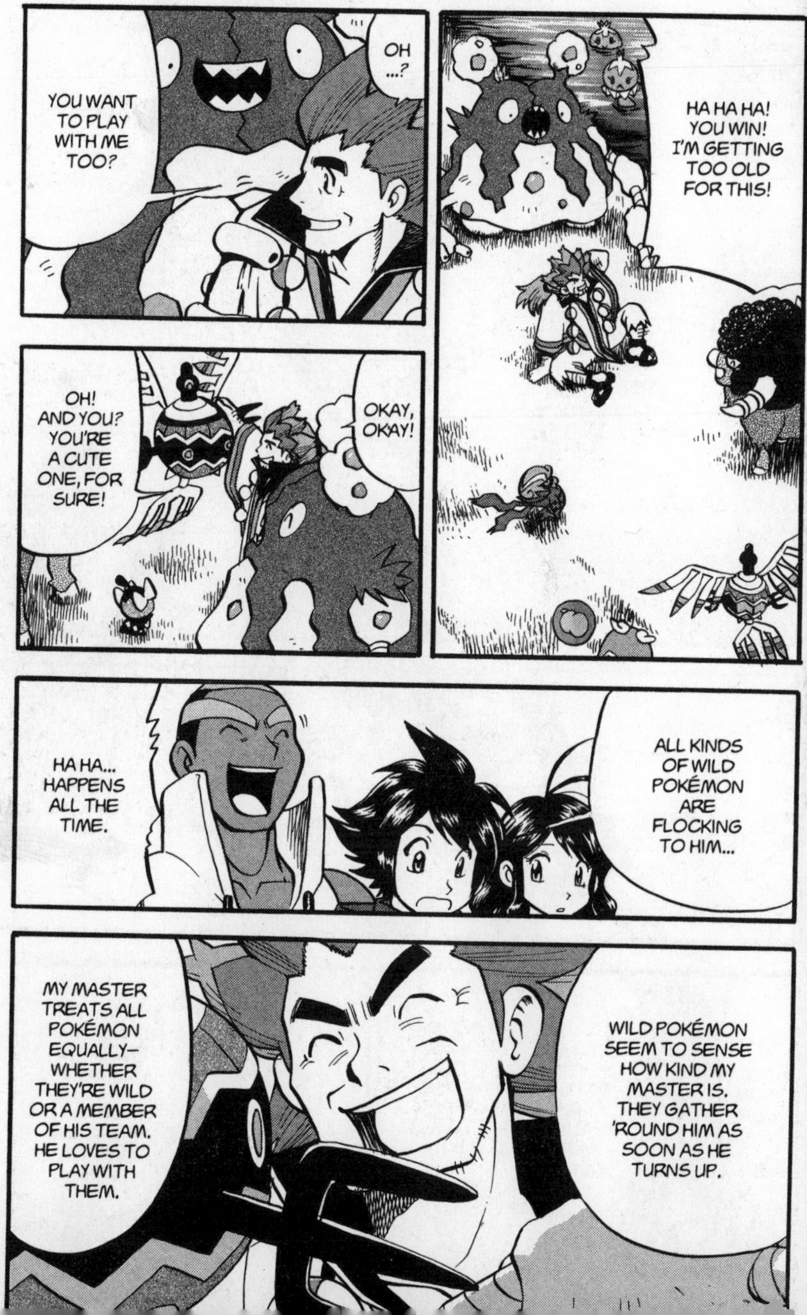
HA HA HA! YOU WIN! I'M GETTING TOO OLD FOR THIS!
OH ...?
YOU WANT TO PLAY WITH ME TOO?
OKAY, OKAY!
OH! AND YOU? YOU'RE A CUTE ONE, FOR SURE!
ALL KINDS OF WILD POKÉMON ARE FLOCKING TO HIM...
HA HA... HAPPENS ALL THE TIME.
WILD POKÉMON SEEM TO SENSE HOW KIND MY MASTER IS. THEY GATHER 'ROUND HIM AS SOON AS HE TURNS UP.
MY MASTER TREATS ALL POKÉMON EQUALLY—WHETHER THEY'RE WILD OR A MEMBER OF HIS TEAM. HE LOVES TO PLAY WITH THEM.

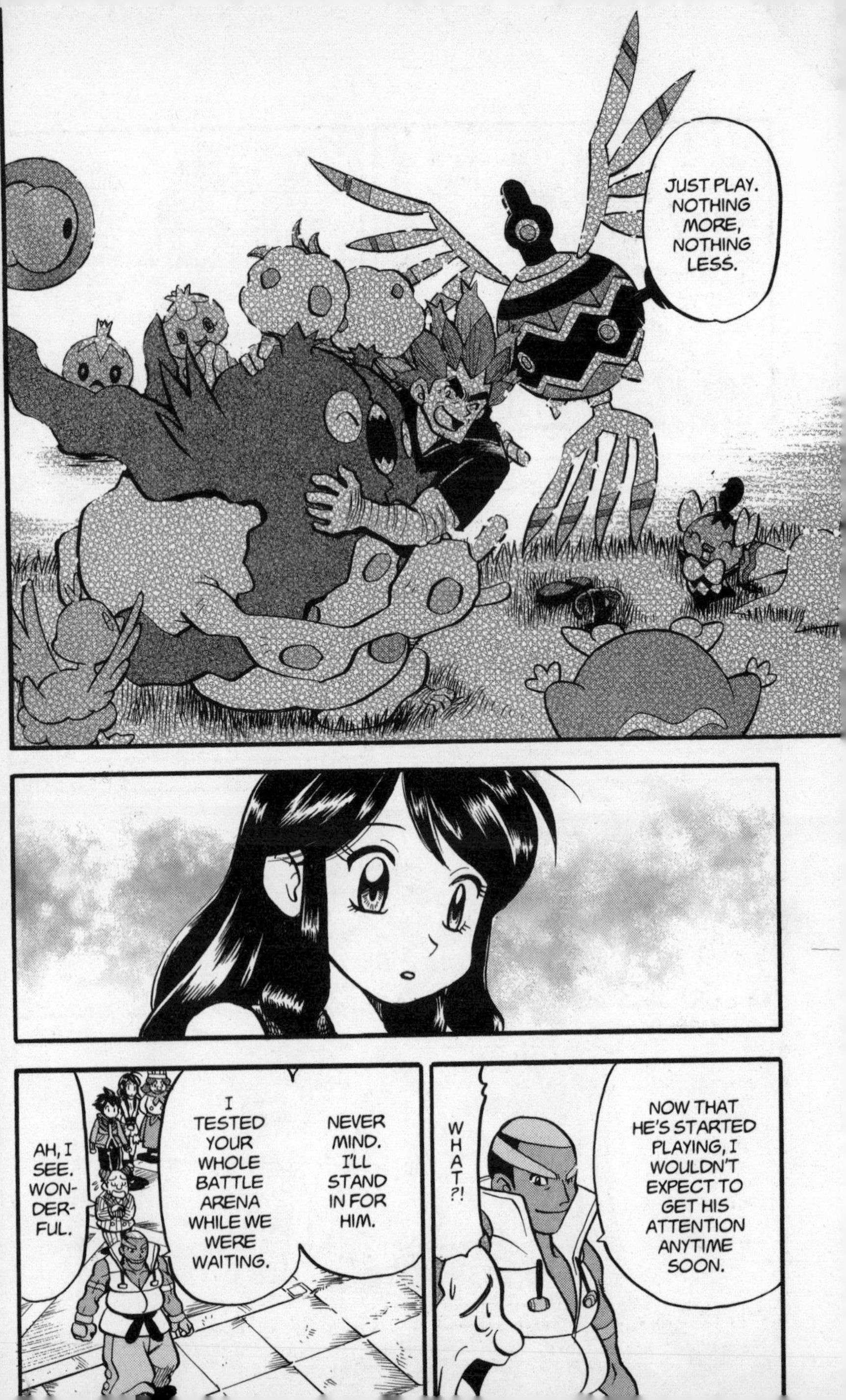
JUST PLAY. NOTHING MORE, NOTHING LESS.
NOW THAT HE'S STARTED PLAYING, I WOULDN'T EXPECT TO GET HIS ATTENTION ANYTIME SOON.
WHAT?!
NEVER MIND. I'LL STAND IN FOR HIM.
I TESTED YOUR WHOLE BATTLE ARENA WHILE WE WERE WAITING.
AH, I SEE. WON-DER-FUL.

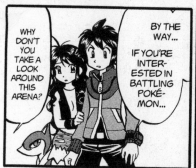

OH, TO AN-SWER YOUR QUES-TION...
ALL I SAW WAS THIS GIRL AND THAT SERVINE.
BY THE WAY... IF YOU'RE INTER-ESTED IN BATTLING POKÉ-MON...
WHY DON'T YOU TAKE A LOOK AROUND THIS ARENA?
IT'S CALLED THE BATTLE SUB-WAY.
THIS IS THE NEWEST ADDITION TO NIMBASA CITY'S ENTERTAINMENT ATTRACTIONS—HOT ON THE HEELS OF THE POKÉMON MUSICAL.
AS YOU MIGHT GUESS FROM THE NAME, THIS BATTLE SYSTEM UTILIZES THE SUBWAY NETWORK CONNECTING THE UNOVA REGION.
YOU BATTLE INSIDE A SPECIAL TRAIN AS IT GOES THROUGH THE TUNNELS.

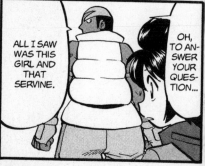

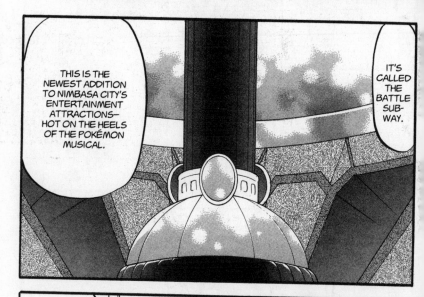

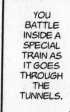

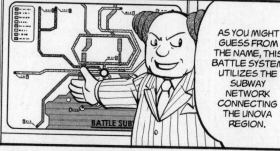

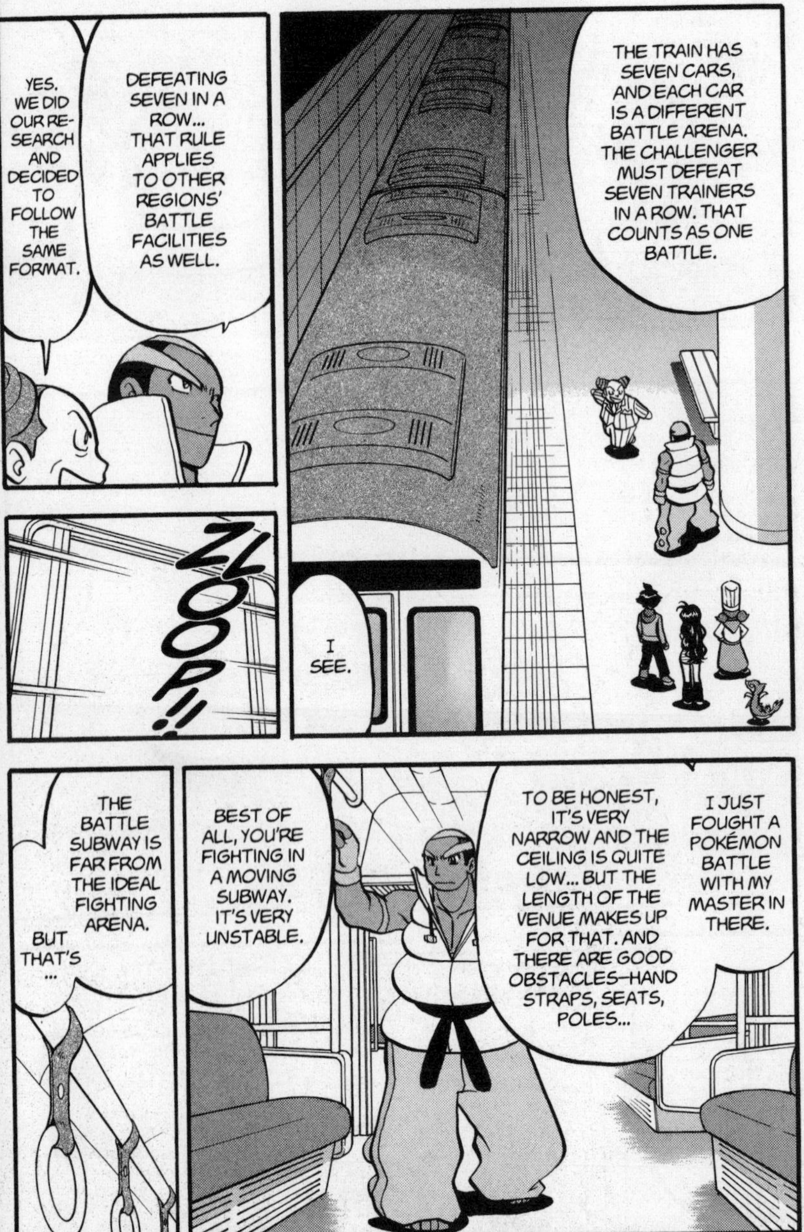
THE TRAIN HAS SEVEN CARS, AND EACH CAR IS A DIFFERENT BATTLE ARENA. THE CHALLENGER MUST DEFEAT SEVEN TRAINERS IN A ROW. THAT COUNTS AS ONE BATTLE.
I SEE.
DEFEATING SEVEN IN A ROW... THAT RULE APPLIES TO OTHER REGIONS' BATTLE FACILITIES AS WELL.
YES. WE DID OUR RE-SEARCH AND DECIDED TO FOLLOW THE SAME FORMAT.
ZLOOP!!
I JUST FOUGHT A POKÉMON BATTLE WITH MY MASTER IN THERE.
TO BE HONEST, IT'S VERY NARROW AND THE CEILING IS QUITE LOW... BUT THE LENGTH OF THE VENUE MAKES UP FOR THAT. AND THERE ARE GOOD OBSTACLES—HAND STRAPS, SEATS, POLES...
BEST OF ALL, YOU'RE FIGHTING IN A MOVING SUBWAY. IT'S VERY UNSTABLE.
THE BATTLE SUBWAY IS FAR FROM THE IDEAL FIGHTING ARENA.
BUT THAT'S ...

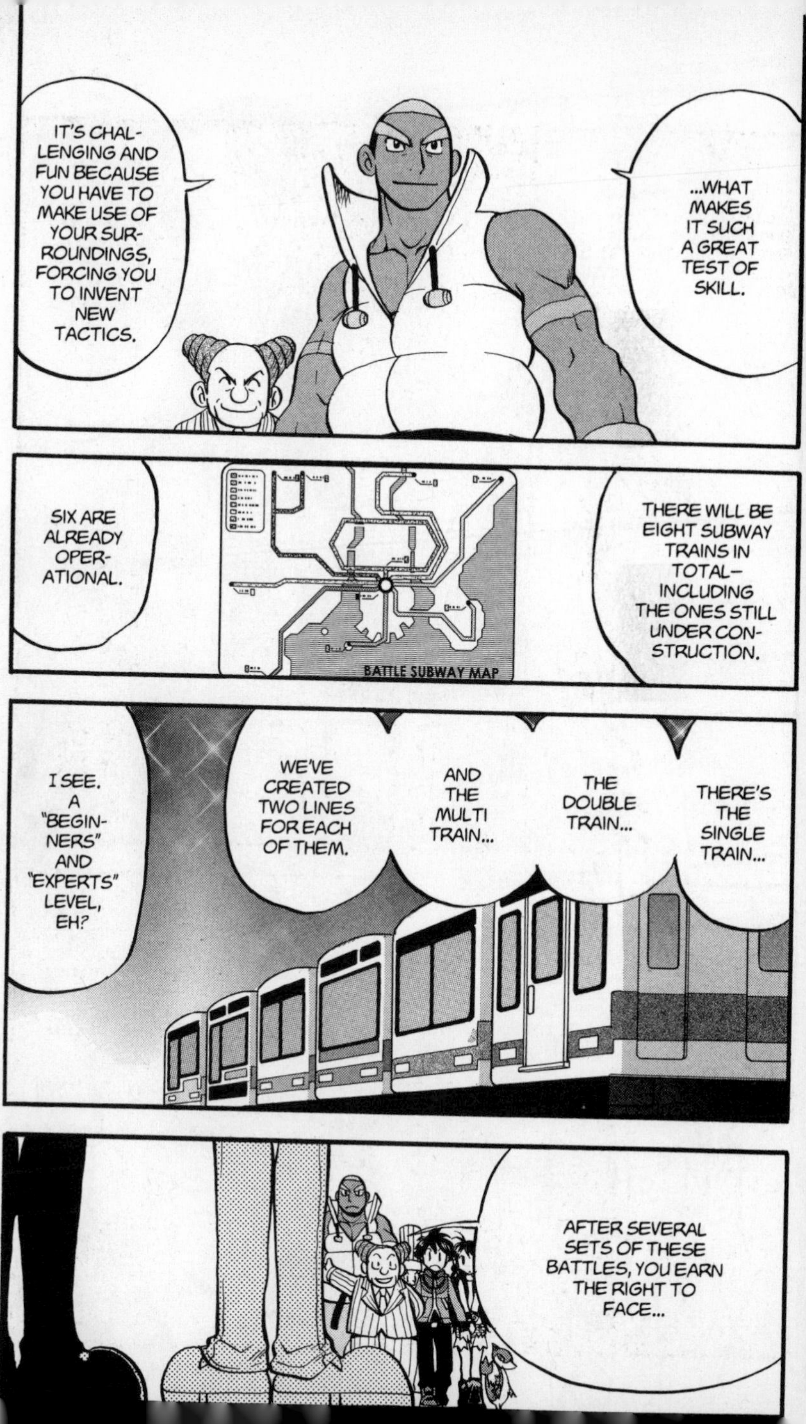
...WHAT MAKES IT SUCH A GREAT TEST OF SKILL.
IT'S CHAL-LENGING AND FUN BECAUSE YOU HAVE TO MAKE USE OF YOUR SUR-ROUNDINGS, FORCING YOU TO INVENT NEW TACTICS.
THERE WILL BE EIGHT SUBWAY TRAINS IN TOTAL—INCLUDING THE ONES STILL UNDER CON-STRUCTION.
BATTLE SUBWAY MAP
SIX ARE ALREADY OPER-ATIONAL.
THERE'S THE SINGLE TRAIN...
THE DOUBLE TRAIN...
AND THE MULTI TRAIN...
WE'VE CREATED TWO LINES FOR EACH OF THEM.
I SEE. A "BEGIN-NERS" AND "EXPERTS" LEVEL, EH?
AFTER SEVERAL SETS OF THESE BATTLES, YOU EARN THE RIGHT TO FACE...

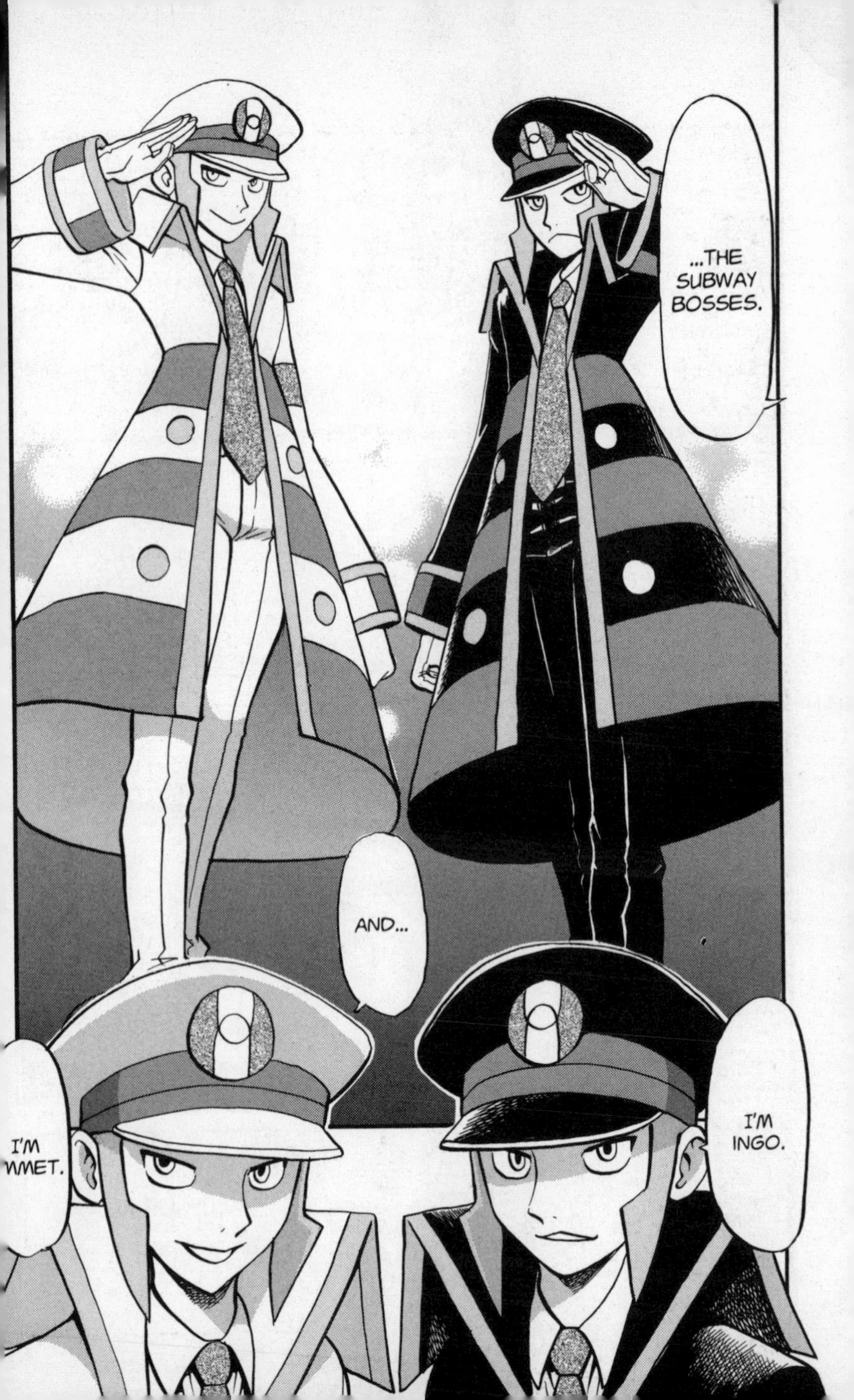
...THE SUBWAY BOSSES.
AND...
I'M INGO.
I'M MMET.

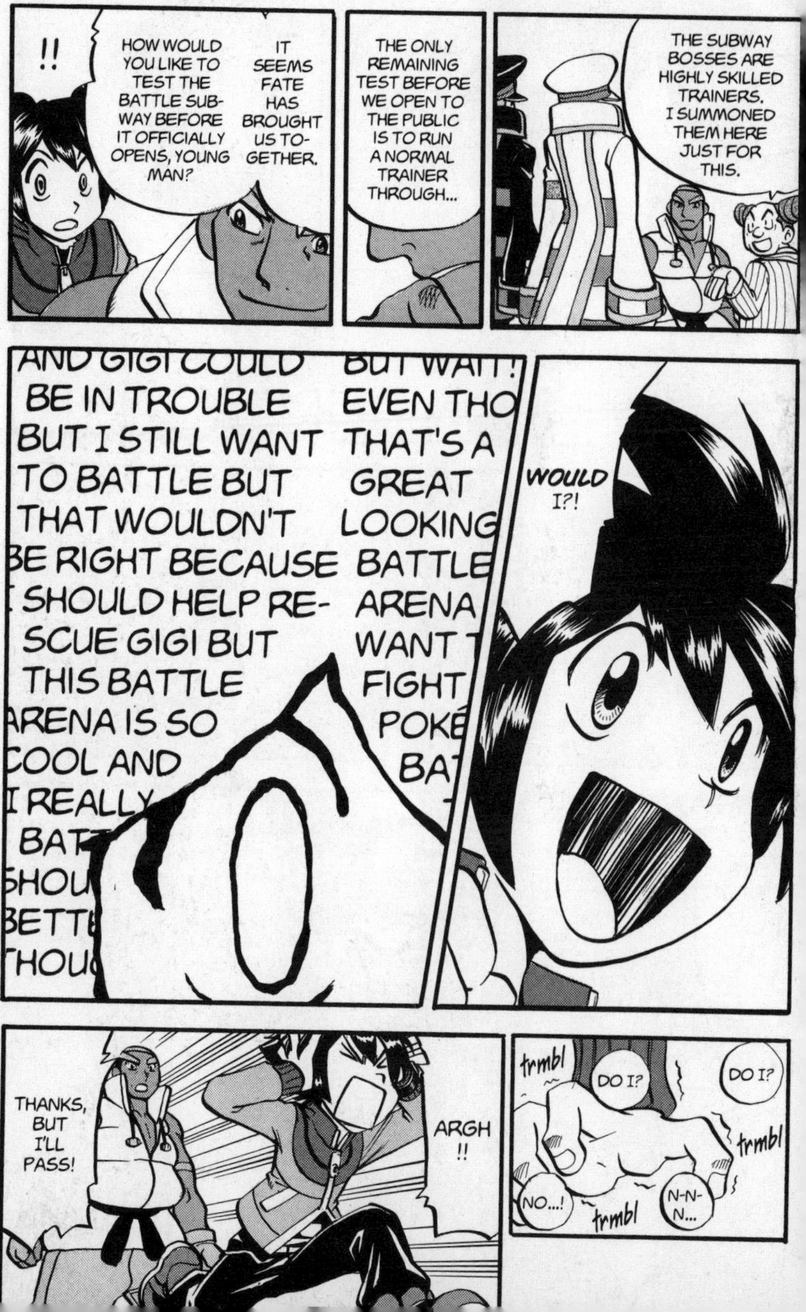

THE SUBWAY BOSSES ARE HIGHLY SKILLED TRAINERS. I SUMMONED THEM HERE JUST FOR THIS.
THE ONLY REMAINING TEST BEFORE WE OPEN TO THE PUBLIC IS TO RUN A NORMAL TRAINER THROUGH...
IT SEEMS FATE HAS BROUGHT US TOGETHER.
HOW WOULD YOU LIKE TO TEST THE BATTLE SUBWAY BEFORE IT OFFICIALLY OPENS, YOUNG MAN?
!!
WOULD I?!
BUT WAIT! EVEN THO THAT'S A GREAT LOOKING BATTLE ARENA WANT FIGHT POKÉ BA
AND GIGI COULD BE IN TROUBLE BUT I STILL WANT TO BATTLE BUT THAT WOULDN'T BE RIGHT BECAUSE I SHOULD HELP RESCUE GIGI BUT THIS BATTLE ARENA IS SO COOL AND I REALLY BAT SHOU BETT THOU
DO I?
trmbl
DO I?
trmbl
N-N-N...
trmbl
NO...!
ARGH!!
THANKS, BUT I'LL PASS!

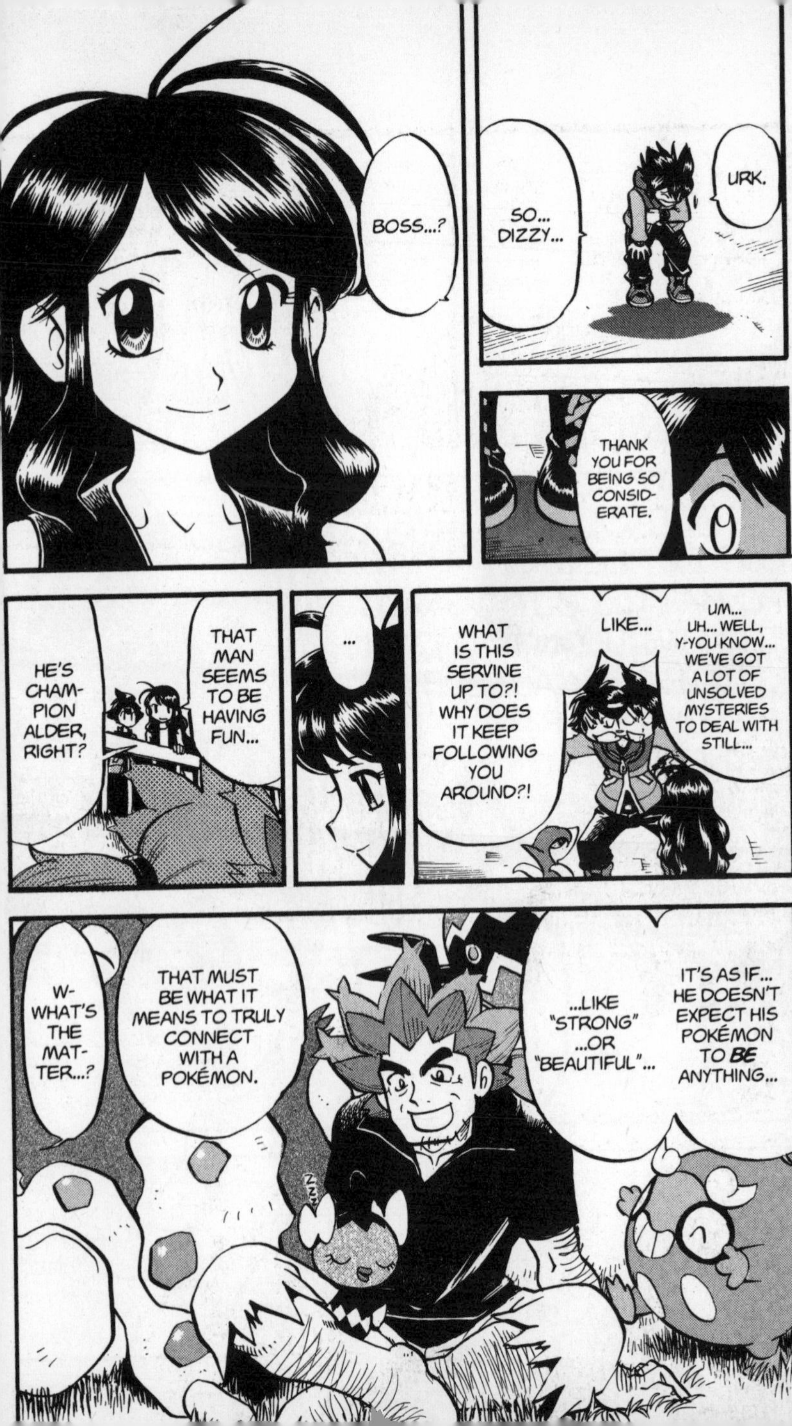
URK.
SO... DIZZY...
THANK YOU FOR BEING SO CONSIDERATE.
BOSS...?
UM... UH... WELL, Y-YOU KNOW... WE'VE GOT A LOT OF UNSOLVED MYSTERIES TO DEAL WITH STILL...
LIKE...
WHAT IS THIS SERVINE UP TO?! WHY DOES IT KEEP FOLLOWING YOU AROUND?!
...
THAT MAN SEEMS TO BE HAVING FUN...
HE'S CHAMPION ALDER, RIGHT?
IT'S AS IF... HE DOESN'T EXPECT HIS POKÉMON TO **BE** ANYTHING...
...LIKE "STRONG" ...OR "BEAUTIFUL"...
THAT MUST BE WHAT IT MEANS TO TRULY CONNECT WITH A POKÉMON.
W-WHAT'S THE MATTER...?

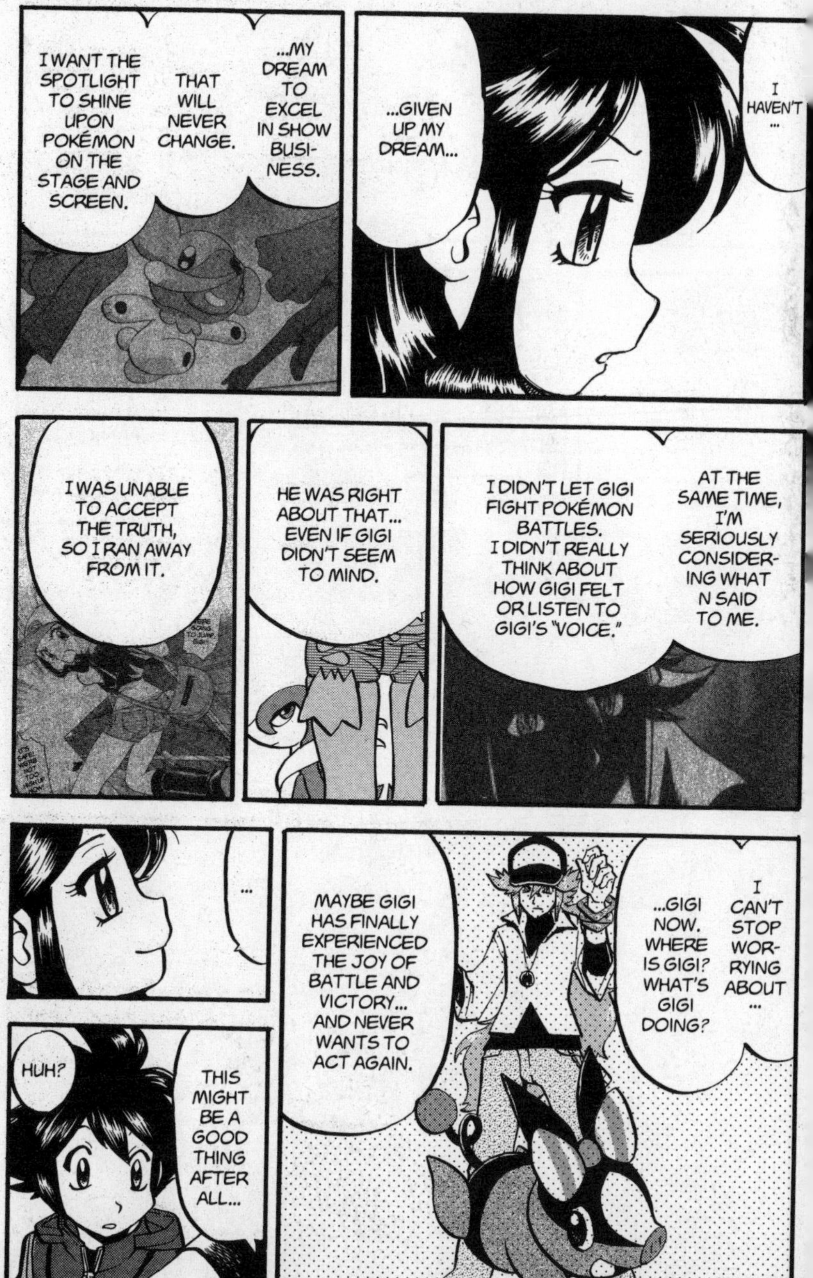
I HAVEN'T ...
...GIVEN UP MY DREAM...
...MY DREAM TO EXCEL IN SHOW BUSI-NESS.
THAT WILL NEVER CHANGE.
I WANT THE SPOTLIGHT TO SHINE UPON POKÉMON ON THE STAGE AND SCREEN.
AT THE SAME TIME, I'M SERIOUSLY CONSIDER-ING WHAT N SAID TO ME.
I DIDN'T LET GIGI FIGHT POKÉMON BATTLES. I DIDN'T REALLY THINK ABOUT HOW GIGI FELT OR LISTEN TO GIGI'S "VOICE."
HE WAS RIGHT ABOUT THAT... EVEN IF GIGI DIDN'T SEEM TO MIND.
I WAS UNABLE TO ACCEPT THE TRUTH, SO I RAN AWAY FROM IT.
I CAN'T STOP WOR-RYING ABOUT ...
...GIGI NOW. WHERE IS GIGI? WHAT'S GIGI DOING?
MAYBE GIGI HAS FINALLY EXPERIENCED THE JOY OF BATTLE AND VICTORY... AND NEVER WANTS TO ACT AGAIN.
...
THIS MIGHT BE A GOOD THING AFTER ALL...
HUH?

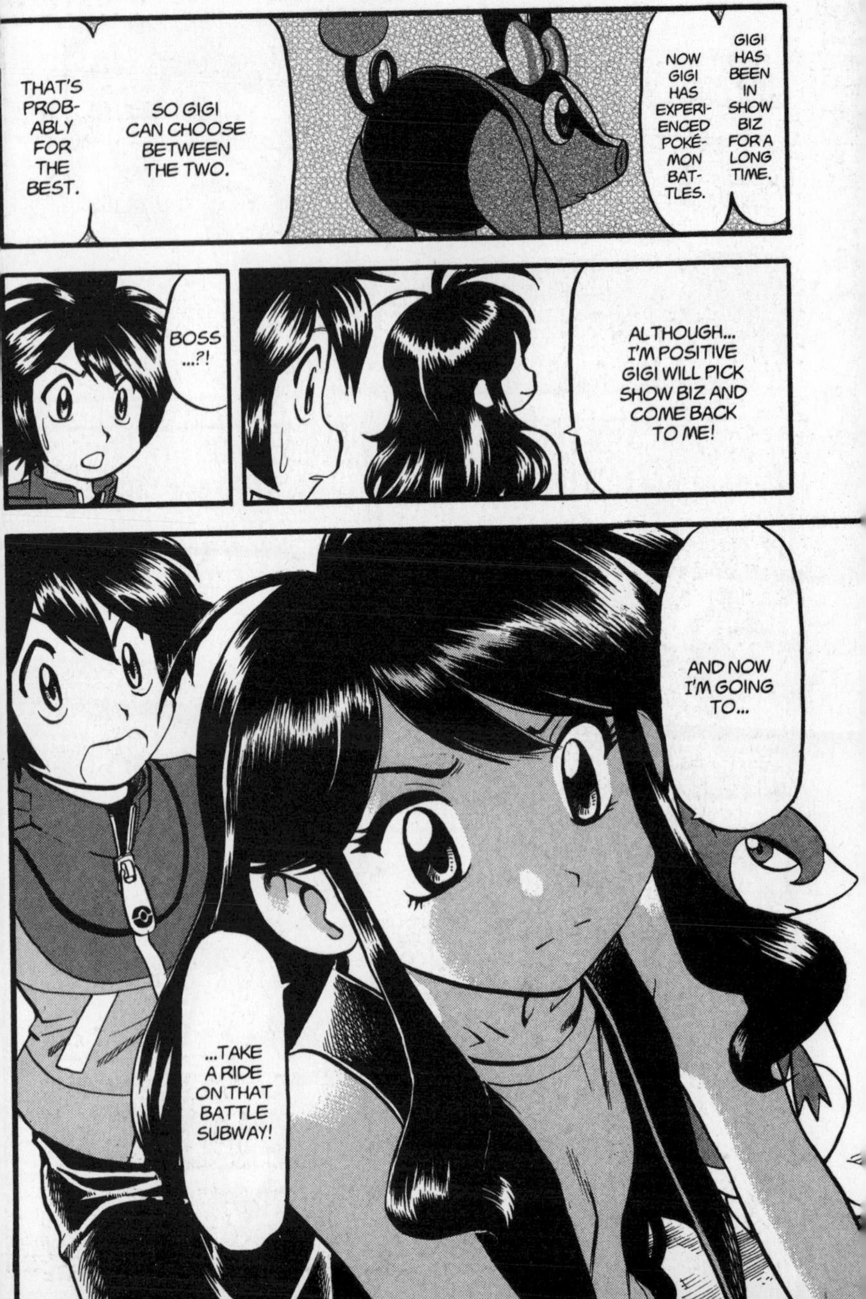
GIGI HAS BEEN IN SHOW BIZ FOR A LONG TIME.
NOW GIGI HAS EXPERIENCED POKÉMON BATTLES.
SO GIGI CAN CHOOSE BETWEEN THE TWO.
THAT'S PROBABLY FOR THE BEST.
ALTHOUGH... I'M POSITIVE GIGI WILL PICK SHOW BIZ AND COME BACK TO ME!
BOSS ...?!
AND NOW I'M GOING TO...
...TAKE A RIDE ON THAT BATTLE SUBWAY!

ADVENTURE MAP

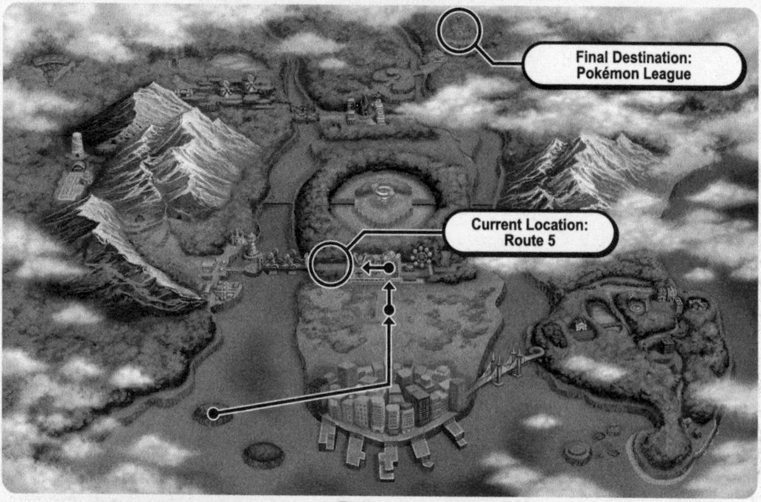

Final Destination:
Pokémon League
Current Location:
Route 5

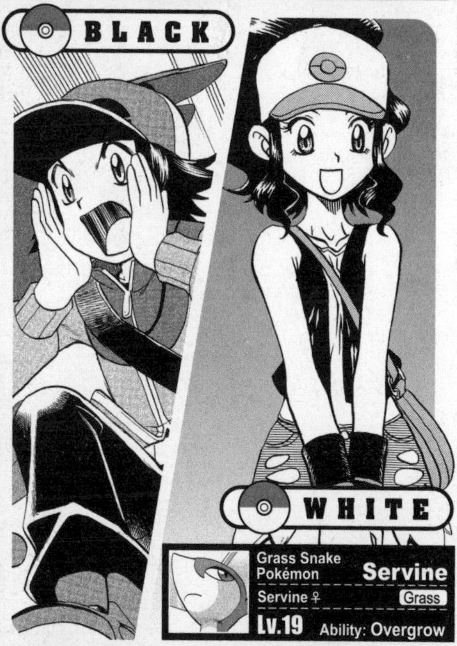

BLACK
WHITE

Fire Pig Pokémon **Nite**
Pignite ♂ Fire Fighting
Lv.27 Ability: Blaze

Dream Eater Pokémon **Musha**
Munna ♂ Psychic
Lv.47 Ability: Forewarn

Valiant Pokémon **Brav**
Braviary ♂ Normal Flying
Lv.54 Ability: Sheer Force

EleSpider Pokémon **Tula**
Galvantula ♂ Bug Electric
Lv.50 Ability: Unnerve

Grass Snake Pokémon **Servine**
Servine ♀ Grass
Lv.19 Ability: Overgrow

TRIO BADGE · BASIC BADGE · INSECT BADGE · BOLT BADGE · ? · ? · ? · ?

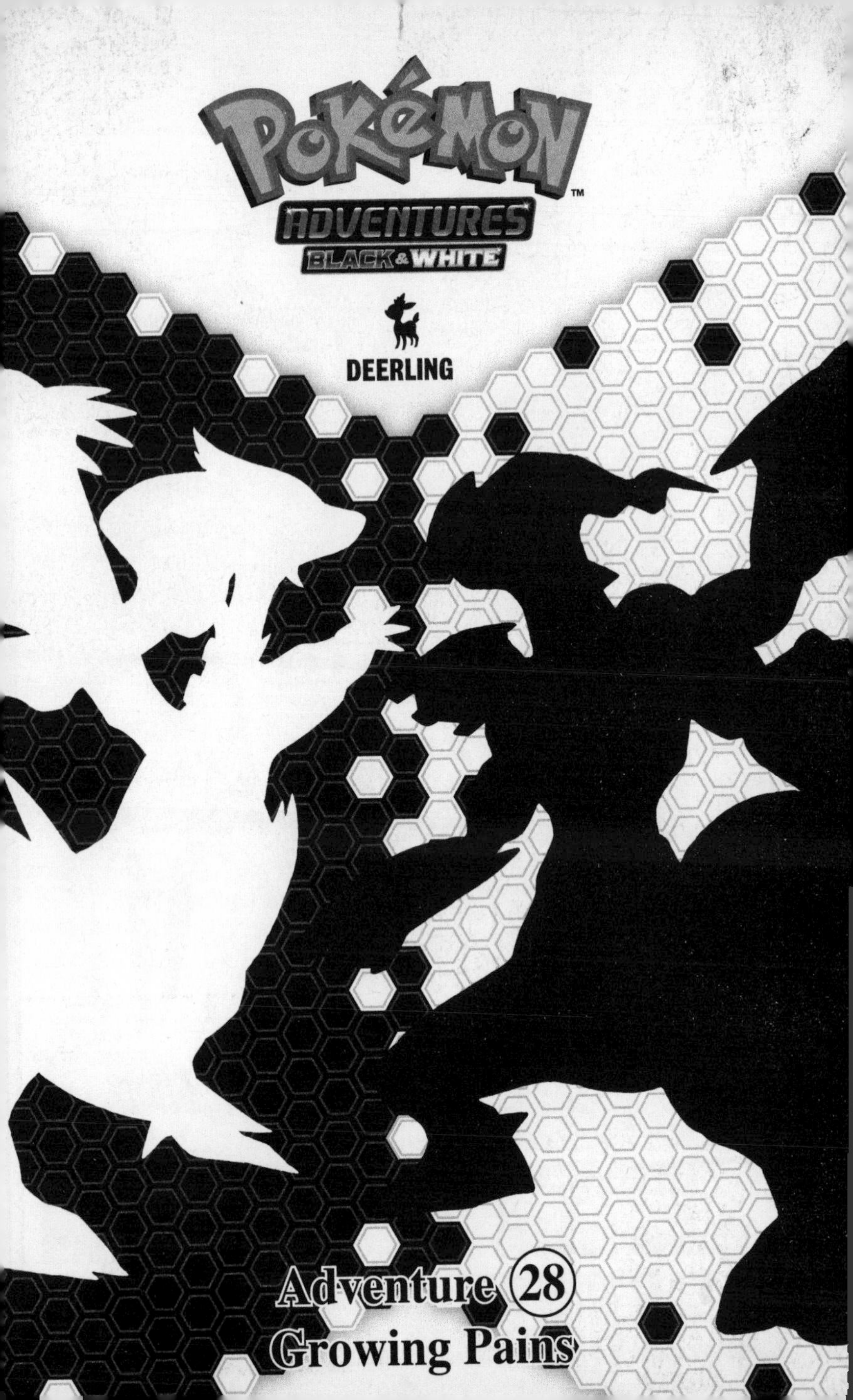
POKÉMON™
ADVENTURES
BLACK & WHITE
DEERLING
Adventure 28
Growing Pains

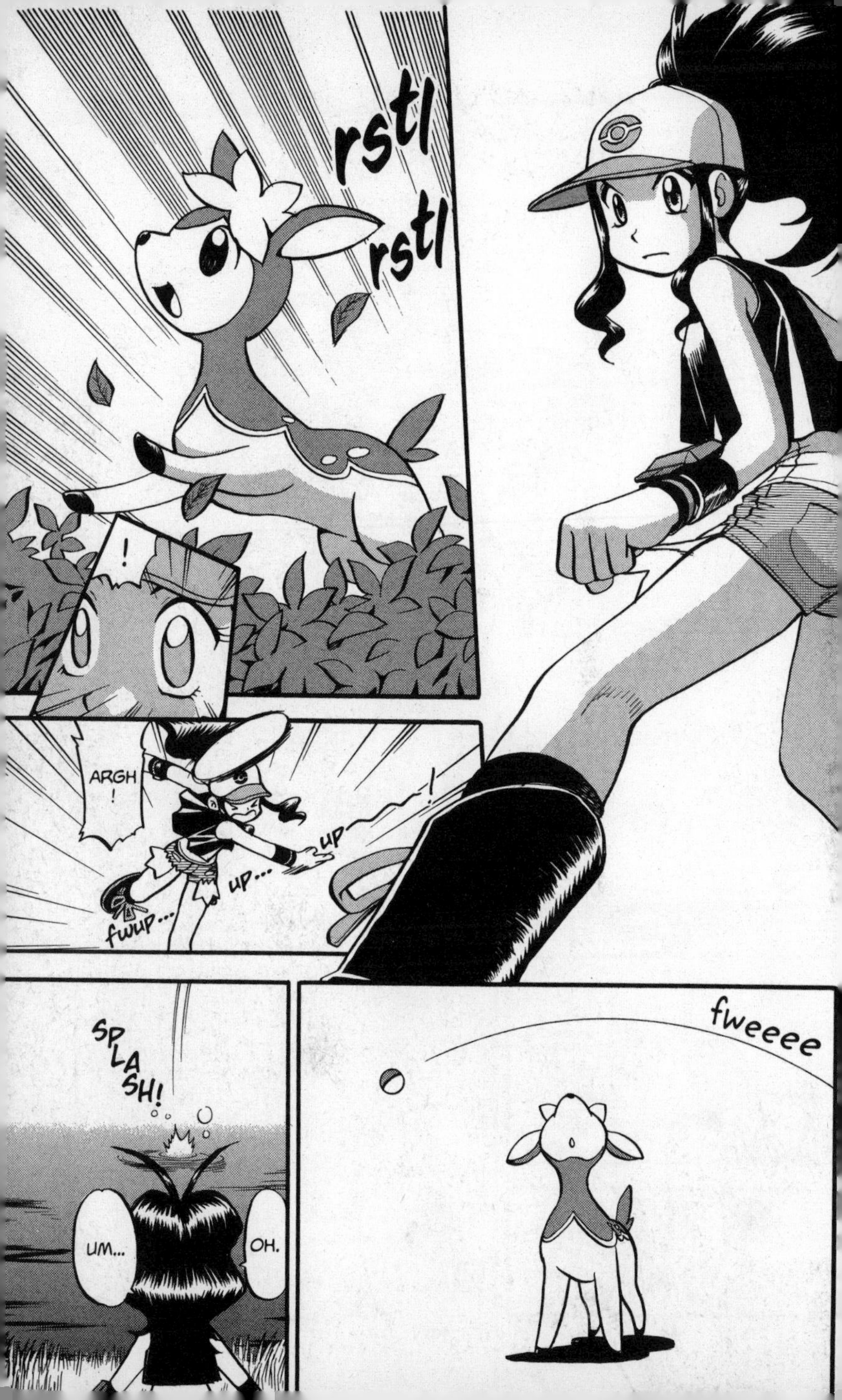

rstl
rstl
!
ARGH!
fwup... up... up~~~!
fweeee
SPLASH!
OH.
UM...

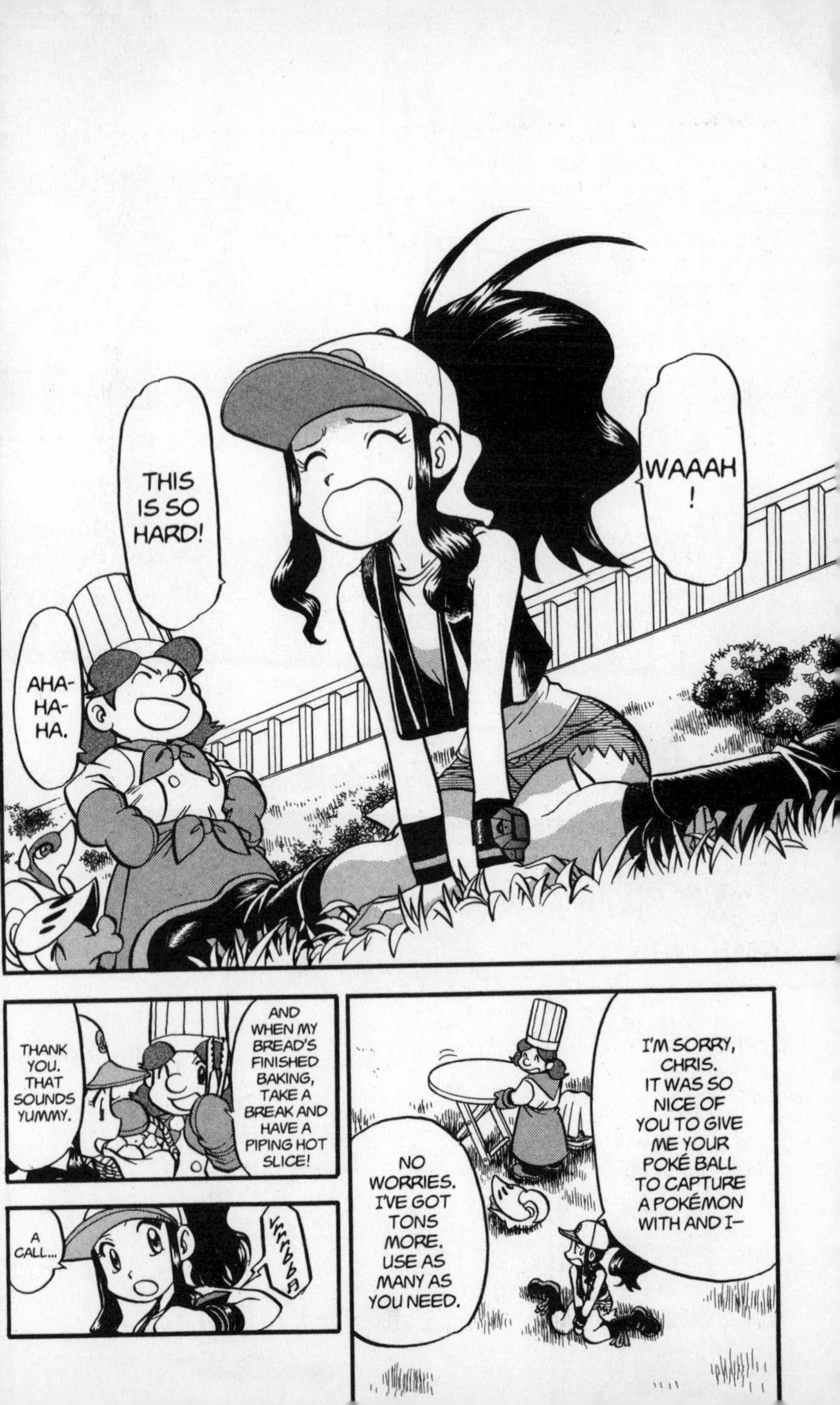
WAAAH!
THIS IS SO HARD!
AHA-HA-HA.
I'M SORRY, CHRIS. IT WAS SO NICE OF YOU TO GIVE ME YOUR POKÉ BALL TO CAPTURE A POKÉMON WITH AND I—
NO WORRIES. I'VE GOT TONS MORE. USE AS MANY AS YOU NEED.
AND WHEN MY BREAD'S FINISHED BAKING, TAKE A BREAK AND HAVE A PIPING HOT SLICE!
THANK YOU. THAT SOUNDS YUMMY.
Vrrrbb
A CALL...

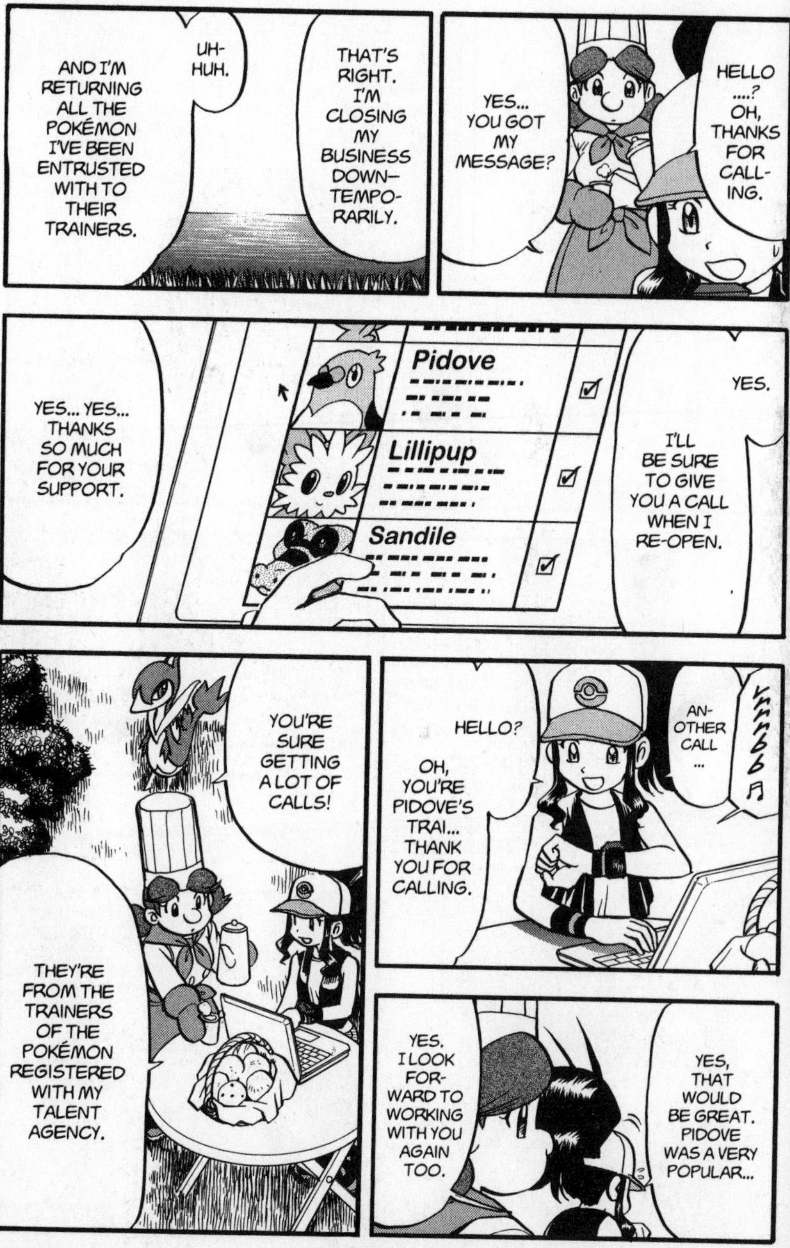
HELLO ....? OH, THANKS FOR CALLING.
YES... YOU GOT MY MESSAGE?
THAT'S RIGHT. I'M CLOSING MY BUSINESS DOWN—TEMPORARILY.
UH-HUH.
AND I'M RETURNING ALL THE POKéMON I'VE BEEN ENTRUSTED WITH TO THEIR TRAINERS.
YES.
I'LL BE SURE TO GIVE YOU A CALL WHEN I RE-OPEN.
Pidove
Lillipup
Sandile
YES... YES... THANKS SO MUCH FOR YOUR SUPPORT.
AN-OTHER CALL ...
HELLO?
OH, YOU'RE PIDOVE'S TRAI... THANK YOU FOR CALLING.
YES, THAT WOULD BE GREAT. PIDOVE WAS A VERY POPULAR...
YES. I LOOK FOR-WARD TO WORKING WITH YOU AGAIN TOO.
YOU'RE SURE GETTING A LOT OF CALLS!
THEY'RE FROM THE TRAINERS OF THE POKéMON REGISTERED WITH MY TALENT AGENCY.

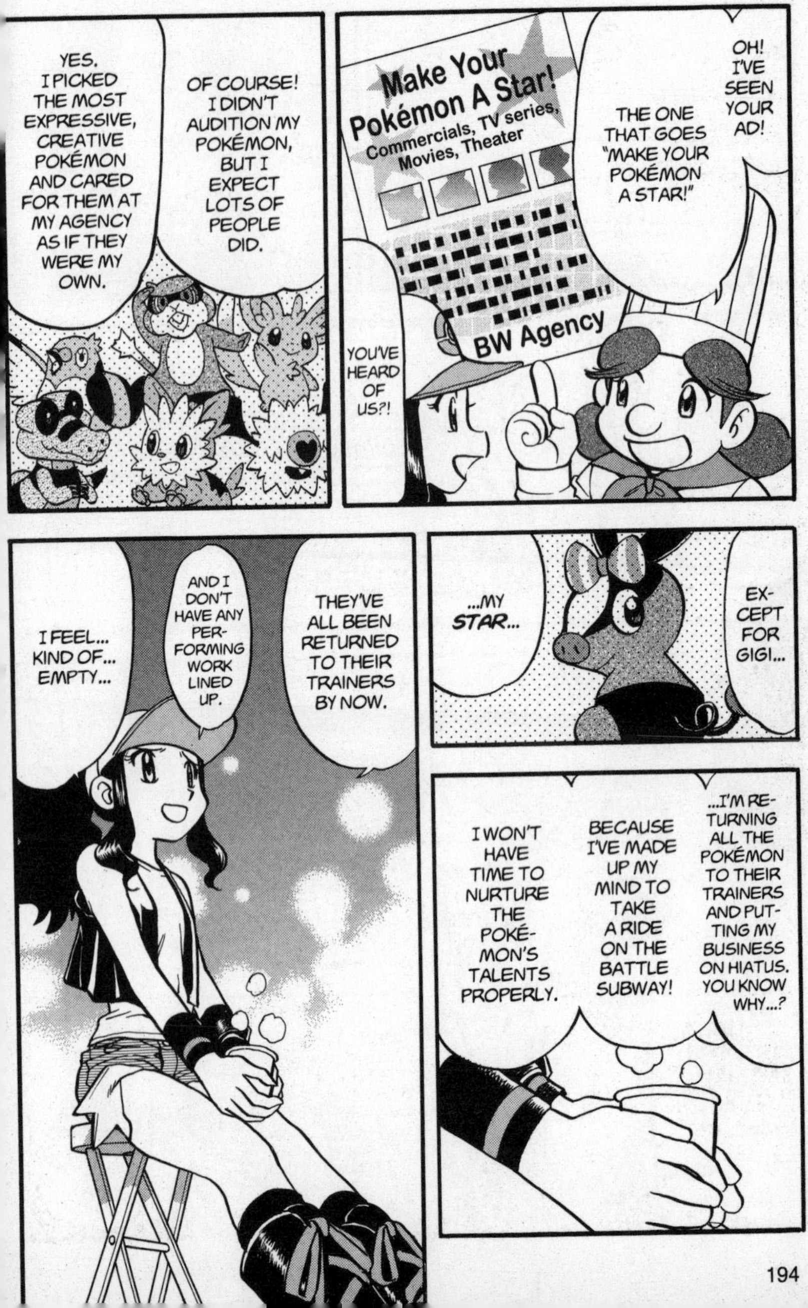
OH! I'VE SEEN YOUR AD!
THE ONE THAT GOES "MAKE YOUR POKÉMON A STAR!"
Make Your Pokémon A Star!
Commercials, TV series, Movies, Theater
BW Agency
YOU'VE HEARD OF US?!
OF COURSE! I DIDN'T AUDITION MY POKÉMON, BUT I EXPECT LOTS OF PEOPLE DID.
YES. I PICKED THE MOST EXPRESSIVE, CREATIVE POKÉMON AND CARED FOR THEM AT MY AGENCY AS IF THEY WERE MY OWN.
EX-CEPT FOR GIGI...
...MY *STAR*...
...I'M RE-TURNING ALL THE POKÉMON TO THEIR TRAINERS AND PUT-TING MY BUSINESS ON HIATUS. YOU KNOW WHY...?
BECAUSE I'VE MADE UP MY MIND TO TAKE A RIDE ON THE BATTLE SUBWAY!
I WON'T HAVE TIME TO NURTURE THE POKÉ-MON'S TALENTS PROPERLY.
THEY'VE ALL BEEN RETURNED TO THEIR TRAINERS BY NOW.
AND I DON'T HAVE ANY PER-FORMING WORK LINED UP.
I FEEL... KIND OF... EMPTY...

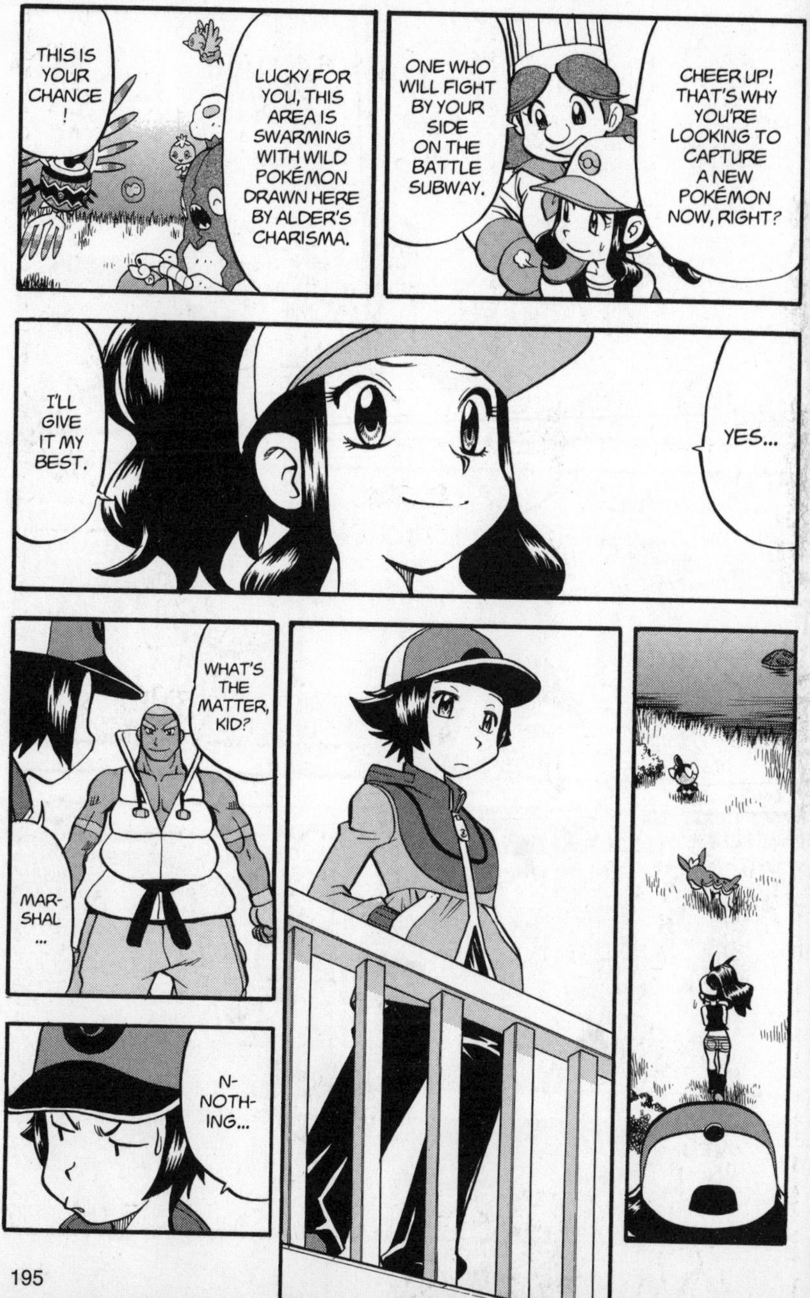
CHEER UP! THAT'S WHY YOU'RE LOOKING TO CAPTURE A NEW POKÉMON NOW, RIGHT?
ONE WHO WILL FIGHT BY YOUR SIDE ON THE BATTLE SUBWAY.
LUCKY FOR YOU, THIS AREA IS SWARMING WITH WILD POKÉMON DRAWN HERE BY ALDER'S CHARISMA.
THIS IS YOUR CHANCE!
YES...
I'LL GIVE IT MY BEST.
WHAT'S THE MATTER, KID?
MAR-SHAL...
N-NOTH-ING...

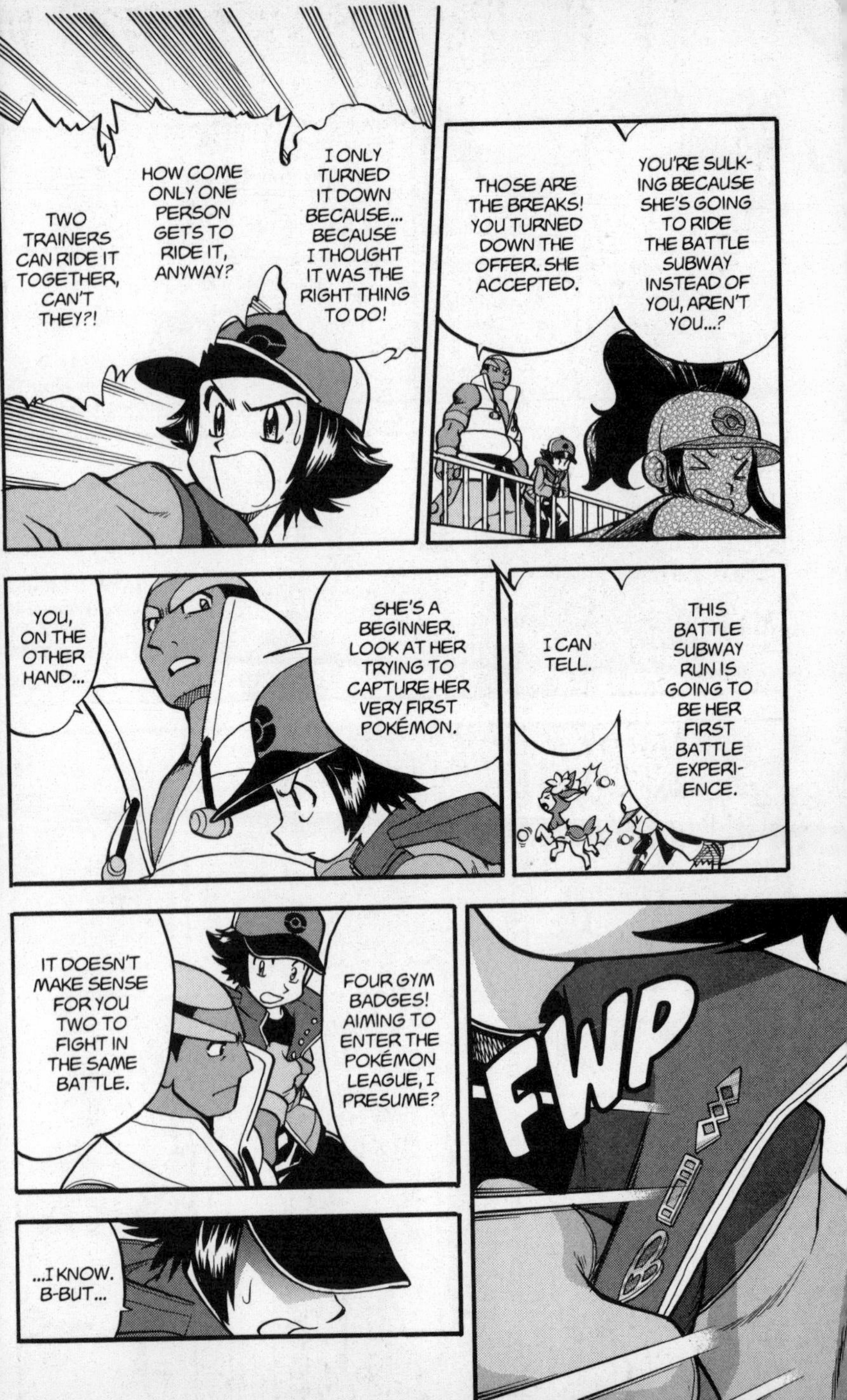

YOU'RE SULKING BECAUSE SHE'S GOING TO RIDE THE BATTLE SUBWAY INSTEAD OF YOU, AREN'T YOU...?
THOSE ARE THE BREAKS! YOU TURNED DOWN THE OFFER. SHE ACCEPTED.
I ONLY TURNED IT DOWN BECAUSE... BECAUSE I THOUGHT IT WAS THE RIGHT THING TO DO!
HOW COME ONLY ONE PERSON GETS TO RIDE IT, ANYWAY?
TWO TRAINERS CAN RIDE IT TOGETHER, CAN'T THEY?!
THIS BATTLE SUBWAY RUN IS GOING TO BE HER FIRST BATTLE EXPERIENCE.
I CAN TELL.
SHE'S A BEGINNER. LOOK AT HER TRYING TO CAPTURE HER VERY FIRST POKÉMON.
YOU, ON THE OTHER HAND...
FWP
FOUR GYM BADGES! AIMING TO ENTER THE POKÉMON LEAGUE, I PRESUME?
IT DOESN'T MAKE SENSE FOR YOU TWO TO FIGHT IN THE SAME BATTLE.
...I KNOW. B-BUT...

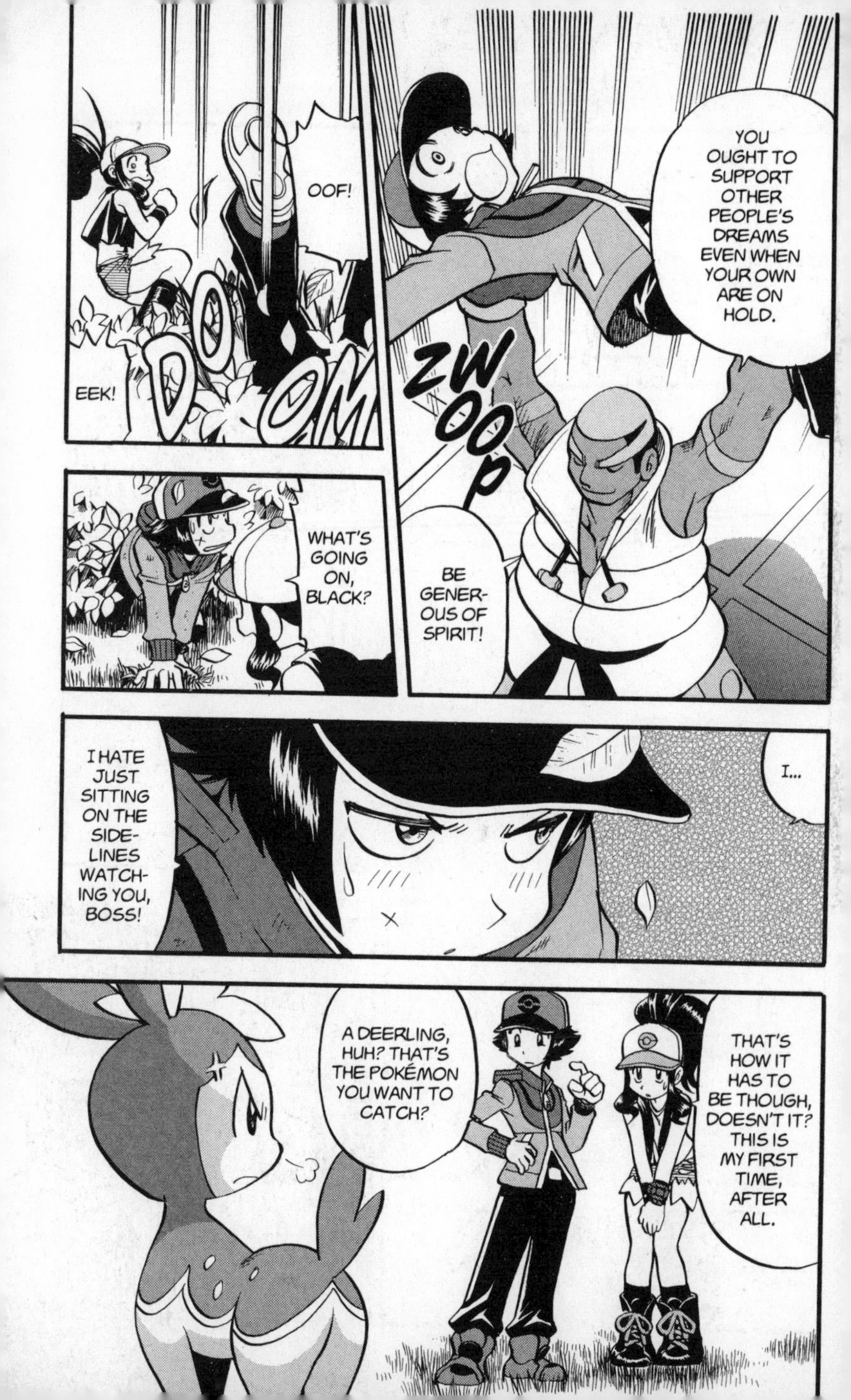
YOU OUGHT TO SUPPORT OTHER PEOPLE'S DREAMS EVEN WHEN YOUR OWN ARE ON HOLD.
ZWOOOP
BE GENER-OUS OF SPIRIT!
OOF!
DOOM
EEK!
WHAT'S GOING ON, BLACK?
I...
I HATE JUST SITTING ON THE SIDE-LINES WATCH-ING YOU, BOSS!
THAT'S HOW IT HAS TO BE THOUGH, DOESN'T IT? THIS IS MY FIRST TIME, AFTER ALL.
A DEERLING, HUH? THAT'S THE POKÉMON YOU WANT TO CATCH?

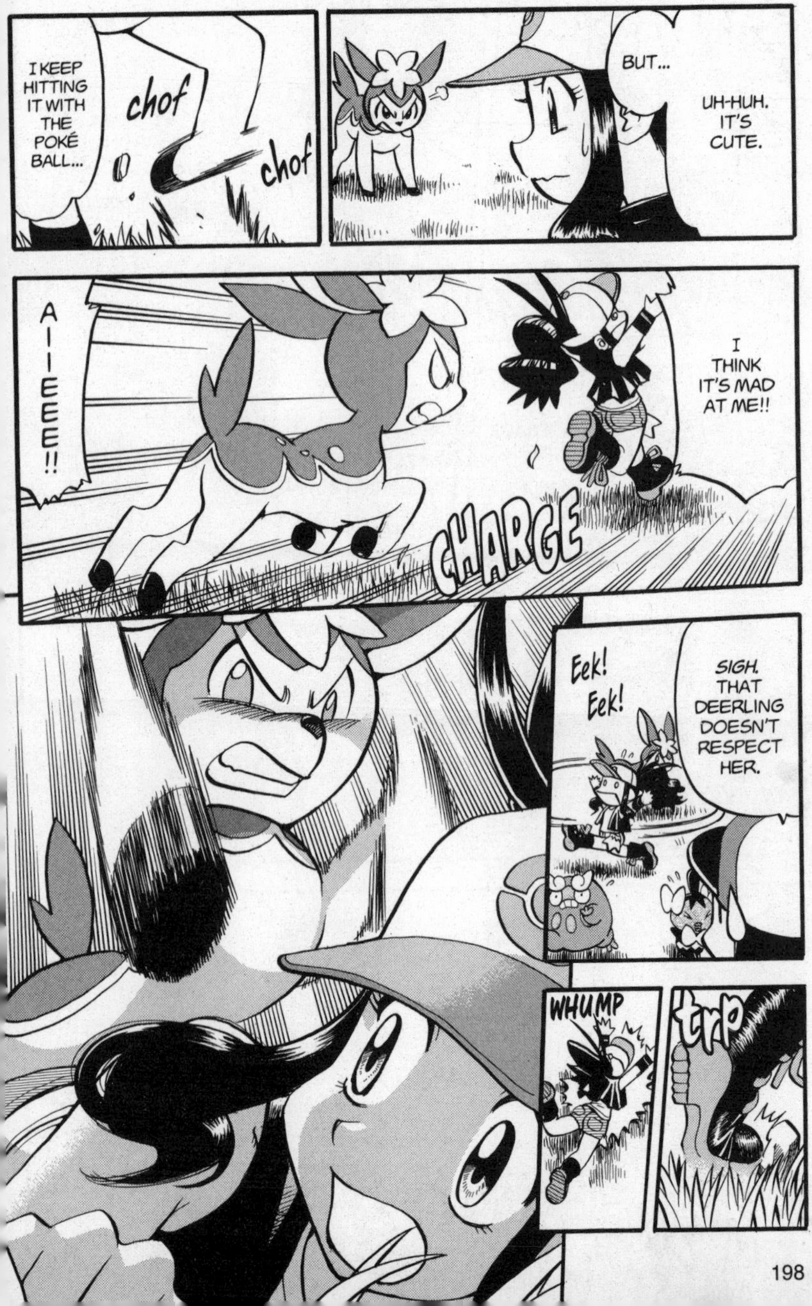
BUT...
UH-HUH. IT'S CUTE.
I KEEP HITTING IT WITH THE POKÉ BALL...
chof
chof
I THINK IT'S MAD AT ME!!
AIIEEEE!!
CHARGE
SIGH. THAT DEERLING DOESN'T RESPECT HER.
Eek! Eek!
trp
WHUMP

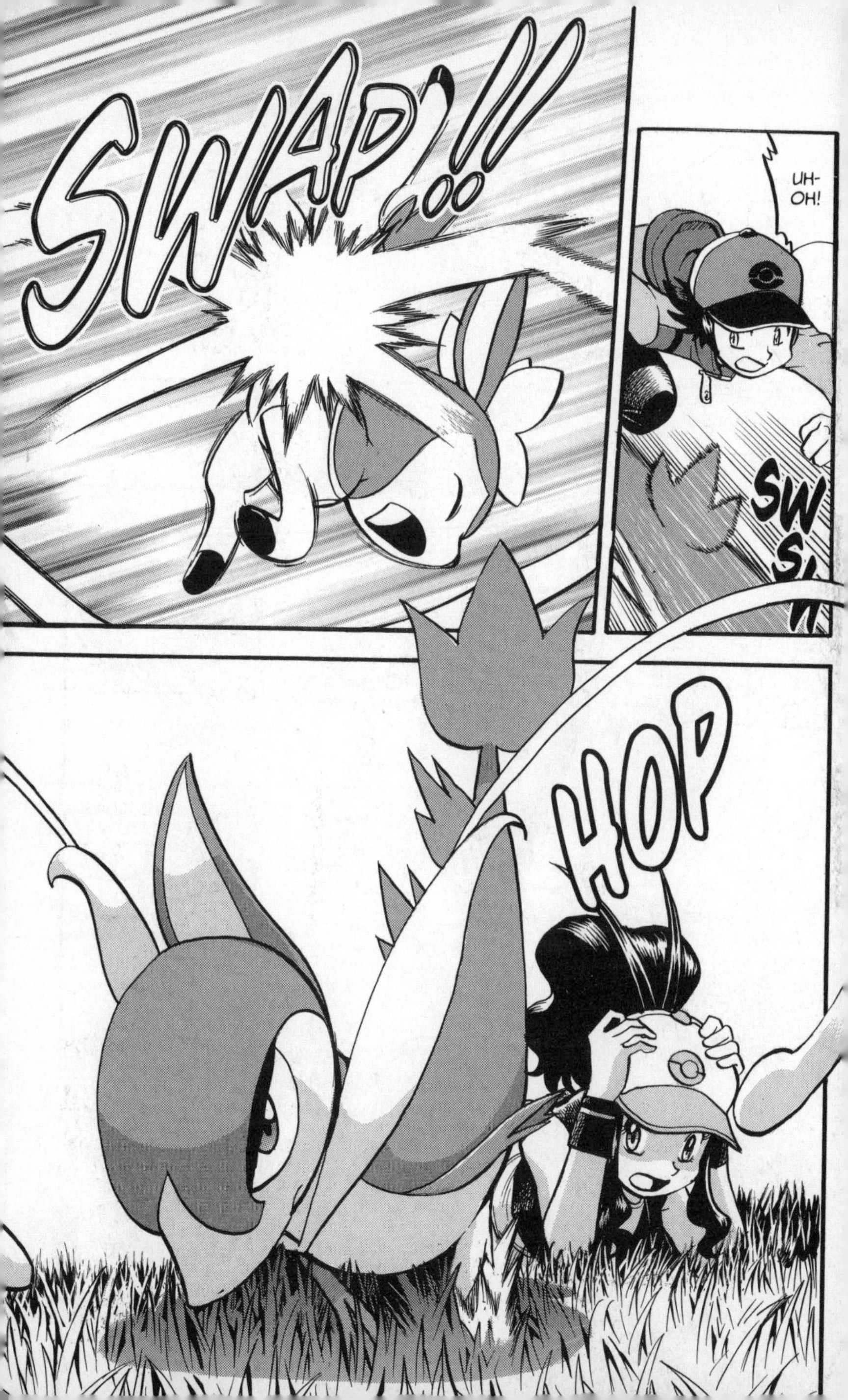
UH-OH!
SWSH
SWAP!!
HOP

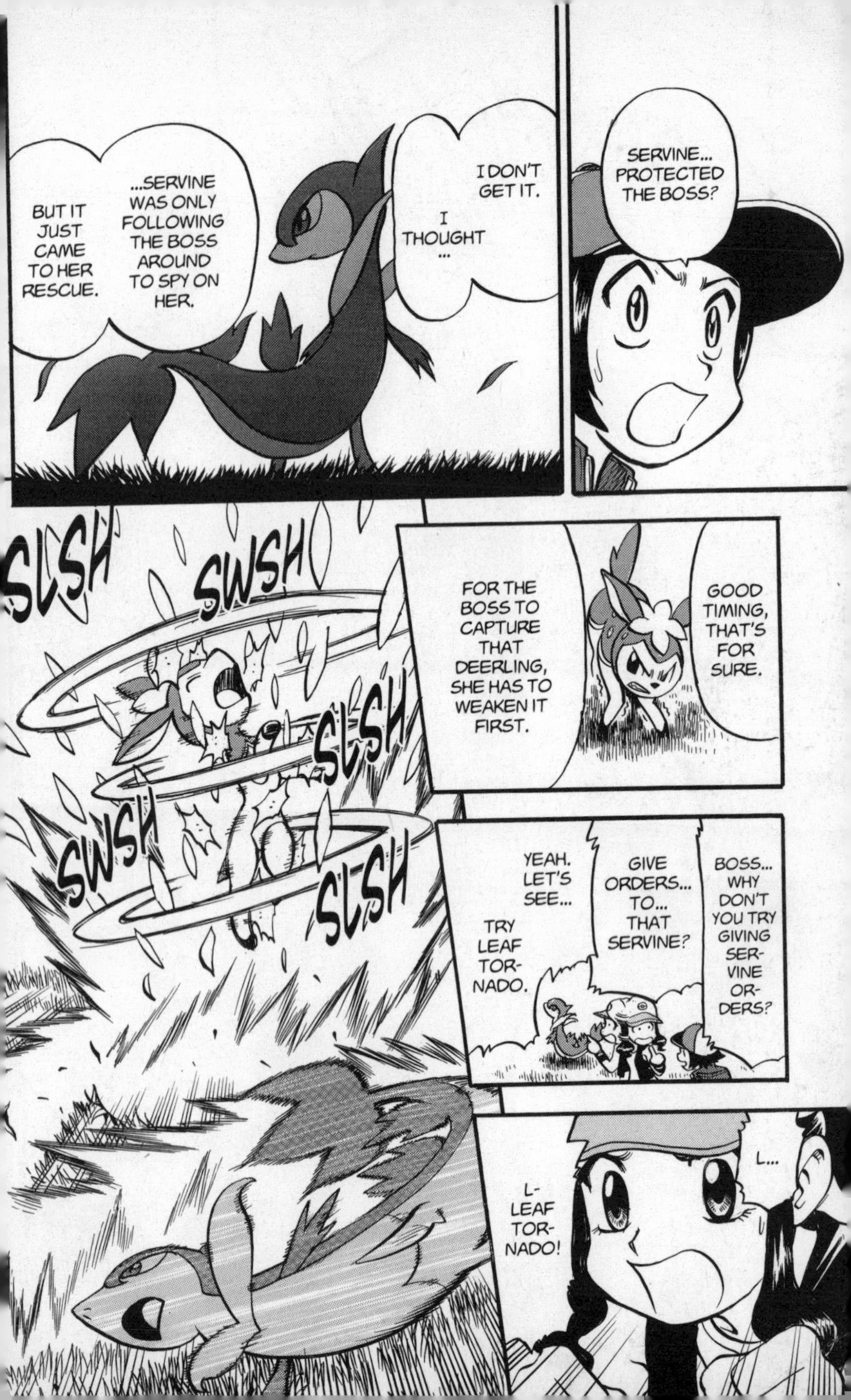
SERVINE... PROTECTED THE BOSS?
I DON'T GET IT.
I THOUGHT...
...SERVINE WAS ONLY FOLLOWING THE BOSS AROUND TO SPY ON HER.
BUT IT JUST CAME TO HER RESCUE.
GOOD TIMING, THAT'S FOR SURE.
FOR THE BOSS TO CAPTURE THAT DEERLING, SHE HAS TO WEAKEN IT FIRST.
BOSS... WHY DON'T YOU TRY GIVING SER-VINE OR-DERS?
GIVE ORDERS... TO... THAT SERVINE?
YEAH. LET'S SEE...
TRY LEAF TOR-NADO.
L...
L- LEAF TOR-NADO!
SLSH
SWSH
SLSH
SWSH
SLSH

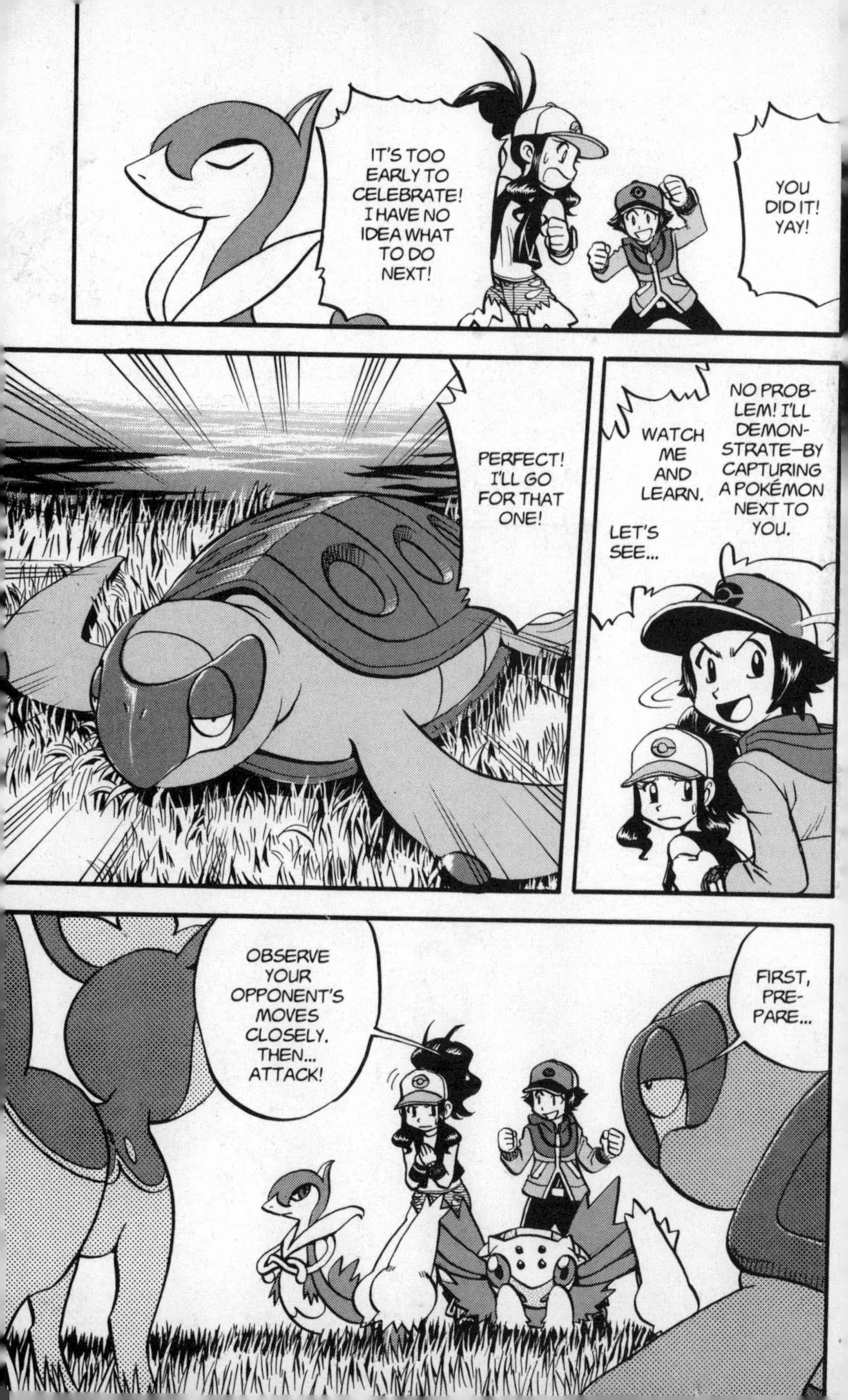
YOU DID IT! YAY!
IT'S TOO EARLY TO CELEBRATE! I HAVE NO IDEA WHAT TO DO NEXT!
NO PROBLEM! I'LL DEMONSTRATE—BY CAPTURING A POKÉMON NEXT TO YOU.
WATCH ME AND LEARN.
LET'S SEE...
PERFECT! I'LL GO FOR THAT ONE!
FIRST, PREPARE...
OBSERVE YOUR OPPONENT'S MOVES CLOSELY. THEN... ATTACK!

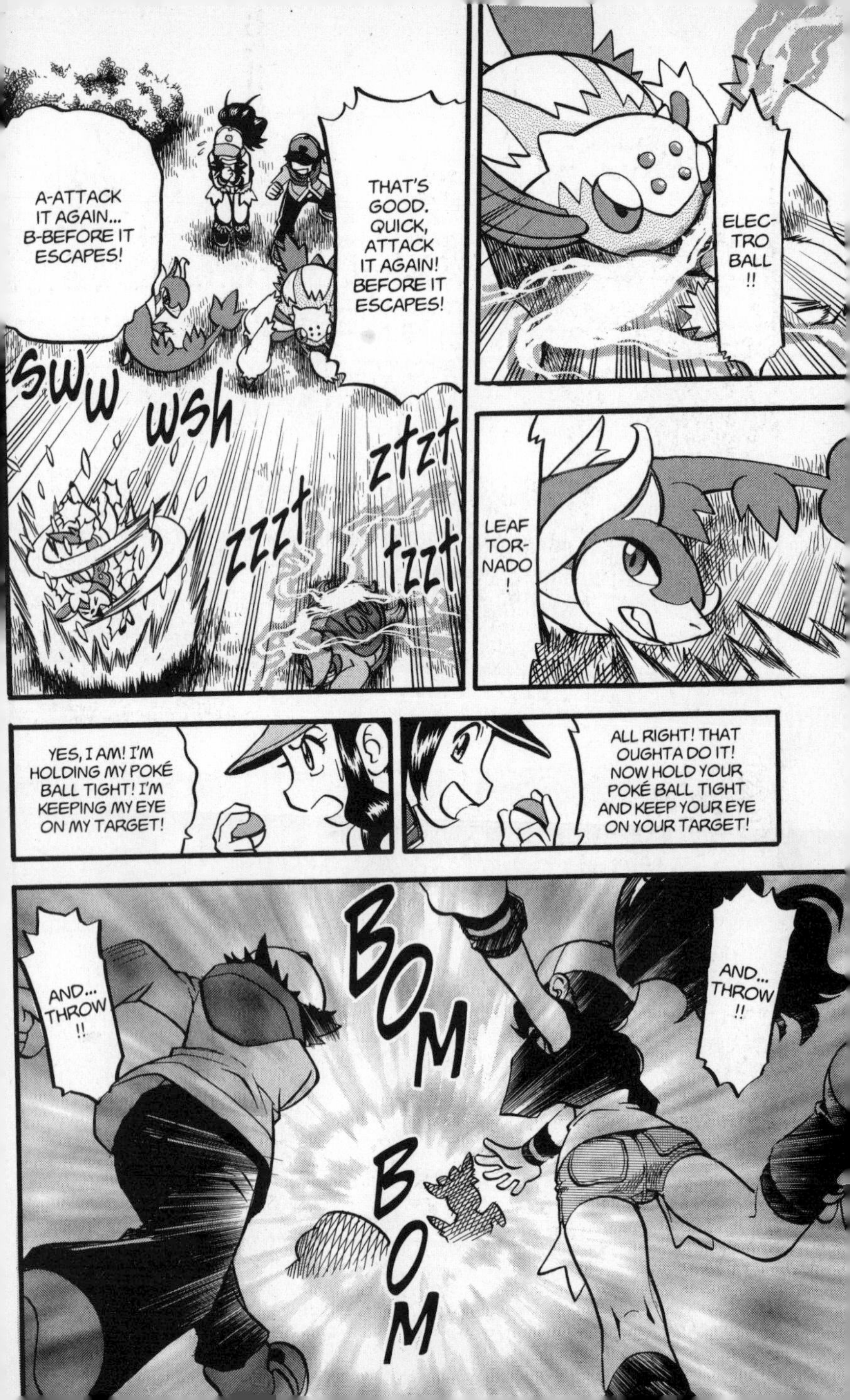
ELEC-TRO BALL !!
LEAF TOR-NADO !
THAT'S GOOD. QUICK, ATTACK IT AGAIN! BEFORE IT ESCAPES!
A-ATTACK IT AGAIN... B-BEFORE IT ESCAPES!
SWWWSH
ZTZT
ZZZT
TZZT
ALL RIGHT! THAT OUGHTA DO IT! NOW HOLD YOUR POKÉ BALL TIGHT AND KEEP YOUR EYE ON YOUR TARGET!
YES, I AM! I'M HOLDING MY POKÉ BALL TIGHT! I'M KEEPING MY EYE ON MY TARGET!
AND... THROW !!
BOM
BOM
AND... THROW !!

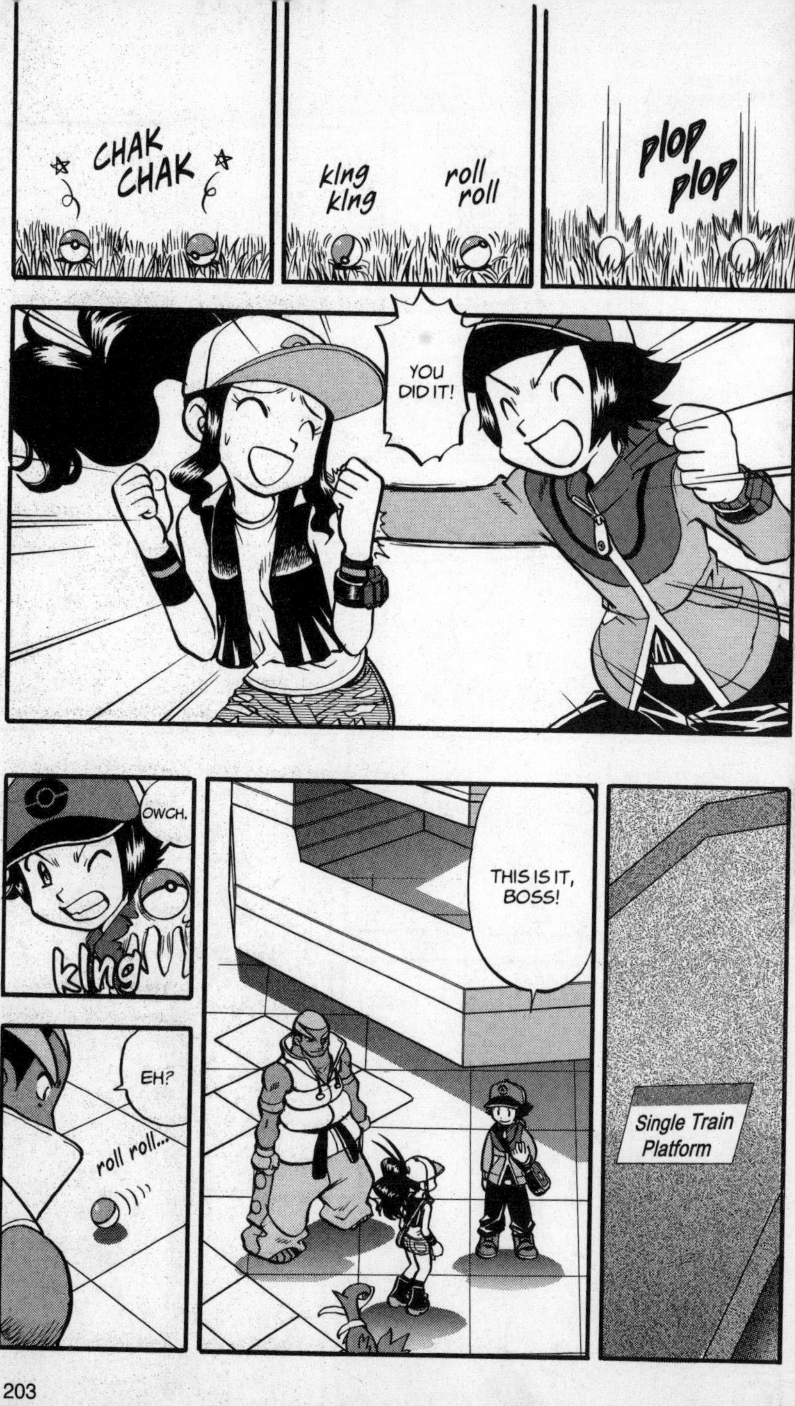
plop plop
kling kling
roll roll
CHAK CHAK
YOU DID IT!
Single Train Platform
THIS IS IT, BOSS!
OWCH.
kling
EH?
roll roll...

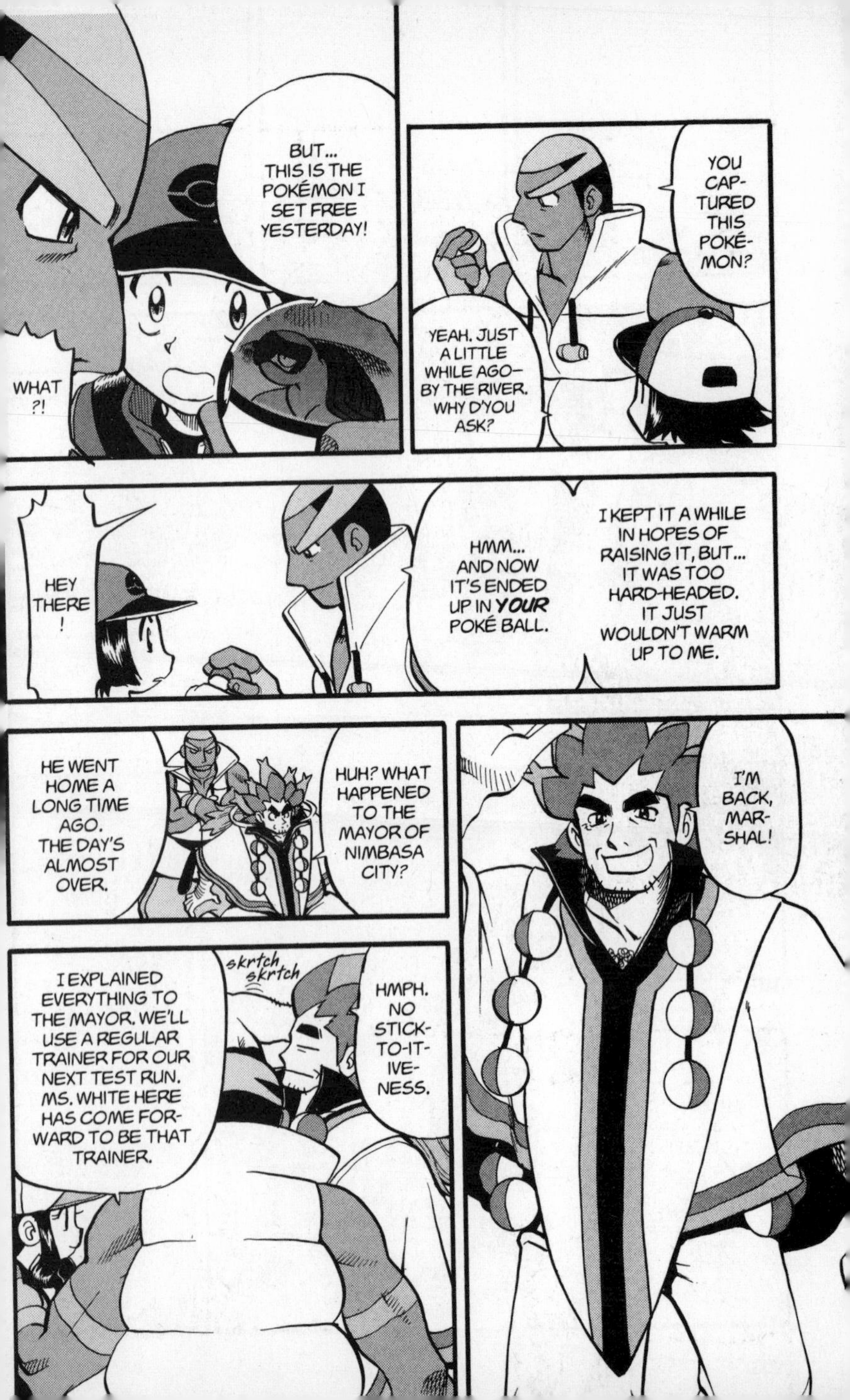
YOU CAPTURED THIS POKÉMON?
YEAH. JUST A LITTLE WHILE AGO— BY THE RIVER. WHY D'YOU ASK?
BUT... THIS IS THE POKÉMON I SET FREE YESTERDAY!
WHAT ?!
I KEPT IT A WHILE IN HOPES OF RAISING IT, BUT... IT WAS TOO HARD-HEADED. IT JUST WOULDN'T WARM UP TO ME.
HMM... AND NOW IT'S ENDED UP IN YOUR POKÉ BALL.
HEY THERE !
I'M BACK, MARSHAL!
HUH? WHAT HAPPENED TO THE MAYOR OF NIMBASA CITY?
HE WENT HOME A LONG TIME AGO. THE DAY'S ALMOST OVER.
skrtch skrtch
HMPH. NO STICK-TO-IT-IVENESS.
I EXPLAINED EVERYTHING TO THE MAYOR. WE'LL USE A REGULAR TRAINER FOR OUR NEXT TEST RUN. MS. WHITE HERE HAS COME FORWARD TO BE THAT TRAINER.

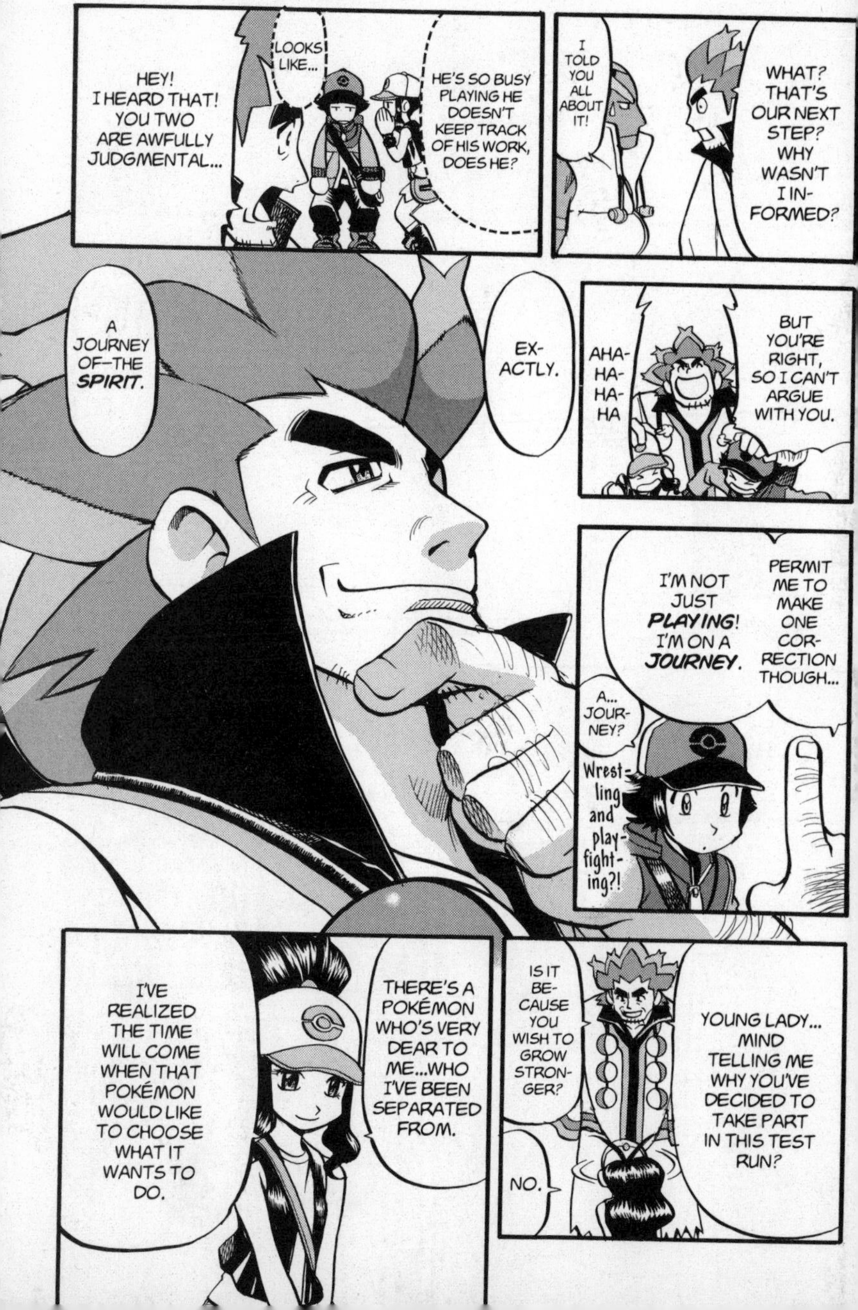
WHAT? THAT'S OUR NEXT STEP? WHY WASN'T I INFORMED?
I TOLD YOU ALL ABOUT IT!
HE'S SO BUSY PLAYING HE DOESN'T KEEP TRACK OF HIS WORK, DOES HE?
LOOKS LIKE...
HEY! I HEARD THAT! YOU TWO ARE AWFULLY JUDGMENTAL...
BUT YOU'RE RIGHT, SO I CAN'T ARGUE WITH YOU.
AHA-HA-HA-HA
PERMIT ME TO MAKE ONE COR-RECTION THOUGH...
I'M NOT JUST PLAYING! I'M ON A JOURNEY.
A... JOUR-NEY?
Wrest-ling and play-fight-ing?!
EX-ACTLY.
A JOURNEY OF—THE SPIRIT.
YOUNG LADY... MIND TELLING ME WHY YOU'VE DECIDED TO TAKE PART IN THIS TEST RUN?
IS IT BE-CAUSE YOU WISH TO GROW STRON-GER?
NO.
THERE'S A POKÉMON WHO'S VERY DEAR TO ME...WHO I'VE BEEN SEPARATED FROM.
I'VE REALIZED THE TIME WILL COME WHEN THAT POKÉMON WOULD LIKE TO CHOOSE WHAT IT WANTS TO DO.

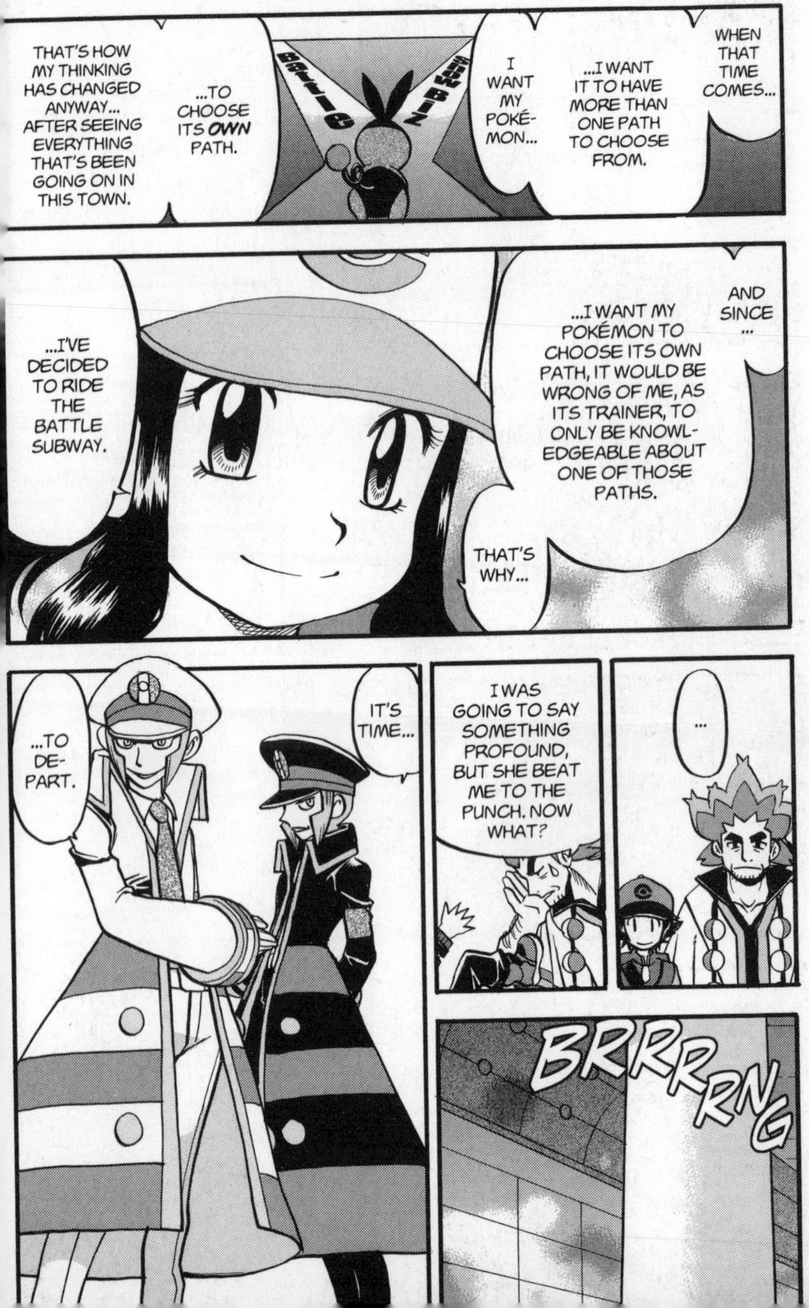
WHEN THAT TIME COMES...
...I WANT IT TO HAVE MORE THAN ONE PATH TO CHOOSE FROM.
I WANT MY POKÉ-MON...
Battle
Show Biz
...TO CHOOSE ITS *OWN* PATH.
THAT'S HOW MY THINKING HAS CHANGED ANYWAY... AFTER SEEING EVERYTHING THAT'S BEEN GOING ON IN THIS TOWN.
AND SINCE...
...I WANT MY POKÉMON TO CHOOSE ITS OWN PATH, IT WOULD BE WRONG OF ME, AS ITS TRAINER, TO ONLY BE KNOWL-EDGEABLE ABOUT ONE OF THOSE PATHS.
THAT'S WHY...
...I'VE DECIDED TO RIDE THE BATTLE SUBWAY.
...
I WAS GOING TO SAY SOMETHING PROFOUND, BUT SHE BEAT ME TO THE PUNCH. NOW WHAT?
BRRRRNG
IT'S TIME...
...TO DE-PART.

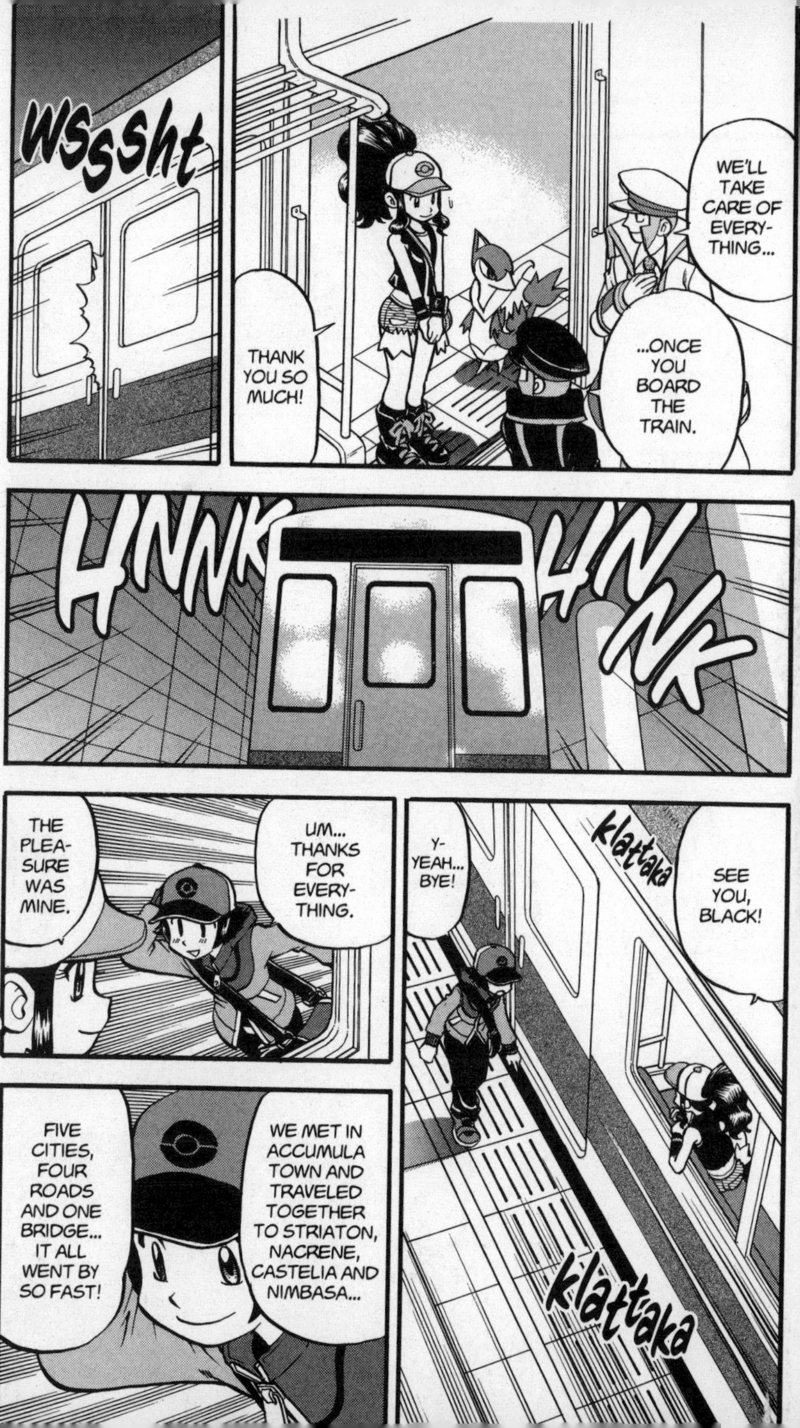
WE'LL TAKE CARE OF EVERY-THING...
...ONCE YOU BOARD THE TRAIN.
THANK YOU SO MUCH!
WSSSht
HNNK
HNNK
klattaka
SEE YOU, BLACK!
Y-YEAH... BYE!
klattaka
UM... THANKS FOR EVERY-THING.
THE PLEA-SURE WAS MINE.
WE MET IN ACCUMULA TOWN AND TRAVELED TOGETHER TO STRIATON, NACRENE, CASTELIA AND NIMBASA...
FIVE CITIES, FOUR ROADS AND ONE BRIDGE... IT ALL WENT BY SO FAST!

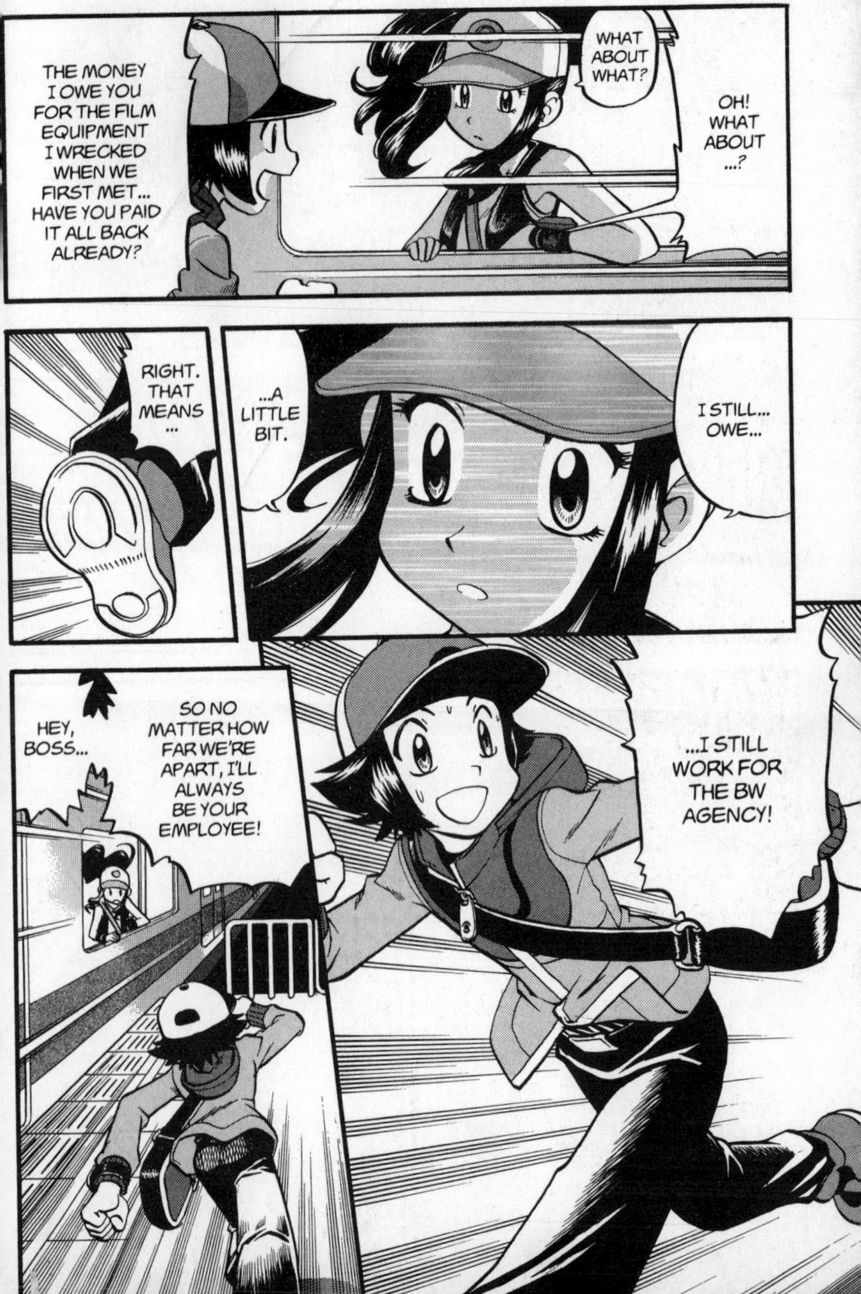
OH! WHAT ABOUT ...?
WHAT ABOUT WHAT?
THE MONEY I OWE YOU FOR THE FILM EQUIPMENT I WRECKED WHEN WE FIRST MET... HAVE YOU PAID IT ALL BACK ALREADY?
I STILL... OWE...
...A LITTLE BIT.
RIGHT. THAT MEANS ...
...I STILL WORK FOR THE BW AGENCY!
SO NO MATTER HOW FAR WE'RE APART, I'LL ALWAYS BE YOUR EMPLOYEE!
HEY, BOSS...

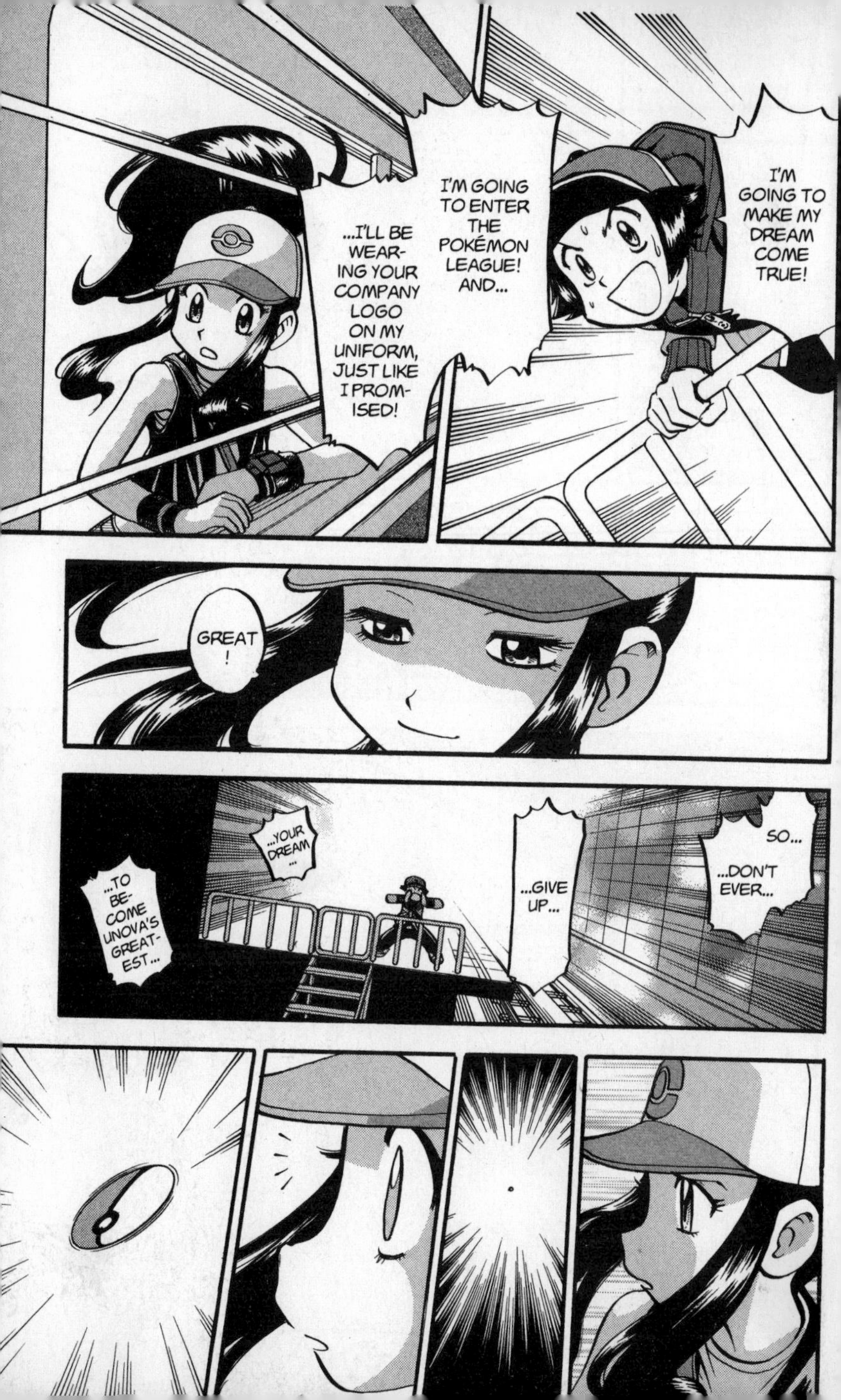
I'M GOING TO MAKE MY DREAM COME TRUE!
I'M GOING TO ENTER THE POKÉMON LEAGUE! AND...
...I'LL BE WEAR-ING YOUR COMPANY LOGO ON MY UNIFORM, JUST LIKE I PROM-ISED!
GREAT!
SO...
...DON'T EVER...
...GIVE UP...
...YOUR DREAM...
...TO BE-COME UNOVA'S GREAT-EST...

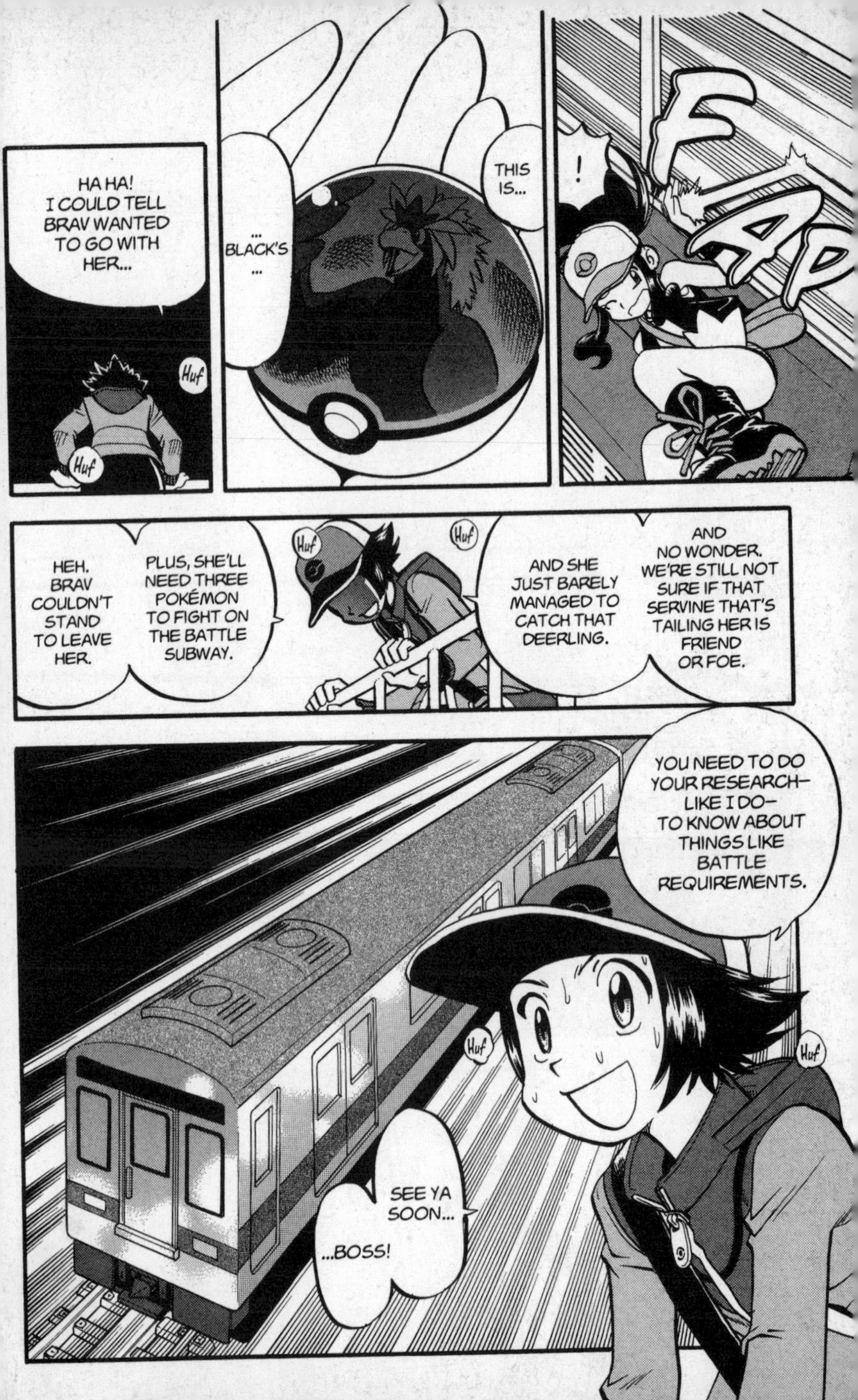
FAP
!
THIS IS...
...BLACK'S...
HA HA! I COULD TELL BRAV WANTED TO GO WITH HER...
Huf
Huf
AND NO WONDER. WE'RE STILL NOT SURE IF THAT SERVINE THAT'S TAILING HER IS FRIEND OR FOE.
AND SHE JUST BARELY MANAGED TO CATCH THAT DEERLING.
Huf
Huf
PLUS, SHE'LL NEED THREE POKÉMON TO FIGHT ON THE BATTLE SUBWAY.
HEH. BRAV COULDN'T STAND TO LEAVE HER.
YOU NEED TO DO YOUR RESEARCH— LIKE I DO— TO KNOW ABOUT THINGS LIKE BATTLE REQUIREMENTS.
Huf
Huf
SEE YA SOON...
...BOSS!

TO BE CONTINUED

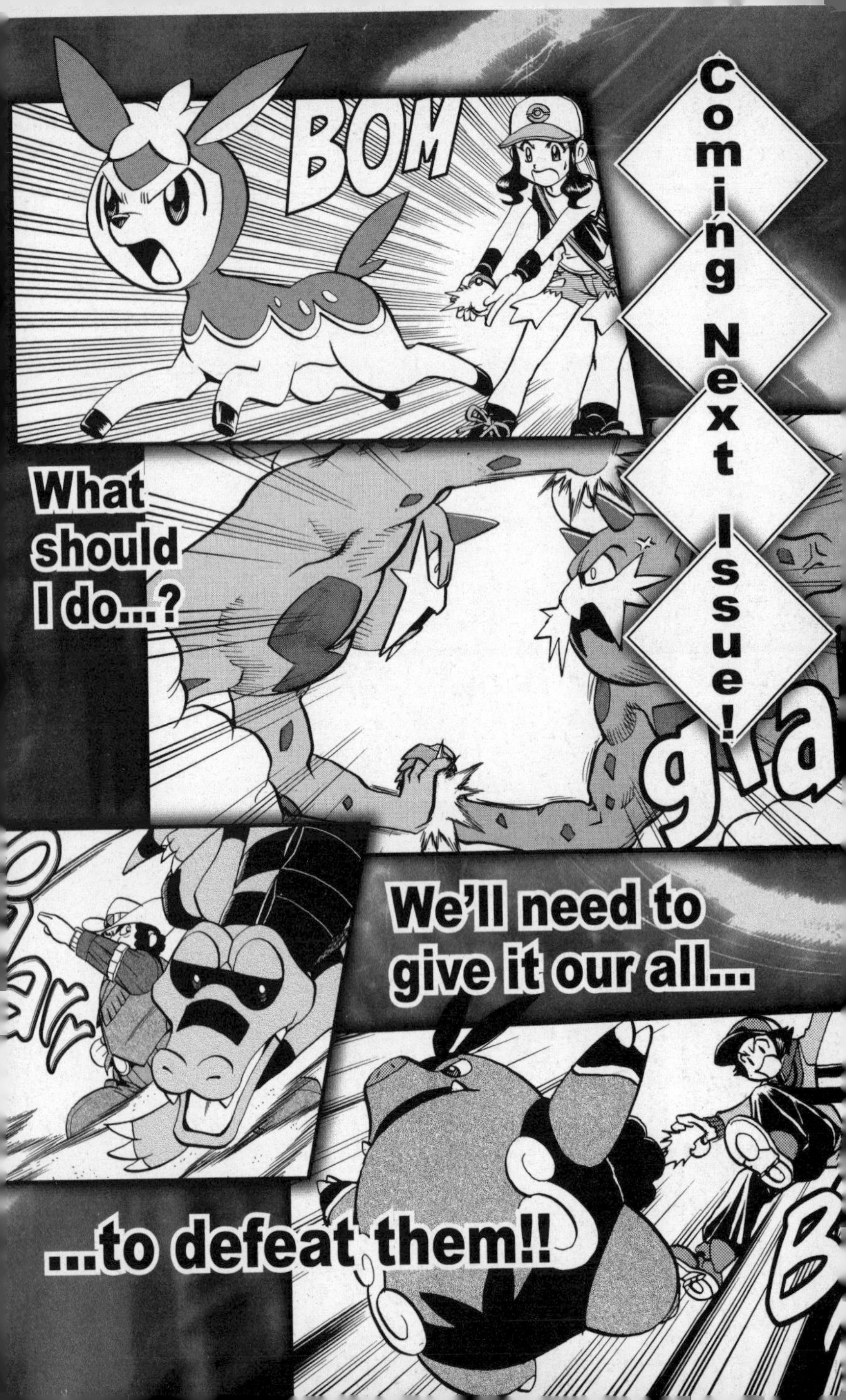
Coming Next Issue!
BOM
gia
What should I do...?
We'll need to give it our all...
...to defeat them!!

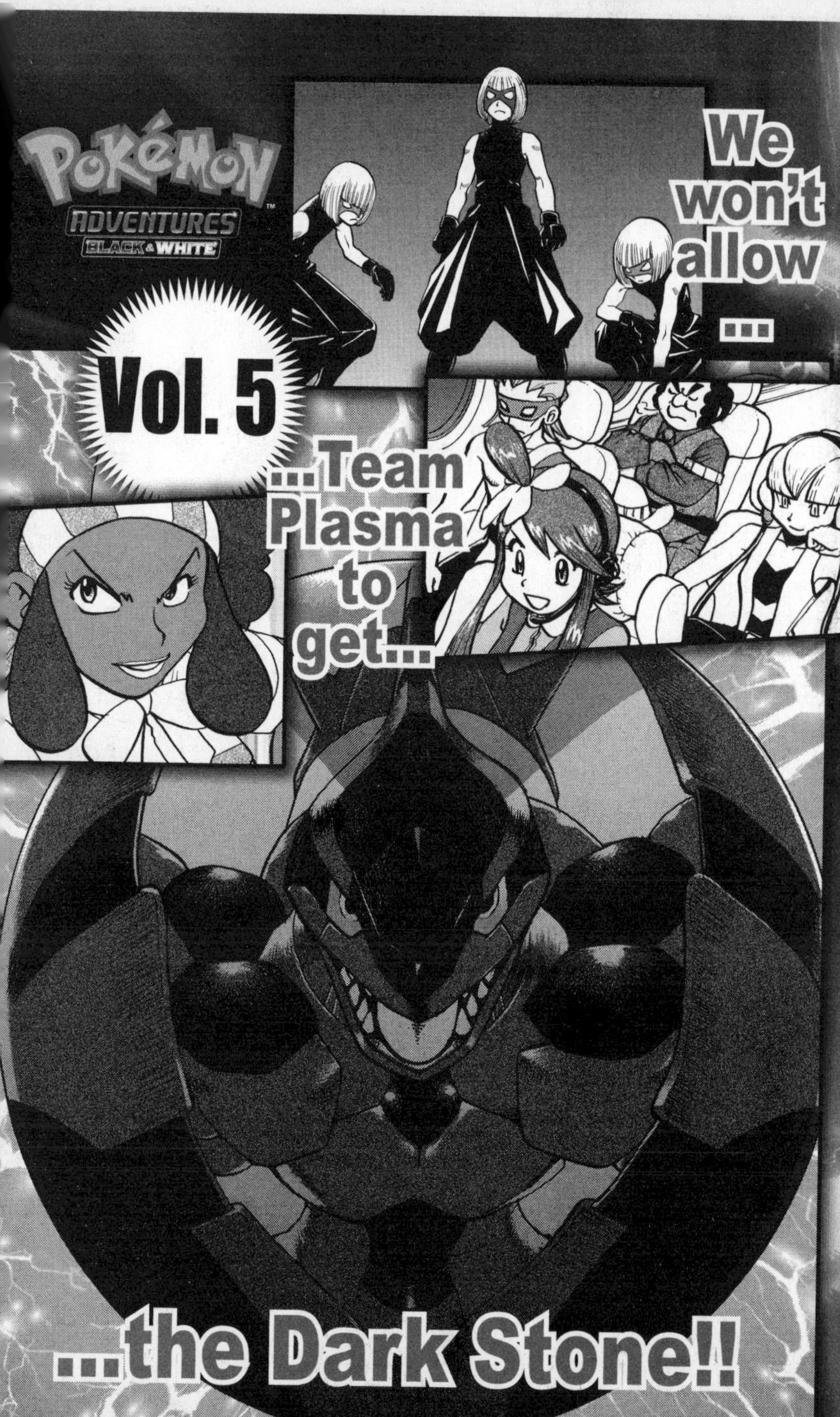
POKéMON ADVENTURES BLACK & WHITE
Vol. 5
We won't allow...
...Team Plasma to get...
...the Dark Stone!!

Special Feature

NIMBASA CITY

Unova's Bustling City of Entertainment

Filled with all manner of entertainment facilities, you'll need more than a day to visit them all. A must-see destination for your family's next vacation!

Fun & Games Guide

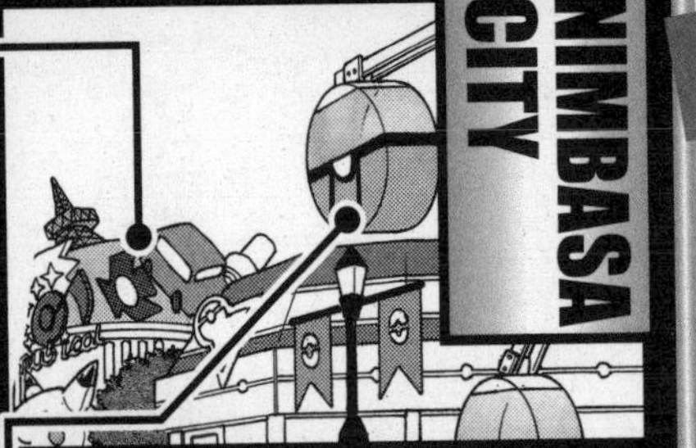

Musical Theater

A new entertainment facility where you can watch the dazzling Pokémon Musical! Dress up your own Pokémon and join in!

Amusement Park

The major entertainment facility of Nimbasa City. The Nimbasa Gym, run by Gym Leader Elesa, is also located here.

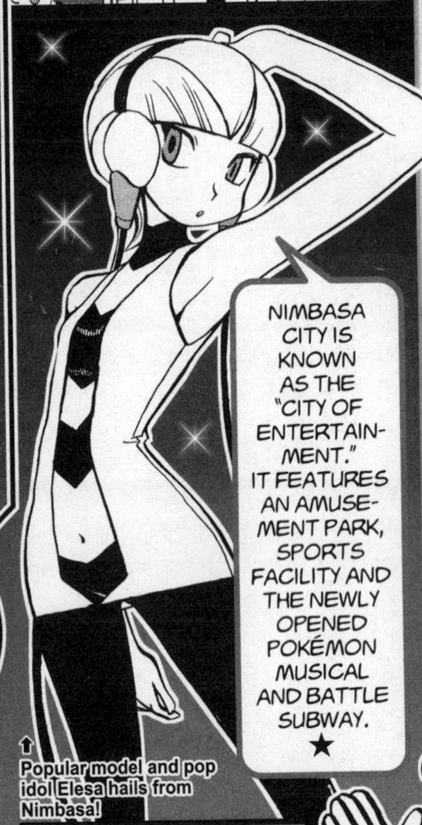
NIMBASA CITY IS KNOWN AS THE "CITY OF ENTERTAINMENT." IT FEATURES AN AMUSEMENT PARK, SPORTS FACILITY AND THE NEWLY OPENED POKÉMON MUSICAL AND BATTLE SUBWAY. ★

⇧ Popular model and pop idol Elesa hails from Nimbasa!

Goal: To become the most popular destination for entertainment.

Professionals in the entertainment industry from various regions attend planning meetings to create events. ➡

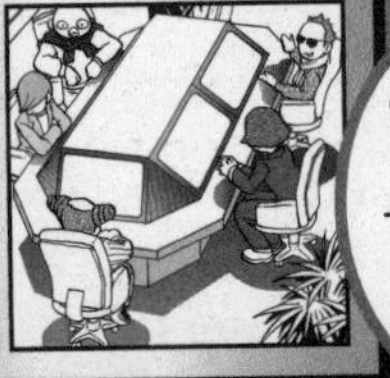

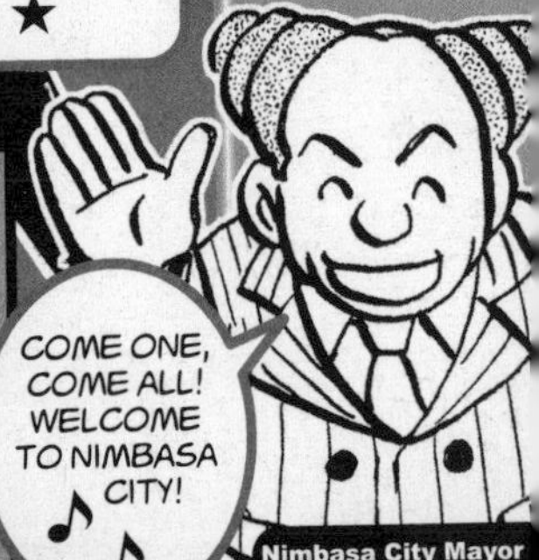
COME ONE, COME ALL! WELCOME TO NIMBASA CITY! ♪ ♪

Nimbasa City Mayor

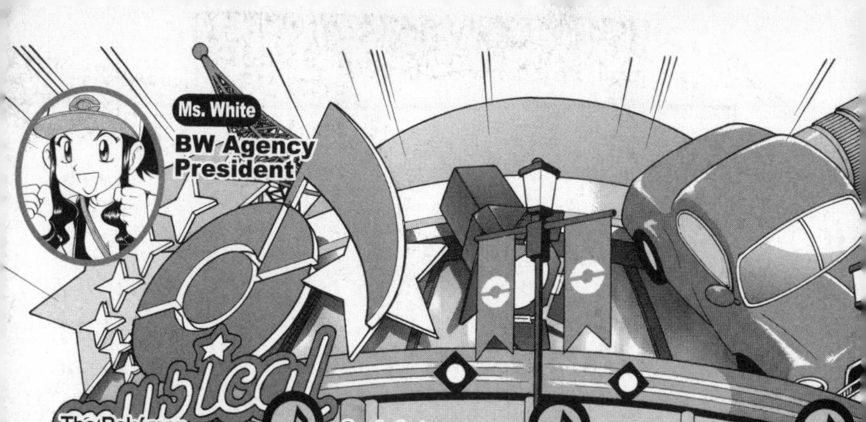
Ms. White
BW Agency President

Use Props to Dress Up

Dress up your Pokémon with props! Show off your fashion sense!

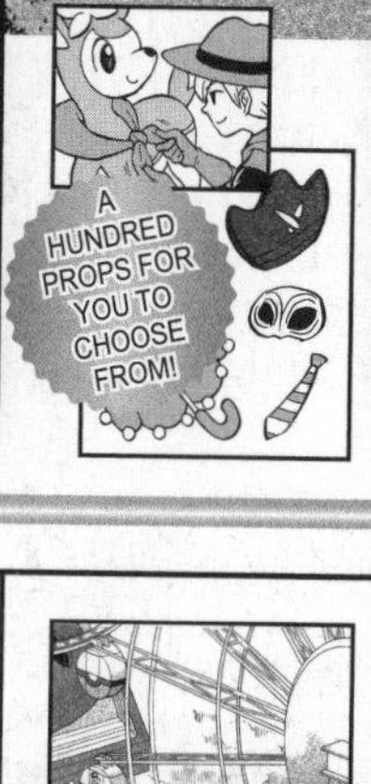
A HUNDRED PROPS FOR YOU TO CHOOSE FROM!

Four Musical Shows

Cool, Cute, Elegant and Unique. You may choose from four different musical performances.

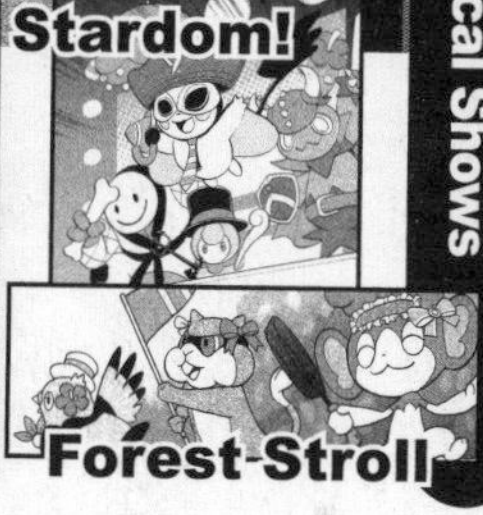
Stardom!
Forest Stroll

Perform... Or just enjoy the show from the audience.

The Pokémon dance upon the stage. ♪ Appeal to the audience with your dance routine, and their eyes will be hooked on your Pokémon.

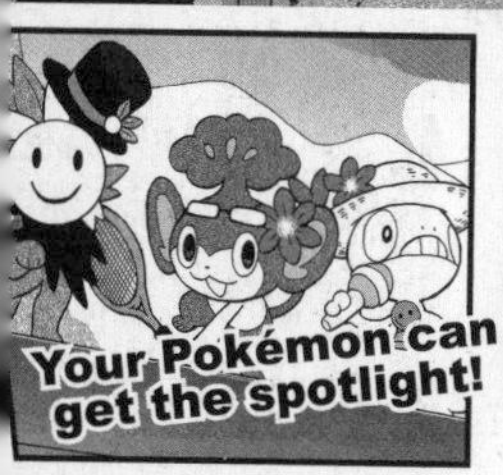
Your Pokémon can get the spotlight!

■ Rondez-View Ferris Wheel

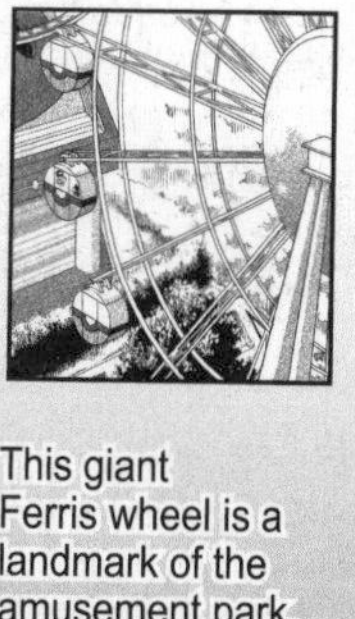

This giant Ferris wheel is a landmark of the amusement park. Enjoy a 20-minute aerial ride and take in a spectacular view of the Unova region.

■ Bouncy Pikachu House

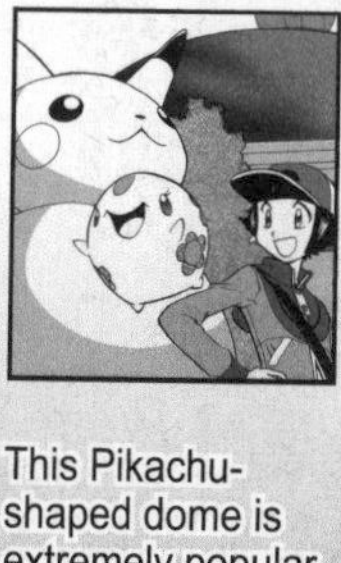

This Pikachu-shaped dome is extremely popular with children. Jump and bounce around on the soft air mattress inside. ♪

■ Shining Roller Coaster

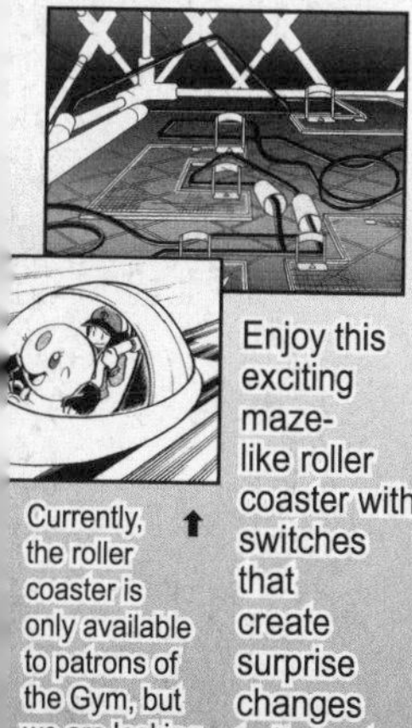

Enjoy this exciting maze-like roller coaster with switches that create surprise changes to its route.

↑ Currently, the roller coaster is only available to patrons of the Gym, but we are looking into ways for others to ride it as well.

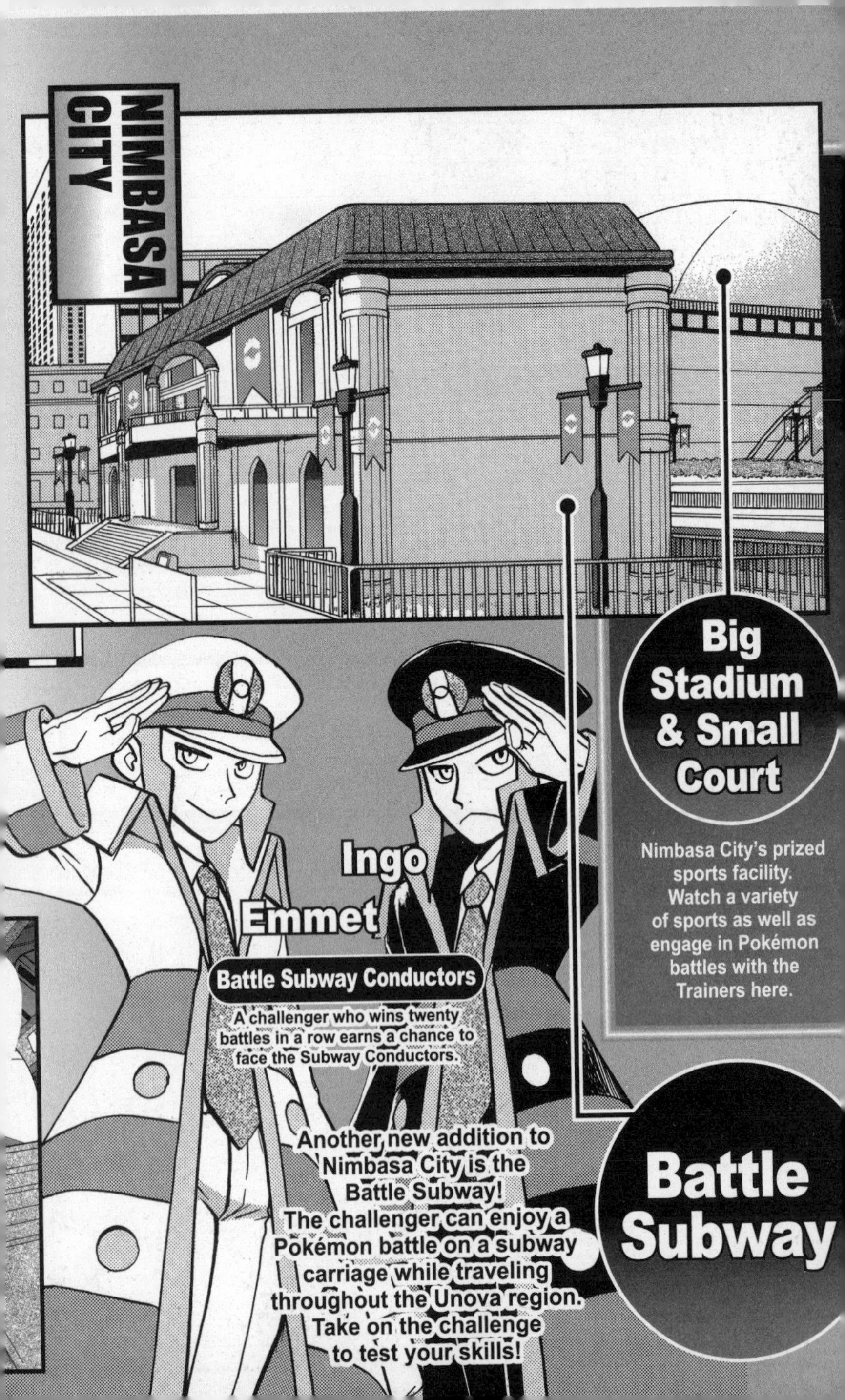
NIMBASA CITY
Big Stadium & Small Court
Nimbasa City's prized sports facility. Watch a variety of sports as well as engage in Pokémon battles with the Trainers here.
Ingo
Emmet
Battle Subway Conductors
A challenger who wins twenty battles in a row earns a chance to face the Subway Conductors.
Battle Subway
Another new addition to Nimbasa City is the Battle Subway! The challenger can enjoy a Pokémon battle on a subway carriage while traveling throughout the Unova region. Take on the challenge to test your skills!

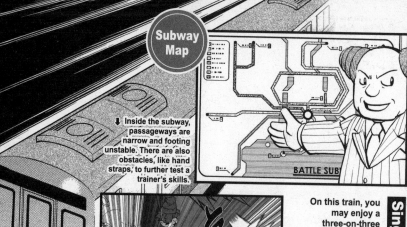

BATTLE SUB

↓ Inside the subway, passageways are narrow and footing unstable. There are also obstacles, like hand straps, to further test a trainer's skills.

Single Train

On this train, you may enjoy a three-on-three single battle. The Super Single Train is also available for expert trainers!

↓ The Elite Four and the Champion personally supervise the Battle Subway.

Double Train

On this train, you may enjoy a four-on-four double battle. An even more challenging Super Double Train is currently under construction.

↓ The station is filled with trains waiting to depart. Including the routes still under construction, there will be eight routes in all.

Platform for Trains to Anville Town

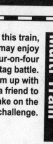

VISIT NIMBASA FOR YOUR NEXT VACATION!

Multi Train

On this train, you may enjoy a four-on-four tag battle. Team up with a friend to take on the challenge.

Message from
Hidenori Kusaka

Roller coasters and Ferris wheels... Rides that take you high up in the air and rides that go super fast... The rides at amusement parks nowadays are pretty amazing! I used to like them, but recently, I have to admit, they're getting a bit scary for me. It depends on who you ride them with, of course. If the person you happen to be riding with turns out to be a total XYZ, then it'll be a lonely, fearful ride even with company. As for the Ferris wheel, the last time one appeared in *Pokémon Adventures* was vol. 10! (´ ▽ `)ノ

Message from
Satoshi Yamamoto

I work harder when I'm criticized than when I'm praised. That's why I can't help putting a lot of effort into stories where the main character is thrown into the depths of despair...only to finally rise up again in triumph. I think you could say that the main character of this volume is White. I hope you enjoy watching her train hard and the change in expression on her face at the end!

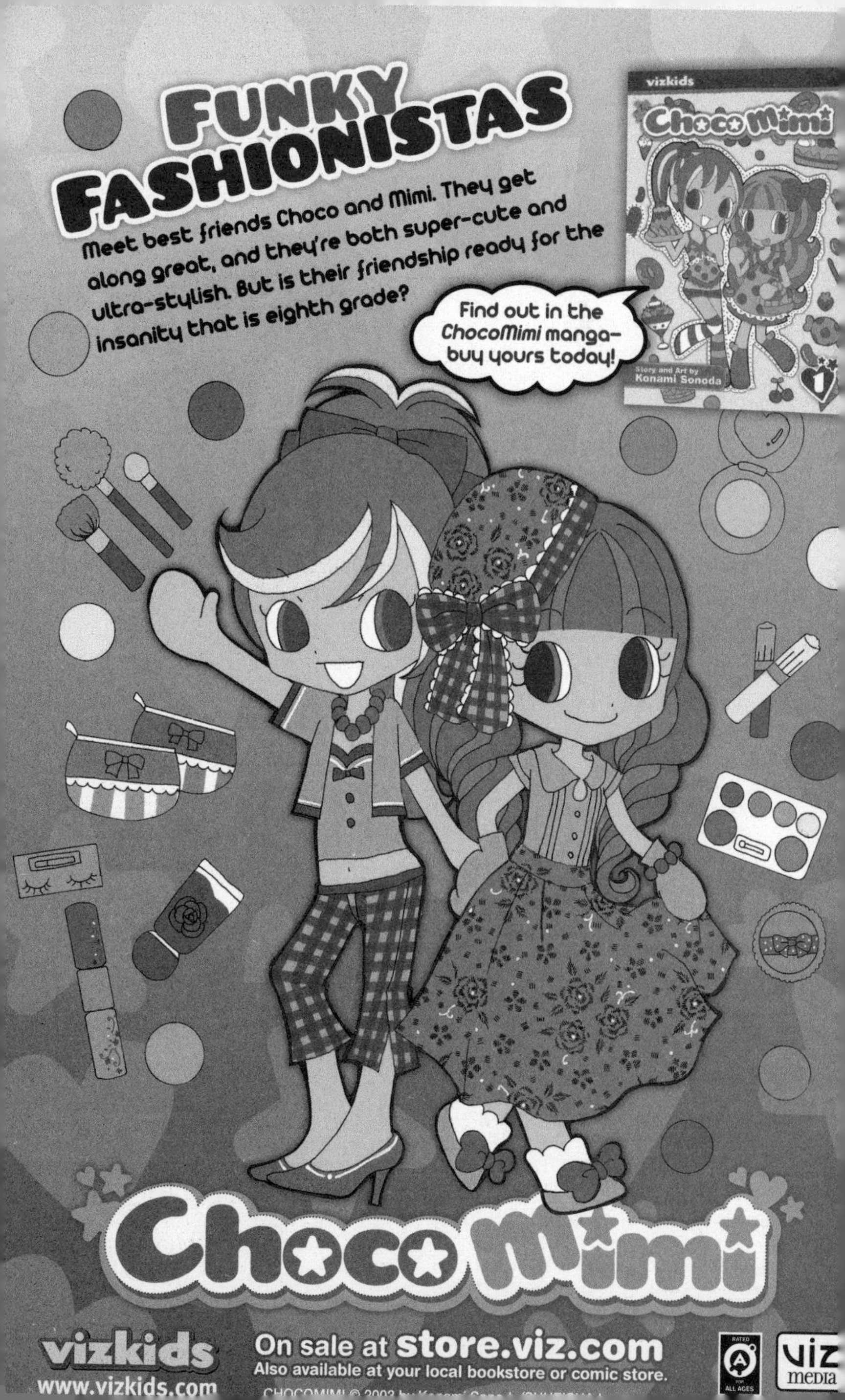
FUNKY FASHIONISTAS
Meet best friends Choco and Mimi. They get along great, and they're both super-cute and ultra-stylish. But is their friendship ready for the insanity that is eighth grade?
Find out in the ChocoMimi manga–buy yours today!
vizkids
ChocoMimi
Story and Art by Konami Sonoda
1
ChocoMimi
vizkids
www.vizkids.com
On sale at store.viz.com
Also available at your local bookstore or comic store.
RATED A FOR ALL AGES
VIZ media

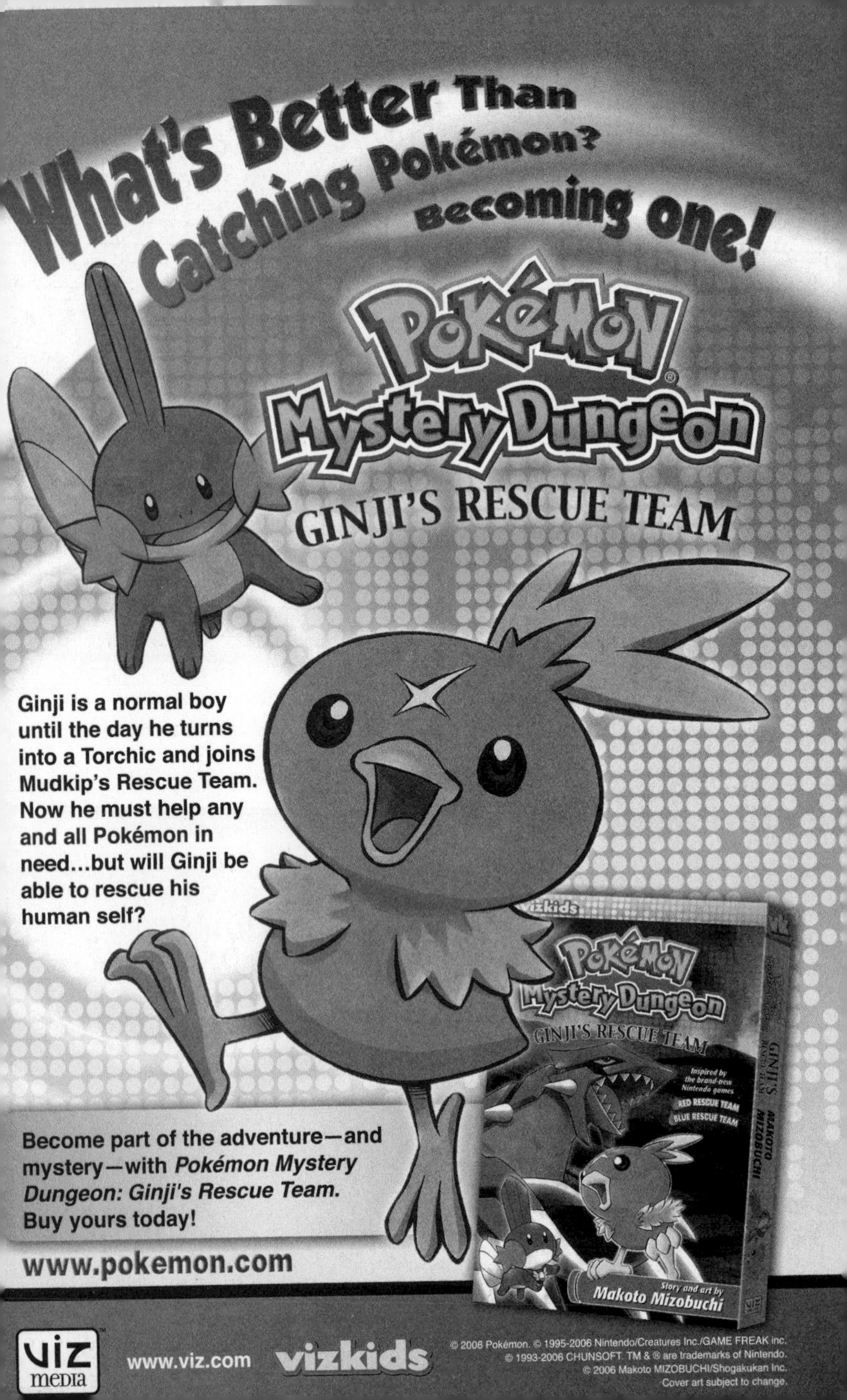
What's Better Than Catching Pokémon?
Becoming one!
Pokémon®
Mystery Dungeon
GINJI'S RESCUE TEAM
Ginji is a normal boy until the day he turns into a Torchic and joins Mudkip's Rescue Team. Now he must help any and all Pokémon in need...but will Ginji be able to rescue his human self?
Become part of the adventure—and mystery—with *Pokémon Mystery Dungeon: Ginji's Rescue Team.* Buy yours today!
www.pokemon.com
vizkids
Pokémon Mystery Dungeon
GINJI'S RESCUE TEAM
Inspired by the brand-new Nintendo games
RED RESCUE TEAM
BLUE RESCUE TEAM
Story and art by
Makoto Mizobuchi
viz media
www.viz.com
vizkids
© 2006 Pokémon. © 1995-2006 Nintendo/Creatures Inc./GAME FREAK inc.
© 1993-2006 CHUNSOFT. TM & ® are trademarks of Nintendo.
© 2006 Makoto MIZOBUCHI/Shogakukan Inc.
Cover art subject to change.

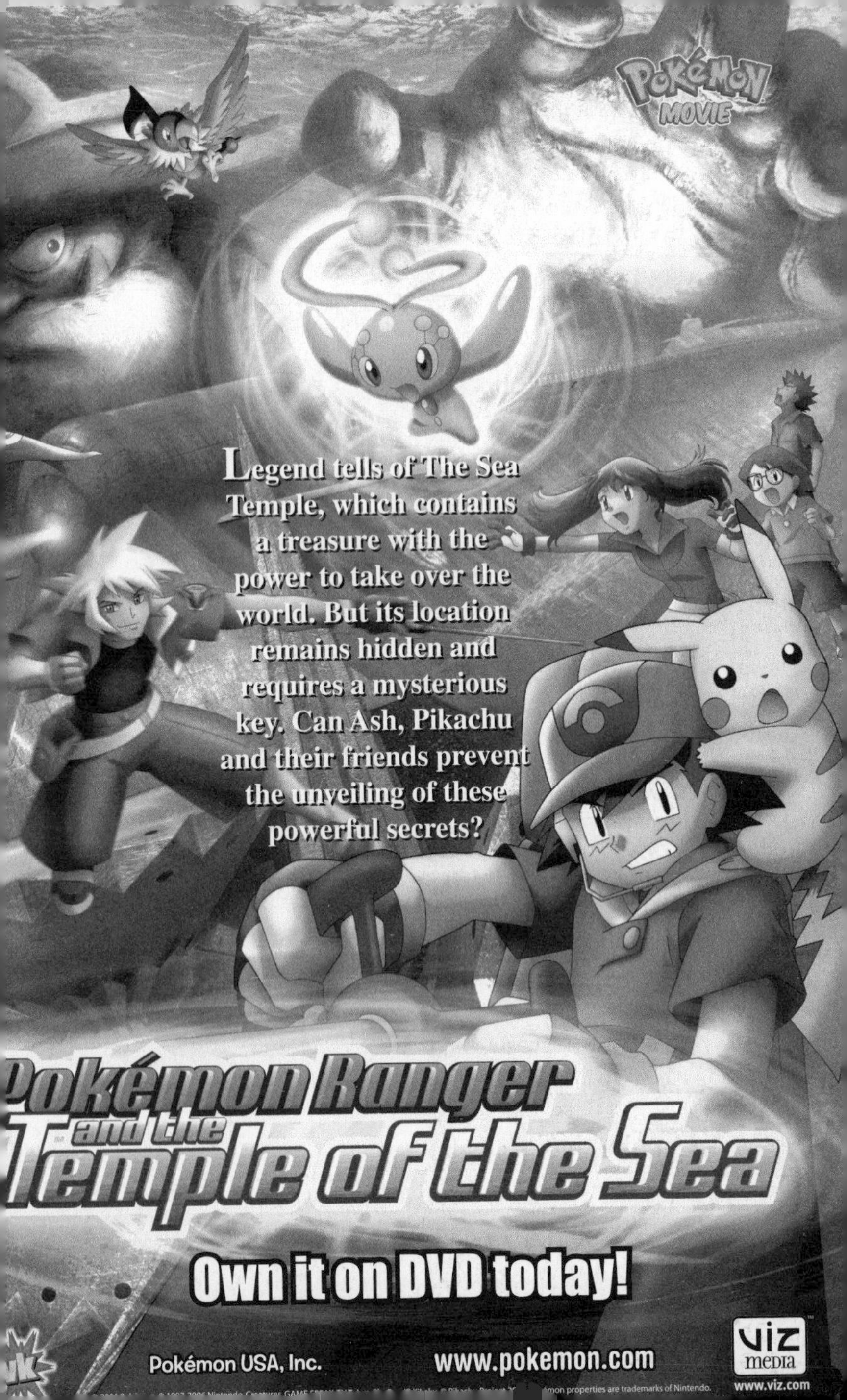
Pokémon Movie
Legend tells of The Sea Temple, which contains a treasure with the power to take over the world. But its location remains hidden and requires a mysterious key. Can Ash, Pikachu and their friends prevent the unveiling of these powerful secrets?
Pokémon Ranger and the Temple of the Sea
Own it on DVD today!
Pokémon USA, Inc.
www.pokemon.com
VIZ media
www.viz.com

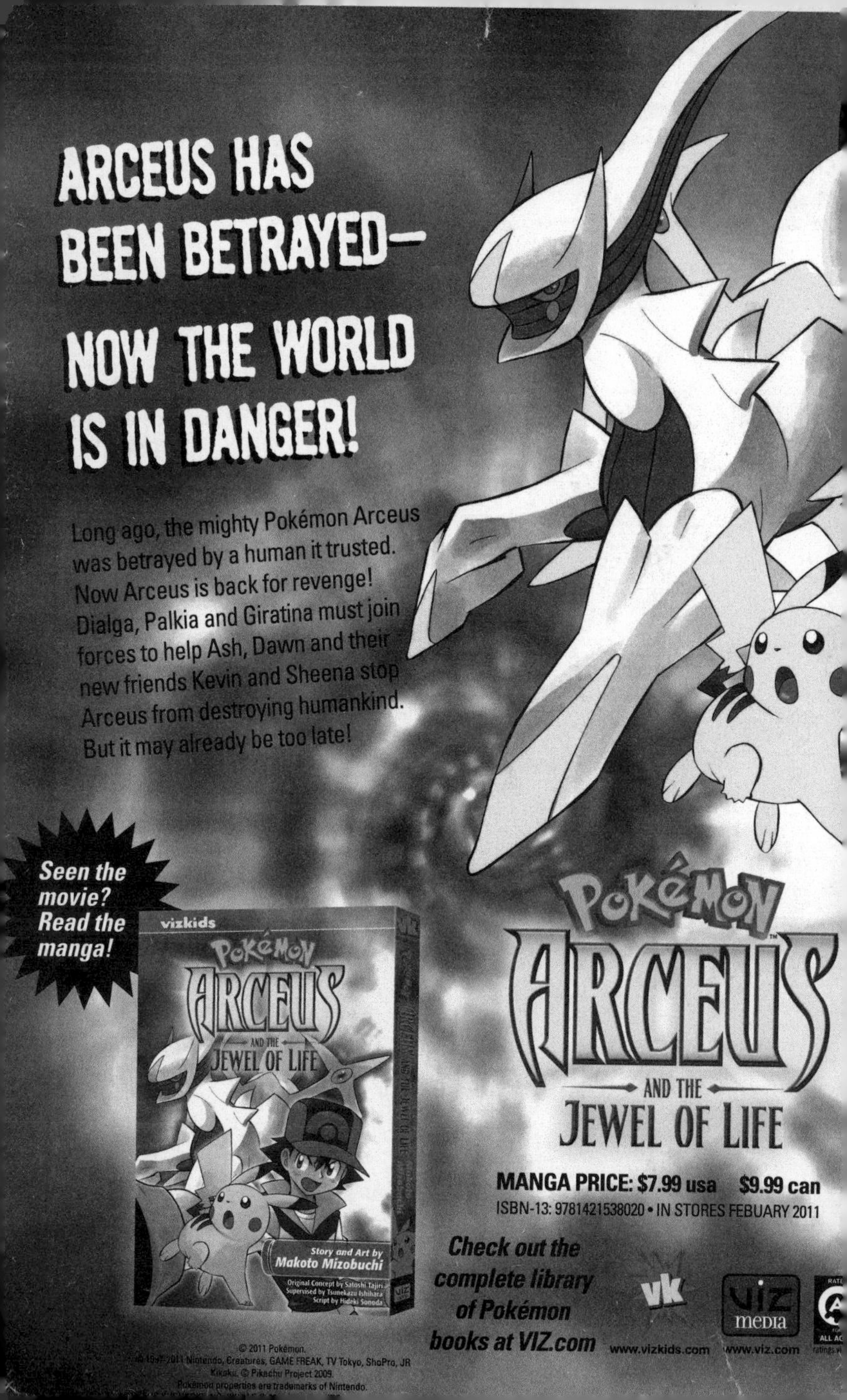

ARCEUS HAS BEEN BETRAYED—
NOW THE WORLD IS IN DANGER!
Long ago, the mighty Pokémon Arceus was betrayed by a human it trusted. Now Arceus is back for revenge! Dialga, Palkia and Giratina must join forces to help Ash, Dawn and their new friends Kevin and Sheena stop Arceus from destroying humankind. But it may already be too late!
Seen the movie? Read the manga!
vizkids
Pokémon
ARCEUS
AND THE
JEWEL OF LIFE
Story and Art by
Makoto Mizobuchi
Original Concept by Satoshi Tajiri
Supervised by Tsunekazu Ishihara
Script by Hideki Sonoda
Pokémon
ARCEUS™
AND THE
JEWEL OF LIFE
MANGA PRICE: $7.99 usa $9.99 can
ISBN-13: 9781421538020 • IN STORES FEBUARY 2011
Check out the complete library of Pokémon books at VIZ.com
vk
www.vizkids.com
VIZ media
www.viz.com
© 2011 Pokémon.
© 1997-2011 Nintendo, Creatures, GAME FREAK, TV Tokyo, ShoPro, JR Kikaku. © Pikachu Project 2009.
Pokémon properties are trademarks of Nintendo.

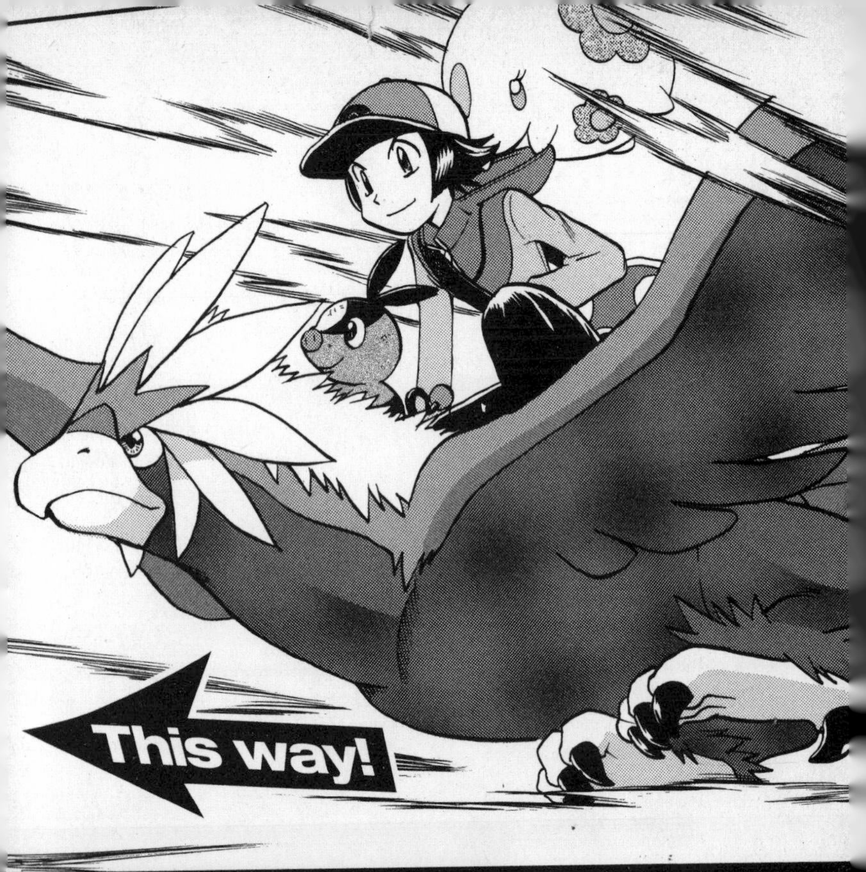
This way!

THIS IS THE END OF THIS GRAPHIC NOVEL!

To properly enjoy this VIZ Media graphic novel, please turn it around and begin reading from right to left.

This book has been printed in the original Japanese format in order to preserve the orientation of the original artwork.

Have fun with it!

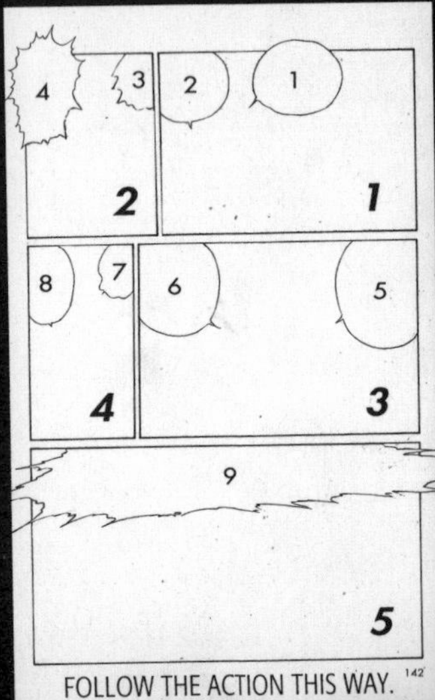

FOLLOW THE ACTION THIS WAY.